twenty percent

STUD

eighty percent

MUFFIN

ALIEN FATED MATES ✦ BOOK 1

CHRIS ✦ REDD

AF265777

Copyright © 2024 by Chris Redd

All rights reserved. No portion of this book may be reproduced in any form without written permission from the publisher or author, except in the case of brief quotations embodied in critical reviews and certain other non-commercial uses permitted by copyright law.

This is a work of fiction. Names, characters, events, incidents, places, businesses are either the products of the author's imagination or used in a fictitious manner. Any resemblance to actual persons, or events is coincidental. For permission requests, contact Chris Redd at chris@chrisredd.ca.

Cover and Graphic Design by Chris Redd at www.chrisredd.ca

Formatting by Chris Redd at www.chrisredd.ca

Editing by Kate Wood at www.katewoodproofreading.com

Proofreading by Libby Hunns at www.libbyhunns.com

Special thanks to Critique Circle

Spelling, punctuation and grammatical errors are the fault of the author and can be reported to Chris Redd at www.chrisredd.ca

To a partner who understands what it means to be supportive in *all* the ways.

And to Stef, Ang and Heather—willing guinea pigs.

Content Warnings

Skip right on over this section if content warnings make your eyes roll or give too much away for you.

Alien genitalia

Off-page rape (non-graphic)

Past childhood neglect

Off-page cheating (non-graphic)

Dubious consent (base instincts of alpha/omega relationship)

Possessive Alpha male

Submissive Omega male

Contents

1

Earth...the not-too-distant future

IS RUNNING AWAY TO another planet really the best option?

"Earth to Geo." Ginger tapped her manicured nails on the café's darkened vid-screen table, scrolling the breakfast menu. I squinted. How did she paint those tiny little cherries on them?

Saturdays at Toni's Café with Ginger were nonnegotiable. Every booth was packed, and the air was thick with the tang of toasted sourdough and cinnamon-dusted lattes. Toni's was the only place in this dive town with espresso that wasn't too sour or acidic—Ginger's words, not mine—and it was a tradition going on eight years.

Dressed in silver lamé, she literally shone as she sipped her Italian espresso. Her black-tipped bangs were framed by stick-straight silver-white hair. Opposites in so many ways, I scuffed my worn steel-toed boots against the floor and fingered the hole in my frayed jeans, sighing as I recalled loosening my belt another notch that morning.

She pushed the off-planet employment brochure toward me the same way she did every week. Constantly scanning them for costume design inspiration, Ginger always had the latest one. "C'mon. Now's the time."

At least three of these brochures lined the bottom of my recycling bin at home, and I'd unstuck one from under the popcorn bowl earlier.

She leaned over the table between us, knocked the brim of my Space Invaders cap from my head and rustled my overgrown curls. "You're too cute and just too amazing overall to let Cameron keep bringing you down."

My ears grew warm as I pulled my hat back down over them.

"You need a change. It's time to kick that douchebag to the curb." Ginger didn't sugarcoat.

"You trying to get rid of me, Ging?"

"Not in a lifetime, but it's resonating in my bones. You'd be so perfect for this. They're recruiting an archbuilder..." She paused before her eyes grew cartoon-character wide. "Plus"—her voice softened—"I know you don't want to hear it, but Cameron looked awfully cozy in his social feed last weekend." Her knuckles turned white around the tiny espresso cup. "Who the hell is that guy anyway? Wasn't Cameron away on business?"

I shook the numbness from my fingers, but my stomach roiled. Whenever Ginger pointed out one of Cameron's indiscretions, I folded my emotions and refolded them before safely slotting them into a locked box, like a ballot to be dealt with never.

I sighed, the earnestness of her words hitting harder than usual this time. "'Kay, you got me. What the hell's an archbuilder?"

"I researched the shit out of this, Geo." She smacked the rolled brochure into her palm. "It's a home builder. You'd be doing what you love, acting as a project manager, but on another planet. How cool is that?"

My mind flicked from one far-fetched image to the next and landed on a picture of Tatooine—beige, plagued by windstorms, sandworms and...fictional.

"You could try it for a year. It pays so well, you'd have enough to start up your own construction company when you got back."

My fingers drummed the table. Could I really leave it all behind?

Outside of my work crew, if I were kidnapped tomorrow, I could count the people who would notice on one hand—two fingers, to be exact. Ginger and Cameron. And Cameron wouldn't miss me so much as he'd miss how much I babied him.

"They have an orientation session this weekend at the Center for Interplanetary Accessibility." Ginger's sing-song voice carried over the sharp whistle of the café's milk steamer.

My jaw tightened and I twisted my fingers around my coffee mug. "Ging." I swallowed the hard knot in my throat. "You think they would let me take Charz and Pika?"

Ginger reached across the table and took my hand. "Maybe...you could negotiate it into your contract?" Despite her lethal fingernails, a wave of comfort filled me. She paused for a second. "You know I love those little rats. I could keep them for you for a year."

My eye twitched over leaving my dogs behind, but no matter how unlikely, visions of aliens with large teeth and no manners swallowing them whole horrified me more.

Besides her persistence about sending me off-planet, Ginger's advice had always been sound. Still, the outrageousness of this proposition blindsided me as if I were the star of a blooper reel. My resolve weakened, and my heart raced at what the future might hold. Cameron would finally appreciate me if we had time apart. Right? Plus, my own company, shiny and new—just a year away.

"But what about my house?"

Cameron loved living in my house, but he sure as hell didn't take care of it.

Ginger's brazen smile, hidden behind her espresso cup, flashed in her eyes the way it always did when she got her way. "You just leave that to me."

I scratched my three-day-old stubble as Charz and Pika pawed at my legs. The two eager Jack Russells yipped for my attention. I crouched low, and my socked feet slipped on the kitchen tiles. "Damn it."

Cameron always put the dog treats in the far reaches of the floor cabinet. As I struggled to reach them, his fresh-from-the-shower scent drifted down the hall. Next, he'd pull on some sweats—the ones that dipped low enough to show his v-line and perfect abs—pocket his cell phone off his bedside table, then turn the house upside down to find his glasses. Lastly, he'd dig through the dryer for some socks. Good luck there. I hadn't done the lazy bastard's laundry this week.

"Gah, that man turns me into a raging bitch."

I tossed chicken sticks, their favorite, to Charz and Pika. My empty hand clenched. Their tails slapped like happy whips, heedless of my annoyance. Without Ginger, the only unconditional love and acceptance in my life would've come from them.

So what if their love is artificially bolstered by treats?

"Geo, did you put my glasses somewhere?" Cameron called from the laundry room.

No, I didn't put your glasses anywhere.

"They're on the kitchen counter."

Where you left them last night, after conveniently ignoring that it was my turn to pick the show? Instead, we watched three episodes of yet another athletic endurance competition, where every contestant had the same over-the-top charisma to match their over-the-top ego. Now that other planets had contacted Earth, the contestants might be green or horned, but not much else had changed since my grandmother's time.

I picked up his glasses and pushed the silent vacuum cleaner to the laundry room before I passed them to him.

He glanced up. "Thanks."

My head used to rush when he pushed the frames over his long, straight nose. A Superman to Clark Kent moment—his perfect features made more human. But that old lightheadedness was gone.

"Er, did you happen to throw any of my clothes in when you did yours?" His eyes flicked a little sheepishly to the vacuum now stored in the wall hanger.

"No." I stood there, rocking from one socked foot to the other, as he maneuvered around me out of the laundry room. The clink of the leashes and the harnesses he knocked together alerted Pika and Charz of an imminent walk. Their tiny nails clicked like a troupe of miniature tap dancers across the hardwood floor. The floor we'd agreed *he* would clean today.

Mired in defeat, I reminded him again. "So...you said you'd do the floors today?"

"Damn it, Geo." He eyeballed the too-small shirt I'd put on this morning. "Isn't it enough that I walk your dogs for you? You could use the exercise."

I pulled back my shoulders and sucked in my belly, even though no amount of sucking in would prevent it from poking out under the hem. Daily physical labor at the construction company I co-owned built muscles, but I enjoyed bread and beer, and my abs were buried under a thick stomach. "*Our* dogs."

"Whatever." He dragged out the 'er.' "I do enough things I don't want for you." Cameron strode away.

Like a happy family, the three of them slipped out the door without a backward glance, and yet again, cleaning the house fell on my shoulders. This time with my heart cowering like a kicked dog's.

Is he worth it?

The corner of a familiar off-planet employment brochure peeked out from under the vid-screen controller on top of the coffee table. After I'd resolutely blocked all the electronic junk mail Ginger spammed me with, these paper versions still showed up on the regular.

An out-of-place image of two aliens stood out among all the pictures of space shuttles, foreign landscapes and heavy equipment. Blue, with long tails, the taller one had an arm wrapped around the shorter one's shoulder. The goofy grin he wore transcended species. I wasn't sure if it hurt more to know love existed beyond Earth or if it hurt more to hope.

Inhaling deeply, I raised my gaze to the vaulted ceiling and scanned my home. A smile formed on my lips. House proud, I'd renovated the entire upstairs, removing the second bedroom and adding a huge en suite bathroom and a walk-in closet. I walked over to the open window and inhaled the sweet fragrance of the native plants I'd relandscaped with. Honeysuckles, wild roses and overripe blackberries wafted through the screen.

Slightly calmer, I finished cleaning the shit out of the house. And because Cameron wasn't home, I did it blasting retro Lizzo remixes. Forty minutes of pondering intergalactic love later, the house shone, and now with the busy work out of the way, reality returned.

I scrubbed my palm over my beard. On more than one occasion, Cameron had said, "There are more important things in life than a clean house, Geo. I'll do it later."

Maybe he was right. I threw together a quick picnic lunch and hoped for the best. Roast beef on fresh sourdough for me, microbe-infused spinach wraps and kimchi for Cameron. After filling a water bottle for us and the dog water bottle Cameron had forgotten, I placed everything in my backpack.

Dahlias bloomed alongside my driveway. Not wanting them to nosedive with nothing to cling to—a metaphor for my life—I reminded myself to buy supports. Then, I headed to the local park.

Winding up the path to my favorite hilltop perch, I spotted my little family on the multi-purpose track below. I placed the picnic pack on the ground and sat on the manicured grass. Spectators cheered for a soccer game on the nearby pitch, and fried onions lingered in the warm breeze from the hotdog vendor beside the fountain.

Excited yips narrowed my focus to Charz and Pika, where they tugged on the leash Cameron held, trying desperately to get to me. The cropped shirt he wore highlighted the swath of golden skin above his low-riding sweats as he not-so-absently scratched his six-pack.

Damn, why hadn't I changed my shirt? My hand automatically reached to stretch the fabric away from my gut.

Oblivious to the dogs, Cameron chatted up a jogger stretching beside him. His grin glowed in the distance. He'd done this before.

My heart lurched, but I always gave him the benefit of the doubt. Cameron loved me.

The jogger rose from where he stretched, leaned in, then held Cameron's bicep as he tapped his number into Cameron's phone. My toes curled against the soles of my flip-flops, bracing for impact. He'd never taken it that far before. Not in front of me, anyways. It usually amounted to harmless flirting—part of Cameron's personality.

I tucked my knees into my belly and rested my chin on them. A cold shiver ghosted over me despite the midday sun.

He says he loves me, but...

When we'd first met, he'd showered me with attention. I never could quite grasp what a guy like Cameron, with his charm and supermodel good looks, wanted with me.

Yanked by our yapping dogs, he turned in my direction. He jumped back from the jogger when he spotted me.

I gasped. His guilt hit like a virtual punch to my gut. His fingers fluttered at shoulder level in an awkward wave, then his long stride ate up the distance between us, his mouthwatering smile firmly in place.

Running his fingers through the long part of his hair, he raked it out of his eyes and sat beside me. A trail of goose bumps pricked my skin where he bumped my arm with his. Then he cupped my calf as he wrapped his other arm low around my back, and my muffin top squished in his hold.

Cameron kissed my cheek, all smiles, as if I hadn't witnessed his obvious attempt at a pickup. "Hey, I didn't think you were joining us today."

Give him the benefit of the doubt. Although I wanted to reply with a snarky 'clearly,' instead, a shy "I made us a picnic" came out.

"Yes, I'm starved!" He pumped his arm, dove for the backpack and passed me the doggie water bottle. I opened and filled the shallow dish compartment. The pups attacked the dish before I placed it on the grass, slopping cool water into my lap.

Cameron rolled his eyes when I dabbed my lap with a napkin. "You're such a mess." He dug in.

I shifted closer to kiss his temple, and my soft belly pressed into his hard side before I murmured, "Cameron, did you give that jogger your number?"

He sighed so long that both dogs chimed in. "About that..." His forefinger circled idly around my kneecap. "Remember our conversation about going non-exclusive?"

Ah, no. What conversation?

The lump in my throat grew so large I could barely swallow. "You've been dating other people?"

I shifted out of his reach, my skin stretched too tight, like a snake near shedding.

"Don't make me out to be the villain, Geo." Cameron stood abruptly, jutting one hip to the side, framed by dramatically placed bent arms. "You agreed."

What's he talking about?

How long had he been, to use his words, "non-exclusive?" "When...when did I agree?"

As much as I didn't want him to answer that question, I needed him to say it. My hands fisted at my sides as I rose to stand. The dogs circled my ankles, whining at my distress. Cameron's elbows locked, his nonchalant gaze narrowed to one of concern.

"Why so serious, silly?" He reached up and booped me on the nose. "I still love you."

But how many others do you love?

"When. Did. I. Agree?" The words bit like venom and pumped adrenaline through my veins.

Cameron stumbled back a step. "For my last conference. You...you said it would be...fine if I went with Mikiao."

"As fucking friends, Cameron! To share a room and costs. Not to sleep with."

Months. He'd been dating other men for months. My heart pounded inside my ribcage, imprisoned behind bars. I shook off his hand when he reached for me. He'd been my jailer for too long, and his time to return the keys had expired.

I seethed but steeled myself against his charm. There would be no second-guessing myself this time. "I'm going to Ginger's." My chest heaved as I attempted to keep the emotion out of my voice. He would get nothing else of mine. "I want you out of my house by Monday morning."

His mouth gaping as I spun away from him would be forever etched in my memory.

The mirrors that covered two walls of Ginger's studio, now an impromptu guest room, told me nothing I didn't already know. Peering back at me was the same short, hairy guy with a short, fat... Finding another man who would love this package—so not happening.

I flicked the corner of the brochure I'd brought to bed to study. The idea of a new job on another planet took form under my fingertips. My eyes laser-focused on the two blue bodies in an embrace on the front, drawn in like a magnet. Cameron may have shoved me over the line, but Ginger's dogged persistence had finally found a foothold. A quick search on my phone led me to an online application. Two minutes later, the 'successful orientation registration' notification flashed.

2

Planet Tern…the not-too-distant future

MY LONG TAIL WHIPPED the ground and splooshed into one of the many puddles that littered my hovery's shop floor. Water dripped into scavenged buckets, and a narrow stream trickled into my nest. I hated sleeping above ground, but drowning in my nest would be infinitely worse.

"Blant." I kicked a scrap of tin, which careened into the wall and remained stuck in the mud. "Not again." I squeezed out the no-longer-fluffy tip of my tail.

How would I repair a fleet of hoverbikes when I couldn't even keep the blanting rain out of my dwelling?

Without a hovery, there was no business and, more importantly, no profit. I glanced at the red light flashing on my wristport and cringed. The credits I had brought with me were long spent. Used to a life of luxury, I had no idea how to manage finances.

If the situation got any more dire, I might need to reconsider one of Raz's many offers and move into my creepy neighbor's guest room. Berating myself for the thought, I lifted my chin and banished the notion. Not in a million annums would I move in with an alpha, even if he was another species. Learning to swim sounded more fun. I shivered. What I needed was to establish myself as a quality hovic, and soon.

When I'd applied to be a hovic on Tern, I was informed that recolonization would be slow. I hadn't cared. The promise of a fully equipped hovery and a personal dwelling in exchange for repairing the hovercrafts in Yurstille had been too enticing to question. Now, hindsight was all too clear. With no hovery or dwelling in sight, asking more questions earlier would have been more than appropriate.

My stomach still twisted every time I recalled my brother's pleas. Bonic's gaze had dropped away from mine with every mention of relocating to Tern. He hadn't wanted me to leave Lorne, let alone move to the farthest outpost in the Reiner System. But in the end, he'd relented and supported my need for a fresh start.

If I was awarded the future contract for Tern's enforcers, that would change everything. Their fleet of hoverbikes would require constant maintenance, and I knew from experience on my home planet that having the ear of law enforcers was a powerful weapon.

My neighbor's green head poked through my doorless entry, all sharp-toothed grin. "Hey, hey, Mak."

I squeezed out the damp tip of my muddy tail again and pressed my lips into a smile of sorts. "Raz, how is your first crop of graneth?"

Raz's toothy grin grew wider, and I shuddered at the number of teeth on display. "Like liquid gold." His sharp talons stuck out from under his slicker and dug into the pink soil doubling as my floor. "It's growing faster than I dreamed pos-s-sible. I can hardly believe the first harvest's next week, and there is a queue to purchase."

Raz was contracted by Yurstille, Tern's first settlement, to cultivate grain. He was one of the lucky ones. He often reminded me of his warm and dry dwelling, built before the archbuilder had fallen from a ladder to his unhappy demise. Boastful credit signs all but shone in my neighbor's eyes, and I couldn't stop mine from rolling. Our daily encounters had grown tiring.

I'd left behind the alpha males of my home planet for a reason. And while I'd never encountered Raz's species—Lizzards—before, that personality type was more familiar than the back of my blue hand.

Before I'd agreed to start a new life on Tern, I'd promised to stay as far away from alpha assholes as possible. My scars made it abundantly clear that I wouldn't survive more of their *love*. Thank the goddess Sola Raz didn't have the alpha pheromones that had blindly led me astray in the past.

"Will this rain ever stop?" I grumbled.

"Let's hope not." Raz's voice rattled and dragged out the 's.' "The heat from the Fires That Cleanse burned through the protective seed coating, and graneth is popping up everywhere thanks-s-s to the rain."

Three weeks earlier, Tern hadn't been peppered with tiny blue graneth flowers. If I weren't forced to constantly shake water from my blue fur, I might've appreciated the rolling hills dotted with star-shaped blooms springing from pink soil. With the first graneth harvested, starving to death could be removed from my list of worries while waiting for the newly arrived archbuilder to build my dwelling and hovery.

I peered through one of the many gaps in the tin sheets that formed my walls. The rolling hills were coming alive with plants, and I still found it impossible to believe that a thriving city had stood here less than one annum ago.

My fingers worked through a knot in my mane. "Can you believe there's nothing left? No wonder people are afraid to recolonize here."

Raz's long jaw snapped resolutely. "It's-s-s working out fine for me. If the medic team had arrived on time and saved the citizens of Tern, they wouldn't have had to deploy the Fires That Cleanse."

Led by my brother, Lorne had recently aided planet Hotner. Legions of refugee Lizzards—Raz likely one of them—sought new homes. Bonic had cautioned me about Lizzards, who were renowned for valuing profit above all else, but learning this secondhand was worlds different than hearing it straight from the source. A coldness that had nothing to do with the rain worked through me, and my tail stood as stiff as a flagpole.

"You're joking, right? Hundreds of thousands of people died, and all organic matter on the planet was destroyed." The electric green flames had burned everything in their path. The video footage had haunted my dreams so much that I deleted the download.

Raz flicked his wrist as if swatting at a pesky bug. "It's all a natural c-c-cycle of life."

My omega inclinations leaned toward being the voice of reason, but they walked a tightrope-thin line right now. I wanted to lay into him for his callous disregard for life, but this was my new neighbor. And although he didn't have the pheromones, his behavior was all alpha. Treading carefully around alphas was the bane of every omega's existence.

Who knew how many annums I might have to live next to this scaly asshat?

"I would like to be the first to offer you a breakfast of graneth cakes-s-s come new week," Raz proclaimed, not quite a question. His taloned toes inched toward me, and his forked tongue scented the air.

I backed up right into a puddle.

What the blant is he scenting?

My tail wound around my calf, a comfort among the quiver that plucked at my nerves. A familiar alert to stay away rang strong and clear—an alpha warning system. The same internal warning that had driven me to the Reiner System in the first place. Nothing had quieted the alarm more than moving as far away from my home planet as possible, but alphas lived everywhere.

As much as I would've loved a good breakfast that didn't come from a ration wrapper or my makeshift kitchen, there was no way I trusted Raz enough to accept his offer. My wristport chimed.

Appointment with the archbuilder: new week at seven suns

My tail unwound from where it hugged my calf. I wanted to hop on the spot but held back. I couldn't wait to talk about my dwelling plans.

I flashed my wristport at Raz. "Looks like I'm already booked."

Thank the goddess Sola.

I sighed. A meeting with the new archbuilder at last. My unfortunate reality couldn't be kept from my brother much longer, as overprotective as he was. Omegas were always protected by the alphas in their families until a complete bond with their soul-linked was made. He would board the next shuttle to Tern if he knew my living situation required me to scour the wastelands for parts to repair the few hovercrafts that did come my way. And if he knew my slipshod hovery also acted as my dwelling...

"Another time then, Makir?" Raz's voice rattled as he hissed out my name. "I'll leave you to your"—he looked around with open disdain—"hovery?"

I wasn't aware my shoulders had tensed until they slumped after his departure. My table tilted as I rested my elbows on it, scanning my dwelling. The walls were riddled with so many holes that they could've been the grounds of a blaster battle. The new archbuilder had his work cut out for him.

Under a drip-free corner stood a makeshift table covered in drawings for my dwelling and hovery. My now-dry tail bounced behind me as I added storage compartments and extra hover bays to run by the archbuilder. All set for new week, I hovered my wristport over the drawings and scanned the imagery with a smile on my lips.

With one problem solved, the next reared its ugly head.

I peeked through the holes in my wall, searching for Raz. All clear. I settled on my hovercraft and flew out through a gap I hadn't had the supplies to patch yet. My earlier encounter with my neighbor had left me on edge. For the first time in my life, I was not under the care of an alpha. My brother couldn't protect me here.

The images of Tern pre-cleanse flashed before my eyes, the wreckage below me transforming into what once was. Towering buildings with hovercrafts swirling around spiky pyramid-shaped roofs. The former hive-like world had been reduced to rubble.

As I searched the wreckage for a flat enough place to land, I planned how to win over a few enforcer friends. A twisted ankle tromping through the wastelands would be worth the risk for the protection I coveted.

The remnants of buildings, hovercrafts and daily life formed a treacherous maze of sharp-edged caves and collapsed arches as far as the eye could see. The wastelands.

I laced up the thick-soled boots Bonic had gifted me. They muffled my steps as I picked my way through the twisted piles of wreckage. Today's mission to salvage material for windshields was part of my plan to win the contract to repair the enforcers' hoverbikes and make an impression. Every market weekend, they complained about the extreme cold encountered in the Starry Mountains on their patrols. I could earn their favor if I outfitted their hoverbikes to protect them from the frigid temperatures.

A warm breeze lifted my damp mane off my shoulders. The honeyed scent of graneth blossoms filled the air alongside the odd chirp of the woodskies. It transported me back to my youth, when Bonic and I would set traps in the rocky outcroppings for bush-tailed monties and listen to the chirps on the hillside around us. We'd held the prize for the most monties trapped five years in a row and had won a hefty pile of credits each time. We'd used them to buy our first hoverbike.

Post Fires That Cleanse, crawling through the wastelands was like crawling through a graveyard. I stood and kicked through the remains. Pots were buried in warped steel beams, curled by the extreme heat of the Fires. Massive fan blades draped in wires and broken concrete mesh littered the ground.

When half a buried hovercraft came into view, my heart skipped—it was like winning the lottery. I stuffed my backpack with the smallest of its parts and noted the coordinates to return to on my wristport.

My boot-clad toe caught on a wire loop, throwing my weight to the left and landing me on my ass. "Blant!" My tail twinged when a jagged edge cut into it from below before I could jerk it away. I quickly sealed it with the healing energy from the suction buried in the tip of my tail and resolved to be more careful.

My wristport pinged—almost out of range. Trapped out here, I'd be all on my own. My squished tail righted itself with a swish, and when I pried my thick boot from under the wire, the motion dislodged a metal panel, revealing thick sheets of lamar. A contented purr rumbled in my chest.

On Lorne, lamar covered the openings on walls that allowed light in. Thin, transparent and lightweight, and most importantly, it stood up to the seasonal windstorms that had blasted my former dwelling for months. Nothing could be more perfect for hoverbike shield fabrication.

I jumped on the spot, grinning for half a second before grabbing my tail and stilling it. A glance over my shoulder ensured there were no witnesses to my youngling-like behavior.

I'm the only idiot salvaging in this mess.

I straightened my shoulders and jumped one more time for good measure, finally free from the restrictive decorum my parents expected. A lightness I hadn't felt since my departure ballooned in my lungs, and I walked back to my hovercraft with a spring in my step, planning out how to extract my bounty.

The archbuilder would undoubtedly agree that lamar could be incorporated into my living quarters and hovery. It let in natural light—every archbuilder's dream. At least, it worked that way on Lorne. My tail twirled all the way home as I mentally added lamar into my drawings for our upcoming meeting.

3

MY ARRIVAL IN YURSTILLE was not earth-shattering, and meeting Mayor Yurst, the settlement's namesake, was unremarkable, but convincing myself to take the leap had been giant. Still, I questioned my decision to leave Earth for the fifteenth time today as I leaned back against my creaky chair. My new office extended off one side of the shared sono like an afterthought. Haphazardly built, it did nothing to extol the virtues of an architect.

My mind drifted—a defense mechanism to avoid the overwhelming amount of work that needed to be caught up on—and thoughts of my first day on Tern took over.

Mayor Yurst had greeted me in the arrival port, shaking my hand like he was drawing water from an old-fashioned pump. "Welcome to Tern and the settlement of Yurstille." The tufts on his catlike ears shook.

With every arm crank, my stomach had roiled, and I'd longed for a breath of fresh air now that I stood on solid ground once more. Nausea had been my worst enemy, shuttling through space, and I'd remained locked in my small cabin, heaving, for most of the journey.

Yurst cranked my arm up and down again. "Thank you, Archbuilder Geo. So many thanks for accepting this very important role."

Saliva pooled in my mouth as I swallowed down bile, but I plastered on a smile and nodded at the man who stood a head shorter than me, wearing an outfit befitting a leprechaun, minus the top hat. I exhaled when he dropped my hand at last. The hangar we were walking through was a blur as I focused on the daylight I'd spotted ahead.

An overhead bay door stood open halfway, and we ducked underneath it. Immediately, a gust of wind coated me in a layer of fine pink soil, and I choked, coughing to clear my throat. *Damn it, it* is *like Tatooine.*

"My, my," Mayor Yurst said, patting my back. "It does take a bit of getting used to, but before you know it, you'll feel like you've been here forever. I'll just give you a bit of a tour and leave you at the sono to settle."

The list of new colonizers who required homes unfurled in front of me, across my desk, like a never-ending story. My head throbbed. The Tern equivalent of Tylenol would barely take the edge off my growing headache. It was as if quicksand was slowly sucking me under.

'Install fountain around statue' was at the top of the list, underlined and triple asterisked. Under the list of all the colonizers' names—most unpronounceable to me—it said 'school, library, recri-plaza and jail.' The more I thought about designing a jail that could contain winged, behemoth-sized and knee-sized aliens, the more my head ached. At least it was last on the list. Mayor Yurst would have put it at the top of the list if he were concerned, right?

What I really wanted from the mayor was a few words of wisdom on where construction should begin. Who was next on the list? Instead, his obsequious thanks for coming to Tern curdled my stomach, and I remained clueless about whose house to build first. The homeowner with the biggest teeth?

The previous archbuilder, a white-winged Nacer, had lived in an aviary on a cliff top before his demise. As a human with two legs, claiming it as my own was impossible. Instead, I had to share a sono, much like a dormitory, with my work crew of Rock Dwellers. Giant, gray-skinned and bald, their snores were so loud they rattled the floor my bed stood on.

Fortunately, I'd worked out a system with my foreman, JayJay, in my first week here. He was quickly becoming my go-to Rock Dweller for all things alien. He constantly chirped at me about how my mouth hung open whenever a new alien species approached. Or when I stared slack-jawed at the hollow squawk of the tiny flying woodskie, no bigger than a hummingbird. He especially loved when the lunal weed that grew under the moon's light trapped me in its snare. But JayJay was a building machine, and his math skills were off the charts by Earth standards.

JayJay and I filed outside to the warehouse to complete the weekly inventory—JayJay in his head and me on my wristport. My mouth watered when I swallowed honey-scented air. I forced my wide eyes back to normal, hoping he wouldn't notice as a species with a lizard tail trailing along the ground walked by.

"I can count your teeth," JayJay joked as he jostled my shoulder, nearly knocking me on my ass.

"Yeah, yeah. You got me, funny guy." I casually nodded toward the alien species new to me. "What planet is he from?"

Every day I witnessed something new. Yesterday, it had rained so hard it turned the unpaved streets into pink mud, not unlike the river of strawberries on the Candyland board game from my childhood.

JayJay's brow ridges popped. Though his long, bony protrusion didn't have any hair, it seemed to function just the same as eyebrows as he scanned the alien in question. "That is Raz S'Lant. He is from the recently war-ravaged planet, Hotner. Lucky for you, his dwelling is already built."

When would I stop acting like the new kid on the block?

I recited Ginger's words in my head. "Do not criticize yourself in any capacity for the first three months, and even then, do so with kindness. Promise me, Geo. You've been your own worst enemy for too long."

"Bish, I know that look, boss man. Cheer up." JayJay dragged me back to the task at hand. His slow speech sent a wave of calm through me.

I pressed the translator embedded behind my ear when "bish" didn't register. It had been injected on the shuttle to Tern. The instant ability to communicate in intergalactically recognized languages was mind-boggling. Every time I said a word that went untranslated, JayJay listed all the synonyms to fill the gaps in our translators.

We walked back through the arched entrance of my office. The list that kept me awake at night remained spread across my desk like a tablecloth that could span three more tables, and I tipped my head to the side. "Bish?"

"You know, boss man, like, c'mon, or forget about it, or no big deal."

He was right I did need to loosen up a little. Though I'd never been as laid back as JayJay, his affirming head nods and constant laughter told me I was doing okay so far. One person liking me was enough of a start. I'd goggled at his giant size for far too long in the first week, but he hadn't appeared to mind. The other inhabitants only had a few months on me, anyways. Tern leveled the playing field. Everyone started new here, and from the way a young Nacer had tripped over his wing tips a couple days back, many had never seen a human before.

JayJay's three fingers spread over my desktop where he leaned. "Time idles when you live in the past."

I still grew weepy-eyed over leaving Pika and Charz behind. The only thing that had stopped the downward spiral of depression caused by moving to another planet was Ginger moving into my house. A win-win for all.

My dogs weren't the only thing I'd left behind. Cameron had sweet-talked me into letting him stay, but when I'd broached the subject of him taking good care of the house, his lips had curled into a snarl. *"You want me to take care of your grandma's house and your dogs for a goddamn year?"*

Our house. Our dogs.

"Geo, I always knew you were delusional, but if you think I'll wait a year for your fat ass and small dick, think again. Think again."

The memory of Cameron's caustic reply still burned the ragged edges of my heart.

So instead, Ginger had moved into my home with my dogs. I exhaled and pushed my hands into my overall pockets. Everything I loved on Earth would be cared for in one tidy package. Now, I needed to move on—a nearly impossible concept when my brain drifted to Cameron's last words every second thought.

"Call me when you get back. Maybe we can meet for a coffee or something."

Fat chance!

Even if the linen scent of his shirt—freshly laundered by me—still lingered in my nose, I was done with Cameron. He could turn dramatically on one foot all he liked, and all I would say to him was sayonara.

JayJay drummed his fingers on my desktop, refocusing me. "Stop thinking of those dodges you left behind."

"Dogs, pups, puppies, doggies—all names you can use for Charz and Pika. A Dodge is like a type of hovercraft."

So far, responding with variations of the unrecognized word had confused us more than helped, but I couldn't wait to hear JayJay, an eight-foot behemoth with muscles the size of boulders, say, 'doggies.'

"Here comes our first appointment," JayJay announced as my wristport pinged.

Ayla Rowtee smoothed a hand over the long dress covering her pregnant belly, then clasped her husband's hand. They sat angled on a wooden bench, so their wings wouldn't brush the roughly finished wall.

Her head tilted to the side like an owl, and she opened her short beak to speak. "The previous archbuilder had approved our plans already and was just about to build when he fell from a ladder."

Mayor Yurst had been tight-lipped when he'd discussed the former archbuilder. "I wondered what happened to him."

Her husband, Tarik, snapped his wings together tightly. "His wings were bound from the beam he was carrying on his back, and..."

Ayla shuddered and clutched her husband's hand tighter. "We really need something rather soon." She pointed a long finger at her belly.

Tarik clacked his beak at his wife, then turned to face me where I sat behind my desk. "You must be under a lot of pressure." He glanced at the long roll of paper. "We trust you've scheduled us according to our arrival date."

The husband and wife chattered back and forth, her with urgency, him not wanting to offend. It was cute that they thought there was a method to the scheduling madness. According to arrival date wasn't a bad idea though. I'd have to run that by JayJay.

"Let me sum this up. You're interested in a dwelling." JayJay and the rest of the crew had drilled the term 'dwelling' into my vocabulary over the last week when I'd drawn one too many blank looks after saying house. Did I find it odd that the translator could translate chandelier perfectly but couldn't translate house? Yep. But I wasn't going to complain. It was one hundred percent more effective than charades. "Up high, fairly remote, but where you can see what's happening around you? Also, time is of the essence."

Their wings fluttered behind them, their eagerness uncontained as both feathered heads bobbed in agreement. I caught my foreman's gaze, and Jay-Jay's grin echoed mine.

"Well, Ayla and Tarik, I have fantastic news." The bigger my smile grew, the more their feathers quivered. "As the previous archbuilder can no longer use his nearly new dwelling, I'm pleased to offer you the cliff-top aviary to make your own."

Ayla and Tarik's heads turned directly toward the aviary like homing beacons. "Thank the goddess Sola," she muttered. "Archbuilder Geo, you have made us so happy." Ayla's face shimmered as tears wet her face.

Tarik wrapped his winged arms around her and stood proudly. "When our first youngling is brought into this world, we would be honored for you to attend the naming ceremony."

I tipped my chin and stood to shake their hands but stopped at the last minute. Handshakes were not always welcome, and I couldn't remember the Nacers' practice at that moment. "It would be my pleasure."

Ayla and Tarik departed my office before immediately flying to the aviary.

JayJay crouched low beside my desk. "That is a rare offer for a Nacer to make. The value they place on the privacy of their younglings is known throughout the galaxies."

I pressed a hand to my aching ear. "Were you trying to whisper that?"

"Bish. I can be quiet." JayJay shrugged.

Quieter than what? A jetliner?

The marker skidded satisfyingly across the paper covering my desk when I struck a line through the Rowtees' names. I enjoyed the comfort of paper for a visual tally, but I also logged it in the more sophisticated digital system for official record keeping.

"That was an easy one." I nudged JayJay with my elbow.

Like the static air surrounding Dorothy before the tornado pulled her into the Land of Oz, a frisson of energy pricked the hair on my forearms. A tall, tailed silhouette appeared in the doorway, haloed in sunlight.

Life experience had taught me to pay attention to these moments, because something life-changing always followed, but this was a new level of awareness. Each hair follicle tingled—the nerves beneath lit up by a bone-deep vibration.

"Is this the archbuilder's?"

The smooth voice raised the frequency of the vibration, honing it until my entire body hummed. Then a strong-jawed male, blue-skinned, with a face trimmed in a multi-hued blue mane, walked into the office. My mind went blank for two seconds before registering that he must be our next appointment.

What was his name? Makir?

Yes, Makir. His name was next on the list that puddled around my feet. His mane fanned out and reached the center of his back, and when he turned his hand to check the time on his wristport, he showed off smooth blue palms. Everywhere else he was uncovered appeared to be furred in my favorite color: blueprint blue.

One of the reasons I had studied architecture, I often joked with Ginger, was because of the stacks of blueprints old world architects' desks used to be buried in. Little did I know that I would end up with a similar stack of papers on my own messy desk.

Makir's long, thin, fur-tipped tail coiled around his waist and hugged him as he approached the table where I sat, widening at the base where it breached the jumpsuit he wore. His silver eyes met mine, then flashed to lavender so quickly I wasn't entirely sure it had happened before his gaze immediately slid to the floor. I couldn't put my finger on it, but there was something familiar about him.

How could that be? My mind had turned to jelly.

I'd never met an alien before my interview, and not face to face until I'd set foot on the shuttle to this planet. I snapped my fingers.

Makir jolted, his eyes glued to my fingers.

He was the same species as the pair depicted on the brochures Ginger had force-fed me weekly for the last couple of years.

I jerked upright and bumped the table that acted as my desk, sending a shower of papers flying over Makir. I thrust my hand out in the worst unreciprocated handshake ever as my notes floated down. My tingling skin drove away rational behavior, and before I had control of my voice, I barked, "Archbuilder Geo."

JayJay's brow ridges furrowed as if to ask 'What's wrong with you?'

I gave myself a mental smack. How stupid could I get? I knew handshakes were not universally acceptable greetings.

My new client took two strides backward and fully clamped his arms to his sides. His focus turned to his pant legs, which were caked in pink mud and matched my office's unfinished floor. I dropped my hand and gripped the edge of my desk until my knuckles turned white.

Stop acting like a clown.

Everything I'd learned about respecting the customs of different species had flown out of my head. Still, for some reason, I yearned to know how soft the fur on the back of his hands was. The prickly sensation doubled under my skin.

"I'm Makir," he muttered as his tail snapped behind him. "I have an appointment about my dwelling and hovery." He paused, then stood tall—well over a foot taller than me—and after he spoke, his tail abruptly stilled as if forced. His eyes met my nose and rose no higher. I wanted to see the silver again.

My stomach pitched and soured the same way it had on the two-week shuttle to Tern. Once gravity had been reinstated, I'd stopped puking and acclimatized. Still, every time the shuttle had stopped to pick up colonizers for Yurstille, my stomach had dipped and hollowed, threatening to spill once more.

"I have drawn up some ideas." Makir pressed the button on his wristport, displaying the images he had worked up. Into the air, he projected what looked like a well-planned mechanic's shop with bay doors, and a bedroom and kitchen appeared hastily added, as if an afterthought.

"What type of material is this?" JayJay's slow drawl eased some of the tension as he pointed to what looked like windows to me.

Makir shifted onto the balls of his feet, and his tense shoulders dropped as he focused on his plans. "I've yet to retrieve them, but my last trip to the wastelands uncovered sheets of lamar. I can supply them. If you can install them."

The room filled with an enticing juniper scent. Inhaling, I settled back in my chair, my hands loose in my lap.

JayJay's lawnmower-like laugh echoed through the bare-bones office. "Rock Dweller building crews can install anything."

I thrust out my chest. "And now that a human is in charge, no job is impossible."

Fuck, could I have sounded any more arrogant?

JayJay's head whipped toward me, but he said nothing. I tried again, leaning across the table to inhale more of Makir's fragrant juniper scent, but the tingling under my skin undermined coherent thought.

"What I mean is humans have a long history of building incredible things. The Great Pyramids used thousands of enslaved people..." I stalled, quickly backtracking, searching for a better example. I swallowed hard. "Coast-to-coast railways crisscross the largest continents on Earth. Oppressed minorities built most..."

My subconscious was working against me. Obviously, there were some repressed emotions I was dealing with at the moment, now that I was one of the smaller species and the lone human around. Formal hierarchy on Tern was nonexistent. A hodgepodge of species across the Reiner System had answered the call to recolonize. But if shit hit the fan, razor-sharp teeth and boulder-sized muscles would out-compete any skills I had to offer.

"Maybe you best stop there, boss man," JayJay said, widening his eyes, and Makir stepped farther away.

Makir muttered under his breath, barely audible, "Great, the new arch-builder comes from a long line of power-hungry alphas."

Instead of digging myself into a deeper hole, I forced my butt back into my chair and loosened my hands in my lap. I filled my nose with the juniper scent saturating the room. Like a balm, it soothed the prickling itch under my skin, drawing me into a trance-like state.

Typically the taskmaster, I kept meetings on time. My foreman tended to get carried away digging into the minutiae of what the dwelling owners wanted. But today, I would have happily let JayJay and Makir carry on if it meant I could openly observe this blue alien. When he relaxed, the fluid grace of his tail was beautiful to my eyes, and his voice lulled me into complacency. The more I watched him, the more I wanted to know him. Was the fur tip of his tail silky? Or was it brittle and impossible to run my fingers through, like Cameron's gelled hair?

My wristport pinged and I shot upright in my chair. I needed to schedule longer meetings.

If Cameron's nephew had been there, he would've said Makir resembled Glaceon, his all-time favorite Pokémon next to Charizard and Pikachu, whom my dogs were named after. Only Makir was bigger, much bigger, and much more human-like. I smiled. Maybe there would be a picture from Ginger of my puppies' latest antics today.

A second notification startled me. The next client would be waiting. Back rigid in my chair, I lifted my chin. "I'll send you an invite for two days from now at seven o'clock." I cleared my throat and corrected myself, "I mean, seven suns...to review the final drawing before your build proceeds on Monday. Please com me if you need to reschedule. If you'll excuse me, I have another matter I must attend to." The prickly sensation deepened to a vibration that rolled through me, and I dug my heels into the floor to combat it.

What's with the deep voice?

JayJay's brow ridges scrunched, and Makir locked his eyes on my nose.

JayJay's gaze bounced from Makir to me. "You mean new week. Right, boss man?"

Makir nodded at my nose and quickly scurried out of the office.

I mumbled, "Yeah, new week."

"You have another matter you must attend to?" JayJay teased in his rumbly voice. "What stick crawled up your ass?"

"Did you feel that?" I ignored his jab.

"You mean your small male syndrome?" JayJay rumbled at the same time he slapped his knee.

"The tingling. Did you feel the vibrations under your skin?"

He shook his head as he walked to the adjoined kitchen. "Are all people from Earth short and crazy?"

The strange, prickly vibrations that had intensified the whole time Makir was near quieted. With some respite to think, I cringed. Apparently, my haywire brain had turned me into a trumped-up politician who'd dismissed Makir like he was nothing. Maybe I could apologize with an upgrade on the house? Would he like a heated towel bar?

Slumped in my chair after the final appointment of the day, I sipped a glass of water. JayJay passed me a slice of graneth bread smeared with peanut butter-type spread, munching one of his own. The flavor took me back to elementary school, where I could find a version of the same sandwich in my Spiderman lunch kit most days.

"Do you think our plan is too ambitious?"

"Bish, boss man. The crew is solid." His slow speech helped to unwind my bunched shoulders. "Eight dwellings a month, no problems."

Before I could finish my food, my head lolled. JayJay's chortle woke me. "Real food, then bed. Bish, let's go."

I blindly followed JayJay to the kitchen we shared with the rest of the crew. They'd been on-site all day, building. While I listened to the loud but happy chatter surrounding me, the first stirrings of friendship took root, spreading warmth through my chest.

Convinced that something in the alien air had caused my erratic behavior this morning, I brushed off the warnings my body had sent earlier. Instead, I declared

I would act perfectly normal the next time I saw Makir. There would be no skin tingling, no deep voice and no handshaking, no matter how much I wanted to know how soft his fur was.

4

"**I**'M NOT GOING TO run," I chanted quietly, power walking as cold sweat broke out on my forehead. The walk back to my dwelling from the archbuilder's office took twice as long as it should have, my legs growing stiffer with each innocent sound I flinched at. Squawking woodskies, doors closing... A squelch in the mud behind me revealed a passerby on their way to the bakery. Blanting bad luck. I'd left Lorne to escape alpha assholes—one in particular—and here they were, popping up all around me. First Raz, and now the archbuilder.

The fear of starting somewhere new was nothing like the terror I'd experienced at Reinik's hands. I thanked the goddess Sola every rotation that our bond had never been completed. Now, it only took the presence of an alpha male to set me on edge—any alpha male.

Small puffs of pink dust kicked up around my feet on the path. The safety of my unfinished dwelling was three steps away. The thrown-together walls barely kept out the rain, but it was home, nonetheless. My drumming heartbeats would slow in a moment, and I'd fall apart where no one could see.

"Hey. Hey, Makir, I've finally caught you."

I jumped. Raz's toothy grin chilled me. My lungs strained when his hand clamped around my wrist, taloned fingertips clicking together where they circled. I had no recollection of holding my breath until my lungs screamed for air.

"Don't you think it's time to take a meal with me as you promis-s-s-ed?"

Promised? Did I promise?

I froze in his grip. In my panic to leave the archbuilder's, I'd forgotten to try and avoid Raz. I was tired of declining his increasingly less polite offers to provide me with more suitable living quarters. Even if I only had one ration bar left and it rained daily for the rest of my life, I would still not agree to move into Raz's guestroom. No one would have that kind of control over me again.

My breathing grew shallow and rapid while my mind blurred. My parents had passed my raising to my brother, but they had drilled into me from an early age how serious promise contracts were to Lornians. The thought of breaking a promise sent my stomach spinning.

I must have nodded because before I knew it, Raz had pulled me into his dwelling and firmly closed the door behind him. The next minute I was seated at his table with a cool drink in front of me to accompany the fresh cold sweat breaking out behind my blue-furred knees.

Around Raz and the archbuilder, I was prey. Nothing more than a hunted bush-tailed montie. Only, with the archbuilder, my desire to submit was so amplified that eye contact was as much of a problem as my voice. I could barely eke out a three-word sentence. My escape from the archbuilder had left me fumbling for a reason to escape this dinner. Alpha males would be my demise, but a bully I could deal with. And Raz was a bully. The archbuilder though… He was something else altogether.

I had to avoid touching the archbuilder at all costs.

Raz plunked a dish down in front of me. Now that I was out of the archbuilder's presence and Raz's scaly grasp, I could focus a little. The honey-scented flowers in the center of his table filled my nose, mixing with the savory smell of herbed meat. The tiny graneth flowerheads drooped over a tall container and bounced when the table jostled, dusting it in pollen. Covered with a blue cloth, the table was the same color as me.

I gulped. The dishes were patterned with stars, and the tart and sweet hiscus I favored filled fluted glasses. My tail swished over Raz's polished floors. Not a speck of pink dust lingered anywhere except where it fell in small clumps off the ankles of my jumpsuit. Warta, the stringed instruments Boola played, thrummed from a speaker in the background.

This is not a neighborly meal.

"How was-s-s your meeting with the archbuilder?" Raz asked tightly.

My accommodations proved to be a sticky topic. "G-ood." My voice wavered. "We meet again in two days." I sipped my hiscus, the coolness of the glass causing condensation on the outside, wetting the skin on my palms. The rigid set of my shoulders loosened when I filled my fancy glass a second time. Raz's house smelled of roasting meat, and my stomach rumbled.

"Ah, glad you enjoy that. Hiscus is a new offering at the market—I thought I'd splurge." He leaned toward me. "No expense is too high to celebrate our special occas-s-sion."

What special occasion?

He lifted his glass to mine. "And when will your dwelling be ready? I'm looking forward to seeing your nest."

You're never seeing my nest, asshat. "I must get my own then. Who is the hiscus seller?" My tail-wrapped calf would've revealed how fake my confidence was to anyone who knew me, but Raz bought it.

Creep.

"No need for that, Makir. I would love to sh-sh-share with you." His toothy mouth widened over my name, and a cold shiver straightened my spine into a steel rod. I wondered if his jaw completely unhinged, like those of some of the lizard-like creatures on Lorne did when they captured extra-large prey.

He pushed the mouthwatering meat toward me on its star-patterned plate. "Please try some mantu. One of the hunting parties had fresh meat for sale and gave me some excellent advic-c-ce on preparation."

Since my arrival on Tern months ago, I'd been starved of fresh meat and living off ration bars. The hovery—or should I say, lack of a hovery—had returned little profit. Bonic would, no doubt, top up my credits if I asked, but I was doing this on my own. The savory aroma of the mantu filled the air, making saliva pool in my mouth like a wild beast.

"Oh, and the lovely things the baker did with my graneth. You mus-s-st try one." A puffy triangle of bread was placed on the side of my plate, perfect for soaking up all the flavorful juices from the mantu.

The conversation was pleasant enough, but the way Raz's forked tongue flickered on every 's' heightened my urge to run. Fast.

I barely stopped the eager purr in my chest as the perfect combination of saltiness and pungent umami flavor melted on my tongue. "This is fantastic." I forked up another mouthful. "The graneth puff is a perfect sponge. My compliments."

Raz leered, his scaly torso all too visible with his top three shirt buttons undone. He reached to caress my hand. Little did he know how practiced I was in avoiding this particular move. A glass of hiscus was in my hand before any offense could be taken.

My mother would've been appalled at how I shoveled the rest of my dinner into my mouth, but it was so much better than my mealy ration bars, I couldn't let it go to waste.

"The archbuilder has given me homework, and it's been a long rotation." I yawned, genuinely exhausted. "I'll have to take my leave. I enjoyed the meal, thank you." My chair glided back smoothly against Raz's polished floors as I exited in a way that could only be construed as polite and neighborly.

"Leaving so s-s-soon? My guest room awaits you. Would you like to see it?" He gestured down his hall, his shirt gaping open farther as he maneuvered in front of the exit, blocking it.

Throat dry, my gaze darted around the room, hoping that a decent alpha would magically appear to rescue me. A heady disappointment had me swallowing hard. My promise to myself lingered beneath the fear. On Tern, you will be more than just an omega. You will be a successful hovic. You will make friends. You will be all the things you never knew you could be.

Chin high, I braced myself. With a grace inherited from my Tuniga lineage and reinforced by the High Hold's defensive arts instructor, I spun on my heel, tail high. Raz's hungry gaze ate up every movement. A smile twitched at the corner of my mouth before I crouched low and sprang up, deftly dodging under the arm barring my exit.

A stunned Raz called out, "Very well. Good night, Makir. I will see you s-s-soon. The offer still stands. You are welcome to use my guest room until your dwelling is complete."

Adrenaline waning, the promise of that "s-s-soon" haunted me, and I ran the three steps to my door. The old tin stopped and stuttered when it caught on the uneven ground, but at least it acted as an alarm when someone entered. I expelled a tight breath and plopped down into a wobbly chair, my tail wrapped around my waist in a hug.

You did good. Be proud of yourself.

The moonlight streaming through the gaps in my walls only highlighted my need for a functional hovery, and my shoulders slumped. Why was my future in the hands of the archbuilder? When would my dwelling be ready?

The archbuilder abruptly ending our meeting flashed clearly in my mind. He had something against me, but my omega needs didn't care. They went haywire around him and his summer fields scent. If only he weren't an overbearing jerk. A round, furless jerk who barely came to my chin.

Something's deeply wrong with my omega instincts.

My teeth chattered in the cold. The nest I'd hastily dug in the corner was too shallow and poorly lined for Tern. Curled into a ball, I contemplated my desire to submit to a human. Such an unattractive species. Damn, alpha pheromones baffled me.

He didn't even have a tail. If my brother, Bonic, were here, he would compare his color to the tasteless paste we cleaned our teeth with as younglings and dismiss him with a flick of his tail. That option didn't exist for me. I needed to get in the archbuilder's good graces and get my business off the ground.

I jacked the last bolt into the wrap-around lamar windshield on Sisip's hoverbike and slapped the dust off my jumpsuit. My clothes collected the dirt off my floor like rocks to an asteroid field. The polished floor of my dreams sparkled in my imagination, five hoverbike repairs out of reach.

The fuzzy tips of Sisip's upright ears twitched. "Thank the goddess Sola, for the new windshield, Makir!" the lead enforcer exclaimed. "The windchill up the Starry Mountains has me close to donating a frost-bitten nose to my hometown cantina."

What would her cantina want with a nose?

I laughed, dropping my torque wrench into a bucket of charging liquid. "Remind me to never visit that cantina."

Sisip's tawny ears twitched on top of her head. "I'd have your back. They wouldn't put any of your lovely, furred appendages into drinks on my watch," she said with a sincerity I appreciated, even if we both knew I would never visit that cantina.

"That crybaby, Warren, has the next patrol in the Starry Mountains sector." She smirked. "I can guarantee you will see him soon." She rolled her hoverbike out of what would one day be a bay and muttered, "Now, if only there was something to keep my hands warm."

"Spread the word. I have plenty more lamar," I shouted to Sisip's retreating back, and she replied with an over-the-shoulder wave. So what if I didn't have any more lamar physically in my shop? I was only a few spare parts away from outfitting my hover trailer to haul as much lamar out of the wastelands as I could find.

My wristport pinged. I lifted my wrist, read the message, and exhaled. Then, with my eyes fixed on the ceiling's overlapping tin sheets, I thanked the goddess Sola. To my great relief, my credit account icon turned from a dismal red to a gratitude-filled green. The timing couldn't have been better. My fingers itched. No time like the present to purchase supplies for an extended trip to the wastelands.

The market was cheerfully busy, species of all colors: giant gray Rock Dwellers, white-winged Nacers and dark-skinned Boola chatted behind tables draped in the bounty the first season of Tern offered.

An enforcer armed with a blaster, a smile and no sense of urgency, leaned with one foot bent against the bakery's wall. Crumbs littered the ground by his feet.

"Makir, Raz passed along your compliments." D'ovey, the baker, gestured toward the door he stood in, drumming up business. "A graneth puff on the house."

Still warm and smothered with honeyed graneth flower oil, the puff melted in my mouth. "Excellent strategy," I teased the dark-skinned Boola, who handed out samples from his storefront. "I'll take a dozen, please." The baker's lips pursed as he held in a knowing chuckle and returned from behind his counter with a still-warm paper-wrapped package for me.

My nose steered my steps toward the stand that boasted grilled mantu as my stomach grumbled. I purchased and then devoured a mantu skewer in two bites. Rich and smoky, it melted like velvet on my tongue. While I licked my fingers, I recited the recipe the stand proprietor, D'irk, told me back to him. "You ferment the mantu in fungus paste in a cool dark place for three days, then add graneth honey and char?"

"Yep. Three or four days, depending on how soft you want the meat."

D'irk shared more recipes, but my focus narrowed on a dagger strapped to a fabric-covered wall of hunting supplies behind his grill.

Can I afford that?

Would a weapon in my possession give me the sense of security I longed for? Who knew what I would find in the wastelands? Or my own neighborhood, for that matter? As it turned out, the Fires That Cleanse hadn't eradicated everything organic on Tern as initially thought.

"I'll also take a reel of that thin line. How many credits for that dagger?"

D'irk tipped his head deeply, a Boola trait I'd picked up on. "Thirty-eight." He unstrapped the dagger from the wall and held it out to me to inspect. "Are you a hunter?"

I gulped at the cost. It wasn't unreasonable, but my credits were spread thin. It looked like I'd have another month of ration bars. "My brother and I used to trap bush-tailed monties on Lorne." I deposited the dagger in my satchel, holding up my wristport for D'irk to scan. "Not the largest of prey, but they were tricky little beasts." Even though my account was treacherously close to red again, I beamed as I shared my story.

"You should join us." D'irk flipped his skewers on the grill. "I'm planning a hunting trip, new moon, with a couple more enforcers. We could use a fourth." Many of the enforcers charged with policing Yurstille, the first and only settlement to be recolonized on Tern, held side jobs. Their shifts were so long that they were compensated with extended time off.

If I got lucky on the hunt—my tail twirled—it would mean no more ration bars. "Count me in. Sounds like an adventure." I'd committed to trying new things, it was part of starting over on a new planet, and the weight of my worry over alphas and hoveries had lightened already. I added D'irk's contact info to my wristport. With a hunting trip in the works, a knife was a must. It was a well-made purchase. I licked the last of the mantu from my lips and savored every drop.

About to turn around and walk back to my dwelling, I jolted to a stop. My skin tingled and my tail stood rigid, hyperaware of the attention suddenly on me. I found my fingers wrapped around the handle of my new knife inside the satchel that crossed my body.

Across the path from D'irk's grill stood D'ovey's bakery, and exiting it was the archbuilder. His eyes were locked on me and his lips were pressed into a rigid line. I don't know how long he'd been standing there, but when he recognized my matching glare, he fumbled his fresh baking. His bag split open just as a Rock Dweller walked past and churned the baked goods into the ground. I snickered as I walked back to my dwelling.

With the final touches added to the bay doors for my hovery, I'd finished brushing up my drawings to include JayJay's suggestions in preparation for tomorrow. I double-checked my alarm and emptied the containers collecting rain. It was forecast to come down hard this moon. Finally, I settled into my nest to sleep.

The meeting with the archbuilder was at seven suns, and I wanted to depart immediately afterward to maximize the rotation in the wastelands. I would desperately need the solitude to recharge after a sun in the archbuilder's presence.

5

Bent over a shared sink in the cramped bathroom, I scratched my beard after another sleep-deprived night. "I really need to get my own place."

Tino, one of my Rock Dweller crew, bumped into me, still half-asleep, and toothpaste dribbled from my chin. "My apologies," he rumbled extra slowly as he washed his smooth gray face with three-fingered hands.

Sully was the next to stagger into the wash-up area. My deodorant shot across the smooth floor like a hockey puck when he knocked over my toiletry case. "Apologies, boss man." His deep voice resonated as he spread moisturizing paste over his bald head with one hand and dozily crouched to retrieve my deodorant with the other.

My work crew was great, but I no longer wanted to live with them. The behemoths put up houses quicker than ten crews back home, but unfortunately, Rock Dwellers had deep, rumbling voices. Putting ten of them into a room together was like sleeping in an airport hangar. And I was entirely too familiar with their grooming habits.

JayJay slammed straight into me, sending my toiletry case flying again as I left the wash-up area. I put my hand up to stop him from speaking. "Yeah, I know. Apologies, boss man." I mimicked his deep voice. These guys were worse than Cameron without his coffee when he first woke up, bumbling around like drunken sailors. Every morning it was as if I were launched like a pinball and shot between a minefield of sleepy boulders.

Intentionally setting my alarm for half an hour earlier tomorrow, I strolled outside through the arched doorway into a peach-tinted sunrise. The first woodskie squawks spiraled through the air, and the earth was dampened under a layer of dew. I inhaled deeply before the air filled with choking pink dust.

The morning sun warmed the back of my neck and my knees creaked as I settled into the opening pose of my tai chi sequence. Meeting with Makir this morning would require complete control of my mind, and if I skipped my practice, I'd be even more hopeless.

I took another deep breath. I will present myself as nothing but relaxed and approachable.

I didn't know why Makir would be crucial for my future, but the way my hair stood on end in his presence lingered in my mind, and brushing off my instincts yesterday had kept me up half the night. This sixth sense had never led me wrong, except when I ignored it.

Sweep arms forward... Hold the ball... Pivot... Brush hands with knee... Ward off left...

"You dancing, boss man?" JayJay interrupted me halfway through my set. More awake now, he cupped a thermos full of the syrupy coffee-like drink Rock

Dwellers preferred in his three-fingered hand. His thick brow ridges twitched in question.

"Funny, JayJay." I paused with my legs spread and arms mimicking a crane. "I'm trying not to act like a jerk at Makir's appointment, and I'm doing tai chi to focus my energy." My mind still reeled over how robotically I'd spoken to him yesterday.

The corner of JayJay's lips twisted up. "Does it work?"

I tipped my head side to side and lunged. "When I'm focused and not distracted by the over-curious." Then I gave up on tai chi altogether.

"Curious?"

My gaze caught a tiny woodskie flying by. "Inquisitive, nosy, questioning."

JayJay's brow ridges dipped and rolled as if he was silently laughing before he sipped more of his morning sludge. "I'll help you," he drawled as we walked companionably toward the office.

Before I could question whether JayJay's offer to help me with Makir was a good thing, the fine hairs on my arms stood on end. Unseen, I knew Makir was around the corner.

My teeth clenched, and I forced my jaw to loosen. "You don't feel that?"

"Feel what?" The corner of JayJay's mouth turned down in concern. "You feeling all right?" His thick palm brushed against my forehead.

I swatted his arm away. "Quit it."

What the hell is wrong with me?

Any positive energy I'd managed to channel earlier was now locked up tighter than Cameron's passcode to his bank card. My shoulders were so tight I might as well have had a hockey stick strapped across them as I walked to the warehouse.

Makir straddled a hoverbike hauling a trailer. They floated, barely skimming the ground in front of the warehouse. Our eyes met and a sudden jolt of energy forced me to step back and steady myself. His eyes flashed from silver to lavender, then immediately refocused on the dry ground.

Fuck. How am I going to build this guy a house?

Makir's tail lashed back and forth behind him. The propulsion from the hoverbike clouded the air with bursts of pink dust.

"Is this the lamar you spoke of?" JayJay ambled over to the trailer that hovered behind Makir. On it were thick sheets of a translucent material similar to plexiglass, and a well-worn backpack.

Makir turned off the ignition, and the bike and trailer drifted softly to the ground. His eyes were silver when he murmured a quiet greeting, "Happy morning, JayJay. Yes, I brought some to leave with you. It can be reused to allow light into the dwellings you're building." Makir looked at my nose and nodded. "Archbuilder."

"Salutations, Makir." I rubbed my palms over my tingling arms and up to my beard, hiding my grimace. I'd never greeted anyone with 'salutations' in my entire life. This wasn't an episode of Star Trek.

JayJay smoothed his hand over the lamar and knocked on it like a door. "I understand now. I think this could be repurposed quite easily and with high demand. What do you think, boss man? We would be happy to pay Makir for supplying us with lamar, wouldn't we?"

I nodded my agreement, rolling my lips inward, fighting the tingling vibrations that lit up my nerves and avoiding speaking altogether. There would be no more word-vomit from me.

I am calm. I am in control.

Makir's tail, which had stopped twitching while JayJay admired the new building material, now whipped against the ground. It hit the dirt so hard that the cloud of dust he dislodged triggered a coughing fit as he dragged his gaze to my nose. "That won't be necessary."

Hmmm... Is he offended that I want to pay him?

"I'm heading out today to collect more lamar after we finalize the details for my dwelling and hovery." He brushed the pink dust off his clean but worn jumpsuit, highlighting his long, lean limbs, and absently combed the dirt off the back of his hands. "I anticipate the enforcers will request it once they see Sisip's windshield." His voice was too loud, like an announcement.

My mind drifted. Does Makir's entire body have blue fur?

JayJay nudged my elbow and smirked at me.

I cleared my throat. "The Intergalactic Federation of Architecture and Building Authority will cover the costs of a basic dwelling and a no-frills hovery. However, as we discussed, if you require anything beyond the standard, my crew will complete the work at an additional charge to you."

His silver gaze flicked over his worn backpack and patched jumpsuit, and his shoulders stiffened. "You have my promise you will get your credits." His firm delivery lost some impact when his gaze still didn't rise above my nose.

I hadn't thought otherwise, but chose to not offend him more. "Very well then. Show me your design."

Why is my voice so deep?

Makir projected the images from his wristport into the air without moving any closer. "I would like three hover bays"—he pointed to each arched doorway—"a wash station, secure parking, a front counter and a small seating area." He drew a long finger over the projection. "This wall divided into tools, parts storage and a lamar skylight."

The more features he listed for his hovery, the more his fur captivated me. Soft and downy-looking, it covered the backs of his palms and traveled up his wrists, disappearing under his jumpsuit. A tuft of blue peeked out from the top of his zipper, where my imagination conjured velvet-muscled pecs. His face was a lighter blue, the color of blue raspberry cotton candy, and entirely humanoid except for the silver color of his almond-shaped eyes.

He shook his head, stirring his shaggy mane like a caged lion while he impatiently waited for my response. Once again, the intensity of his steady gaze was laser-focused on my nose.

Shit. I'd totally tuned out after skylight. What was the last thing he said?

The back of JayJay's palm neared my brow, and I pushed it away. Usually, this giant boulder of a man's maternal instincts were funny, but not right now. I had no desire to be the smallest guy in the vicinity, and *hell* no to the childlike treatment on top of it. I sucked in my big belly, forced out my chest and stood as tall as possible before walking toward Makir. He shuffled backward with every step I advanced.

Was he afraid of me?

I rubbed my forearms, then forced my hands to my sides. Tingles be damned. My construction company on Earth had thrived under my professionalism. This shouldn't be a problem. I could be professional with Makir.

"The IFABA will cover the cost of two bays. You will need to create the storage or hire our crew for your shelves and the third bay. Also, the skylight would be considered an extra."

Makir's silver eyes swirled and his square jaw tightened.

"However, as we have to complete the roof anyways, we could install it at no cost with you providing the lamar," I barked, then internally cringed when Makir stiffened. I'd meant to come across as accommodating.

"I don't think the tai tai is working, boss man." JayJay snickered, more lawnmower than giggle.

"Tai chi," I corrected stiffly.

JayJay's cheeks twitched as he reached toward my forehead, his grating laugh adding to the vibrations racking my body.

"And your bedroom?" The words were out of my mouth before I could think. Heat raced up my neck.

Makir's soft voice barely carried. His silver eyes were on the ground once again. "My bedroom?"

"I mean dwelling." I shook out my fingers and tried to dissipate the tingling.

Great, he probably thinks I'm a recovering addict or prone to seizures or something.

"Kitchen, washroom, bedroom," he mumbled, loosening the strap over the lamar on his trailer and stacking it neatly in the warehouse with JayJay's help. "I require a round depression in the bedroom for my nest," he added, so quietly I could barely hear him.

He sleeps in a nest? Tell me more.

"Big enough for two?" I'd meant to say it in my head.

Makir wrung his hands in front of his stomach before firmly placing them on his hips. "For one."

"I…I didn't mean anything by that." I frantically rubbed at the prickles needling under my skin. "Fuck, I think I might be allergic to something in the air."

JayJay scrolled through his wristport, all smiles, likely looking up human allergies, and Makir eyed me dubiously. The tingles increased as he faced away from me and continued chatting with JayJay.

Makir's jumpsuit pulled taut over his curvy ass. In my mind, the plump globes were tight, with just enough give to sink my hands into. Occasionally, part of their discussion would surface in my mind. Wastelands…lamar…hover trailer… But the subtle sway of his tail as he talked—tick tock, tick tock—hypnotized me like a cobra's dance to a snake charmer's tune.

JayJay's "Right, boss man?" snapped me back to reality. Once again, I'd missed half of the conversation. I rolled my shoulders, realizing JayJay was expecting a reply to something about the wastelands…maybe? Nodding firmly would show I'd been paying attention, so I did. I was professional and in charge of the situation.

I am calm. I am controlled.

"Good, it's settled. You will accompany Makir to collect lamar. In exchange for the materials, we will install his third bay and storage system." If Rock Dweller brow ridges could smirk, his were.

Accompany Makir?

With the lamar stacked, Makir stood near the wall, toeing the ground awkwardly. Clearly, this was not part of his plans.

What's JayJay thinking?

"Have you traveled in the wastelands?" Makir asked, not meeting my eyes.

"No." There was no way I was admitting that I couldn't fly a hoverbike. I'd explored our settlement, Yurstille—the only one on Tern—by foot. A tacky statue of Yurst stood in the village's center, and I'd learned he'd named the town after himself.

Makir thumbed something inside the satchel on his hip. "The unexpected can happen."

Like finding myself on another planet attracted to a blue alien?

Makir turned toward JayJay. "I cannot guarantee the human's safety. He said he might be allergic to the air, and it's not a good idea for us to spend time to—" He snapped his jaw closed as if he hadn't meant to say that much.

I thrust out my chest. "I can take care of myself." All the excuses I'd formed to stay back vanished. The tingling vibrations battled with my ego. I would prove myself to Makir. How hard could it be to collect plexiglass?

In the minutes it took for my pride to determine my course of action, JayJay had packed my duffel bag, thrown it at my feet, and would have picked me up and lifted me onto the trailer if I hadn't leveled him with a glare.

"Bish, don't you worry. I know the drill. Check on the progress with Tino's crew"—he lifted one thick finger—"follow up with Sully"—then a second—"and meet with Mrs. Towhee about the plans for her nursery." Then he waved us off. His rumbling voice carried over the loud hum of the hoverbike as we slowly flew toward the wastelands. "No need to hurry. Take all the time you need." His ear-to-ear grin vanished in the dust.

6

With Geo sitting on the hover trailer behind me, I flew well past the stash of lamar I'd found on previous scouting missions. To avoid thinking about his presence, I let my mind drift to my brother and how proud he would be of me as we passed the shells of empty buildings below us. I'd extended the hover field around the trailer late last night when I couldn't sleep. We had taken weeks to accomplish it as younglings, but the magnets I'd found in the wastelands had done the trick. Working with what little was available had become my specialty, and I'd awoken with renewed confidence and an operational hover trailer.

My confidence blew away like a flower heavy with feathered seeds in a windstorm when I couldn't put off landing any longer. The puny Earthling would likely fall in a hole, get lost or, um…run his fingers down the length of my tail. I stopped that line of thought. I wasn't responsible for him. This was a mutually beneficial work arrangement. Bay doors and storage for me, and lamar for him.

Debris was scattered around us in rickety towers too tightly packed to navigate the hoverbike and trailer through. Forced to land, I lowered us into unfamiliar territory.

"Blant," I muttered under the engine's whine. "Blant. How did I let this happen?" I groaned, leaning forward on my handles. The archbuilder would be with me all rotation.

This is it, I mouthed. Time to face the unavoidable. He still sat on the wide, flat deck, but his presence loomed so large he felt glued to my side. I turned off the ignition, leaving the air devoid of sound. The silence heightened the tension between us. Heat from the sun, now high in the sky, radiated off the tin and steel, adding weight to the moisture in the air. Like the inside of an oven, we would slowly bake in it throughout the day. I lowered tinted goggles over my eyes to protect them from the glare.

"This the spot?" His deep voice sent a shiver through me. The archbuilder eyeballed the busted concrete slabs interwoven with wire mesh. They were piled high, a teeter-totter of twisted steel and crumbling rock all that remained of skyscrapers long gone.

I fanned my face with my tail. This spot is fine. I wished I didn't second-guess myself whenever the archbuilder came close. "I've never been here before, but today's about finding new stashes of lamar, and this place seems likely to me."

Geo squared his broad shoulders as he approached. I thought he sucked in a breath to hold his belly in as well. What odd behavior. Could that be how humans kept themselves cool? My nerves skittered as he neared, but we were going to be working together all rotation, so I needed a strategy. How close could I get before his pheromones turned me into a mindless omega?

One step...two steps... Too close! My knees weakened, and heat spread low in my belly. I grabbed my tail to stop it from reaching for him. A sheet of dislodged metal a few steps away caught my eye. It should prevent my omega from taking control. I retreated behind it.

From my safe zone, I pointed in the opposite direction. "Why don't you start over there?" I winced when my chest rumbled. The archbuilder advanced, inching his way forward, drawn in by my omega purr. But he would be the perfect height to tuck under my chin. Past alphas had told me I had an irresistible purr.

Unfortunately, I had no control over my purr in the presence of an alpha pumping out pheromones. Why was he pumping out pheromones anyway? He reacted like a new alpha did when exposed to his first omega—with no control. Tin panels clattered together in a symphony of trash as I scrambled backward.

"'Kay." He dragged his gaze away from me, grunting and moved in the direction I gestured to.

I cleared my throat. "Try searching under the thickest panels. They seem to have protected the lamar and preserved it the best." The increased space helped, but my reaction to this human set my mind spinning. I would have to work hard to keep my distance. His summer field-scented pheromones drew me in like a magnet.

He shook his round head right and left as if to empty it, and his face turned a dark pink shade. Geo's skin was as unprotected as a newborn youngling's, with only the hair on top and around his chin to shield it from the sun.

A short while later, he returned with a large stack of lamar. The balls of his shoulders bulged under the weight. And once he put it down he took a long drink from his container before he removed his short-sleeved shirt from under his overalls and wrapped it around his head. My mouth watered when I stared at the dark, sweat-matted fur covering the blocky muscles of his chest. Even though he stood far enough away to keep me from going into total submission, I could scent him. My nostrils flared as I inhaled sun-warmed fields and a male not afraid of physical labor. Divine.

"What are you staring at?" he growled, sticking out his chest and sucking in a deep breath.

No matter how divine his aroma, his personality screamed alpha asshole—everything I needed to steer clear of.

Remember, he's an ugly, angry human, the color of the paste younglings eat.

Mentally scrambling for a neutral topic, I asked, "Do all humans turn pink in the sun?"

He glanced at his bare arms and stomped over to his duffel. After rifling around, he pulled out a container and spread white paste over his reddening cheeks, nose and arms.

"Ah..." My imagination cranked into overdrive. I swallowed the saliva pooling in my mouth when his lotion-slick hands smoothed over his ropy forearms. Heat swamped my lower belly when his thick fingers spread the cream along his straight nose. When he rubbed back and forth over his bristly cheeks, I practically drooled.

"Happy now?"

He glanced at me, his fists squeezing open and closed before he cleared his throat and thrust the container toward me. "You want some?"

"Um..." His muscles shimmered in the sun. I coughed. "Thank you anyway, but my skin is not dry at the moment."

"It's sunscreen."

"Sunscreen?"

I stacked a pile of lamar on the trailer and tried to piece together the broken translation. Sun checked out, but a screen kept flying insects out of dwellings. Flying insects were always worse at night. "Maybe tonight."

Geo's nose scrunched up, and he tossed the container back into the bag. "Whatever." He turned his wide shoulders away from me and lifted an enormous steel beam, grunting before uncovering a hill of lamar. The puny human was much stronger than he appeared.

When my attempt at small talk failed, I busied myself collecting as much lamar as Lornianly possible. Many suns later, my hands ached from where the rough edges had pressed into them. Not heavy, but unwieldy, the clear sheets stretched my arms to the limit and left me walking the way I did after being on a double-wide seat on a hoverbike all rotation. I massaged my palm with my thumb. Maybe the sunscreen would help.

Geo sat on the edge of the trailer, his sweat-soaked shirt wrapped around his head, summer field scent oozing. Naked shoulders on display. He sipped from his water container, and his unnerving gaze fixed on me as I approached, arms loaded with lamar.

Focus, will you. So what if he's strong and has nice shoulders?

I stumbled over a dip in the ground, but before the lamar could fly out of my hands, Geo stood opposite me, holding the other end of the pile together. He rebalanced the load and, in turn, me. "Thanks," I said.

Silently, he walked backward, and I walked forward until we reached the trailer, where he grasped the top sheet, unloaded it from my arms and placed it on the trailer. Then he did it again...and again. Each time he turned to grab a new sheet, his eyes caught mine, until I stood there empty-handed and empty-brained.

Geo fidgeted with the shirt he'd wrapped around his head. "You're staring again."

Right, yep, I couldn't keep my eyes off him. "I'll...ah...get far away from you." The corners of his mouth turned down while I stammered. "I-I mean...I found a good stash over there. I'll just..." I jerked my thumb over my shoulder.

His chin lifted, and he screwed the lid shut on his water container. "Do what you gotta do."

The archbuilder may have been an asshole, but we made a good team. By the time the sun was casting long shadows over Tern's graveyard of remains, the hover trailer was loaded high with lamar. My half would be enough for my skylight with plenty left over for windshields. I could even put some in my dwelling. My tail danced behind me.

The archbuilder unwrapped the shirt from his head, slipped the straps of his overalls down, exposing the nearly black fur on his belly, and pulled his shirt back on. Though lazy, his gaze lit a fire in me, like the lowering sun's rays that lengthened the shadows around us. I grabbed my traitorous tail before it swayed.

"Ready to head home, Archbuilder?"

His shoulders slumped but quickly rolled back again. "Call me Geo." His voice, rough as gravel, slid over me. "Yeah, let's hit the road. I need to check in with JayJay." He inhaled another belly-sucking breath and widened his stance.

Hit the road didn't quite translate, but he sounded civil, so I went with it. "Great work today, Archbuilder." I could still be pleasant, even if he didn't know how to engage in polite conversation. Not in a million annums would I call him by his name. That level of familiarity would not be wise.

After I secured the load and straddled my bike, I signaled the archbuilder to jump on the trailer. I turned the ignition and...nothing. The rump, rump, rump of my heart deafened me. No matter how often I depressed the lever, the familiar whoosh and hum never came.

"Blant." I lashed my tail against the thick leather of my tall boots and bit my lip at the sharp sting. Why hadn't I pulled my bike into the shade?

The newer model hoverbikes had integrated cooling systems. Unfortunately, after many suns under Tern's hot rays, my standard model ignition was fried.

I knew better. As a blanting hovic, my job included fixing messes like this, not causing them. How many times in the past had I rescued Bonic when his starter mechanism had melted? Too many to count. I'd cherished the role reversal—me saving him for once. I stiffened my spine. I could handle this.

The archbuilder's gruff voice interrupted my thoughts. "What's with the delay?" His face had turned alarmingly pink. It looked as though it had swallowed the sun, and for a moment, I wanted to place my palms on his cheeks to soothe them.

"Melted starter." With a glance over my shoulder, I jumped off the bike and headed to the closest scrap pile in search of the perfect trash to repair the starter.

The archbuilder reached for his wristport—to call JayJay, I presumed.

"Don't bother. We're out of range." My voice wavered at our predicament. The situation was bad enough already, and now the archbuilder had to be dealt with too. The sinking sensation in my guts told me he wasn't the 'don't worry, we'll figure it out together' type.

With every tormenting step, his footfalls echoed the way a giant ringa's might—the often-mentioned, never-seen beast of Lorne. Although now that I thought about it, the ringa's depiction in books uncannily matched my neighbor, if he were giant-sized. No wonder I had an aversion to Raz.

"Why the fuck are you over here playing in the dirt?" His voice rumbled, and the scent of summer fields and male overwhelmed me.

I scurried behind a thick sheet of metal to gain some distance. "I need to…"

"You're a mechanic. Fix the damn bike." His hands were on his hips as if to stop them from trembling.

"Listen." I wanted to insert the word asshole, but if I'd learned anything from my parents, it was to always behave with the utmost decorum, so I held my head high and breathed deeply. I didn't have to take his shit. "I need to fabricate a part, and I need to do it before the sun sets. It has to dry before installation." My tail stood high above my shoulder. "Now, if you'll sit over there and wait, I'll get it done." Uncurling each of my fingers by force of will, I pointed to some random place. Distance mattered, and he needed to move far away. Otherwise, I might drive my fist into his chin.

He stomped back to the trailer and leaned against it with a huff.

The sun dimmed to a beautiful velvety red, and the temperature dropped with the change. Even though I found the perfect mold in what appeared to be a previous sink drain, the clay disk I prepared resembled a youngling's mud pie. As much as I willed it to be true, the spare wouldn't be dry anytime soon. I carefully placed it on a flat piece of steel where it would collect the morning's sun. Then, braced for the storm, I walked away from the archbuilder to break the bad news.

The archbuilder's eyes followed my every movement. I cleared my throat unnecessarily to announce my arrival. Resolved, I forced my gaze to his face and worked my eyes up to his beard, but no matter how I tried, eye contact wouldn't come. Would the rasp of his beard along my neck send me to my knees? I straightened my spine, stepped backward, and shook away those mutinous thoughts. "Archbuilder…"

"God damn it, will you call me Geo?" he growled.

The red velvet of the sky deepened further to a ripe purple. Sundown on Tern unfolded with more drama than on Lorne. The glowing orb resembled the pulse of blood through a heart, as if the sky wished to embrace it before it shut its eyes to the dark of night.

I swallowed hard. "We have to spend the night. The part I fabricated needs time in the sun to bake and dry." My shoulders slumped.

"You can't be serious. Do you even know what to expect spending the night out here?" With a voice like thunder, he would have scared away any lurking bush-tailed monties if we'd been back on my home planet.

"No, I don't, but all your blanting shouting will only draw attention to us. Yelling at me will not change the fact that we are stuck here for the night. Are Earthlings always so whiny?" My tail flicked rapidly behind me.

Take that. I can stand up for myself, alpha asshole. I'm more than just an omega.

He tipped his chin to the sky and rolled his shoulders back—praying for divine intervention?—then walked back to the trailer, where he upended the bag JayJay had packed for him.

"Thank fuck." The archbuilder stuffed everything back into the bag and scaled a concrete slab, then another, then another. To escape some unknown entity that might reach him in the night? He stopped when partially sheltered by a sheet of tin overhead and laid out a frame of bendy sticks.

Ridiculous human and his tree-top nest. Did he think he was a winged Nacer?

He glanced down at me every now and then. He opened his mouth to speak, or perhaps invite me to join him, but in the end, he wrapped some noisy fabric over his sticks and climbed into the dome without another word.

With nothing better to do, I set up for the night too. My body was tired, but my mind buzzed, so I busied myself with the spool of wire I'd purchased from D'irk at the market. I quickly transformed it into a line of snares circling my camp. I didn't really expect any creatures to come in the night, and the traps wouldn't be useful for anything too big, but the act helped settle my nerves.

I scratched out a dip in the center to bed down in, filled it with the tall graneth grass that had sprung up all around and settled in. My nose twitched. The spring-fresh odor lifted my glum spirits. Then, I pulled one of the soft graneth puffs from my backpack. A cold wind blew strands of hair across my face, urging me to put on the warm sweater in my pack. Much warmer, I bit into my meal but stopped after swallowing the first mouthwatering bite.

"Archbuilder," I called out, "do you have any food?"

"My name is Geo." He paused, then said, "I'm fine."

Fine then. I was fine too. Only trying to be polite. I finished the puff and sucked on a strip of mantu. He was missing out. With the rest of my food tucked carefully away for tomorrow, I closed the latches on my bag.

"Night." My voice echoed through the valley of junk.

The archbuilder grunted.

My lumpy nest left me tossing and turning, but sleep eventually found me. A series of ear-piercing squeals rang out, jolting me upright into the inky black night. Sharp teeth pinched my tail, shooting needle-sharp pain through the flesh, and I yelped before whipping it about, only to find a thickly furred creature the size of my forearm latched on to it.

"Makir?" The archbuilder's sleep-roughened voice yelled.

"Get the blant off of me, you little ringa." I danced around, my tail whipped furiously, trying to shake the creature off. My tail wrapped around its neck and squeezed, dislodging the toothy monster, and it scampered into the dark shadows.

"Makir!" A zipper came undone. "I'm coming ..."

Rocks crumbled, followed by a loud "Fu-u-uck" and then nothing. The nothing had me scrambling toward the archbuilder. My night vision kicked in and fixed on Geo's body where he lay motionless in the dirt. Adrenaline pumped through my veins while I begged the goddess Sola for Geo to have landed with no serious injuries. What had he been thinking? He'd walked straight off the concrete slab on which he'd perched his tree-top nest.

The clouds slipped away, exposing a bright moon as I rushed to his side. I scanned the fluffy tip of my tail over him to ensure nothing was broken, then cradled his neck with one arm and slipped the other behind his knees before carefully lifting him, my heart fluttering like a bird. As my flesh met his, a hot bolt of fire seared my veins.

Blant! Everything I'd been avoiding had launched into motion.

Geo moaned as the tether lashed at our contact like a wild beast, and my arms trembled under his weight.

Leave him! Run!

My forehead broke out in sweat and a desperate fear swelled beneath my skin. As much as I wanted to pull away and run as fast as I could in the opposite direction. I couldn't drop Geo. He needed me.

My final fight for independence had all been in vain. The connection wound around my heart, sheathing it in a heady warmth my omega craved. Despite giving up my freedom, I sighed as waves of contentment trickled down my spine. The bond tethering me to an alpha had been initiated.

"It's okay." I panted. "The archbuilder's not so bad." I gulped hard. "His roundness is cute. He's a million times better than Reinik."

Warm breaths against my neck assured me Geo was alive, but I much preferred him biting off my head to soaking my jumpsuit with hot blood.

I placed him inside my ring of snares. "I'll be right back. You're safe here." I swept my hand over his gritty hair.

Though the air was cool, I continued to sweat—not from exertion, but worry—as I climbed over a ledge, then another and one more, until I reached his nest. My fingers fumbled with the zipper to his dwelling, where I crouched before I wiggled inside and snatched his puffy nest, water container and duffel.

A moment later, I was back at his side, arranging him under his crinkling nest. With careful fingers, I probed the back of his head and neck, then feathered my hands down his body, seeking anything broken. A significant swelling above his right eye and a deep gash along his thigh, the blood already thick and clotted, worried me.

I sucked moisture into my dry mouth and swallowed down a hard knot. His injuries needed to be treated quickly. He groaned when I smoothed my palms along his ankle, his skin hot to the touch.

I had no choice.

With great reluctance, I spread the fluffy tip of my tail and exposed the healing disk hidden inside. Lornians were forbidden from revealing this ability to outsiders for fear of exploitation. My stomach plunged as I fought against everything I'd been taught.

With my mind made up, I dabbed the suctioning disk over the worst of his injuries. His bleeding slowed, the swelling went down, and the skin around his gash closed.

I hauled his crinkly nest next to mine and lay beside him, my tail's suction still in place over his heart to monitor him through the night. The tether between us hummed, the first step in completing a mating bond in place. I stared at the stars and sorted through all my emotions, trying to narrow down how bad it was. The thing was, no matter how much I wished to prepare for the worst, hope shone through. Maybe this time it would be okay?

Most Lornians dreamed of this moment their whole life, but my past experience with an incomplete bond had been a nightmare. My tail wrapped around my wrist, a bandage of comfort, and returned to Geo's heart. The tether, though a thin connection for now, still anchored an unwanted alpha at the other end. A warm tear spilled down my cheek.

Please let this time be different.

7

I SUCKED THE ROOF of my mouth, searching for moisture. It was drier than the Sahara. Holy shit, my head throbbed. I brought my hands up to remove my helmet. Only there was no helmet, just soft, silky fur.

What the hell?

"Coach, I can't get my helmet off," I murmured.

A soft purr answered me. "Geo."

The low timbre of his voice soothed the wild parts of me.

"Geo, you had a fall." A velvety thumb stroked my temple.

Pain racked my leg as I attempted to twist my body. "Shit, that hurts." Sweat broke out across my forehead.

"Stay still. Let me help."

"Makir?"

His gentle rumble settled me, cocooning me in its warm embrace. The beats of my heart were slow and syrupy.

"Yes, it's me. I'm going to help with the pain, and then you can sleep."

Am I hallucinating?

Something fluffy brushed over my forehead and gently sucked. The tingly sucking kisses spread down my leg, and a whisper of silk circled my ankle. Then darkness.

I dragged a knuckle over my eye and groaned. The remnants of a strange dream about a hockey game and a basket of purring kittens lingered as I woke.

"Ah, you're awake." A low, soothing voice, the loveliest I'd ever heard, came from slightly behind me. "I filled your container with the morning dew. You're going to be very thirsty after your accident."

Inch by inch, I propped myself up on one elbow. My body came alive with aches, and my sleeping bag crinkled and shifted beneath me. Makir passed me my water bottle and I gulped it down.

"What happened?" Something smelled delicious, like juniper and ginger snaps, and my mouth watered.

"Well, I believe we may have found the solution I was looking for to keep the enforcers' hands warm." Makir chuckled, dodging the question.

"Huh?"

Makir pointed to a line of glossy white pelts hanging in the early sun. They looked like beavers. Wow, he'd been busy last night. Then it came back to me—the squeal, Makir's shout, my stumbling around...

"Did I fall?" I turned toward Makir, slopping water all over his shirt. "Hey, are you okay? Why did you yell out last night?"

"I'm fine, but you fell a long way."

Makir's tail skimmed over my ankle and arousal swamped my gut, heating my groin. What was happening?

"And it felt even longer getting you over here." He flexed his biceps, teasing.

Damn, he carried me all that way?

I sucked in my big belly and mentally scanned my body. Everything appeared intact for a guy who had essentially dropped from a second-story window. Although I was sore and scraped raw from the jagged concrete, my head was clear, and I could get on with my day.

Makir pointed to one of the white pelts. "They may look cute and cuddly now, but those things have sharp teeth."

Makir's ears twitched. I'd never noticed them before, but with his face curled toward me from above, his long mane parted and his velvety blue ear peeked out in the same place as mine. It had a small, pointed tip I longed to touch, just out of reach as he tipped back on his haunches.

"Hey." I reached out to cover his hand with mine, the blue fur silky against my palm. "About last night…"

The small clearing where we'd stacked the lamar filled with the buzz of hoverbikes and as they quieted, Sisip shouted, "Makir! Geo!" Two other enforcers followed closely behind.

"Looks like we've been rescued." Makir's eyes met mine, and the silver shifted to lavender, then back again.

Something was different.

When Makir slipped his fingers from beneath mine, he stole my heat with it. I hadn't realized I'd been brushing my thumb through his soft fur until my hand was empty. If I snatched his back, would I seem desperate?

"Sisip, I'm so glad to see you!" Makir stood from where he'd been sitting cross-legged at the end of my sleeping bag. I could hear him explaining about the melted starter, the attack of the beavers and my fall. He played it up.

"It was terrifying. Out of nowhere, sharp teeth sank into my ankle, and Geo rushed to my rescue."

If by rushed, he meant I'd fallen off a cliff. Why was he making me out to be a hero instead of an idiot? Whatever the reason, I could have kissed him for it.

Hmmm. How would those blue lips feel? Soft and buttery? Would they melt against mine and taste of the ginger cookies my mom baked at Christmas? Or would they be the kind of firm that gave with just the right amount of pressure? Either way, they would yield to mine somewhere in the very near future. That knowledge resonated in my bones.

D'irk, one of the enforcers, climbed the tower of debris where I'd set up my tent last night and brought it down for me. With my supplies gathered, I packed them into my duffel bag while mentally thanking JayJay for his foresight in throwing in my tent and sleeping bag. Then I pinched myself. There would be no thank-yous for JayJay. He was responsible for this forced wilderness adventure. I would never have signed up for an impromptu camping trip on a planet where no one really knew what had survived the Fires That Cleanse.

Makir's soft purr echoed in my memory, along with whispers of a remembered touch. "Nah," I muttered. I pressed my fingers to the bump above my eye. That couldn't have happened, but Makir's eyes *had* changed from silver to lavender—that was real. Something had changed during the night.

My name in his soft purr had been real too. I would focus on that. If anything good had come from this unplanned adventure, it was Makir finally calling me by my name. No more archbuilder.

Makir rushed to my aid as I limped toward the hover trailer. The vibrations turning me inside out in Makir's presence had disappeared entirely and been replaced by a cozy blanket of contentment.

"How's your ankle?" Makir purred, a soft question, as the tip of his tail gently brushed over my boot right at the tenderest spot.

With the slightest hitch, I clambered up to where the enforcers were gathered and leaned against Makir. My head throbbed and my ankle ached, but when I paused and strained my eyes to look up, my heart stuttered. That was a long fucking way down.

"Way better than it should be."

His purr drew me closer, his body warm and solid against me.

"Thanks for last night, Makir." My voice rumbled. Fuck, he smelled good.

His eyes met mine and held. The silver and lavender swirled and drew me so close I could've unzipped his jumpsuit with my teeth.

Sisip cleared her throat and adjusted the high collar of her uniform, and I forced myself to step away from Makir's delicious pull. Then, with an amused twist to her split-lip cat's mouth, she looked between Makir and me, then at the stacks of lamar on the hover trailer. "I need to put in a request to your building crew, Geo. I wish for an opening to allow light into my dwelling now that you and Makir have sourced all this lamar."

I scanned the horizon, and inventoried the scene around me. The wastelands were shockingly beautiful in the morning light. Sun refracted light in a kaleido-scope over stacks of lamar, casting sunrise-peach prisms where it touched.

"How did you find us?" Makir twisted his hair into a braid. It was extra unruly this morning, and as soon as he bound it, I wanted to unravel it and run my fingers through it until it was messy again. Plus, his ears were exposed. They were for my eyes only.

Sisip logged a note on her wristport. "Your neighbor, Raz, filed a missing person report."

Makir immediately tensed and his eyes turned a solid silver. He grabbed his tail. "That was...kind."

What was going on with Makir's neighbor?

Sisip's tawny ears twitched as her gaze scanned the wastelands, constantly on alert. "Let's get you back to Yurstille and over to the medic. Makir said you took quite the tumble."

I rolled my eyes. "I don't need to see the medic."

"It's Intergalactic Federation policy. You must seek medical attention if you're injured on the job." Her no-nonsense voice brooked no further discussion.

It only took moments for Makir to repair his hoverbike with their wealth of spare parts, and just like that, I was back on the trailer behind Makir's hoverbike, heading toward Yurstille with an entourage of enforcers guiding our way.

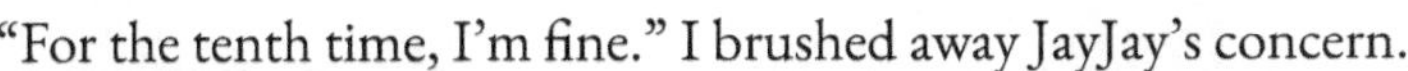

"For the tenth time, I'm fine." I brushed away JayJay's concern.

When he wouldn't stop his mothering I showed him the report, trying to convince him the doctor had given me the all clear. We'd both questioned Dr. Ten's notation about "unusually accelerated healing."

I spent the afternoon blissfully alone while JayJay checked in with the crews. I reviewed the progress report from yesterday, and everything was on track. A few emails for extra projects had come in. Sully, my only married crew member, saved every penny for his elaborate house plans. His family was expected on the supply ship due in three months. He would be up for a side project, so I scheduled him for a few weekend jobs.

I typed out a quick email to Ginger. Pretty please, more pictures of Pika and Charz. As much as I hated to admit it, my head hurt. Though not as much as it should have. Fingertips massaging my scalp ghosted through my memories. "I think I overdid it," I muttered, shaking my muggy head and resting on my bunk.

A couple of hours later, I woke to a rumbling chorus of "Boss man." My crew, finished for the day, lazily gathered fresh clothes and shower gear from their bunks.

My appetite was off, so I turned down dinner with my crew. I needed something to ease the restlessness crawling through my body, though.

I peeled myself out of bed and walked outside to the space in front of my office, widening my stance and clearing my head for some tai chi. Sparse vegetation pricked my ankles as I flowed into a twist, and I wished for the shelter of the oak tree I was so used to practicing under. I'd never thought about trees creating privacy before, but the distinct lack of personal space ruling my current life left me yearning for trees.

Before I finished my set, a gentle tug compelled me to move. The hit to my head must have messed me up more than I'd realized. I pressed my fingers to my temple, trying to dull the thrum. I tried to force myself to work through my tai chi set and refocus my energy, but after the fourth repetition of the same brush knee sequence, I wrote it off as a lost cause. The compulsion to follow the tug was too much to ignore, so I walked instead.

The warm evening sky, painted a liquid gold, provided an idyllic playground for the woodskies strange squawking. Pink dust kicked up over my boots. I waved to the Rowtees as they passed, and we firmed up plans for their youngling's naming ceremony.

I wandered the paths of Yurstille and followed the persuasive tug while mentally designing plans for the Rowtees' nursery. If I incorporated the lamar into a series of tiny round sunlights, they'd create a pretty honeycomb pattern.

The tug increased in strength, and so did my pace. When I rounded the corner and saw Makir, the urge to run to him grew so intense I had to force my heels into the dry earth.

A Lizzard invaded his space. Its long, taloned fingers pinned Makir to the side of a ramshackle building. Makir's head was down, and his tail whipped ferociously around him. His short blue fur stuck straight out on his arms as if he held a static electricity ball.

Makir's whine immediately dislodged my heels from where they were planted. The Lizzard loomed even closer to Makir, and I short-circuited. He ran one of his talons up and down Makir's chest, his forked tongue slithering too close to Makir's ear.

Possessiveness burned through me like a lit fuse. *Alligator lips dares to touch what's mine?*

A gust of warm wind sandblasted everything pink, and a panel dislodged from the shack Makir was pinned against, rattling through the air like shrapnel.

Instinctively, I pulled in my gut and stood taller. "Makir," I barked, jogging toward him. His silver eyes met mine, briefly flashing lavender, and my heart galloped when his tail reached for me.

"Geo, what are you doing here?" The relief in his voice was palpable as Makir took advantage of the distraction and ducked out of reach of the scaled arms trapping him.

My name on his tongue was like melted chocolate. "Is there a problem here?" I growled at the Lizzard. Testosterone pumped through my body, and I glared at the much larger man encroaching on Makir's space.

A rational thought tried to fight its way through my testosterone-fueled rage but fled when Makir pressed his long, lean body to my side. Why wasn't he wearing a shirt? The fever subsided to a simmer, and the persistent tug was gone.

Instead, what was there was a sense of rightness so complete I'd never known the likes of it before. His scent flooded my nose, like my favorite ginger snaps mixed with crisp juniper needles. I was wide awake and on full alert.

"There's-s-s no problem, right Mak?"

Makir cringed at the pet name Lizard Lips called him.

When Scaly moved toward us, Makir clung closer, his lavender eyes asking me for something I couldn't quite decipher. Was he aware of his tail wrapped around my ankle like a coil and what it was doing to my aching dick?

My fists yearned to show this creep a lesson.

"S-s-simply a friendly neighborly conversation." His wide mouth opened in a razor-toothed smile, the opposite of friendly.

Ah, so this was Raz, the neighbor who'd alerted the enforcers to our absence. I changed my plans about thanking him.

"In fact, Mak was-s-s about to come over for a late evening dinner, weren't you, Mak?" Raz eyeballed Makir as if he were dessert.

I stepped between Makir and Raz. "Unfortunately, I've discovered some last-minute changes to Makir's hovery I must go over with him before to-morrow." My voice bristled with forced politeness as I dismissed him.

I placed one firm palm on Makir's bare lower back, and warmth spread through my fingertips.

Shirtless, the defined muscles of his arms and the dips and gullies of his abs begged to be traced. His torso was longer than mine and covered in the same fur as the backs of his hands. The color blended and matched the sky blue of his face when it reached his stomach. My fingers wiggled, and I yearned to smooth my palms over his velvety skin.

"Where's your house? I mean, dwelling?"

When he nodded toward the heap of lashed-together trash he'd been pinned against, my neck flushed and my fists clenched. I led him through his pieced-together doorway, Raz's deflating hiss lingering behind us. Raz was just as I suspected—all bully and no bite.

"Makir, this isn't secure," I snapped. Urgency itched over my muscles as they pulsed, and my skin grew taut. I had to keep him safe.

With a hand on Makir's shoulder, I turned him to face me. I smoothed my hands down his bare arms, over his hips, and patted his legs, ignoring the sparks igniting along my skin where it met his.

"Are you okay?" My voice was so deep I was surprised Makir understood it enough to nod.

I stood and inventoried his dwelling. A patchwork of tin and steel intermixed with some type of adobe-like building material. The ground was bare and uneven, and a dip was tucked away in the far corner, filled with graneth grass. It poked out from under the pile of white pelts from our trip to the wastelands. That must be his nest. I gulped as the scent overwhelmed me. I rubbed the tight skin over my bicep as I sucked in a deep breath, held in my gut and calmed myself.

His tail unwound from around my leg and swooshed as he backed away, leaving a hollowed out feeling in my chest. "I'm doing the best I can." His voice wavered as he pulled up the top half of his beat-up jumpsuit, zipping it over all his luxurious blue skin.

Fuck, I didn't mean to be critical. I kicked the ground in frustration. Damn it, he'd gone from one asshole straight into the arms of another. As archbuilder, I could provide Makir with a secure dwelling. I didn't give a rat's ass if he was next on the list or not. His house was going up one way or the other.

"We're starting your dwelling tomorrow."

Makir jumped at the force of my voice. "What?" His tail tapped agitatedly on the ground.

"You heard me. Tomorrow at seven suns." My voice echoed off the tin walls like thunder.

Makir straightened his shoulders, and his silver eyes flashed at me. "I need my hovery completed first." His voice was firm but threaded with a delicious purr that weakened my knees.

"You will have a secure home, and that is final."

On that order, I abruptly turned and left his home. The tug immediately resumed, and with it, the overwhelming need to act as a sentinel and stand outside his door all night. Against my better judgment, I forced myself to return to the sono. The cooler night air did nothing to soothe my hot skin.

I stomped home in the dark and promised to be kind to Makir tomorrow.

8

M Y TAIL STOOD STIFF and proud by my shoulder as I walked toward my shower for the second time. "Domineering, self-righteous, arrogant do-gooder," I grumbled. With Geo far enough away, coherent thought had restored itself.

How dare he insult my dwelling? So what if it wasn't much to look at? I'd pieced together a somewhat habitable space. Even if it was far from perfect, it belonged to me, and only I could insult it.

I stripped off my jumpsuit, dusted in Tern's pervasive pink soil, and hung it over the chair that doubled as my towel rack. A shower would help me reset.

The patch of skin Raz had trailed his talon over earlier burned under the lukewarm water, and I scrubbed the offended area raw. I should've known better than to run outside half-dressed, but the wall panel had shifted where I'd built my shower, and a cold breeze had been blowing in. When I'd gone outside to fix it, Raz had found me.

Alphas were meant to protect and cherish their omegas. On Lorne, that was the way it worked—in theory. Raz descended from planet Hotner. I didn't know which clan of Lizzard he belonged to, but my brother had recently led a mission aiding their planet. While there, he'd witnessed many alphas of the third clan misusing their power over weaker omegas. That behavior would be criminal on Lorne...unless you were best friends with the regent.

My tense muscles loosened as I shook out my fur and toweled dry. Would a hot shower have felt a hundred times better? Bless the dess Sola, yes, but I could live simply if it meant not moving into Raz's guest room. I'd heeded my brother's warning about Lizzard alphas and avoided Raz whenever possible. His sway over me was weak. I wasn't drawn to Raz in any capacity, but I always faltered when he caught me by surprise.

Thick furs lined my nest, lustrous and pearl white. Warm and sumptuous, they called my name. Even my parents would have been proud to have furs like these blanketing their nest.

Wrung out from the previous rotation's hard labor, followed by a sleepless night nursing Geo and another hijacking from Raz, rest was long overdue. Sleep, however, proved hard to come by. My mind cycled between what I would do about my bully neighbor and what I would do about my partial tether to Geo. Add in the fact that anybody could walk in on me since my dwelling was so poorly secured, and it was no wonder I couldn't sleep.

I checked the time on my wristport. Ten moons. Bonic might still be awake. Maybe he could help me sort out my head?

"Makee!" One warm greeting from my brother and I relaxed into my nest. No matter if his voice was garbled and broke up through the audio on my wristport.

"How are things on Lorne?"

Usually the epitome of self-control, Bonic's voice wavered. "Jast is pregnant! Can you believe I'll be a father?"

My eyes welled with tears, and I choked on my words. "Congratulations." Why had this happened so soon after my departure? I wanted to be there for Jast for her pregnancy. I yearned for Lorne for the first time since I'd arrived on Tern. "I can picture you and your youngling with traps full of bush-tailed monties already."

Bonic's laugh rang through the speaker. "Now I know you didn't call to ask about Lorne. What is it?"

I bit my lip. "It's happened again. I feel the tether." My voice quieted and nearly disappeared.

"There are Lornians on Tern?"

My mental picture of him was clear. Bonic's eyes would turn inward in confusion, an expression as familiar as the scar near my thumb. He sat behind his glossy black desk, the portrait of our prestigious family line proudly hanging behind him. In the image, we stood shoulder to shoulder.

No, there were no Lornians on Tern, but Raz would have fit perfectly in my parents' grand living quarters. All show and no substance. My brother's alpha voice commanded my attention, but with a temporary bond in place, it held much less power over me than usual. "It's not with the Lizzard, is it? I thought I told you to keep away from him. They're strong, but easily intimidated. Just shout at him or something."

Thank the goddess Sola, no, a tether to Raz would be a nightmare. And Bonic was just as aware as me that omegas didn't shout at people. "Er…it's with a human."

"You're tethered to a…human?"

I hesitated. "The connection's weak." My fingers wove through the fluffy tip of my tail, where I played with it idly. "But I've also…healed him."

Bonic hissed. His disappointment swooshed through me like a spiral of water down a drain. Technically, my father should have been the alpha in the family protecting me, but his disappointment over my omega designation and quick abandonment after learning of it had left that role to Bonic.

"Makee," Bonic said, voice softer, his judgment tempered.

I swallowed the knot in my throat while my tail enclosed me in a hug. "What do I do now?"

Bonic cleared his throat. His rational demeanor returned along with his strong instincts to care and provide for an omega, especially one related to him. "I need to investigate whether there are cases of Lornians and humans with tethers and determine if a complete bond is possible." The way his keyboard keys whirred in the background, I could visualize him already delegating tasks to his team. "You'll be the first to know, Makee. In the meantime, stay away from the human, and the Lizzard too." He directed his staff in the background to investigate. No matter the time of rotation, there was always someone on duty. "Call me if anything unusual happens. We shall speak again soon." The dead line hummed in my ear.

I snorted. "Unusual?" My new and improved life occurred on a planet surrounded by species I'd never mingled with. A place where I slept in a slapdash hovel on the good nights and on the bad ones, fended off unknown creatures in the wastelands. And I planned out my days to avoid alpha males. Most days, my credit icon blinked red. I snorted again. "Unusual is my usual."

My tail wrapped around me tighter. With all his resources, my brother would find out if a full bond with a human was possible.

I forced positive thoughts into my head: a contract with the enforcers, graneth puffs, pale green eyes... I nestled into my furs. Come new week, my accommodations would improve tenfold. With a temporary tether, I didn't have to think about a true bond yet. And a true bond with a human had to be impossible. No matter how much I longed to touch Geo's sweet, round stomach. Before sleep took hold, I imagined my head lying on top of it like a pillow.

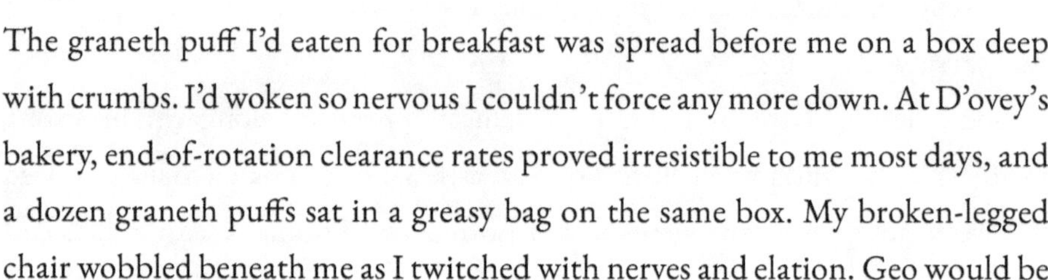

The graneth puff I'd eaten for breakfast was spread before me on a box deep with crumbs. I'd woken so nervous I couldn't force any more down. At D'ovey's bakery, end-of-rotation clearance rates proved irresistible to me most days, and a dozen graneth puffs sat in a greasy bag on the same box. My broken-legged chair wobbled beneath me as I twitched with nerves and elation. Geo would be here any moment. My dwelling's construction started today.

My tether pulsed—Geo was close. I brushed the crumbs off my jumpsuit, then ran my fingers through my mane, hurriedly braiding it.

Were humans and Lornians even sexually compatible? My tail swayed behind me as the low grumbles and reverberating chuckles of Geo's Rock Dweller crew approached.

JayJay boomed, "Morning, Makir." He drank from a travel jar then set it on my workbench.

A couple of Rock Dwellers stood outside, chatting. "Did you see him trying to pull his shirt over his stomach earlier?"

One of them chuckled, the sound like one of my torque drills. "Then he stormed over to JayJay and demanded he feed him only vegetables?"

JayJay's lips tipped up before he shouted for his crew. "Tino, Sully, get in here."

"Happy Morning, JayJay." I nodded and introduced myself to the other Rock Dwellers. My space turned infinitesimal as it filled with their massive gray bodies. Still, the human whose tug zinged through my tether, tickling my awareness, was nowhere to be seen.

"Wonder why boss man wants to throw both crews, JayJay and himself, at this job," Tino, whose name I'd just learned, said to Sully. Like JayJay, both were large, appeared to be hairless, and had shiny gray heads. Sully peered around my room, eyes skipping from my nest to my crate to the gaps in my wall.

The tether pulled tight just before Geo pushed through my door, his pale green eyes fixed on mine. Now that he was in my line of sight, the tether grew slack. Bonic had told me a complete bond relaxed when mates shared the same space, and long-distance separation physically hurt, especially after the mating ceremony. The tether urged togetherness. Although the zing had dulled, the tension remained weighed down by the intensity of his stare.

In three…two…one, and right on cue, Geo sucked in his belly and puffed out his chest. Great, now the next sun would be spent torturing myself over what it could mean. His broad shoulders supported a thick neck, and his short-sleeved shirt clung to his muscles in a way that outlined every round bulge.

His blocky pectorals appeared to pulse.

Why did he always suck in his belly?

The small space grew warm, and the scent of summer fields filled my lungs. My thoughts sloshed around like soup.

"Boss man?" JayJay cleared his throat. A grin curled his upper lip as he watched Geo, mesmerized by my swaying tail—stupid, impulsive tail. Geo's cheeks pinked, and he pushed out his chest even farther before he barked a series of orders without even a hello.

"Clear all this out. We need to pour a solid foundation." He pointed to the bits of furniture and equipment strewn about. "Tino, work with Makir. Discuss how he built that low wall. See if we can work it into the design. I like it. When you're done, I want JayJay and Makir together on lamar installation. The rest of you—with me. We're getting the framework up and a goddamn secure door on this place by the end of the day if it kills me." He sucked in another gut-holding breath.

Geo pumped out alpha pheromones that wreaked havoc on my mind. Adding a compliment to boot? I was in shambles. Who cared if it had been buried among gruff orders? He'd said he liked my wall. I pressed the heel of my hand over my heart. It took everything in my power to not stand at attention and salute before I scrambled to do what I was told.

"Sully, careful with Makir's bedding," Geo snapped. "Never mind, I'll take care of it."

Geo stomped over to my nest and proceeded to fold and stack all my pelts and wrap them in a neat bundle with the utmost care. His nostrils flared as he inhaled the scent. The distraction softened his belly, and his relaxed stomach squeezed through the gaps in the sides of his overalls. My heart melted a little. I wanted to squish his soft flesh.

The rotation passed in a whirlwind of activity. It shouldn't have surprised me what five behemoth Rock Dwellers, a human on a mission and a Lornian could accomplish in such a short time, but it did. They built my walls in Lornian fashion, mixing Tern's soil, the tall, rain-soaked grass I'd dried and water into sturdy walls. Except, on Lorne, you would never catch sight of a pink wall, and mine were undeniably pink. They interspersed the circular walls with thick split logs, and lamar filled the small, round holes where wall met roof. The lamar honeycombed the entire back wall facing the courtyard, and streams of warm sunlight cascaded through.

I stood in a beam of sunlight with my hands clasped over my chest and lifted my chin. The importance of the moment swelled in my chest.

The dwelling was one hundred percent better than my initial plans and way bigger, but my jaw clenched when unbidden reality cracked my newfound joy. The truth was, I didn't have enough credits to cover this. My profits from installing lamar windshields for the enforcer's hoverbikes would not be enough.

Raz's voice slithered up my spine, startling me from my financial woes. "Hey, hey, Mak." A chill rolled over each vertebra of my backbone.

"I've brought your favorite." He handed over a jar of hiscus juice, so cold that moisture beaded on the outside. The talons at the ends of his fingers raked through the fur of my hand, and the icy drink spilled when I jerked backward.

"Thank you." I ducked my head. My submissive nature to alphas repulsed me, but I accepted the cold drink anyway.

Geo had avoided me all rotation. By some miracle, his work always took place outside, even when his crew called him in to deal with a problem, but just then, the tether yanked taut.

Raz wandered across my new floor with a proprietary air. Why he was interested in a Lornian baffled me. I wouldn't fit in his neat and tidy world any better than in my parents'. His thick tail dragged through the mud and sawdust before leaving a trail across the polished surface.

"This-s-s...is an Intergalactic Federation-funded dwelling?" Dark vertical pupils, encircled in yellow, elongated when they dropped to my floor, widened further at my high walls and turned black when he snapped his scaly neck through the courtyard opening. He'd obviously compared my construction to his dwelling, and his steady low hiss highlighted his displeasure. He was not pleased my rooms already surpassed his in both workmanship and overall design.

Honestly, I had no idea how many credits I would owe for all the extra features Geo had built into my new place, but I wouldn't change one thing. The smell of warm summer fields drifted my way, and I immediately relaxed. Geo's arm brushed mine, his presence solid at my side.

"Raz. It seems we meet again." Geo's words welcomed, but his tone did not. "Not that it's any of your business, but Makir has agreed to be my lamar supplier. We have arranged to use his dwelling to showcase lamar." His thick arm was so close to me that his shoulder brushed against my jumpsuit. I looked down and found his hands bunched into fists.

Raz hissed. "An arrangement, you s-s-say?"

Geo's fists squeezed tighter, and I could have sworn his chest muscles pulsed. The heat in the room grew, and my jumpsuit stuck to my body.

"Yes." His voice was so low it rattled in my tightening groin. "The Intergalactic Federation Building Authority has approved Makir's dwelling as a showhome."

It had?

Clouds stirred above, visible through my roofless walls. Then a slow drizzle started, and I shrank into my collar. My shoulders drooped. It took so long for my fur to dry.

"Hmmm, you can't sleep here tonight." Raz switched tactics, his glare softening as he eyed the weather worsening overhead. The clouds darkened to an ominous brown.

"I welcome you to s-s-spend the night with me."

My body drew tight at his exuberant invitation, and I didn't dare look at Geo. If I were an alpha, I would tell Raz to shove it. Heat radiated off Geo in waves.

"In my s-s-second room, of course," Raz tacked on.

Is he deliberately baiting Geo?

"Makir," Geo growled, his emphasis on the 'r' at the end of my name buzzing in the pit of my stomach, hot and eager, "has already agreed to bunk with me tonight." Geo's face flushed red.

I have?

When JayJay chuckled, I surfaced from the dense fog I'd been in. Five Rock Dwellers stood, riveted by the scene in front of them. I'd forgotten anyone else was here.

"I-I meant bunk with the crew," Geo stammered, sucking in a belly-holding breath.

Lornian omegas eased the tension in the room. They didn't cause it. I licked my lips. The time to put my charms into effect had arrived. Raz could do nothing to me in Geo's presence, not to mention the wall of giants who also had my back.

"Thanks so much for the hiscus juice, Raz." I finished the jar and passed it back to him. The sweetness on my tongue matched my honeyed words. "I appreciate your offer and concern for my well-being." I hoped my friendly smile didn't go too far.

I walked toward the empty space where my door would soon be. Would Raz follow? When I looked over my shoulder, he was right where I wanted him, but Geo's stern gaze was not. "Staying with the Rock Dweller crew makes the most sense. That way, we can plan everything out for tomorrow. I hope you understand." I spread my hands open in front of my stomach and shrugged. "Oh, and by the way, D'ovey mentioned he needs another order of graneth at your earliest convenience." With a smile and distraction, I peacefully ushered Raz out, no harm done.

Geo scratched his beard and toed at the construction debris beside me. "What's everyone doing standing around lollygagging?" He stormed outside. "Get back to work."

"Lollygagging, boss man?" JayJay's snicker mimicked a tree falling, its thud like an echo through a canyon. He trailed after his grumpy boss.

In the distance, I heard Geo's voice. "Lingering, loitering, hanging around and not minding your own goddamn business." His anger had ebbed, and through my lack of a doorway I saw Geo bump his shoulder into JayJay's ribcage, teasing his much larger foreman.

I'd observed how he interacted with his crew today: patient, kind, efficient and with good leadership. Was that his usual self? They got along surprisingly well, and he seemed like a good boss.

Why was he an entirely different beast in my presence?

My long tail coiled around my waist, and I spent a brutal sun wondering what would happen if I ran my finger down his sternum and over his belly. Would his stomach soften and relax under my touch, or would his chest expand more? What would a night so close to Geo mean for our tether? Bonic had told me to stay away, but the light rain had already matted my fur, and I didn't have a roof. One night surely wouldn't hurt.

9

I STOOD IN MAKIR'S courtyard, the sun casting a moody red glow over the new construction. The crew, long gone, had taken Makir with them, but I couldn't shake my restlessness. So, I kept going and going, funneling the buzzing energy into finishing the courtyard now that Makir was safe with my crew.

I'd always admired Balinese courtyards and how their water features and lush greenery created an oasis of tranquility. Tern was beautiful in the way new beginnings were—filled with bare earth, stalky graneth and potential. Still, I missed the plants, trees and water from Earth.

The honeycombed windows spread along the back wall of Makir's house like lace trim, framing the view of a soon-to-be sparkling pool. In my mind, the leafy gardens would skirt a perimeter dressed in bamboo-like plants and surround the stone walkways that led to private nooks. Would Makir love the courtyard of my dreams? Honestly, the bamboo plants were a bit of a long shot. I hadn't seen anything of that description on Tern yet. But the rough finish of the walls and bare ground glowed, sunset soft.

I placed my hands on my hips, leaned back to stretch the kinks out of my back, and exhaled. Finally, I'd worn out my body enough to return to the shared sono. I grabbed Makir's bundle of furs and headed toward the hole in the wall. Tomorrow he would have a door if I had any say in the matter. And I had all the say.

"Makir, are you out here?" Sisip walked through the opening that would soon be filled with a solid door and whistled. "Now, isn't this something?" Her head swiveled, and the tawny catlike ears all Tigs had on top of their heads twitched. Her eyes widened when she walked outside into the courtyard.

The lead enforcer posed no threat, but why did everyone think they could just walk into Makir's dwelling uninvited? I plastered on a smile and mentally added a deadbolt with an exclamation point behind it to the long list of items I needed to follow up on.

"Geo?" She seemed confused by my presence at first, then shrugged, not caring one way or the other. "I wanted to catch Makir." She rubbed her hands back and forth like she couldn't warm them.

My shoulders tightened, and the muscles in my chest burned as they stretched the bands of fabric around my arm uncomfortably tight. "Yeah, do you normally come by Makir's in the evening? Is he expecting you?" The filter I'd employed regularly on Earth had shriveled and died since I'd met Makir.

Taken aback, her expression quickly changed to amusement. "Calm down there, hot stuff." She laughed. "The only thing I'm after are the hand warmers he hinted he could make for my hoverbike." She rubbed her hands together again. "Looks like we'll be patrolling the Starry Mountains a little more regularly." The corners of her mouth turned down.

I stuffed my hands into my pockets, embarrassed by my obvious attraction to Makir.

"Anyways"—she perked back up—"can't wait to see this dwelling when it's all done. I might have a few ideas for changes to my place."

Proud of the hard work we'd done today, I stood taller. "Absolutely. Get in touch with JayJay, and we can schedule a design consult. I'm heading back to the sono. Makir's spending the night with the crew there."

My gaze wandered before it found the gaping hole where the roof should be. I wasn't sure why I'd omitted that he would also be spending the night with me. I should've said something along the lines of 'I'll tell him to get in touch with you' but I couldn't force the words out. My attraction to Makir was so fragile it might snap if vocalized. Instead, I walked her toward the door like an unwelcome guest, as if Makir's home was my own.

"Anything else?" I grumbled.

"Nah. Tell Makir he'll hear from me soon." She laughed and turned to walk away the same way she'd arrived, ambling under the windows along Makir's roofline, oohing and aahing.

To keep myself distracted, I recorded notes in my wristport while I walked to the sono.

"Talk to the landscaper about plants. Speak with Sully on how to use the lamar to create a massive sliding door opening onto the patio."

The sky turned inky, and I searched for the Big Dipper or Orion among the spray of stars, neither to be found. I swallowed around the lump in my throat, forcing away the thought of my dogs, who currently orbited a different sun in an entirely different solar system. Maybe Ginger would send pics today.

My shoulders slumped with exhaustion, and my stomach growled as I trudged back to the sono. I hoped JayJay had saved me something to eat. Sisip had really thrown me for a loop. Was she competition? If so, I didn't have a chance. Cameron had flirted with men right in front of me. Would it be the same with

Sisip? What was I supposed to think when she'd walked into Makir's dwelling so casually?

I tripped over the ruts in the road and added 'Learn to ride a hoverbike' to my list. In the murky dark, the road heaved and dipped like a freshly plowed field.

With time to think, my self-esteem plummeted as fast as the temperature. I hugged Makir's furs, and a shiver ran through me while my muscles pulsed and ached from inhaling his enticing fragrance. I didn't recognize myself anymore. I'd gone from a doormat in my old life to a raging bear in this one. The only thing familiar was that I could still build a hell of a house.

"In-floor heating and a dual fireplace." I spoke into the wristport, expanding my ever-lengthening list of must-haves. Makir's gingery smell drifted from the bundle I held, and I nearly face-planted in the dirt.

"Fuck," I muttered. "Why do I always go for guys way out of my league?" I said to the ground. Even if Makir was into men, what would he want with a short, fat, hairy guy from Earth who had nothing to offer in the goods department? I groaned. The ground dipped, and this time I fell flat on my ass.

"What are you doing down on the ground talking to yourself?" JayJay boomed. He reached for my hand, and the force of his pull launched me straight into him.

"I can't see for shit out here." I smacked the dust from my butt.

"Why are you looking for shit?" JayJay, never discreet, asked anyone within a half-mile radius. That included everyone in the sono. Cool night air currently drifted through the wide-open windows along with his voice, which was as subtle as a car backfiring.

I dropped my head to my chin. "It's an expression, JayJay. It just means I can't see anything."

"Why do you walk in the dark if you can't see?" The light from the doorway lit JayJay's face enough for his giant grin to lighten the mood.

"Good fucking question," I muttered. Half-smiling, I followed him inside.

"I was coming to see if you got lost." JayJay moved around the shared kitchen and placed a bowl of something savory in front of me. The long table was much too high for me. He glanced at his wristport. "It's two moons. You should have returned long ago."

Of course he was concerned—the guy was a damn saint. Time on Tern was measured in suns and moons. It had taken me weeks to adjust. There were ten sunlit hours, suns, and ten dark or moonlit hours, moons, in a rotation.

Saliva pooled in my mouth. "Thanks, JayJay, this is terrific." I polished off a second bowl. All the while, JayJay assessed me as if his eyes had x-ray capabilities. They scanned up and down, but as far as he'd explained, the only superpowers he had were his freakishly large size and strength. His words, not mine.

All I wanted to know was whether Tino and Sully had carved out a nest in the soft soil of the dirt floor so that Makir would be comfortable for the night, but, nope, not asking. That would have violated my promise to not think about Makir. Thinking about Makir was firmly off-limits, especially when he would be in the same room as me all night.

"Since you are stubborn and want to know but aren't going to ask, Makir's nest has been burrowed out as you requested. He's quite comfortable playing cards with the rest of the crew." JayJay planted his hands on his wide hips. "Now, I must insist you shower and go straight to bed. You've done far too much work for the rotation."

When JayJay launched into maternal mode, there was no messing with him. I forced my aching body out of my chair. I'd put off the inevitable for too long, so with no other choice, I headed into the shared room to gather my pajamas and toiletries.

Instantly, Makir's eyes sought mine. The lavender lingered for a moment before they swirled to silver, and I froze in place. The other Rock Dwellers disappeared. My shirt felt suffocatingly tight as my muscles pulsed and heated.

Be normal.

"Makir," I rasped. "Sisip came by this evening and wanted to talk to you about how you could warm her up."

Rumbling snickers filled the room.

Makir's brows furrowed and my nostrils flared. The room I slept in was entirely saturated with Makir's scent. The crisp juniper and warm ginger muddled my tired mind. The low light darkened the shadows of Makir's strong jaw. His blue mane was pulled away from his face in a damp braid, revealing the velvety tips of his ears. A growl built in my chest. The entire crew could see the tips of his ears. His tail rested casually on his knee as he sat at a table with Tino and Sully, playing cards.

"Hand warmers. She wanted to talk to you about hand warmers," I corrected.

Makir's tail switched against the floor.

"Getting a shower," I muttered before I told a knock-knock joke or something equally terrible.

Makir popped up out of his chair. "About that… JayJay said it would be okay if I used your towel, so it might be a little damp." His words rushed out, and his tail coiled around his wrist. I envied his tail and its ability to measure the thrum of his pulse the way my fingertips so urgently desired.

"S'fine," I grumbled before I put his bundle of pelts on my bed for safekeeping and grabbed the damp towel. Tino and Sully had carved out Makir's nest in the small space that happened to be immediately adjacent to my bunk. Assholes. On legs weakened to the point of jelly, I walked to the bathroom.

The bathroom stall was filled with his ginger and juniper odor. The towel drew me like a bull to a red cape, and I braced my forearm against the tiles before I dropped my forehead on it. "Fuck," I swore at the wood-slatted floor.

The hot water did not remove the ache from my muscles. It agitated the itchy, tight sensation that occurred every time Makir neared. I soaped up, rinsed off and got out of the hot spray as quickly as possible. I wasn't prepared when I reached for the towel to dry off. Makir's scent buckled my knees.

My body shuddered, and my muscles grew tight like they might burst. That wasn't the only thing that felt like it might burst. With the water off now, my cock stood painfully erect as I rocked from foot to foot, swathed in clouds of steam. A leisurely walk to my bed in my pajama pants with a raging boner was not an option. My eyes laser-focused on the towel through the mist—nothing else existed. I brought the towel up to my nose and inhaled deeply. Makir's scent annihilated what was left of my senses, and my cock leaked.

Crisp juniper drifted from the towel, and my arm worked automatically, no longer connected to my brain. I rubbed the nubby fabric, slow and rough, over my plumped cock. The cloth wasn't velvety enough. It wasn't my favorite blueprint blue. But Makir's perfume enveloped me like a hug. I smelled of Makir. It was enough for now.

I dumped shampoo into my hand, dropped my face into the towel and inhaled again, then slicked the makeshift lube down my hot length. With a firmer grip, I fisted the fabric entirely around the nest of curls at my base, our scents mixing.

My mind conjured Makir's smooth blue hands and wrapped them around my iron-hard length. I squeezed my eyes shut. Sex-fantasy Makir worked my erection up and down. His silver eyes so close to mine that my clenched jaw was reflected in them.

I pumped my fist harder. My chin tilted toward the rough-hewn beams on the ceiling. The shower stall walls ended a couple of feet above me. If anyone came in...

Biting down on my lip, I stifled a groan as I came. The fur of his blue chest would drip with ropes of my thick cum. Panting, I leaned my shoulders against the cool tiles, then turned on the faucet to rinse away the evidence. This time I avoided Makir's delicious aroma and dried off with my T-shirt.

"What the hell?" My pajama top buttons wouldn't close, and my thighs stretched the seams of my pants. I did a double-take. Yep, they were my pajamas, the same ones Ginger had bought me last Christmas. The ones covered in retro Pikachu and Charizard Pokémon characters.

"Jesus, what's happening to my body?" I groaned and added a medic visit to my list. Not sure how I could look Dr. Ten in the eyes and tactfully ask why Makir's scent turned me into an animal or why I found my clothes three sizes too small. I walked back to the shared area filled with enormous bunk beds.

"Ungh," Makir whined. His lavender eyes moved up and down my body from where he sat on the empty mattress across from mine. They'd been silver a moment ago in my fantasy.

My shoulders curled inward. Exposed, my muffin top hung over my pants, and my hairy chest stood on display for everyone's eyes, but Makir's disgust hit hard, a direct punch.

Cameron had continually begged me to wax and cut carbs. My Adam's apple bobbed.

My body's fine.

Ginger firmly believed that I needed to come to terms with being happy in my current body. Maybe I didn't believe the words yet, but it was a step.

I gathered the bundle of Makir's pelts and blocked out my self-loathing. Then I gently unfolded them, shook them out and lined the nest Tino and Sully had dug for him. His scent covered me everywhere, burning like a juniper-scented fire under my hot muscles. My skin prickled where I uselessly rubbed over them.

Not bothering to suck in my belly, I called out a quick goodnight to Makir and the crew and rolled into my bunk, safely hidden under the covers. JayJay would be pleased. I'd followed his directions to the letter. This day couldn't be over quick enough.

10

"MAKIR, THIS IS D'ARGON and D'Rasma." D'irk slapped the back of my shoulder where we'd agreed to meet at the base of the winding path up to the Rowtees' tree-top aviary. All three were Boola, had deep brown skin that glistened in the sun and wore enforcer-issued boots. Their heads tipped to the side in greeting. "They're brothers, if you can't tell." The brothers shared the same broad shoulders and tapered hips, but D'Rasma's more rounded chin set him apart. D'irk laughed at his own joke.

They rolled their eyes, and I lifted my chin in greeting. "Happy morning."

D'Rasma's gleaming white teeth shone. "Glad you came. We know you're in the middle of construction. You're luckier than the last winner of the intergalactic lottery." He chuckled as he adjusted equipment on his hovercraft. "I think I'm last on the list for a dwelling."

D'Argon's arm swept out. "Sisip wants us to survey the outskirts of the mapped area of Tern, so we're heading north."

Except where the occasional weed popped up among the graneth stalks with the recent rain and sun, Tern was dominated by pink soil as far as the eye could see.

"Y'up for it?" D'Rasma asked.

I nodded and shook the morning funk off. I'd had the best sleep in a long time last night, but I'd been unsettled since I woke. The tether between Geo and me buzzed in agitation, not liking the distance between us. Disheartened to find Geo's bed empty when I woke, I'd told JayJay I would be away for a couple of days hunting instead. Geo had probably installed a reinforced door on my dwelling before I'd even awoken.

D'Rasma sipped the syrupy dark drink most of Tern preferred. I would stick to hiscus. "D'irk has raved about your skill with a snare, and Sisip has told us nonstop how you'll be her salvation with the hand warmers you're crafting for her. Sisip and her cold hands..." D'Rasma's long lashes trembled when he laughed.

"I think I have something to warm up those hands." D'Argon thrust his hips out playfully.

D'Rasma's narrowed eyes nailed his brother with a near-lethal glare.

Interesting. Sisip has an admirer.

"Quit harrasin' your brother, D'Argon," D'irk said. "Makir, show 'em the pelts you got when you slept out in the wastelands."

My tail loosened behind me as the inclusion into this group settled over my shoulders like a warm blanket. I dropped my backpack full of gear on the rough ground and rooted through it for one of the pelts I'd packed.

D'irk had been part of the rescue crew when my hoverbike broke down in the wastelands. He had eyeballed the creatures I'd snared after they attacked me. The last time I'd seen him at the weekend market, his eyes had dipped to the vest I'd fashioned from them.

D'Argon inhaled and clicked his teeth. "A linobee! A huge linobee! You were right, D'irk." D'Argon and D'Rasma smoothed their fingers over the thick fur, their dark skin a sharp contrast to the pearly white coat. "These are highly prized on our home planet." D'Argon's wide-eyed gaze caught mine. He cradled the pelt in the crook of his arm. "The ceremonial clothing for our mating ritual is entirely crafted from linobee. Only the species on our planet is much smaller."

"Well, boys, are we done with the greetings?" D'irk projected a map of the surveyed area into the air from his wristport. "The sooner we get to where Sisip would like us to scout, the sooner you can get your hands on some linobee." He pointed to a rocky outcrop in the center and tapped the place we'd be hunting in. "Linobee are pretty enough, Makir." D'irk chuckled. "But I'm after a critter a whole lot bigger. Those mantus cook up real nice, plus they earn me a few credits at the market."

I straddled my hoverbike, the trailer in tow behind. "Geo has my plans"—not that he's following them—"and currently, I have no roof, so this is a perfect time to get away for a few days."

Hmmm...maybe the linobees would earn me a few credits at the market.

My shoulders tensed when I thought about Geo as I secured my gear. I didn't know what to expect from him. He'd hammered home the fact that my plans extended beyond what the Intergalactic Federation would provide and then proceeded to completely disregard them and built whatever came to mind. I just wanted a hovery.

I looked at the blue sky. The sun warmed the back of my neck, and I stretched into its heat. The rotation hummed with a sense of adventure. I would not let the emptiness of an incomplete bond between Geo and me ruin it. I turned over the ignition. "Let's hit it," I yelled over the downdraft of my hoverbike.

As I flew in line behind D'Rasma, I couldn't help but worry that Geo had been upset with me when he crawled into his nest last night. He was always growly and aloof, but something had been different. I might have put my finger on it if I hadn't been so distracted by his magnificent chest—especially when he puffed it out. His blocky pectoral muscles, matted with swirls of damp fur, had driven me to distraction.

Deep inside my protective pouch, I grew hard and slippery. I caught Geo's fragrance on my skin, and my bike dipped. When I swiped the sweat off my forehead, his aroma lingered. I had no desire to wash it off anytime soon. I loved that his scent covered me. My erection throbbed, and the channel that extended from my opening lined itself with slippery wax.

Blant!

Every sensation heightened, and waves of arousal rolled through me. I dodged a flock of woodskies. It all pointed to one thing. My heat is here.

My erection quickly deflated at the thought of a bond with Geo, but I couldn't deny the signs of my heat.

Under no circumstances did I want to spend the rest of my life with somebody who constantly bossed me around. I'd had enough of overbearing alphas. Tern was my fresh start—a safe place where my omega traits weren't supposed to be triggered. Even though it was rare for a Lornian omega to move away, Bonic and I had checked the species colonizing Tern and none were Lornian.

Stupid blanting faulty bond tethering to a human.

I needed to tell Bonic that my body showed signs of sexual compatibility. My tail whipped beside me in frustration. What a fun conversation that would be—telling him my breeding passage was preparing its natural lubricant, I was growing hard, and a temporary human tether combined with the full moon had triggered my heat. My shoulders turned inward.

A faint sulfur odor tainted the air. Then a rocky outcropping appeared, a wall of ebony rocks jutting from the ground. The sun rose high, and dust motes enveloped the hoverbikes in a cloud.

D'irk motioned where to park. "We'll set up camp here."

My jaw dropped open as the full scope of the razor-sharp terrain we had to survey spread out before me.

I threw my bag down near the base of the outcrop and hollowed out a nest, a simple job I could wrap my head around. Then we moved forward as a team, the soft thud of my water container bumping my hip as I scouted the landscape. Jagged black rocks rose from the raw pink earth. The sharp contrast transformed the land. A Do Not Enter sign would not have been out of place.

"Strange how it's all mixed up like that," D'Argon said. We stood shoulder to shoulder, admiring the layered striations of silver and charcoal among the ebony that twisted and warped at odd angles.

Although we were only about one sun from Yurstille by hoverbike, the rugged nature of the ground had left this area unexplored until now. Heavy with supplies and weapons, D'Rasma and D'irk joined us.

"This is perfect ground for snaring." I handed everyone a length of wire. "You'll want to hold the wire this way as you create your loop." I wove a long coil over my forearm and around my hand into the perfect snare. "Cover it up a bit when you find the right spot. The snare should be hidden. The rocks will hold many good hiding spots, but it will be tricky to find the right one."

"Especially when we haven't got the goddess clue what the blant we're hunting out here," D'Argon joked, but a sense of unease grew among us.

The expansive plateau we sat on was dotted with flat droppings dry enough to burn. The night air crackled as D'Rasma threw another patty on the fire in front of us. The moon, directly overhead, passed behind a cloud, and our breaths puffed out in cold mist. The sun had long set, the snares were laid, and a trap had been built to take down the mantu. My stomach was full of the mantu strips D'irk had dried, and linobee fur would line my nest tonight.

D'irk tipped his head. "This planet was supposed to be a dead zone. Mantu and linobee should not exist here. Tern keeps throwing all these mutations at us."

"The Fires That Cleanse are not very well studied." D'Rasma's dark fingers tapped his thick pants. "I remember my sister researching it for a proposal she wanted to bid on, and she shared all sorts of anomalies that have come up in the places where it's been used."

"Right, I remember that," D'Argon chimed in. "She didn't get funding because the backers thought it was too risky to complete the on-site investigations."

My tail lashed against my thick leather leg covers. "Well, we wouldn't be here if it wasn't safe. There's no way Mayor Yurst would allow it."

"The mayor..." D'Argon, D'Rasma and D'irk all huffed, displaying pointy white teeth.

Their reactions swayed me to reevaluate my opinion of the mayor. He did talk an awful lot without saying much of anything, but wasn't that a trait of mayors federation-wide? I wondered what he'd done for all these capable enforcers to mistrust him?

"Let's find us some critters to eat." D'irk threw some soil on the fire and swiped the scanner on his wristport, mapping the ground as we walked. He signaled for the rest of us to do the same.

My fingers prodded the latest gash in my leg covers. Scrambling over jagged rocks all rotation had bruised the arches of my feet and gouges covered the soles of my boots, even though they were manufactured from the highest quality material available on Lorne. Worn by the elite protectors, they'd been a parting gift from my brother.

A couple of moons later, when the night sucked the heat from the air, the area well past the rocky outcrop was mapped.

"Let's have a break before the big show," D'Argon said.

"That cliff was something else, wasn't it?" D'irk drank from his container. His mouth widened in a deep yawn. The container held the same slick sludge the Rock Dwellers drank every morning. I guessed Boola liked it too.

"Sprang up out of nowhere. Almost walked straight off it." D'Rasma chuckled and rose from the short springy grass, securing his weapon on the belt at his waist.

Despite the peacefulness of the moment, my tether tugged. Agitation burned through me and beads of sweat broke out on my forehead. I tilted my head to glare at the full moon.

Blanted heat! How would I get through this with no alpha to service me?

The deep lowing of a mantu echoed in the distance. I focused on the crisp air and the looming full moon hunt. If I was firm enough with myself, everything else might fade away. Mind over matter. Denial had been my best friend before, and it was a comfort to hide behind it again. Instead of my heat, my focus would remain on D'irk's plan.

At D'irk's signal, I positioned myself as planned. Borrowed spear secured to my back, I crouched behind the boulder marked with an X. My lungs expanded and filled as I waited in the stillness lit by the pale moon's glow. D'Argon and D'Rasma were tasked with separating a mantu from the herd with the help of D'irk's clever whistle. It mimicked its young in distress.

The thunder of hooves stiffened my spine, and my breaths shortened as the ground shook. Mantu were herbivores, so I was at no risk of being eaten alive, but their long tusks and hard hooves could skewer or crush me in a moment. Adrenaline pumped through me as my heart drummed in my ears.

Here they come.

Then it was on me. Faster than I thought possible I charged forward. Shoulder to shoulder, I ran alongside the snorting beast, our grunts and heavy footfalls in sync. I held my breath, rib cage fully expanded, and felt the hot gusts of air blowing out its nostrils against my skin. Then I tightened my grasp on the spear I held overhead and lunged. A fierce bellow tore from deep in my chest as the spear arced through the sky. The mantu lowed and stumbled as the sharp point struck its target. A blow to the mantu's shoulder forced the beast into the sharp curve of the boulder-strewn path we'd toiled all night to build.

As the anchor of the crew, I would close the deal and ensure the shaggy-coated mantu fell into our trap.

The snorting and pounding of hooves abruptly ended. Straight off the cliff's edge, the mantu soared before it plummeted to the grassy plateau below, its neck at an odd angle. The loss of life left my heart skipping a beat in sadness.

I peered over the steep drop as D'Rasma shouted, "It's a good clean death. C'mon down."

D'irk ran up beside me, his chest heaving. "Worked like a charm, Makir. Couldn't have got it done without you. Those tusks are yours." He tapped his fist twice on his opposite shoulder.

The show of respect made it difficult to swallow. A sense of pride filled me, not unlike when my brother and I had come home with a bundle of bush-tailed monties. "I will mount them in a place of honor." Still flushed with adrenaline, we clambered down the boulder-strewn path to the plateau.

Crouched before the mantu, the suction pad of my tail, still hidden among the fluff, touched the space between its lifeless eyes. "From the soil to the land, thank you for what you give to nourish us."

D'irk bent one knee to the trampled grass and passed his sharp blade through the mantu's thick, shaggy coat. The spilled blood from its neck soaked the dry soil below, a tribute to its time on this planet.

The somber moment was yanked away. Below me, the plateau vibrated, the sensation rolled through my knees, and four heads cranked toward the source. A herd of mantu stampeded directly toward us. Their panicked lows and snorts neared. And taking up the rear, chasing them, a creature the size of a tower wreaked havoc.

My shoulders tensed. The air tasted metallic with spilled blood. Every muscle coiled, strung tight as a bow. "W-what the blant is that?"

"Seek cover!" D'Rasma yelled over the din, already in motion. He grabbed my jumpsuit.

"C'mon." D'Argon pointed to the base of the cliff among the boulders and stones.

A long, flat space emerged as we raced closer. On our stomachs, we wiggled through a narrow cleft. All too soon, sandwiched between three Boola, it became an unwelcome cage to watch the gruesome scene play out in front of us. My tether tightened, prickly and itchy. It twanged, like humming feedback along a taut wire. Geo's concerned face flashed through my mind.

D'irk gawked. "Blant me, look'a the mouth on her."

My heart raced, but crammed side by side on our stomachs, we were relatively safe. Just above our heads, a stone shelf extended over us like a roof.

D'Argon's teeth clicked in time with his bouncing foot. "It looks like some type'a mutated worm."

"Goddess, no." I trembled as an enormous, pale, round-mouthed, eyeless creature tore through the herd of mantu. Gore dripped from rows of pointed teeth, circling the black hole of its gaping maw and extending down its throat. Mantu were flung from the creature's mouth, their death screams haunting the herd left behind. Broken bodies littered the grassy plateau. The steam from their snorting noses turned into white clouds in the cold air, and the moonlight cast an eerie glow across the macabre scene.

The bloodshed, too gruesome to process at the moment, would haunt me later while I lay safe in bed. I scanned the carnage as if I were watching it on a screen, not like the all-too-close, terrifying reality I could almost reach out and touch.

Time ticked by while I lay frozen in fear. So much gore. I flashed back to the worst night of my life. Tremors racked my body. "Reinik. No. Stop." I pleaded. "You're hurting me! Bonic, h-help..." My vision grew black, my breaths so shallow it felt like I was suffocating.

My hand clamped so tightly onto the rocky ledge in front of me that my skin broke and bled. My vision tunneled as the giant worm-like monster gulped down one more mantu, then sank back into the earth, purple with blood, a geyser of soil rising in its wake.

"I guess it's had its fill," I distantly heard D'irk mumble.

"Makir." D'irk's hand rested on my shoulder. "Take a deep breath now." He spoke to me in a low voice. "You're calm and safe. Breathe now. Listen to my voice... Good. Focus on my voice. Keep breathing."

The two brothers chatted in the background, faint at first, then louder. "She's as pale as the moon. My guess is it's nocturnal," D'Rasma whispered. "I think we should wait 'til morning before we move."

My mind finally stopped its freefall. I drew in a long breath of air. Hunting I enjoyed, but single-minded destruction was something else altogether.

D'irk's hand remained a solid presence on my shoulder. "You okay now?"

I nodded and drank from the water container he offered. "Th-thanks. How did you know what would help?" This wasn't my first panic attack, but my brother was the only one who had successfully brought me out of one.

"T'isn't somethin' new to me...." He stared into the distance.

Wedged between a stone slab above me and one below, the hiding place was eerily similar to the graves on Lorne rather than a haven. How would I spend the rest of the dark hours in this tiny shelter?

When I stared into the moonlight, its glow electrified the tether's vibration and pull. I felt hot all over, my face flushed, and it had nothing to do with the lingering effects of the panic attack or the warm bodies on either side of me.

I closed my eyes and prayed to the goddess Sola to let me get through this night.

11

"J ESUS!" I JUMPED AS a fountain of hot water heavy with sulfur doused me from head to toe, then I wiped the stream of water from under my eyes as it pooled in my steel-toed work boots. "What next?" I muttered, then turned toward the small backhoe digging out Makir's pool. "Stop digging. We need to cap it!"

My crew stood buried to their ankles in Pepto Bismol-colored muck, and the geyser continued to jet into the air like an artesian spring. Bright moonlight glinted off a length of copper in my periphery. The long, wide tube I'd cleared out of Makir's hovery lay beside a pile of excavated dirt. I raced through the courtyard, shouting, "Tino, Sully, with me."

By the time we'd augured the tube deep into the hot water and capped the top with a temporary faucet, MacGyvered from parts Makir had salvaged from the wastelands, my arms were trembling with exhaustion.

JayJay, knee-deep in the milky slurry, rolled his eyes. "Still think it was a good idea to work through the full moon to get ahead?"

Maybe I'd been a little too ambitious in wanting to have everything perfect before Makir returned from his hunting trip. I pulled a bandana from my overalls and mopped the sweat from my brow. "Nice work. The orzfoam is on me this week."

The Rock Dwellers bumped fists and cheered. Dang, my credits would take a hit this week. Those boys could throw down some beer. Totally worth it, though.

As my crew worked their way out of the thick goop, I burst into exhausted laughter.

"Boss man, you good?" JayJay asked, slogging toward dry ground.

Nearly bent over with laughter, I choked out a few words. "You look like you've been dipped in pink chocolate." Mud dripped down their legs and speckled their bodies.

"You think that's funny, huh, boss man." Tino's teeth flashed, and he scooped a handful of mud from his bald head.

"Chocolate?" JayJay's brow rose, and a rivulet of grime tracked down his smooth gray cheek like a clown's tear.

"Hey!" I called out, my breath stolen from me as Tino and Sully, huge hands slippery with mud, picked me up and threw me into the pool. I sat there for a moment, admiring the horizon where a soft yellow line separated earth from sky as the sun prepared to rise. All the while, globs of cotton-candy-colored silt dripped from my beard and oozed between the seams of my coveralls.

If Ginger were here, she would capture the moment on her phone to revisit and torture me for eternity. Complete with narration. 'Here lies Geo, a man in search of his identity. Will he find it at the bottom of this idyllic watering hole alongside the mystical unicorns that drink here or...'

More like a pig in a sty than anything remotely magical, I slid to the edge, where the same giant hands pulled me out. Their lawnmower-like laughter nearly deafened me.

"Very funny." I flicked mud at Tino, then turned to JayJay. "Chocolate's one of the greatest creations of humankind." I wiped the mud from my arms and legs. "Creamy, sweet, delicious—"

I jerked to a stop. The hairs on my arm stood on end. Something was wrong. Makir was in danger and the need to get to him rattled through my bones.

The strange pull that connected me to Makir vibrated with tension. Alarm bells rang in my mind. I bit down on the inside of my cheek, drawing blood. Who the hell hunted in uncharted territory on a planet that hadn't been studied since the Fires That Cleanse had been deployed? As soon as I saw him, I would shake some sense into Makir's perfect blue head.

"Shit. Shit. Shit." I pressed the heel of my hand over my heart to relieve the pressure.

JayJay lifted one of his pronounced brow ridges. "Boss man?"

Already jogging toward the sono, I shakily replied, "Something's wrong with Makir."

Sully hauled me back and hosed us all off in no time, washing away the mess but not the urgency.

"Com Sisip," JayJay told Tino.

I clenched my fists. "Damn it, I couldn't get to Makir even if I knew where he was." Without a hoverbike, I was useless.

"I think you know how to find him, boss man," JayJay said in a low voice. "Use your tether."

Something poked at the recesses of my mind. Like a sixth sense, long dormant, newly awakened. "Tether?"

"Can you not sense your connection to Makir?" JayJay's brows nearly sank into his forehead. "Human courtship must be very difficult if you can't identify your mate."

A spike of fear jolted me back into action, and I ran toward JayJay's hoverbike. "Let's go. I can't let anything happen to him."

Tino bumped my shoulder. "We're a team, boss man. We've got your back."

I paced like a helpless idiot, eyeing the hoverbike I had never learned to fly. The morning sun turned the sono's pink walls an orange that reminded me of vomit.

The reply from Sisip was taking much too long. It grated on my nerves to ask Sisip for help, but my crew backed me up one hundred percent without bombarding me with a million questions, keeping my fraying sanity in check.

All the waiting left my imagination running wild to place my Makir in the evil clutches of an alien villain, about to be eaten.

My Makir?

Tino took a long drink from a container of javae as he exited the sono. "Sisip is putting together a team. We'll meet them at the base of the Towhees' aviary in one moon." Tino relayed Sisip's com, and three determined heads nodded back at me.

Damn it! It will take forever to assemble a crew this early in the morning.

"Bish, you need food." JayJay gripped my elbow, yanking me out of my stupor.

In dry clothes and armed, the Rock Dwellers bristled with knives. Sully tucked me in front of JayJay like a child on his hoverbike. My cheeks burned, but I stuffed my embarrassment into the deep recesses of my mind as I white-knuckled the handholds. My unease grew so great I rocked forward on the seat, wanting to take control and leave everyone behind. I needed to protect Makir all by myself. Prove myself to him.

The downdraft of the engines coated us in a cloud of pink dust, and we lurched ahead. My connection to Makir hummed with tension and pulled directly toward the Towhees. Tether. I rolled the label over in my mind. We were tethered?

Though I was one step closer to Makir, my foot bounced so hard against the hovercraft that JayJay clamped his boot over it to hold it down.

At last, the steep trail to the Towhees' aviary, perched high above us in the shadows, opened before us. My foot resumed its restless tapping while we waited for Sisip, and once again my mind played havoc with my nerves conjuring visions of Makir in the venomous mouth of some giant alien.

In a haze of dawn-lit dust, three enforcers arrived with Sisip and dismounted. Loaded with gear, a blaze-orange spinal board hovered behind one of the bikes. Fuck! My heart drummed. Would Makir need to use that? A clock appeared in my mind. The second hand hung suspended, paused, and the next tick would mean detonation. We needed to fucking go.

After what felt like hours, Sisip stood before our search party on the dusty ground, legs spread wide, and spoke in a voice that demanded attention. "Thanks for volunteering to search on such short notice. I know for many of you, you're sleep—"

"Let's go! We need to go!"

"Can you lead us to him?" Sisip's hand rat-a-tat-tatted against her thigh.

"Yes." The word flew out of my mouth before I considered what it meant.

Sisip ignored my biting tone and placed JayJay and me at the front of the search party. Her gaze dropped from my shoulders to my waist before she pulled a belt out of her gear bag and wrapped it around me. Silently, she tucked a long dagger into the sheath that now hung at my side and patted it before her eyes caught mine. Though her face remained free of judgment, my cheeks flushed red.

I can't even protect myself. How am I going to protect Makir? Trying to remain neutral, my eyes scanned Sisip up and down. She oozed confidence, and her hair was nice, I supposed. Is this what Makir finds attractive? She's much more competent than me.

"Thanks," I growled, "Let's go." The hoverbike vibrated between my legs and JayJay formed a solid wall behind me. To our left, Sisip's hand circled in the air in a signal to head out, and the rest of the team shot off, filling the air with a loud drone.

With Makir's rescue in motion, I focused one hundred percent of my attention on the strange link between us and slowly led the caravan. JayJay quickly figured out my hand directions and flew where I guided him, taking my cue from the tether's strong pull. The dangerous vibes quieted, but replacing them was something just as urgent. I shook my hands out, trying to relax, but they wanted to grip the tether as if it were physical and yank Makir straight into my arms.

I can't see a thing, so why do I know where he is?

"Doesn't look like they camped here," Sisip said as we arrived at their base camp. Four hoverbikes stood neatly parked below a giant rocky outcrop, and Makir's beat-up duffel bag sat next to a dip in the ground that hadn't yet been slept in. I fingered his pelts. His scent was too old to be fresh.

The Rock Dwellers' sonorous humming broke my increasingly disturbing train of thought—jaws clamping over Makir's head.

One of the enforcers approached me. "What are they doing?" he asked, as if I had a clue.

The Rock Dwellers caressed the rocks as if they'd found a long lost family member. Sisip sidled closer to me. "They've been here nearly a year now, and all they've seen is the silty pale pink earth of Tern." She idly thumbed the holster on her hip. "I've seen pictures of their home planet, and it looks a lot like this."

Spikes of ebony stood before us as if they'd erupted from the ground. The morning sun glistened on the rocks and would have been beautiful on a different day. Right now, it was nothing more than an obstacle course made up of shattered rock so sharp it cut like glass.

My eyes fixed on where JayJay, Tino and Sully stood humming. Not unlike a holy pilgrimage, it was as if they were reconnecting and recharging their spirits, worshipping the rocks. My skin itched, a fire spread through my chest, and my muscles bunched and grew. Makir was close.

Enough of this singing already. It's time for action.

A flash of white caught my eye, and I scrabbled up the rocks, cutting through the calluses on my hands for a closer inspection. The tiny pricks of pain were not enough to compete with the agonizing pulling of my muscles as they stretched to their fullest. My bicep expanded to the point it almost tore into two. First a tether, now this?

A white beaver, the same type of creature Makir had trapped when his hover-bike had broken down and trapped us in the wastelands, lay dead in the snare in front of me. My imagination concocted an alien creature strangling Makir in the same way, a sharp wire against his neck.

"This way," I shouted, breaking the Rock Dwellers' trance and capturing the enforcers' attention. "This is Makir's trapline. We need to follow it."

An enforcer bent to collect the beaver from the snare. "Leave it," I commanded, my voice shockingly deep, "we'll collect it on the way back."

JayJay's long legs caught up with me in no time. He wove effortlessly through the jagged boulders beside me like a trained soldier. "Slow down, Geo." JayJay grabbed my shoulder and placed leather gloves on my tattered hands. Tino and Sully were nearly invisible they trailed so far behind.

The enforcers' voices rose and fell as they grumbled about the terrain cutting up their boots and exclaimed over the white beavers caught in the snares of the trapline we followed.

I leaped over boulders and stumbled over shale-like shards of rock. All force and no finesse, I battled against the final grains of sand as they dropped through the hourglass.

JayJay grabbed the back of my belt, jolting me. "Stop," he rumbled.

I gasped, searching for an elusive full breath. We stood at the edge of a sheer drop-off, a vast plateau spread as far as the eye could see. Early morning mist parted, revealing a patchwork of wispy brown clouds intermixed with green grass.

JayJay's brow ridges relaxed and almost disappeared into his forehead. "It's beautiful." A chorus of awe-filled breaths followed closely behind.

"Let's go," I grunted.

Panic consumed me. The bond rattled like a prison chain, and the fiery itch spread to my pulsing forearms. My internal GPS told me the most direct route would be straight off the cliff edge. I was tempted to jump and hope for the best, but the rational part of my brain took control, aided by JayJay's quick save, and logic prevailed.

Tino lurched to a stop beside us overlooking the cliff, shading his eyes with a giant hand. "There! I see movement. Four bodies."

My heart soared as I sped toward the blue fuzzy one. Rocks skidded out from under my feet as I descended—the curves of the winding path brought me closer with each expansion of my rib cage. Yet, my senses still warned of danger.

"Hello there, is all well?" Behind me, Sully's baritone carried down the cliff to the plateau below as I surged forward.

"They're waving us down." Sisip's voice grew distant as she directed everyone to continue along the same path.

A rock shot out from under my foot as I sprinted, nearly faceplanting and I slowed for a second to catch my breath and wipe the sweat from my brow.

Finally, my boots sank into short grass. "Makir?" I shouted.

I rounded a boulder and my gaze landed on him, desperately assessing. Bent over with my hands on my knees, panting, I swallowed around the lump in my throat.

His arms dripped with blood, yet even amid the gore, my heart skipped a beat at the sight of him. His glorious blue mane framed his face in a messy knot, highlighting the sharp angles of his cheekbones and square jaw. Deep shadows darkened his eyes, but he appeared fine. Crouched on his haunches, he butchered what must have been a mantu. Long and shaggy, its coat wouldn't have looked out of place on a highland cow.

"Geo," he groaned. His lavender eyes swirled and locked on mine, tail erect.

"You can't be here! Blant this temporary bond," Makir muttered.

My head spun. It felt as if I'd been shoved over the cliff's edge. He didn't want me here?

12

THE SMELL OF WARM summer fields assaulted my senses. "Geo." I inhaled deeply, unable to fight against my instincts any longer. Heat swamped me. Every nerve tingled and needed to be soothed by my mate.

My mate?

No! Geo was not my mate. The bond was incomplete. I wrestled against my omega's base needs, struggling to regain control of my body. With the rag tucked in my pocket, I wiped my arms and hands clean of mantu blood.

Last night's gruesome feeding frenzy had left the grassy plateau soaked with blood and strewn with bodies. In the safety of the daylight, the four of us butchered as efficiently as we could, but with so much waste, my heart hurt.

The tether snapped and settled. When Geo approached, hesitant step by hesitant step, mind-numbing heat spread low in my groin, and my passage relaxed and grew slick with wax. "You can't be here." I moaned and clamped my hand over my nose to block his scent. That never worked.

The need to get Geo somewhere alone before my omega instincts completely took over consumed me. With my heat near its peak, it left no room for playing shy. We needed privacy. "D'irk," I called out, "Me and Geo are mapping out the cave we found earlier."

With only minutes of clear brain function remaining, I no longer cared how much sense I made. D'irk tipped his head deeply to the side. Geo's hands spread palms up in front of him as he inched toward me. He appeared equally confused at my words. D'irk's expression morphed into relief as reinforcements flooded onto the plateau. So many more animals could be preserved now with all the extra hands.

"Hope you boys and girls are ready to get dirty." D'irk chuckled in the distance, but I only had eyes for Geo.

I'm ready to get dirty. Past ready.

When I rose, my nose filled with Geo's powerful aroma, sending my tail swaying. My knife fell to the ground, and I walked with an exaggerated tilt of my hips, prowling toward Geo. As much as I didn't want to believe it, denying I was in full heat right now would be stupid. Without the cold baths, heat suppressants and confined quarters of home, only one thing could slake my need. He happened to be three steps away and smelling of warm summer fields.

The cloth covering his bicep had split, and I wanted to rub my cheek along the round bulb of smooth muscle. His massive pectoral muscles bulged under his bib overalls, the clasps at their breaking point. Pale green eyes were riveted on mine, and his nostrils flared. He stood still, drugged by me. My omega traits pulled him in hook, line and sinker, and for now, he remained mine for the taking.

"This way." I crooked my finger and sauntered toward the cave we'd found earlier.

He blindly followed my swaying tail. Right where I wanted him.

A smooth gray-and-white marbled stone ramp replaced the springy grass beneath my boots before it reached a narrow entrance. Once inside, the cave opened into a dome. Warm and humid, it reeked of sulfur, and an escape from the ever-present pink dust of Tern proved impossible. It sparkled like glitter where sunlight streamed through the tiny, pockmarked holes in the curved ceiling.

The air crackled with tension. Locked eye to eye, we stood facing each other, suspended in time.

Geo lunged for me, pressed his nose to the soft spot behind my ear where my scent was the strongest and huffed deeply.

"Yes," I moaned.

He pulled his gloves off and flung them to the ground before he slid his rough fingers down my tail. "Soft," he growled. His arms bulged as he pinned me to the side of the damp wall. Calloused palms traveled over my hips and ribcage and feathered over my neck, where his fingers twisted into my tangled mane. Sparks erupted over my skin everywhere he touched. I sighed when he cupped the back of my head, freeing the tie holding my mane away from my face.

"Are you okay?" His voice dipped so low it landed in the pit of my belly, stirring up need. Geo's neck flushed red, and one blunt tooth held down his lower lip as if to punish it. "I was worried."

I licked my lips, nodded, and bared my neck in submission. Warm summer fields had never smelled this good.

"I'll tell you later." The heat built under my skin, impatient for this conversation to end.

He leaned in, and his hot breath skimmed my neckline as he pressed against me from thigh to chest. My knees grew weak when his beard rasped against the thinner skin over my collarbone. "Like velvet." His deep voice rasped. The point of his tongue tapped against the sensitive skin, a Morse code plea to...

I lost the last vestiges of control when he nibbled up my neck to my jawline. "Oh, goddess," I moaned. His pheromones drove me past delirium, and I clung to his muscled arms.

Geo grasped my hips and pressed his lips against mine. The little sucking kisses shot directly to my tightening groin. My passageway throbbed, the waxy coating building.

It needed to be filled.

Geo's tongue coaxed my mouth open. When I yielded to him, his blunt teeth grazed over my lips. Our tongues tangled and untangled—a promise of things to come—muffling my moans until I gasped for air.

"Makir? Geo?" JayJay called from the cave entrance.

Not now. I can't hold back any longer.

"Fuck." Geo lurched away from me. His pupils were dilated, and only a tiny sliver of pale green remained when he forced his gaze away. He rearranged himself under his overalls before walking stiffly to the cave entrance while I swayed in a lusty haze.

Geo returned, holding a bag. He rocked from side to side, an arm's length away. "Told him we found a hot spring, and you wanted to explore the cave a bit more for future hunting trips. To go on back without us."

"Did he believe that?" I asked cheekily, one brow raised in question as I eyed his rumpled state and swollen lips.

"Not one bit." Geo's face flushed red. "He gave me this bag"—Geo tossed the bag to me—"and told me to have fun. They're leaving and taking your trailer." His foot traced circles in the soil where it drifted inside the cave and formed ridges.

I smiled to myself. If Geo didn't know the drill, at least JayJay had caught on.

"Everyone has as much mantu as they can eat, so they're not too upset about being woken up before dawn to rescue you," Geo said.

"I didn't need rescuing." I peeked into the bag. It held two large containers of water, dried mantu strips and graneth puffs.

Geo's eyes narrowed. "Ah, did you see the bloodbath out there? What the hell happened?"

"Hot," I groaned as I shamelessly wiggled my boots free and unzipped my jumpsuit, kicking them both to the side. The demands of my heat overpowered my need to explain the events of the night before. Geo's pectoral muscles pulsed with each piece of clothing I shed. His gulp was audible when I dumped the water from one of the containers down my arms and over my hands to wash away any lingering blood from the mantu I'd butchered.

"Jesus Christ," he groaned. "I guess you are into guys," he said with so much reverence I laughed.

I needed to see him, free of clothes. I wanted him as bare as me. He stood still when I approached and stiffened when I popped the clasps of his overalls.

"Kick off your boots," I whispered into his ear, nibbling on the soft lobe, so different from a pointy-tipped Lornian's.

Geo growled and tore at his straps. His overalls stuck where they met his belly. Slowly unbuttoning the sides, I caressed my tail over his wrists to his round shoulders. No wonder he has no trouble with manual labor. The fluffy tip lingered on his bulging bicep and shifted down to dust the ropy veins of his forearm. His eyes locked on mine in a daze. A quick tug freed his overalls from his belly, and they fell to the floor.

"Step out," I purred.

Geo's wide eyes were enraptured by the soft rattle of my purr. "Why do I feel like this?"

The roundness of his belly peeped out below his torn shirt, and his hard bulge pressed against his tight white underclothes. I scratched my blunt nails through the sparse hair peppering his exposed belly. Back and forth, scritch, back and forth.

"Jesus." Geo groaned, shifting onto his tiptoes, taut as a spring. "I'm going to jump out of my skin."

His body trembled when I pulled his shirt over his head, exposing his pale stomach and the dark fur on his chest. His peppery musk was incredible. I dove in nose first, rubbing my face up his sternum and nuzzling into the soft tufts of fur in his armpits. They smelled spicy. My hands kneaded his soft belly like a kitten.

"I'm in heat, that's why."

Geo dipped forward and suckled first one nipple, then the other, giving each the same treatment as if the other might get jealous. Then, he brushed his thumb around the velvety fur there. Each aching nipple he nursed ramped up my lust. A rush of heat flooded through me all the way to the tips of my ears.

"Geo, I need you."

"Softer than I imagined," Geo murmured. My skin sizzled like a drop of water in a hot pan.

Geo fumbled between my legs and brushed over my sensitive pouch. "Where is it?"

With my knees in danger of collapsing, I grabbed his wrist and guided him to the top of my protective pouch, where my erection ached for his touch.

"What the..." He hummed as both of our hands plunged inside to pull my cock out. "So warm." Exposed to the humid air, my length stiffened further. He murmured something about a kangaroo, but I was too deep into this wave of my heat to make sense of the image the translator showed in my mind. "And blue, too," he said with awe as he licked his lips.

Of course it's blue, what other color would it be?

Before I took my next breath, he dropped to his knees and drew my long blue shaft between two plump lips. "Blant, Geo, what are...ungh."

He pumped my length in and out of his mouth with one rough hand, cradled then massaged my smooth sac with the other. This is the most amazing... When my legs gave way, he wrapped his solid arm under my butt for support. Eons later, he released my cockhead with an audible pop before he twisted his hand around my base and squeezed up, forcing out a pearly bead of liquid.

An inferno built inside of me. I swiped moisture from my brow. The demands of my heat required penetration and his release inside me, but... Goddess, why does this feel so much better than normal? His fingers circled my tine as I panted.

Blant, I loved it when a partner played with that little spot. Past alphas had paid no attention to the pleasure my tine gave me. Instead, they'd made my heat about what I could give them.

My fingers sifted through his dark hair. "Bless the goddess Sola. Why don't more alphas suck?"

"What's this?" He gently pinched the bump halfway up my erection before circling my engorged head with his tongue and sucking it till it grew dark and purple with need.

"Huh?" I moaned. My fingers spread over the back of his damp neck—softer than a bush-tailed montie. His broad tongue ran up the length of my throbbing dick as his rough beard brushed against the sensitive fleshy bump halfway up.

"Ungh... It's my tine. For your pleasure." I groaned as Geo squeezed another drop of seed from my engorged cock. "Stimulates your gland inside. No more, please..." I begged. "Need you inside." I was burning up.

He grazed his teeth over my tine and said, "Maybe I like sucking because I'm not an alpha."

That's cute. With no time to explain, I crouched, gathered our clothes, wove them into the most haphazard nest imaginable, and walked on hands and knees into it. Then I tilted my hips and presented my ass to Geo as an omega in heat to his tethered alpha.

"Jesus Christ."

That name again. I'd have to ask Geo who Jesus Christ was later. Didn't humans understand it wasn't proper to call out another's name when I was presenting myself?

My heightened senses picked up the *swoosh* of fabric over skin when he slipped out of his tight white undergarments. I regretted not taking the time to feast my eyes on Geo's hard bulge, but I would burn up if he didn't get his cock into me right this instant. I arched my back more to entice him and purred deeply.

"Fuck, you're slippery." One finger circled my passage and timidly entered up to his knuckle. His body loomed over me, encapsulating me in his summer fields' scent, driving me to my elbows.

"More, please, Geo. I need all of you."

A second finger entered my passage and scissored, opening me further. When his thumb dipped in, I shivered.

"What the fuck?" Geo groaned.

I turned to see him smear my wax over his plump head. His cock was slightly darker than the rest of his skin and deliciously thick. Bonic no longer needed to confirm whether humans were compatible. I trembled as our scents mixed. "Geo. What's wrong?"

"It's just that my dick seems to have grown." He wrapped his hand around it with wide eyes and pumped once before releasing it. "Never mind."

The way he fisted the sensitive base of my tail with one hand as he fingered my opening for an eternity was obscene. My knees shook as he tested how ready I was for him. I trembled, more prepared for him than for any alpha who had serviced me through a heat. Not sure what the holdup was, I groaned in relief when Geo's plump head tapped my opening.

My body quaked with anticipation. Then, with a long groan, he pressed his fat cockhead firmly into my puckered hole. The tension before the give—like ecstasy.

He held himself still, breaching my tight ring, and groaned. "You're so slick."

One impressive thrust later, my slippery passage stretched to a delicious fullness. My hips loosened, and my back arched more. His cock stretched my opening so wide, that any farther and I thought it might split. The perfect blend of pain and pleasure.

"So good." I pushed my hips back and ground down. "Faster, Geo. I'm ready." A purr rattled deep in my chest.

His fat cockhead popped all the way out, and he pressed it through my clinging hole again before he shifted his hips ever so slowly. Shallow thrusts forced my legs wider. The cave's humidity slicked my skin with sweat and heightened his summer field aroma. His thumb circled the bump of ridges around my pucker in a mesmerizing thrum, thrum, thrum as he plunged deeper. My whole body turned liquid—the sex was so good. It couldn't possibly have gotten better... but it did. The broad, round head of his erection bumped the entrance to my sensitive womb.

I whined.

Geo sucked on my shoulder blade. "You taste as good as you smell."

My opening was so shallow that most alphas forced their way into my womb before I was ready. But, for the first time, the nerve endings lining the entrance to my womb hummed in pleasure. Each exquisite hit from his short, wide cock knocked against it, begging for entry. I moaned at the intense pleasure and melted deeper into the nest of our clothes. My greedy ass lifted.

"Let me see those ears." Geo withdrew and flipped me so I faced him. Then he nuzzled into my temple before the pointy tip of his tongue traced the shell of my ear. I swore he muttered, "Mine." He bit the tip sharply, and when I jerked up, his beard rasped over my nose.

Sweat dripped from Geo's brow. His knees spread wider as he gripped my hips firmly, hiking my legs up before he thrust inside in one long stroke. The air smelled like my favorite place in my most scandalous dream. Summer fields and a peppery musk that was all Geo. His harsh breaths hit my collarbone. I was burning hot, his hands fused to my hips like a brand. Only an orgasm would provide relief from the unbearable inferno.

"Please, Geo."

"What the..." Geo growled. The furry tip of my tail reached between Geo's legs, and I applied suction to the spot right behind his balls.

"Holy mother of god."

"Geo," I gasped his name in ecstasy as he jolted forward, his rock-hard cock finally pushing through the entrance into my womb.

His cockhead grew even fatter. When he finally locked himself inside my warm chamber, I erupted. Glorious relief pulsed through my limbs. My release marked his stomach, the tether thickened as if pleased, and the incomplete bond grew more substantial.

With a hoarse shout, Geo surged upright, hips hilted, and threw his head back. streams of cum sprayed the inside of my womb, dousing the fire of my heat. Each of my muscles shuddered and turned languid, the volcanic heat replaced by cool satisfaction.

Although I wanted his lock, my jaw tightened in anger unconsciously when he gave it to me. An alpha should never lock without permission. They were trained not to. While in heat, an omega could become pregnant. My shoulders pressed into the nest and the hard ground below. Good thing I was broken.

Still, I loved the floating sensation. Plus, I was in no position to blame my worst enemy for impropriety at the moment, let alone a human who likely had no idea he'd overstepped.

Geo tugged at his lock, pulling a groan out of my liquid body.

"Relax, give it a minute. It will unlock," I mumbled, drugged by pleasure.

"What have you done to me?" Geo's hoarse voice rumbled.

Done to him? What's the matter with this guy? He's no virgin.

"What are you talking about?" My bliss faded away much too soon for my liking. Geo wrecked the moment of quiet before the storm, because if this was like any other heat, things were just getting started.

"Why can't I get out?" He jerked at the lock again, and my womb shuddered.

"Be still. It's your lock. It will let go from my womb in a few minutes." My tone may have been a little firmer than necessary.

His eyes narrowed to slits. "I don't have a lock."

"Erm, I beg to differ." I gazed into his pale green eyes. Only to find confusion, the desire of moments before long gone.

"Womb?" Geo's pinched brows furrowed further.

Oh, boy. What planet is he from, anyway?

I sucked in a breath. That was it. Only Lornian alphas had serviced me before, and Geo was from Earth. The flutterers and the buzzers were clearly a little different on his planet.

Geo fell flat on his ass as the lock broke. His soft belly rose and fell rapidly. He looked bewildered and muttered something about condoms that didn't quite translate.

13

MY ALARM BINGED, ALERTING me it was time to wake up. The dim cavern light illuminated the lavender in Makir's eyes. His lean body was spread, enticingly naked, on top of the few articles of clothing he'd bunched into a makeshift bed around him, like a strange bird's nest. He would not have been out of place in a harem with slaves to fan him and feed him grapes. His posture, his enticing fragrance, the crook of his smile all screamed 'serve me, and you'll be rewarded with endless pleasure.'

I'd be first in line.

His gaze on me forced my cramped muscles to flex, stretching my skin taut. The tether hung lax and languid between us, heavy but content with our forced proximity.

My mind was like mud, so muddled I couldn't recite the alphabet, let alone make the smart choice to return to Yurstille yesterday with JayJay and everyone else. Compelled to protect and provide for him, I wouldn't be leaving this cave any time soon with Makir in the state he was.

Sex with Makir was the best and strangest of my life. The scents of ginger, juniper and…sex overpowered the cave's sulfur smell. My cock stood at attention as if performing tricks for Makir's steady gaze. Dizzy with lust, I jammed the heel of my hand into my erection for relief.

As I sat, transfixed by his swaying tail, I contemplated the wack changes to my body. Something serious was wrong with my penis. Yesterday, it had not been fatter than a beer can. Also, my cock did not have a lock. I was one hundred percent certain that if my dick had a lock, I would know about it. I tore my gaze away from Makir and glanced at it. Still short but alarmingly fat, I pinched what appeared to be an extra band of muscle at the base between my thumb and forefinger. "What the ever-loving fuck."

Makir's devouring gaze followed my hand, where I prodded at my new endowment. "Problem? You need me to hold that for you?"

Nope, nada, I'm good. This was happening a little too fast and a lot too strange. Sweat broke out along my hairline, and I reached for my overalls, twisted up with Makir's jumpsuit beneath him. I really needed to revisit the medic.

Doctor, I appear to have an allergy that fattened up my penis, grew every muscle of my body and triggered an obsessive attraction to Makir. Oh, and I have a dick lock too.

At least the conversation wouldn't be with Ginger. The corner of my mouth twitched.

"What's got you smiling?" Makir purred, and when his tail swayed, it drew my attention to the smooth blue muscles of the stomach he fanned. His eyes no longer switched to silver but remained the lavender I adored. He tucked his long erection back into its protective pouch. It didn't hide the fact that he was stiff. Then he pinched my side, his eyes twinkling with mischief.

Great, how long have I been standing here staring like a lovesick fool?

"Aren't you male?" I barked, my voice uncharacteristically deep, and I winced. I wished I'd paid more attention to the interspecies relationship module in my Intergalactic Federation orientation, because I was freaking out. My toe tapped as if I were jacked up on caffeine. In my wildest dreams, I'd never imagined Makir would desire me this way, but the waxy coating, the tine, the womb... It was a lot to process. "Are you related to a kangaroo?" My stomach churned and turned into a queasy mess.

He has a pocket for his dick, for fuck's sake.

Makir's pretty eyes turned to slits, and his tail lashed his leg. "Was I not male enough for you a moment ago? Is it Jesus you want instead, or Christ?"

"Huh?" I tilted my head.

"The names you shouted while you used me?" Makir shoved a leg into his jumpsuit and reached for one of the water containers JayJay had dropped off. JayJay and I were long overdue for a chat.

"Used you?" I growled and tried to put my T-shirt on. It wouldn't even fit over my shoulders.

Did he mean I used him because I didn't wear a condom?

"I should've used a condom, you're right, but I'm negative I've only had one partner before this." Fuck, I hadn't meant to divulge that much information. Now he would believe I was some insecure little boy. Damn it, and he would be right—except for the little part. I cupped the heavier weight between my legs.

The cave's humidity agitated my skin, and Makir's alluring scent consumed me from the outside in. I needed space, or I wouldn't be able to control myself. Again.

I threw my useless shirt to the ground before storming off. "Going to explore the cave."

Makir launched himself behind me as if compelled to remain close. His hand trembled when he grabbed the bag of supplies. "Sounds good. I'll just…join you." His voice wavered.

My stride faltered. I did not like his insecurity one bit. Hadn't he enjoyed the sex? I'd thought he was into it.

Shoulder to shoulder, we moved through the cavern. It gradually narrowed and sloped deeper. The smooth ebony walls along the tunnel sank into pink earth, where humidity coated them with a thick vegetative slime. As we descended farther underground, the light dimmed, and the moist air turned oppressive.

I stumbled and dragged my hand along the wall. "Jesus Christ isn't a guy I've dated. It's a swear word." My toe caught on another lip of the uneven ground, and I tripped. "Damn it, I can barely see a thing." I hoped a little conversation might make this whole heat thing a little less slam-bam-thank-you-ma'am. "Damn's also a swear word on Earth. Kinda weird, but a lot of swears are based on religion, and believers get pissed when you use them. But they're just words to me."

Makir hummed. "Like when I call out 'thank the goddess Sola.' Okay, I see what you're saying."

The tunnel curved, and the passageway opened up, revealing a large spring. The sulfur stench of it overtook Makir's crisp juniper scent, and steam rose from it in veiled sheets. I dipped my finger into the pool to test the temperature, then jerked it out with a hiss. A hot spring. A cold plunge would've been preferable to keep my attraction under wraps, but I welcomed a good wash.

Makir leaned in and grasped my wrist before he brought my tender finger to his lips. And then he blew. "Did you burn your finger?" His tail skated over my calf.

I was hard as a rock in an instant. His breath had a direct line to my dick, but trying to discern the 'come-hither' expression from the 'back-off' look, I had no idea how to respond. One moment he leaned closer, the next, he dropped my hand and spun around. A second longer, and I would've devoured his lips. Talk about mixed messages.

Makir marveled at our beautiful surroundings. "Wow, this is spectacular!"

It really was. I stuffed my hands into my pockets. "Stay turned around."

"What? Why?" Makir twisted his neck toward me. He held his stomach, wincing while his pupils dilated into pools so dark I could drown in them.

He's suffering, but why?

"I want to take off my overalls." My voice deepened as my self-consciousness grew. Yes, my actions were ridiculous. I'd been naked not long ago. But my mind was still operating at fifty percent capacity, much too aware to let my muffin top flop around in front of Makir and his long, lean body.

"Goddess Sola above, what have I got myself into?" Makir muttered to the dripping ceiling as he turned to face the slimy wall and placed the supplies on a dry rock. "Crazy human." He gripped his stomach again and moaned.

Hot water sloshed over my skin. "I'm in now. You can turn around."

Naked, Makir whimpered behind me, then he followed. Water lapped around his trim waist with each stiff step he took. His eyes were as big as saucers and flickered toward the shoreline before he squeezed them shut. His tail slapped frantically where it broke through the surface.

"Is your species related to cats?"

Why couldn't I ask him what I really wanted to know? Why can't I stay away from you? What are you doing to my body?

His lips pursed, and his lavender eyes narrowed and flicked to mine. "Cats? The little Earth creatures that meow, claw your laps and don't listen?"

The translation was remarkably accurate, so I nodded, then cringed at my insult and tried again. "Your tail is similar..." Grasping at straws, I added, "And they don't like water."

"My tail..." His nostrils flared. "Is not in any way similar to a cat." His teeth bit down on the T. His mane curled around his face in long, wet coils I wanted to slip my fingers in. His tail flicked—in irritation? He stopped, panting, trying to catch his breath. "And what...is it about me...that resembles the giant vermin...you called a kangaroo?"

I stepped toward him as his breathing grew shallower. "Are you okay?" No way would I mention the part of him that reminded me of a kangaroo. Not with a ten-foot pole. Also, I don't think he would have appreciated me telling him that lions were among Earth's most majestic and fierce beasts. The way his hair spread around his head, over his pointed ears and down his back looked leonine.

Would I tell him that? Hell no. He could envision himself as a domestic kitty that purred for affection and kneaded my lap all he liked.

When he stood there, unresponsive, I couldn't resist teasing him. "You like the water then?"

He took a defiant step toward me, then his slitted eyes leaped from irritated to panicked as he plunged in over his head.

I chuckled. He must have found a pothole.

Makir's arms and tail splashed desperately above the surface of the hot spring.

A moment later, the hairs on my arms stood at attention. The tether snapped taut, like an alert from a flashing red beacon.

Fuck, he can't swim.

I dove forward, grabbed his flailing limbs and pulled him through the water to me. My arms wrapped so tight around his chest that I'm sure it took him longer to recover from his coughing fit because of my stranglehold. But I couldn't let go.

He pushed against my shoulder for release. "I'm fine," he sputtered.

I pulled him back into my arms. "You're not fucking going anywhere."

Soaked lashes rimmed sparkling lavender eyes. "Aww, isn't that cute?" He coughed. "You do like me." Then he pecked me on the nose.

He looked like a drowned lion. Beautiful. "Why didn't you tell me you can't swim?" I growled.

He looked away. "It didn't seem necessary."

"Didn't seem necessary? You almost fucking drowned!" My voice rumbled, my body vibrated, adrenaline pumped through me and my internal temperature rose to match the hot spring. Under normal circumstances, tai chi would alleviate my restless energy, but no amount of tai chi could abate this.

"Let's cool you down a bit, shall we," Makir purred, as if the soft rattle in his chest was driven by a sixth sense. Makir led us deeper into the spring, toward a second pool of cooler water that soothed my fevered skin.

His pulse hammered where I grasped his wrist.

I sighed in relief. A perfect alcove opened before us. A cool spring fed it and tempered the water, and when a shelf carved from ebony stone revealed itself, I sucked in an awed breath. The previous inhabitants of Tern must have used these hot springs.

Makir shook out his fur, showering me in a spray of water droplets. "Sorry." He ducked his head sheepishly. "It's involuntary. Blanted water. I hate it."

I'm such an idiot. Why didn't I talk to him before filling his courtyard with a giant-ass swimming pool?

Makir's purr grew louder. The deep baritone reverberated from the tips of my toes to the top of my head. The fur on his tail parted and sucked over the bare skin of my ankle, still tender from where I had twisted it over a week ago. It awakened every nerve, and I about drowned in his alluring ginger scent.

Lost again to the frenzy pumping through my veins, I inhaled long drafts of smoky juniper from behind his ear and along his collarbone as I sucked the wet nape of his neck.

"You smell so good, little lion." I nuzzled the smooth blue skin where it met the fur of his torso.

Makir was so gone he didn't even comment on the endearment. Instead, he swung a leg over my lap and straddled me on the bench. Water sloshed between us. His erection stiffened inside his dick pocket and pushed into my belly. His nose dipped to my neck, and he inhaled. His body shuddered where it pressed against mine, and he licked cool water from my beard.

Makir lowered his hips and he ground against my rigid length, sending waves of desire deep into my stomach. His tail jumped everywhere—first, one nipple, *zing*, then the other, and finally around my belly button. The wet fur swished inside it, a direct line to my groin.

"Mmm..." I groaned while I grabbed the firm globes of Makir's ass, spread and kneaded them. My erection bumped against the base of his pocket and his tail fluttered over my relaxed belly. I didn't care in the least. He reached into his pouch with his tail, and his leaking dick emerged.

Yes, to the magical powers of a tail!

Water swirled around us like hot tub jets, drowning out my moans. My fingers worked their way into Makir's crease, and I rubbed my thumb around his softening pucker, occasionally dipping in to collect the slippery wax.

"I'm... I need you in me." The lavender of his eyes swirled, and he closed them on a whine. His tail wrapped our shafts, and the tip feathered over them as the water lapped at our legs. The fur on his tip spread, and he lifted his tail until the small suction pad latched on to one nipple, sending a burst of electricity over it, then the other. My knees quaked, the drawn-out suction and low vibrations pushing me to new heights.

Too soon, my hips jerked up. "Shit. Stop, or I'll cum."

Makir's tail released me, and his hand wrapped around the thick band circling my base. Then, with his hot grip, he positioned my erection at his entrance. "Geo... Need you so bad. I'm sweltering. It hurts. I need..."

Makir's eyes dilated. Perspiration beaded his brow, and his hips circled like crazy, chasing my cock when I took control. I traced his pucker with my cum-smeared head.

I nibbled the tendon on the side of his neck and licked it with the flat of my tongue. Unable to get enough of his crisp juniper scent, I inhaled a drugging breath. Makir's wet curls trailed across my cheeks. They left rivulets of water that I sucked into my mouth. I continued to rub his rim with my cockhead, waiting until he was as crazy for me as I was for him.

My words were guttural. "I'll give you what you need."

"Geo, please... It hurts." Makir moaned, forcing himself down on me.

I kneaded his ass cheek with one hand, spreading him further, preventing him from lowering himself as I kept up my slow rub. "I'll give you what you need.

When you're ready." My arm trembled, not from holding him but from holding back. Instinct drove me.

Makir's high-pitched whine echoed through the cavern. "I'm ready. So...ready. Now, alpha!"

I wrapped my hand around the base of his tail and lifted until every muscle in his body submitted to me. "Not until I say."

But the truth was, the moment he'd screamed alpha, my control had evaporated. My lips blindly met his in a sloppy kiss, and I inserted my well-lubed head into his needy hole.

"Ungh..." Makir jerked and relaxed down my length, muttering something to the goddess Sola the whole time.

My pelvis tilted, and I pushed his hips down until my full balls settled against his fur. "Hell yes!"

Makir dropped his head to my shoulder, and his whine transformed into a deep purr, like a rumbling engine. Like white noise, his purr blocked all sound, heightening my senses. The tip of my tongue dipped into the water droplets sprayed over his face. A zing of ginger hit my tastebuds. Then I traced the circle of his lips and dipped in. My tongue synced to the same rhythm as my plunging cock. Makir undulated his spine—it rippled long and limber, turning sex into dance.

Holy hell, it had never been like this. I'd never imagined it could be so good.

Makir panted as I gripped his hips so hard there would be bruises under his gorgeous blue fur.

"More, alpha, more," he gasped. "I need it all. Give me everything. Don't hold back."

I leaned back against the cool wall. Grasping his shoulders, I guided his body away from mine to change the angle of penetration. "I know exactly what you need."

I pulled out and thrust back in with one hard push. And there it was again. My cock bumped against that... spot. With each clench of his passage, it begged me to enter, called me, and told me how much better it would be if I could only be…inside.

But I hesitated. Last time, I got the impression I'd done something wrong when I entered his…womb.

He grunted and jerked as I ran my thumb around his slippery pucker.

"Christ, why does this feel so good?" I swallowed as saliva pooled in my mouth. Makir's tail latched on to my nipple—zing—and that was all it took. I punched through to heaven.

Fuck! I'd been trying to stop that from happening, but it felt incredible. It took every ounce of control I had to pull out again.

Makir whined, grabbed my dick and slotted me back into his hot channel. "No. Need you."

He bounced up and down on my dick, coaxing the entry to his womb with each downward motion. I closed my eyes in ecstasy for a moment, then, with a sharp inhale, I gripped his hips and held him still. "Tell me exactly what you want."

His lavender eyes, ravenous with lust, met mine. "You, Geo. Just you."

My mouth went dry, and I could barely swallow. Water sloshed between us, maintaining the pumping rhythm of the past moment, and his resonant purr blocked all attempts at reason. But I persevered. "Do you want me inside? All the way inside?"

Makir nodded.

This was the precipice of something bigger. "Say it."

"Your lock." His tail trembled like a leaf where it lay in the crease of my elbow. He lifted his finger to my lower lip. "I've never wanted another's lock as I want yours. Geo, I need you inside my womb." His finger drew a line across my lip. "I trust you."

I sucked his finger into my mouth and drank in the red-hot need in his eyes. "I'd give you every star in the heavens if I could."

Makir gasped. My hands released his hips, and he plunged down my length. I'd never been harder in my life. Sweet bliss enveloped me, and I knocked my head back against the smooth stone as my neck curved. I lifted his leg and rocked my hips harder. My dick surged, plumped and again locked me inside. "Fuck, yeah." I ground my teeth as I came.

Makir almost tipped out of my lap as I opened my eyes, and I slung my arm behind him. He arched backward, his long mane dipping into the water, exposing his pretty ears. His eyes flickered shut as he savored the pull of my lock.

Makir's erection stood tall over his stomach, and I couldn't resist brushing my calloused thumb over his tine, then pinching it a little.

His eyes snapped open. "Oh, goddess…"

Near boneless in my arms, his ejaculate dripped from his softening length down the muscles of his abs. I blinked twice and inhaled. Dim light drifted through long, thin holes pockmarking the stone ceiling, sending slivered sunbeams over the water. They played over every inch of Makir's body, highlighting the curves of muscle and shadowing the dips. An image forever saved in my memory.

14

I LEANED INTO THE solidness of Geo as he carried me through the hot spring. Always so gruff on the outside, I now had a little more insight into his inner workings. Under the belly sucking and squared shoulders lay a tender heart.

Blessedly cool after our last mating, I couldn't help but rub the pad of my index finger through the wet fur that covered Geo's chest. The dark, springy curls begged to be touched. I loved the sensation of the coarse locks clinging to the length of my finger.

Though my heat amplified every sense, I longed for our tentative connection to have taken root the same in Geo as in me. With each greedy wave, I rode emotion and parked reason.

"You good now?" Geo placed me on my feet as we reached the shallow shoreline of the hot pool. His hands lingered below my ribs as if he didn't want to put me down.

The sudden temperature drop improved my senses, but I missed his warm solidness. Although my heat wasn't complete, the inferno and tunnel vision had abated for the moment.

How could I do this to myself again? I knew the strengthened bond after a mating frenzy didn't equal love.

Geo filled the void of caring protector so well that I almost forgot that alphas could turn from loving to terrifying in the span of a breath. I shook the water from my fur, along with my dream of a soul-linked mate. That path only ended in pain. Determined to minimize the effects of our bond, I stood tall. "I'm fine, Archbuilder. Thank you for ensuring my safety."

Geo's forehead furrowed. "Back to Archbuilder, huh?"

I grabbed the sack of supplies and headed back up the tunnel toward the cave's main entrance. "Yes. Thank you for servicing me, but we can keep it professional in between." From now on, I would just use Geo as an outlet to satiate the needs of my heat and nothing else. We would not complete the bond—if that was even possible. The full moon would be over tonight, then we'd return to town, and with my hovery complete, Geo would be out of my life. A few more days and this would be over.

He walked beside me, scrubbing his beard before kneading his temples. The softness in his eyes was replaced by a cool blankness. "Whatever you need, Makir.

"Ow! Stupid-ass cave." Geo staggered behind me.

"What are you doing back there? Hurry up so I can put together a meal for us."

The more sex we had, the more the tether thickened and solidified our connection. It vibrated with its own life force. I didn't need Bonic to tell me that humans and Lornians were compatible when my heart pulsed with the truth. But only the grand omega could confirm whether an omega and alpha went beyond compatible. If she blessed a couple as soul-linked mates then the full bond ceremony could happen.

"Oh, you know, just going for a jog with my eyes closed. What the hell do you think I'm doing?"

His night vision was terrible, and I'd forgotten entirely. I backtracked through the dim light. A check of my wristport confirmed dusk neared. My stomach growled. Usually, there was a fully equipped room prepared for my heat, complete with lots of water and high-protein food. I sucked on my lip, envisioning the luxurious swaths of fabric past alphas had provided—they made the loveliest nests.

"Here, take my tail."

Geo jumped, one foot cradled in his hand. "Jesus Christ, you are part cat." He yelped as he staggered back and bumped the wall again. "Make a sound, would ya? Let a guy know when you're in the vicinity." He groaned as he cradled his stubbed toe.

"Quit acting like a youngling." I wrapped my tail around his wrist. "Come on, you big blind Earthling."

Geo huffed but allowed me to tug him along. "Do you think JayJay left us anything good to eat?" He moistened his lips with his tongue and ducked his head as if hiding from his comment.

I'd seen annoyed Geo. Angry, passionate and workaholic versions of Geo had also shown their faces. But shy Geo was new and cute, and it poked at the edges of my resolve to keep our relationship at the acquaintance level.

His eyes flicked to mine, tracing my face and following the trails of water running down my chest and stomach.

"Quit looking at me like that," I groaned as my cock lengthened in its pocket.

Geo's thumb brushed over my tail where it wrapped his wrist.

I snatched it away.

"Fine, little lion, I won't touch your fluffy tail like that. Give it back to me, and I promise to be good." His deep voice sparked a cascade of shivers along my tail that pooled at its base like hot lava.

"Behave," I snapped at him, wrapping my tail around his wrist again. I was soaked, starved and horny. We could not go at it again until I had something other than Geo in my mouth. Plus, I didn't want him to walk into any more walls.

Next morning's light filtered through the pinprick holes in the cave's domed ceiling. The moon had set, and the mating frenzy had come to an end. My eyes traveled over Geo's thick body, peppered with bruises and scratches, up to his face where dark shadows lingered below his eyes. I swallowed hard as I took him in, splayed like an offering, unabashedly naked. Even in my pathetic excuse for a nest he looked magnificent when relaxed, so tired he didn't bother with his belly sucking as he drifted in and out of sleep.

Mayor Yurst had mentioned the full moon lasted two nights on Tern when Bonic had questioned him during my orientation. With no Lornians on Tern, I shouldn't have gone into heat, but my tether with Geo had been enough to trigger it. It would be hard to distance myself from Geo until my next heat. My womb already ached with emptiness.

I felt done in. Wrung dry. Lethargy and depression weighed heavy on my shoulders. Geo would know nothing about omega aftercare, and I wouldn't be the one to explain it. My broken state hit me like a plasma hammer and I dropped to my haunches, burying my face in my hands.

The last alpha I'd mated with had ruined me. In Lorne, unable to bear children, I'd been left an omega with no purpose. Every omega's instincts drove them to nurture a family, and mine would remain forever unfilled. I'd vowed to reinvent myself on Tern, but the burden of my lost purpose overcame me every full moon.

I shook Geo awake, longing for my luxurious Lornian nest. The desire to hide from the world while being pampered by a devoted alpha stirred beneath my skin. Instead, we'd have to manage a long, dusty trek back to our separate nests.

Geo stretched, his voice hoarse after our long night, his fingers idly scratched at the fur on his belly. I passed him the last of the dried mantu strips he seemed to adore. "Archbuilder, my heat is over. Let's head back to Yurstille."

I chuckled as he jumped, shocked at his own nakedness.

"Heat?" He plucked the jerky from my fingers, hunching over as if to hide his body as he searched for his overalls.

I rolled my eyes. "Are all Earthlings so shy?"

Geo rolled his eyes and rubbed the back of his neck with one hand as he hopped around with one foot in his pants.

Without warning, the cave shuddered. Pink dust shook loose from the pock-marked holes in the cave's ceiling, glittering in the early dawn.

Not again.

My muscles grew rigid. "We're getting out of here, now. Before this cave collapses on us." I held Geo's hand for balance as he jammed his feet into his boots, then scooped up his belongings.

"What is it?" Geo latched the closure on his belt, thumbing the knife's hilt.

"I'll explain on the way!" The cave vibrated again, and loose rocks showered down on us. My tail wrapped around Geo's wrist as we ran to the entrance and into the red glow of dawn. Hitting the cooler air was like passing through a wall, and I shivered at the contrast to the humid cave.

Another shudder sent jagged shards toppling over the ground like icicles shaken loose.

"Down on your belly. Now." I gestured with my tail as I squished myself into the narrow slit I'd occupied two nights ago. "We'll wait here until all is clear."

Geo's breath puffed in front of him in white clouds. "Clear from what?"

"Did you notice the field of massacred mantus when you arrived here?" My voice wavered as I relived the awful night and the carnage of the aftermath.

Geo's cheeks pinked. "I was a little preoccupied."

A sharp shriek echoed through the hiding spot, and from our vantage point, a giant worm-like creature slammed its body to the ground.

"Save us, Sola." I clutched Geo's hand, my heart racing.

Geo's eyes widened as his grip grew painful. "Jesus Christ, what the fuck is that thing?"

The enormous worm was nearly translucent. It writhed up on its end before throwing itself over its earlier kill and shredding it with razor-sharp teeth.

"I think it's mad."

"You think?" Geo snarked. "That big bastard is pissed."

Stripped carcasses lay strewn across the plateau. "It must have been planning to come back for its kill." The enforcers and Rock Dwellers had butchered and removed most of the mantu it had annihilated in its earlier killing spree.

With its meager meal, the night crawler reared up and dove under the ground once more.

Geo muttered something about a movie called *Tremors* and his friend Ginger while he rubbed the fur of my tail between his index finger and thumb. Free of his stranglehold grip, I shook my hand out.

"Stop that." I pulled my tail from his fingers. My body quivered from the aftermath of my heat and the fear of the monster buried somewhere below.

"Do you think we'll make it back to your hoverbike?" Geo placed a hand on my back and surveyed the area.

My legs were like rubber, and I couldn't take my eyes off the ring of earth left in the creature's wake.

Geo nudged me. "Can we make it?"

"D'Rasma thought it was nocturnal." My lungs heaved, unable to fill with air. "But...this proves it can get us during the sun's rotation too." My tail fluttered at the edge of my fraying nerves, and I gasped. My lungs contracted as I struggled to take a breath.

"Makir, I've got you. You're safe with me." Geo's voice drifted at the periphery of my hearing, and his pale green eyes narrowed into slits.

My vision dimmed as blackness overcame me.

I awoke cradled in Geo's arms as he navigated the sharp edges of the rocky outcrop.

"Shhh...rest now. We're almost there." He soothed me as I twisted to get free of his arms.

"I'm fine now," I lied. He embraced me, holding me steady as I gathered my feet. I stayed pressed against him because my legs had turned liquid, not because of the warmth of his chest or his soothing scent, and definitely not because of his display of strength. He carried my larger body across the harsh terrain as if I weighed nothing.

"Wanna tell me what happened?"

I swallowed. "Certain things..." The casual air I'd hoped to project fell flat, replaced by a barely there whisper. "Trigger panic attacks in me."

"Yeah... Like giant-ass worms?" The calm he exuded loosened my shoulders, and my arm settled on his lower back.

"No. More like alphas... I mean...things that destroy for no reason." I choked. He swept me into his arms once again before I could protest, and I drifted back to sleep.

"Wake up, little lion," Geo murmured, placing me on my feet, his hold solid on my hips as we arrived at my hoverbike.

Geo passed me the water container JayJay had left for us. "Here, have a drink. Do you think you can drive?" The concern in his pale green eyes made it difficult to hold to my new rules. Acquaintance only. Be professional. When I flicked my tongue out to catch the drop of water on my lip, his pupils dilated, and the blatant desire forced me back a step.

"Yes," I squeaked as I clambered onto my bike. When Geo climbed on behind me, every muscle in my lower back tightened. "Ah, where is your hoverbike?" I gulped.

"Don't have one." He squared his shoulders and sucked in his belly. It still spread around my ribs like a warm hug. "I don't know how to drive one."

His hands seemed unsteady on my hips, so my tail wrapped around his waist and pressed him closer to my back. I loved the push of his soft belly against me a little too much. Plus, he needed to be secure. Right?

Thankfully or unthankfully, the flight home allowed for no discussion, only the hyperawareness that came from having his body flush with mine. My tail pet him, and whenever I grabbed it to hold it still, the next moment it would resume touching Geo, unbeknownst to me.

The hoverbike quieted as I pulled up in front of the archbuilder's office. "This good?"

"Yep." His eyes didn't meet mine. He unwrapped my tail from around his waist, and his hand swooshed through the soft tip, sending a cascade of shivers up my spine.

Thanks for coming to my aid when you thought I was in danger. Thanks for servicing me during my heat.

Those were things that I could have said. Instead, I was tongue-tied as I attempted to meet his eyes.

"Boss man." The boom of JayJay's jovial voice broke the tension. "You made it back." His brow ridges dipped as he assessed Geo. "I thought you would look more relaxed." His laughter drew the rest of the Rock Dwellers out to greet us.

Sully passed me a large satchel and a huge set of mantu horns where I sat straddling my hoverbike. "A gift for you from D'irk, D'Rasma and D'Argon."

Geo growled when Sully attempted to help me situate the satchel across my back. Sully held his hands up and backed away while the Rock Dwellers' rumbling laughter filled the air.

Geo patted my back as he took over. "You're good now. We'll be there at seven suns tomorrow."

I flew the short distance back to my dwelling, missing the warmth of his touch already. The tether grew taut as the distance between us stretched, longing to be near Geo.

15

Ayla Rowtee waited beside me in Dr. Ten's lobby, her hands resting on her belly. "You must be relieved that Dr. Ten is familiar with Nacer youngling delivery?"

Her wings fluttered behind her, brushing below a neat line of framed medical certificates mounted on the wall. "I'm so luck—" She'd started to reply when I was called in for my appointment.

I shrugged an apologetic goodbye. "I'll see you at the market."

With a deep inhale, I braced myself to open the door. The time for getting to the bottom of this...allergic reaction had come.

Doctor Ten was Nacer, the same species as the Rowtees, and his eyes were pinned to his datapad. "Well, isn't that interesting?"

I shifted from one foot to the other. A bead of perspiration rolled down my temple. To sidetrack myself from my increasing nerves, I blurted, "When's Ayla due? I mean...of course, I can ask her myself. Not trying to pry or anything."

The doctor peered down his long beak at me and tipped his head. "Do? I don't believe that is translating correctly."

"The baby. When will it arrive?"

"Right, of course." The doctor's eyes lit up. "The first youngling on Tern. Won't that be extraordinary?"

"I want to add some windows to their nursery as a gift."

The doctor's head lifted from his datapad, and he tipped it to the side again—a gesture with a plethora of meanings, this time it likely meant he was confused.

My hands were so deep in my pockets that the seams started stretching as I rocked back and forth and offered an explanation. "An opening with a clear cover that allows sunlight in."

Doctor Ten scanned his office walls. "How wonderful. I may need some of those myself." His eyes lingered on a few spots as if mentally placing where the windows might go. "Mrs. Rowtee has two months until her youngling arrives."

Doctor Ten scrolled through my results on his datapad. "Isn't that interesting? You say your muscles have increased in size to the point your clothes no longer fit, and that your voice has deepened." Dr. Ten counted out my symptoms on long, knobby fingers. "You seem to lose control of your emotions when you're in the presence of Makir, a Lornian. Anything else?"

I cleared my throat. "My dick, I mean penis, has gotten wider and..."

"And?" Dr. Ten's patient eyes assessed me as he considered all the information I'd laid out.

How the hell do I say this?

His talons clicked across the floor as he walked to a pod-like chair and prompted me again. "And..."

When the words wouldn't come, my eyes focused on a long line of curious shapes. Medical equipment sat on immaculately clean and organized shelves along the southernmost wall. There would be enough room along the top of the wall to install lamar windows that wouldn't affect the room's privacy but would add warmth and comfort to the sterile space.

The doctor cleared his throat, snapping me back to the present.

Jesus Christ, Geo! Just spit it out. "My dick is way thicker than it was on Earth and..." Dr. Ten casually broke eye contact, likely to put me at ease. "Makir calls it a lock. My dick expands and won't release when I'm in his"—I choked—"womb."

Heat flooded my cheeks, washed over my neck and warmed the top of my chest. The mirrored surface of the cabinet across from me reflected a face I barely recognized, besides the embarrassed flush. Why couldn't that have changed with the rest of my body?

"I can assure you everything is perfectly normal." The doctor smiled warmly. "Please take a seat." He gestured to the pod. "The analyzer will perform a full body scan—completely painless, of course—and we will go from there."

Apparently, doctors from across the galaxies had one thing in common. They all agreed that things were perfectly normal when they were about as far from fucking normal as I could imagine.

My fingers tapped the polished armrests. The drumming clashed with the whir of the contraption but masked my deafening heartbeat as the pod sealed around me. With a grip like steel, I steadied myself against the dark and unsettling swoosh, and squeezed my eyes shut. When nothing appeared to happen, I grimaced and chuckled at the same time. What seemed like seconds later, the hatch popped open.

"Nurse Claice will have the analysis prepared in just a moment." Dr. Ten flipped to a diagram on his datapad. "How much do you know about Lornians?"

My face burned hotter. I had no idea what species Makir was, but presumably, he was the Lornian Dr. Ten was talking about.

I knew fuck all about the guy beyond him being irresistibly cute.

"They're blue, furry and have tails," I blurted.

Oh, and he has a dick pocket, a tine and a…womb.

"Yes, that's true." He nodded in my direction. "Makir, however, is a special type of Lornian. He's an omega, an extremely valuable asset to his species."

At my blank expression, he continued, "I can see from my quick analysis of reproductive relationships on Earth that an omega is likely not something you are familiar with. A brief explanation, if I may?"

I nodded. Whenever I tried to speak with Makir about the changes happening to me, I got distracted. His crisp juniper scent, my bossy mouth or…his furry tail would get in the way.

But really, it was just me. Avoidance was my specialty.

"Outside of Earth, many species have omegas. They are cherished and protected in their families until they find a mate. Omegas are often the calm voice of reason in a family, taking on the role of mediator, and of course, they are excellent parents—extremely nurturing."

The doctor projected an image from his datapad of a Lornian family against a shiny bronze wall, tails entwined as they leaned into each other. "They must be matched with an alpha who services them throughout their heat every full moon unless pregnant. It is painful to the omega otherwise, and the household may be distressed if the omega suffers. Omegas can be male or female, and as you mentioned, the males have wombs to allow them to carry younglings."

Perspiration beaded across my forehead. Jesus, is Makir pregnant? Why the hell didn't he tell me he could have kids? Contraception had always been a matter of preventing sexually transmitted diseases. I'd never considered the possibility of getting a partner pregnant.

"Younglings?" I barked.

"Yes. Quite wonderful isn't it? We need so many more here in Yurstille." His beak bobbed cheerily, oblivious to my distress. "That was a rapid-fire ABC on omegas, and every species may have slight variations, but the most important thing to know about omegas is how vulnerable they are under the influence of an alpha."

The doctor continued while I half listened, still hung up on kids. "The pheromones an alpha emits erode an omega's sense of reason. As a result, they are susceptible to every whim of the alpha, and I'm sure you can imagine the negative implications that has had on the lives of many omegas. For that reason, omegas are often cloistered away from society. Additionally, their scent is irresistible to an alpha when they are in heat and unmated."

Irresistible was an understatement.

"What the hell have I gotten myself into?"

I was only aware I'd said those words out loud when the doctor raised placating hands. "Now, now, let me assure you this is wonderful."

The doctor scanned through more information on his datapad. The white feathers along his wings tucked behind his back in a neat stair-step pattern. My heart ticked like the timer on a bomb, and I grew lightheaded and shivery all over. What else could he add to that? It's too fucking much. With stilted steps, I clambered back into the pod. The seat deflated like a whoopie cushion when all my weight landed on it.

"Oh dear." The doctor placed his solid hand on my shoulder, and I shrugged it off. "Clearly, I've distressed you. Is there someone I can call to fly you home? Nurse Claice always tells me, 'less is more, don't overwhelm them with too much information,' but I want to be thorough. Wouldn't you agree it's better to have all the facts?"

The doctor talked to himself as he dampened a cloth and placed it on my forehead.

I tapped out a message to JayJay. "I'm fine. My friend can pick me up." I pushed his hand away. Heat swamped me, and the wilder part of me—*the alpha?*—took over as I wrestled with the new information.

Dr. Ten smiled, all beak. "Yes, yes, you're exhibiting alpha signs," he muttered as he stepped away. "I will send some information to you. Please read through it carefully. We've barely mentioned alpha traits. I encourage you to set up a second appointment to discuss any questions you may have. I will leave you in peace until your friend arrives." The door swooshed shut behind him, and I dropped my face into my hands.

Pink clouds of dry soil puffed up from where I stood outside the doctor's office, toeing the earth with my boot while I waited for JayJay. I stretched into the beginner set for tai chi, desperate to settle my rattled nerves. I'd never dreamed of being a father before. Brush left knee and push. As I rolled the idea around in my head, it didn't strike me as the world's worst idea, but I still wasn't sure it was something I wanted. Grasp bird's tail. Plus, Makir was running hot and cold. He was calling me Archbuilder again, for fuck's sake. Step forward, parry, block and punch.

Would a child tying me to Makir be a good thing? Sex with Makir had been off the charts, but I hated how I turned into an asshole in his presence, and he didn't deserve that. Fist under elbow. He was such a sweetheart. Way too good for the likes of me. Turned out anyone—well, any alpha—would have the same reaction I did when he was in heat. Turn body and chop with fist. I wasn't even someone he found special, just some asshole he'd happened to be trapped with because of pheromones and the moon. Fuck, life on Tern was as complicated as life on Earth—maybe more so. I wished Ginger was here. She'd know what to do.

"Boss man, you dancin' again?" JayJay rumbled as he pulled up on his hover-bike.

I climbed on behind him, leaving as much space between us as his seat would allow. "I'm so tired of riding like a child clinging to its parent on these damn bikes."

"Dr. Ten has put you in a much better mood, I see." His lawnmower-like laugh vibrated the seat.

"What the fuck is an alpha?" I shouted over the downdraft as we flew to Makir's hovery.

"Dominant, assertive, desirable…" JayJay trailed off, reciting a list of words no one had ever used to describe me.

"I don't get it. Dr. Ten said Makir's an omega and requires an alpha to service him while he's in heat." I hated the term 'service.' It sounded so institutional, like I was a dick for hire or something. "I'm not an alpha!"

JayJay's huge palm reached back and clapped my knee twice as his body shook. "Whatever you say." He didn't even have to raise his voice to be heard over the downdraft.

Ten minutes later, the tension had mostly bled from me. As we approached the hovery, the proximity to Makir loosened the tether, and my shoulders eased. JayJay rode his hoverbike through one of the three brand-new bay doors. I barely had a chance to absorb what my crews had accomplished since my return from the cave with Makir before the tether grew taut once more, its urgency pulling me forward.

Laughter spilled out from the courtyard. Apprehension launched me straight off JayJay's bike, and I jumped over the newly installed back gate toward the fear zinging through the tether. The pool, glistening in the overhead sun—no longer a mud-filled hole—teemed with splashing bodies.

I stormed to the pool's edge, fuming. "Tino, Sully, get the hell out of that pool and back to work. The bay doors still need to be installed. Get on it," I barked. My skin was on fire, and the hairs on my arms stood on end. Makir scrambled backward in the pool, where Raz circled him like a shark.

I strode to the pool's edge nearest Makir. Eyes wild, he splashed toward me as I'd anticipated. We were drawn to one another like magnets. As soon as he drew close enough, I squatted low, hooked my hands under his armpits and tugged him straight over the lip of the pool and into my embrace. I didn't care one bit that my overalls were now soaked.

"Enough," I scolded Makir. "You don't like the water and can't swim." I scooped my arms under his legs and carried him like a new bride toward his bedroom, heedless of our audience. "You were going to be over your head in the next couple of steps, and you didn't even know it." I cautioned a bewildered Makir.

Raz's Lizzard tail lashed the water. "But, Makir, you were about to offer to s-s-show me your nest."

Makir whimpered, still cradled in my arms as I turned and snarled, "Over my dead body." I'd deal with our unwanted guest later. Right now, Makir was priority number one.

JayJay's lawnmower laugh rumbled behind us as we moved out of the courtyard toward Makir's room. "Not an alpha. He thinks he's not an alpha." Laughter filled the courtyard and carried down the short hall.

Makir traced a finger down my forearm before looking up at me from under his long lashes. "Geo, are you okay?"

Gently placing him in his nest, I rushed toward the bathroom, pulled a fluffy bath sheet off the heated towel bar and returned to his side. Dabbing softly, I blotted Makir's wet fur. I loved the swirls his velvety fur made as he dried.

"Geo..." He batted my hands away and took the towel. "I'm demonstrating the pool to a few potential customers for you. Raz is one of them."

I stood tall and threw my shoulders back. "I don't need him as a customer."

Makir stood and dried my arms with the towel. His ginger and juniper scent covered me—so good. "Calm down, okay?" he purred. My heart rate slowed, and my muscles relaxed.

Shit. I'm an idiot.

I stepped away and shook out my arms. "Sorry about that," I muttered. With the threat taken care of and my wild side tamed, I focused on every detail of his room. Tino, Sully and their crews had taken my vision and smashed it out of the park. The warm pink walls mimicked the soft curves of Makir's original construction. The mixture of the soil, graneth stalks and water added an organic texture to the walls that I couldn't resist running a finger over.

His nest was lined with thick white linobee furs. I swallowed hard when my mouth went dry. There was definitely room for two in there—it would be like sleeping in a cloud. My nostrils flared. Ginger and juniper perfumed the air, soft rugs warmed the high-gloss floors and a breeze drifted through the high-timbered ceilings. A slab of concrete installed as a desk added a bit of masculinity to all the curves. Along the exterior wall, a sliding lamar door opened into the courtyard.

"I'll...get out of the way and see how things are...progressing in the hovery." I spun on my heel and walked to the sliding door, which I stumbled through before hunting down Tino and Sully. All I did lately was apologize for snapping at people.

Makir's voice followed me into the courtyard. "Geo, you don't have to go."

Hell yeah, I did. I'd likely do something else idiotic if I remained in his vicinity.

Tempted to peer over my shoulder to catch another glimpse of Makir, I forced myself to leave. He'd probably be standing there, beautiful, damp and dumbfounded, dismayed at the asshole he'd chosen to service him during the full moon. Plus, when he stood by that nest, I couldn't stop imagining my naked skin pressed to his luxurious velvet as we sank deep into the linobee furs and each o ther.

Enough of that train of thought. I forced the fantasy out of my mind, stomping past potted plants and Makir's fern-lined walkway. Where had they found the fantastic greenery?

I marveled at the tropical oasis I found myself immersed in. My eyes widened, taking in each frond and leaf. My crew had created this? JayJay's booming voice led me to where the Rock Dwellers were installing Makir's bay doors. "Come on, boys, I need a drink. We're celebrating the bang-up job you did on Makir's place and I'm saying sorry for being a shit."

Tino, Sully, JayJay and the rest of the Rock Dwellers' hairless brow ridges furrowed, but they stowed their tools fast as lightning before I could change my mind. "No need to apologize, boss man." Tino slung his heavy arm around Sully and grinned. "You have a lot on your mind."

"Just got to take care of one thing before we head out." As I expected, when I reached the pool, Raz still lingered. No longer in the water, his scaly limbs were spread out on one of the loungers, like a vacation brochure. His tail looked obscene as it jutted from the rear of his tiny, patterned swim shorts.

Are those ducks?

"Raz! This is a construction site and unsafe for those not working on-site or who are not occupants of the home. I'll have to ask you to leave." I waved my hand magnanimously toward the back gate—the exit closest to his home.

Raz startled upright in his chair. He must have been dozing. "Makir invited me." His jaw unhinged in a long yawn.

Like hell he did.

"I'm sure you understand the liability the building authority would face if any unfortunate accidents were to occur here." My lips may have unconsciously formed a snarl. Raz had overstepped one too many times and had planted himself in enemy territory. My hands fisted at my sides, the urge to drive them into his jaw barely contained.

His wary glance dipped to my hands as I advanced toward him, and he quickly popped off the chair and scooted toward the fence. "Well, I do have a mantu roast on the grill." He tripped over his tail in his hasty retreat. "I'll go and check on that."

But his sneer, combined with the slam of the gate as he exited, sent a loud and clear message.

Fuck, I hope my big mouth isn't going to cause more trouble for Makir.

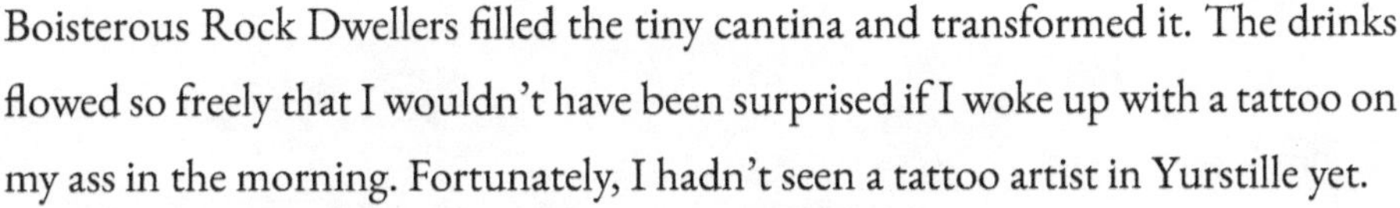

Boisterous Rock Dwellers filled the tiny cantina and transformed it. The drinks flowed so freely that I wouldn't have been surprised if I woke up with a tattoo on my ass in the morning. Fortunately, I hadn't seen a tattoo artist in Yurstille yet.

Tino's elbow nearly knocked me off my stool, where I sat wedged in beside him, but I was curious about the landscaping, so I persevered with our conversation.

"The plants in the courtyard... How did you get a hold of them?"

"Well, you would know if you had returned from the rocky outcrop with us," he teased. Beer spilled from his mug and sloshed through the knee of my overalls. "A couple of the enforcers have green thumbs and brought seeds from their home planets to propagate. Their little nursery is taking off."

After securing a ride to the nursery with Tino the following day, I paid the tab and set my sights on the door. Thoroughly bruised after the back pats from a bunch of half-drunk giants, I departed into the cool night air with my spirits considerably improved.

I vowed to reward my crew monthly with an early day off and an open tab, but the real reason I wanted to escape pressed down on me.

Makir. The tether tugged and urged me toward him. Our brief exchange this morning—if you could call me wrestling him out of Raz's reach an exchange—hadn't been nearly enough to satiate my need.

16

T HE ROW OF ROUND windows skirting the ceiling turned my concrete table purple with the dusk's light. White linobee fur slid softly through my hands. I pushed my strongest needle through the pelt, shaping the mittens I'd promised the enforcers. My gaze passed over the dark beams that framed the ceiling, then caught the glitter of liquid mineral under the polished floors. Thoughtfully planned and beautifully executed, my new dwelling nearly matched the quality of my rooms on Lorne.

My shoulders drooped as I sighed, settling into a state of relaxation I hadn't known in annums. I no longer had to wrestle through a sticky door or fend off surprise visits from unwelcome neighbors, but even if I included my labor and supplied the lamar, this went way beyond a basic model dwelling. And Geo's claim to call this a show home seemed like a stretch to justify all the extra features.

I snipped through the last thread of the mittens, picked up the stack and hugged them to my chest before I placed them on the table. They were ready for delivery to Sisip tomorrow. That reminded me, I needed to come up with a design for the mantu hides stored in my spare room—perhaps a coat for the cooler weather.

My wristport pinged.

Bonic: Are you free for a call?

Before I could respond, the screen flashed 'incoming call.' Typical Bonic.

"And what if I'd been busy, brother?" I teased.

He chuckled warmly. "You'll always make time for me."

Blant, I miss my brother.

"Spoken like an elite protector," I joked. "How's Jast's pregnancy?"

"Well, would you like my words or hers?"

"You know only the omega's opinion counts."

"How could I forget? She'd say it can't be over soon enough. She refers to the youngling as 'a little parasite.'" He crunched something in the background. The snap made my mouth water, and a burst of zilna teased my tastebuds. Alpha asshole eating my favorite snack.

"I wish for the pregnancy to last forever. The youngling moved last night when I pressed my palm to Jast's belly. It's the safest place for the little one." I could sense the awe of creating a new being in his voice. "Enough of me. Tell me how things are with the Earthling?" Bonic's low voice vibrated through my bones.

Ah, there's the commanding alpha voice I know and love.

"Um...will you visit Tern once the youngling's born? I'd love to meet my little niece or nephew."

I could practically see his eyes roll. "Of course. The little one must meet their only uncle. We'll visit when Jast and the doctor agree it's safe." He cleared his throat. "Now, tell me."

I sucked in a fortifying breath. "He's compatible," I blurted.

"Is that right?"

I couldn't tell from Bonic's neutral response whether he was angry. "Er...it was unavoidable. He was injured and I had to heal him. And, unconsciously, I used the healing source...which created a tether...which alerted him that I may be in danger." My head grew dizzy from the lack of air, but I needed to tell him everything. "The hunting expedition coincided with the full moon, and we encountered a giant scary worm, so Geo led a rescue party to me, and my heat took over from there." I exhaled. The weight of my stored guilt was released after my confession, and my shoulders relaxed.

Bonic drummed his fingers, likely against his desk, in the background. "I have a lot of questions." The *swoosh* of his tail as it lashed through the air carried over the line. "You're aware treatment with our tail's source reinforces a tether, so I won't belabor it. But I will remind you—these powers are sacred, do whatever you must to keep our ability hidden. Our people will be exploited otherwise. Off-worlders, especially omegas, will be even more susceptible to manipulation."

My stomach soured, and I swallowed bile. Although he phrased it in general terms, there was no confusion about who the comment was directed at. "Of course, Bonic. I would never put Lornians at risk."

"I know you wouldn't." His voice softened. "Now, tell me about this danger?"

I didn't think he meant falling for Geo. With a white-knuckled grip, I clutched the table's edge. "We encountered a giant worm-like creature. It decimated the herd of herbivores we hunted." I began to pant, and my heartbeat ramped up, but I lifted my chin high and inhaled. I will not panic. "It appeared to track prey through vibration and...attacked," I whispered, "by exploding through the ground." My shoulders shook. "We were forced to hide."

Bonic didn't need to know I'd been having more panic attacks. He had enough to worry about.

The tick of Bonic's fingers against his keyboard, tapping out messages to his staff in the background, guaranteed the problem would be addressed. "The mayor assured us the Fires That Cleanse had wiped out everything organic on the planet. How is it such a creature exists?"

"That's just it, Bonic. Organic life blooms all over the place. The Fires That Cleanse did not eliminate everything as intended. Fortunately, there is no sign of the illness that left Tern at its mercy."

"The High Hold's researchers will investigate the creature you described and send the report to the mayor. Furthermore, I will request Mayor Yurst advances me the management plan for handling the predator. That should be a clear message to him that I expect this to be dealt with."

I snorted. As if the mayor had a management plan.

If I were anywhere near Bonic right now, I'd have cowered under the alpha pheromones he likely pumped out in waves. He'd elected himself my protector alpha when my father hadn't stepped into the role. There was always one in a family, and it had gone against his every instinct to allow me to go to Tern unmated. Even his voice through the phone had my tail tucking between my legs.

My brother's voice grew gentle. "Is your Earthling a kind alpha?"

Geo brushed off my offers to pay for the many extras I hadn't agreed on. My tail snapped. That was garbage. I'd pay what I owed even if it meant spending every hour not in my hovery making mittens. But I wouldn't change how my dwelling had turned out for all the stars in the Reiner System—it had been built as if he could read my mind.

I sucked in a breath. "He'd never hurt me or ask me to do anything uncomfortable. He's a strong protector and a skilled archbuilder. You should see my fabulous dwelling. It rivals my private rooms in the Tuniga High Hold."

A needle of loneliness threaded through my heart at memories of the Tuniga family dining table. It always overflowed with an aunt or uncle and their younglings. My fine table would likely end up more of a cluttered workstation. Family was something I'd left on Lorne.

The background noise had diminished. Bonic's fingers stilled their drumming. "You have no idea the peace it brings me to know you are now protected." Bonic blew out a long breath.

I worried my lip until it bruised. "Ah... He would make a fine mate."

Do I mean that?

The power of saying the words aloud, 'he would make a fine mate,' shuttled through my veins, lighting up each nerve with hope.

With conviction this time, I said, "He'll make the best mate."

The list of pros and cons in my head finally sorted itself, and the pros list tipped the scale. "But he's clueless, Bonic. Geo isn't aware he's an alpha, has no idea what an omega is, and was alarmed, to put it politely, about my womb and...shocked that our genitals are hidden in protective pouches."

Bonic's laughter rang through my empty kitchen. "Teach him our ways, and he will want no other." A notification pinged in the background. "It has been an extremely long rotation and I still need to sort out an incident from earlier. Misinformation caused riots along the northern border."

Blant those councillors! Always meddling with the elite protector's business. Bless the goddess that my brother is in charge of them, not my parents.

"I wish I was there to lend support, Bonic."

"I must go, Makee. May the goddess Sola bless this union. We will speak on the new moon or sooner."

My heart soared at his approval, but he was gone before I could say, "Bye, brother."

The call disconnected, and longing for my brother swept through me. I yearned for a soul-linked bond like the one he had with Jast. In this moment, I wanted nothing more than to place my hand on Jast's belly.

A strange clunk rattled my front entrance—a welcome distraction.

I pushed aside the cover of the tiny lamar viewer, marveling at Geo's ingenuity and concern for my safety. Geo stood on the other side of my locked door, his face strangely distorted. If I hadn't been so focused on Jast's growing youngling, the loosening pull from my tether would have alerted me to his presence. He shifted from one foot to the other as I watched through the little lamar hole. A smile so big my cheeks hurt was plastered across my face.

When I opened the door, Geo straightened his shoulders and sucked in his belly. He said, "For you." Then he pushed a container into my hands as he continued to shift from one foot to the other on the threshold. "Can I come in?" His voice was too loud, but I wasn't startled. "I haven't seen the finishing touches on your house, and I can't market the features effectively if I'm not sure what they are."

Geo stared over my shoulder. We stood so close that his belly bumped me. The heat from his body drew me to him like flying starbugs to a flame. Boozy orzfoam and summer fields scented the air. How could I say no to his scowling face, gruff voice and terrible excuse?

"Uh-huh." I nodded, then twisted sideways, allowing him to step in. His shoulder brushed against my chest and turned my nipples into stiff peaks. "What's this?" I read the label on the container. "Hiscus wine."

"It's a housewarming present," Geo mumbled. He unlaced his boots and toed them off before locking the door. His brightly colored socks had what I assumed were little Earth creatures on them.

With a sway to my step, I entered the kitchen, and Geo followed. He poked and prodded the cabinetry, scent-marking his territory with each touch of his fingertips. His lips tipped up when he discovered the cleverly camouflaged appliances.

I poured us each a container of wine and sipped mine. "It's lovely." A purr rattled in my throat before I tipped my container to him. "To fresh beginnings." I took another sip of the fermented hiscus.

We walked into the hovery side by side. I bounced on the balls of my feet, eager to show off my space. "The three bays are exactly what I asked for. Where did you get the idea for the clever pit with a lift? It will be extremely helpful to be under the hovercrafts for repairs." Nearly twirling, I stopped where my parts were stored. "Oh, and take a look at my storage wall!" My hand brushed across the tools where each hung from a peg. Storage bins and drawers for parts lined the wall. "So much better than I imagined."

"You like it then?" Geo barked, but his shoulders slumped forward vulnerably before he stiffened his spine again.

"No, I love it," I gushed. "It's remarkable. Plus, I have so many appointments for the next two weeks that I stopped taking new bookings." I smiled as I recalled the number of people who'd just happened to walk by and need a little tune-up. Another sip of flowery wine burst sharply on my tongue.

I leaned on my long workbench as Geo opened and closed drawers idly, presumably testing how smoothly they shut. While I chatted away, his shoulders loosened, his legs gave a little more around the knees when he walked, and his belly relaxed.

"Why don't we finish the tour in the courtyard?" I lifted my container.

Geo cringed and followed me with dragging steps. What was going on with him? I was thrilled with the work his crew had completed.

The woodskies' squawking calls drifted in from the courtyard. Greenery perfumed the air with a sweet and spicy scent reminiscent of cold season holidays on Lorne.

Geo sat sideways on the lounge chair, his legs spread wide, facing the lounger I lay on. "So, about that." He jerked his head sideways toward the pool. "It was installed before I knew you...hate water." His cheeks turned a shade of pink that warmed a place low in my stomach. He took a gulp of wine and grimaced. "Anyways, it would be a lot of work to...remove."

Ah, he's embarrassed about the pool.

"Hey, none of that now." My tail wrapped around his calf, and the fuzzy tip brushed up and down. "I don't hate water," I lied. "This is exactly the push I need to finally force myself to swim. My brother has pressured me to learn for a lifetime." I rolled my shoulders back and nodded.

"I can swim..." Geo's pale green eyes lifted to mine.

"Well…great for you." We both knew he could swim. He really was the strangest alpha.

He stood up then paced along the pool's edge. "I'll teach you to swim."

Why was he pacing? The hair on my arms rose, and I shivered as I recalled Raz circling me deeper and deeper until I was on my tippy toes and at his mercy.

He scratched the back of his neck and looked through the lamar ceiling that domed the courtyard. "Maybe you can tell me more about Lornians…" Then, with a sharp inhale, his uncertain demeanor changed, and his chest puffed out. "This time tomorrow…I mean, new week, and every night after until you can swim from there—" He pointed to the shallow portion of the pool, then his arm swept out to cover the entire pool length. "—to there, three times with no breaks."

My heart raced. There to there…three times. I inhaled deeply. New challenges. I'm open to new challenges. I'd already completed my orders for linobee mittens, and I only liked to be covered in hovercraft grease for so many hours in the rotation, so that left a lot of free time.

Plus, there was the incentive of ogling Geo in a swimsuit. "In return for your kind gesture, why don't you come one moon earlier, and I'll make you dinner?" I beamed. "I hope you like mantu?"

Get recipes from D'irk on how to prepare mantu, because asking Raz is out of the question.

Geo met my eyes as he nodded in agreement, but his words were stilted and his face a blank mask. "I like mantu."

Maybe this will provoke a reaction. I leaned back on the lounge chair and lifted the hem of my tunic, exposing my stomach. "I can repay you by feeding you."

Geo's gaze fixed on my hand, where I not-so-idly scratched my tummy.

"So, tonight?" I asked.

His knuckles turned white as he clasped his container. Even in the dark of night, his eyes dilated. But he said nothing. I couldn't get a read on him.

"Not tonight." Geo shook his head, swallowed the rest of his wine in one gulp, and shuddered.

"I've had a few drinks. We'll start in the new week." He pushed back his shoulders again and sucked in his belly. "I'll see you tomorrow, an hour before dark. Thank you for showing me the final product. Sully will be by tomorrow to finish the overhead bay door installation. If you encounter any problems, com me and I will send one of my crew over to make repairs." He tipped his chin in goodbye, a vein throbbing on his neck. Seconds later, he exited by the side gate.

"Geo..." I walked toward the latched gate.

The door swung open, and I swallowed a lump in my throat as his hungry gaze scanned my body. Not so 'all business,' after all. "You forgot your shoes."

He looked down at his bare feet. "Right." Heat radiated from him as he wove around me and stalked toward the main entry. "I'll just get those then."

"Bye, Geo," I whispered into the wake of summer field-scented air. I'd never met an alpha quite like Geo. At times his insecurities overpowered his instincts. Edgy and hot, I stalked to my freezer and stuck my head in.

I made a plan to avoid my terror about learning to swim and control my raging hormones over a confusing alpha. First sun tomorrow, I was heading to D'ovey's bakery and trading some of my mantu for graneth puffs. Worrying over credits and ration bars was in the past. Maybe Lorne wasn't the only place I had a family after all.

17

"**S**ERIOUSLY, YOU HAVEN'T READ it yet?" Ginger's gasp was loud and clear through my wristport.

"Well, I've been a little preoccupied, Ging." A few grinning Rock Dwellers turned to face me from their card game in the corner of our shared room. They didn't even bother to cover their grins with their thick fingers as they eavesdropped.

I really need my own place.

My mind wandered to the list of extra features people wanted for their homes. After walking through Makir's, the damn mayor had decided he could skip the queue and demanded a pool.

"Geo, are you even listening to me?" She whistled to get my attention.

I winced and moved my wristport farther from my body. "Jesus! Ginger, you're going to make my ears bleed."

"SEND. ME. THE. REPORT. NOW." My wristport vibrated with each dramatic pause.

"Geesh, all right. Hold your horses." I scrolled through my email and forwarded the one from Dr. Ten to Ginger. I wasn't sure how they did it, but the Intergalactic Federation had seamless communication technology between the planets in the Reiner System.

Reading Dr. Ten's report topped my to-do list, but it kept getting put off, filed in the same place as building my home.

What kind of archbuilder has no home to show off?

A private shower would be nice. Makir's slick fur in the hot pools of the cave came to mind, and I hardened against the fabric of my overalls—something that happened with increased frequency these days.

Ginger's annoying voice shook me from what was sure to be a pleasure-filled fantasy. "Geo, it says right here the reason your muscles have grown and your"—she cleared her throat—"cock has thickened..." She snickered. "It's due to 'shared DNA with Lornians.' That's Makir's species, right?"

"Uh-huh." Dr. Ten was a crackpot. Me sharing the same DNA as a furry blue alien with a puff on the end of its tail? No way.

Ginger continued to read. "The alpha traits the patient displays stem from latent chromosomes that, while present on Earth, in rare cases have remained repressed until exposed to a compatible omega. When exposed, personality traits consistent with an alpha behavior profile manifest, i.e., increased assertiveness, persuasiveness, desirability." Ginger laughed. "I gotta get me some of this."

Pika and Charz barked in the background, and I longed for my home on Earth.

"I'm going to keep reading this to you because otherwise I know you'll ignore it forever. Among the physical changes that may occur, muscle development and genital adaptations are the most common."

This couldn't actually be a thing, could it? I cupped my cock and stared at the sleeve of my shirt. I'd had to rip it this morning so it wouldn't cut off the circulation to my arm.

"He's got it all laid out for you here, you big doofus. You should've read the damn email instead of worrying up eight thousand fatalistic reasons why your body has gone berserk."

To get a little privacy, I walked outside.

Sully yelled at my retreating back, "Boss man, come back. We want to know more." A chorus of laughter followed, which I casually waved off, but I wished the ground would swallow me.

As I walked, my mind drifted again. What Yurstille really needed were a few green spaces, like a community park, especially if they wanted to encourage new families. I didn't want to hear what Dr. Ten had to say. If I read it, there would be no plausible way to deny the fact that I had the genetics of an alpha. At least when it came to Makir.

"Tune in, Geo," Ginger scolded. "This is your life, and it has gotten exponentially more interesting." She took a sip of something, likely an espresso. "This is straight out of a sci-fi movie. You might have blue babies with beards and fuzzy tails in the future."

"Come on, Ging," I said quietly. "That's not funny. What the hell do I do if he's pregnant? Fuck, I didn't even know he had a brother until yesterday. I know nothing about the guy. Any time we're together, I'm either a barbarian or under the influence of his pheromones." And his hands, mouth and naughty tail. "How does a guy even know what's real in the middle of so many chemical reactions?"

"It can't be any worse than the bad decisions I take home after a night at the club." Ginger laughed. "Geo, take a breath. Do some tai chi and get your Zen on. You need to get out of your head. It's all too close, and you're catastrophizing things."

She tapped her nails against her cup in the background—probably neon with black tips, or something equally bold. Ginger was right, and I didn't want to discuss it.

"I miss Charz and Pika." I sighed.

"An unusual letter came for me yesterday, which is why I called. Someone can't seem to remember my phone number." Her excitement topped her sarcasm. "It turns out I can visit you because you put me as your next of kin. One paid visit a year!"

"Are you serious, Ginger?"

"I know, right? Crazy," she replied. "I can bring Charz and Pika with me..." Her voice softened. "It's not like I would miss them if they ended up—"

"Why didn't you start with this? This is great news. I don't care if I have to build the mayor three pools. I'll do whatever it takes to get approval to bring them here."

"I'll have to wrap up a couple of contracts and set up a house minder. Unlike some people who take far-flung vacations that are a mere flight away, it takes two damn weeks to get to Tern." Ginger soothed my dogs in the background as if they understood the conversation.

My cheeks grew sore from smiling so wide. "Do I need to remind you whose idea it was for me to move here, Ging?" I felt like I'd just won the lottery.

The sky darkened with brown clouds, and the wind kicked up pink dust around me. The tether between Makir and me tugged, a constant reminder of my need to be closer to him.

"I've got some planning to do, Ging. Thanks for making my day. Talk soon."

"Bye, Geo. Send me a list of what I should pack."

I wandered back into our shared accommodation and tripped through the entryway, standing there in a daze.

"Boss man, why are you staring into space?" JayJay's deep rumble brought me back.

I looked around at my enormous roommates. Ginger can't stay here. Then I pictured her sitting with Tino and Sannit playing cards in the corner, owning the table. What was I talking about? She'd love the shit out of staying here.

"My best friend is visiting in two turns of the moon, and she's bringing my dogs."

Sully grinned so big I feared he might swallow a bug. "She'll be on the same shuttle as my family."

"Your puppy doojies are coming here?" JayJay tested out the words, and as I'd expected, it was hilarious.

"That's right. You'll love them." I squeezed into my bottom bunk and scrolled through documents on my tablet. "JayJay, let's rearrange the schedule. We're moving Sully's dwelling up in the queue. Both crews will begin work on his build first sun tomorrow."

Sully cheered, and his thick fist bumped me on the shoulder. The friendly gesture would've had me on my ass a few months ago. Maybe having traces of Lornian DNA was good for something, after all.

"You got it, boss man," JayJay said.

"Now, I need two volunteers to come with me to the mayor's tomorrow." The happy vibe faded as Tino and Sannit trudged forward. "We're putting in a pool and doing it smiling because my puppies are staying in Yurstille."

Stay... Could I stay here? Leave everything behind? Sell my grandmother's house?

My stomach soured at the possibility of selling my grandmother's home on Earth. Nope, not happening. Ginger could live there forever. But a construction company of my own on Earth...that dream seemed to hold a little less weight.

Eventually, I fell asleep compiling a list that had me drooling on my pillow. Cured meats from the deli down the road, dill pickles, dill pickle chips, dill pickle popcorn seasoning, popcorn, chocolate chip cookies, garlic... Would the mayor give his permission to bring chicks, garden seeds and tree seedlings on board? And holy crow did I need some new clothes.

Covered in pink mud, the mayor barked out instructions to Tino, Sannit and me from his plush chair in the cool shade. "Make it a little wider. Makir's pool is twice the size." Sweat dripped from my forehead while ice rattled in the glass Mayor Yurst sipped from.

His nonstop changes turned my smile brittle. The rest of the week had dragged on in the same way. Even the Rock Dwellers, whose optimistic outlook on life could be nauseatingly sweet, had lost some of their natural sugar.

"One more time, boss man, one more time..." Sannit's low voice grumbled when Mayor Yurst had left us for his lunch break. "If he asks me one more time to be careful around his silly statue, it might end up in the pool. What kind of self-important blanting fool has a statue made of himself?"

I chuckled. The mayor was a first-class idiot.

"Bish. Boss man, you aren't buying the story that he happened to be awarded it for his 'exemplary service?'" Tino's deep rumble turned to a high-pitched warble remarkably similar to the mayor's. "Are you?"

I snorted as I tapped down the last paving stone around the pool. "Not a chance. He intentionally had that atrocity made. It's better looking than he is."

In exchange for the pool, an outdoor washroom and a guest house, I had the all clear for my dogs and enough storage space on the next shuttle to accommodate my every whim. Unsurprisingly, the mayor didn't care about me bringing in foreign organic matter from off-planet, as long as he could look out over his pool from a lounge chair and admire his statue.

"Fuck, you guys are hard workers." I slapped the pink mud off my overalls, astonished at what we'd accomplished in four long days. "And have I mentioned patient?"

"Bish, boss man." Tino's gray cheeks purpled. "It's nothing special."

I'd had countless crews over the years and knew good workers when I found them. Rock Dwellers were nothing shy of solid gold.

"Sannit, com the other crews and let's get out of here before Yurst returns and asks us to do anything else. First round's on me."

The small cantina was shoulder room only. The Rock Dwellers took up most of the space along the communal table. A lively tune filled the air where an enforcer played an instrument similar to a guitar in the corner. The holes where windows should have been had sticks in place to prop up their salvaged tin covers. Colored lanterns dangled from the rafters, and the aroma of grilled mantu sizzling outside wafted through on the evening's light breeze.

"Boss man, thank you for the generous gift of timber and lamar. TeyTey and the younglings will love it. We've never lived anywhere of this caliber before." Sully's eyes were glassy as he polished off the mug of orzfoam before him.

"If I can build the mayor a pool house, I can throw in a few extras for one of my guys." I bumped my knee with his. "I'll be at the Rowtees' tomorrow, but I want to see the lazy river you designed. Oh, and I set aside some plants for you at the nursery."

"We'll have you over for dinner every night when my TeyTey arrives." Sully's grin resembled a deranged comic book character's, even though he had about as much malice in him as a lamb.

"You can bring Makir, too."

What? Why would I bring Makir?

"If TeyTey can make something besides graneth puffs and mantu, count me in," I replied good-naturedly, ignoring the bit about Makir.

My mind drifted as I unwound with my crew. Engineers on Earth would go crazy exploiting the geothermal power that showed up in pockets around town. The awe on Makir's face when'd he realized his floors, even the hovery's, were heated by geothermal power had made me all soft and gooey inside. The tether pulled, luring me with the desire to be closer to him.

JayJay's orzfoam sloshed onto my elbow and startled me from my daydream. His deep rumble vibrated through my elbow where it touched mine since we were so crammed together.

With the tab paid, I forced my way out of the pub through a chorus of goodbyes with a bottle of hiscus wine. I had a favor to ask from my favorite blue Lornian.

I zipped up my hoodie and braced for the cool evening air. No one knew how the Fires That Cleanse might have affected the seasons. Nevertheless, my gut told me that summer was nearing its end. A temperate climate had been highlighted in the brochure the mayor had produced to recruit newcomers, but I worried over what a cold winter might present for the unsuspecting.

The tightness of the tether relaxed as I neared Makir's home. Two days with no Makir, and I was about to jump out of my skin. I tripped under the stars' dim light.

I practiced what I would say to Makir as I walked. How are alphas meant to act? Can you get pregnant? Despite the heaviness in my stomach, I wouldn't fail this time.

The knocker on Makir's door was cold against my sweaty palm. Tap, tap, tap.

"Come in the side entrance. I'm out back."

I growled at his response. The whole point of the goddamn peephole was so he would know who stood there, not so he could invite a potential stranger straight to him. Or worse, his creeper neighbor.

"Makir!" I barked as I walked over the paving stones to his pool. "What if I was Raz? Where's your sense of self-preservation? Be sure it's safe before you let someone in, for crying out loud." My hands landed on my hips, and my too-tight shirt stretched across my chest.

Makir's eyes peeked over the tablet he read from, and his tail whipped softly. The fronds from the tropical-looking plants beside his lounge chair jostled when his long legs stretched out.

"And hi to you too, Archbuilder." Makir's quiet voice drew me in. I couldn't quite get a read on him, but he smelled delicious. I inhaled the sharp gingersnap and juniper fragrance that I couldn't get enough of. My arms dropped to my sides, and tension eased from my shoulders.

"To what do I owe this honor?" Makir placed his tablet on the lounge chair beside him, sat up and shivered.

"Here, this is for you." I shoved the bottle of wine toward him. "We're moving to the fire pit. You're chilly." I clasped his long blue fingers in mine and tugged him toward me. The contact sent a heady warmth through my body. "Why don't I start a fire? I don't want you to catch a cold."

The lavender of his eyes swirled.

One of the enforcers had a side business selling graneth husks compressed into pellets that could be burned, and a covered nook housed a neat stack.

"Geo, I'm fine. I just put on a sweater less than a moon ago." Then, as if he sensed my need to be busy, he changed his tune. "However, a fire does sound rather nice. I'll grab us a couple of containers while you get it started."

Don't be a blockhead caveman. Stick to the plan.

My hands clenched as I crouched to light the fire. I hated how I became a bossy grouch every time I got near Makir. I couldn't live here permanently if I lost control every time I got close to Makir.

Makir's chair scraped over the paving stones as he dragged it alongside mine in front of the fire. "You might like this." He passed me an amber-colored drink that warmed my toes and tasted remarkably like whiskey.

I guessed he'd picked up on my dislike of hiscus wine. "This is terrific." I leaned back in my chair, and my muscles relaxed further. My eyes found his, drawn to the blaze-orange flames reflected in his dark pupils. My mouth watered at the endless possibilities lurking beyond the reflection.

"It's from my brother's collection back on Lorne. A farewell gift." His voice sounded a little distant, but his slight purr called to me on a base level. My chair jerked loudly, scraping over the stone, and I backed away before I jumped Makir like a wild beast.

"Well, thank you for sharing." I cleared my throat and stood.

My lungs expanded on a deep inhale, and a button popped off the shirt I'd purchased from the market. I polished off my drink in one final gulp and slammed the glass down. "Dang it, nothing fits right. I can't wait until Ginger gets here."

Makir stiffened in his chair as he passed me my button. "Well, I'm not sure who Ginger is, but I can fix a button. I'm good with my hands."

And his tail. I gulped.

Makir's loose, liquid sway as he walked toward me left my mouth watering. His tail flicked out and brushed the back of my calf. A second later, he unbuttoned my shirt with his long, nimble fingers, his delicious aroma making my knees go soft.

"She's my best friend." I coughed, frozen by Makir's actions. If he shifted any closer, he'd be touching me, but his fingers didn't even graze me as one button after another came undone. I sucked in my belly.

"Quit that." Makir purred, patting my belly as he undid the last button and gently pulled my shirt free. My breaths came so hard that I must have sounded like a freight train. "It will only take me a minute to fix this for you." He turned around and moved toward the kitchen, my shirt in one hand. His tail swayed in sync with his hips as they rocked in a slow saunter, beckoning me.

The bright kitchen light broke my trance. "Makir, if you have no plans for tomorrow, can I ask for a favor?" I blurted.

His gaze rose from my belly before he deftly stitched my button back onto my shirt. The tip of his tail tapped the floor in concentration.

I scratched the back of my neck. "Do you have a shirt I can borrow?"

"Don't be silly. I'll be done in a second. Now, what's this favor?"

"I need a lift to the Rowtees' tomorrow," I barked, more sharply than I had intended. "Also, I need to use your trailer to haul supplies."

Fuck, that wasn't a question.

Makir tucked the thread behind his incisor to cut it off. The tip of his tongue played against his lower lip for a moment.

My mouth turned dry. "My friend Ginger is coming to visit, and she's bringing my dogs." I grinned, my desire tempered as I pictured Pika and Charz dusted in Tern's pink soil. "Plus a few supplies from Earth. I have something perfect for your bedroom in mind." I took a steadying breath. "In exchange for your help."

Makir passed me back my shirt. "Geo, you know there's nothing you could ask for that I wouldn't give you."

My heart thumped.

He leaned back against the counter, his long blue fingers sweeping over the swirled surface the same way they'd caressed my chest not long ago. His gaze was wide open. "I don't want anything in exchange. But, of course, I will help you."

I slipped on my shirt, missing half the buttons as his eyes tracked my hands. "Does nine suns work?"

He nodded, his tail rocking back and forth.

"Welp, good night then." My lips tilted in an awkward half-smile as I turned to leave the charged atmosphere before I gave in to the desire to touch his lips with mine. I needed to learn how to control the alpha first.

Makir continued to lean against the counter, his tail lazily circling in front of him as his gaze ate me up. "See you tomorrow."

Damn it. Shit. Fuck. Another epic fail.

"Why can't I think about anything but the taste of his lips?" I muttered as I stumbled over the rutted pathway home. "Or the smooth nap of his tail under my fingers." The cool air did nothing to ease the heat swamping me. I wanted to touch the soft points of his ears with my tongue. And I still didn't know if he could become pregnant. I kicked a pebble, launching it through the sky in a perfect arch. If I could control my lust with the same precision, I could be with Makir as I yearned to be.

18

T HE TRIP UP THE narrow, winding passage to the Rowtees' cliff-top aviary took forever. Geo clutched my hips hard from behind. He twisted and turned, continuously readjusting himself to keep from slipping off the hover-bike seat. We leaned up into the steep slope, and every time he squeezed his thick thighs against mine, my nerves tingled. I sighed when at last, he just wrapped his arms around me. When we drew to a stop, I clutched my knees to steady my nerves.

The sunlight glinted off the roof panels lining the Rowtees' arched entryway, turning them iridescent. Ayla stood under its rainbow. Her belly extended in front of her, ready to burst, and the feathers on her wings shone glossy and white.

Her head dipped to the side, and she beckoned with a folded wing. "Come in. I'm so excited to show you the nursery."

She stepped between Geo and me, and her serene presence smothered the tension zinging back and forth between us. But when Geo's hot gaze met mine as he rebuttoned the strap on his overalls, lust ignited inside me again, and I longed to reach over and undo the clasp once more.

The Rowtees' dwelling was airy and bright as Ayla walked us toward her youngling's room. "Get started anytime." She clicked her beak. "I'll bring in some lunch a little later."

Preoccupied with our task, the sexual tension between us dimmed to a slow simmer. We worked all morning. Geo cut through the thick external wall—some type of fabric and wood hybrid—and I passed him the lamar. He measured, and I shaped the lamar into rounds of differing sizes to fill the holes.

"These little windows look like swiss cheese." Geo glanced at the openings dotting the wall. He must have noticed my blank look and continued to explain. "It's a saying on Earth when something is full of holes."

That made no sense. I lifted a brow. But he sure looked cute trying to explain it.

"Yeah, well...cheese is a snack... Never mind." He shook his head and gestured to the smallest piece of lamar I'd cut. "Pass me that one, would ya?"

Our fingers brushed as I extended the circle to him, and the tether almost sighed. It was so content in his presence. A glimpse into what life together might look like.

We make a good team.

As my stomach grumbled, Ayla waddled in to check our progress. When I checked my wristport I was surprised to find half the day had passed.

"This is stunning." Ayla's wings fluttered behind her happily as she observed the progress Geo and I had made. "The sunlight has transformed the space."

Her beak pointed from one lamar-filled hole to the next. She passed me a tray of sliced fruit and nuts and handed Geo two steaming containers of tea. "I insist you take a break. You're welcome to come to the kitchen. We have actual furniture there." She laughed.

I took in my sleeves, covered in bits of clear plastic, and the dust from drilling through the walls that coated my boots. "We're fine here." Geo nodded when our gazes met. "No need to track this mess through your dwelling."

Ayla's wings fluttered in a shrug. "Suit yourselves." She took her time looking through each of the eye-level windows while I laid down a plastic sheet on the floor, placed the tray on it, and sat.

Geo joined me. "When I asked for a ride, I didn't mean you had to work all day. I thought you would just drop me off." Geo's low voice rumbled beside me. "I can com you for a lift when I'm done. Probably a couple more hours."

His shoulder brushed mine when he leaned in to grab a slice of hiscus, sending electric sparks up my spine. A trail of red juice dripped down his chin, and I tilted toward him instinctively, wanting to clean his beard with my tongue.

"I'm going to place my nursing chair right here to take advantage of the changing light in the evenings."

I jolted back from Geo, startled by Ayla's voice. How had I forgotten she was here?

"The sunsets are so beautiful here on Tern, and what did you call this effect again, Geo?"

It took a moment for him to respond. "Bubbles…" He paused to suck the sticky juice off his fingers. "You know, like the spheres created when you agitate soap. On Earth, children have little wands they dip in soapy water and blow into the air." He waved his arm through the air with a grace unexpected in a male wearing dusty coveralls. "They create a stream of bubbles that drift through the wind." Cross-legged, elbows settled on his knees and gaze turned inward, he seemed at peace. "Then all the other children run around, popping them." His lips tipped up in a fond expression that made me think he'd be a good father.

A sense of longing I had thought I'd left in the past filled me. I would never be a father, and nor would any partner of mine.

"That represents the idea beautifully. I especially love how they're all different sizes." Ayla brushed off her talons on a mat Geo had dropped by the door. "I'll be in the kitchen if you need anything."

"We'll be out of your hair right away," Geo said.

A curious expression passed over Ayla's face as she fingered the translator behind her ear, just as I did. She adjusted a feather on her head before continuing to the kitchen.

"I like helping you, Geo." My tail swirled around his bicep and squeezed as I picked up the thread of our last conversation. "Plus, I have no plans today. I'm all caught up at the hovery." The nut I crunched burst with a creamy, bitter flavor, and I purred. It tasted so good.

Geo's calloused finger caressed up and down the same section of my tail over and over again, driving me insane. Drawn in by my purr, he tipped onto his knees and crawled toward me. I gulped and his pupils dilated. I purred louder, reeling him closer.

A loud clatter in the kitchen forced us to jump apart. Shortly after, Ayla's sing-song voice rang out. "Don't mind me, I'm nothing but slippery feather-fingers these days."

"Let's get this finished." Geo's thick rasp vibrated over my skin, urging me to touch him. "You're making me want..."

Whatever had been holding him back broke. Our lips met, and the tether's connection grew thick and syrupy between us before he pulled away.

Under his breath, he muttered, "Trying to kill me." Honestly, I didn't know what I was doing when it came to Geo anymore. I was no longer confident the tether could be broken, or even that I wanted to break it. Geo was much more than a typical alpha—he gifted sunlight to nurseries.

Just as the reds of sundown cast their warm glow through the lamar, Geo installed the last bubble window.

This would be the perfect place to raise younglings. I hugged my calf with my tail.

We barely escaped the Rowtees. They were so pleased with Geo's generous gift that they wanted us to stay for dinner. They even invited me to join Geo at their youngling's naming celebration.

Geo stacked the unused lamar onto my hover trailer beside his tools and secured the load before sliding onto the seat. "Keep your tail to yourself," he grumbled as I turned to look at him over my shoulder, slotting my butt between his hips. His V-neck shirt stretched and exposed a patch of fur over skin flushed red. "Or I can't promise I'll be able to control myself."

He sidled up behind me, his considerable bulk pressing against my back. My nostrils flared, inhaling as much of his summer field scent as possible. It aroused me so much that I almost tipped the hoverbike over. I'd considered offering him riding instructions, but now I wasn't sure.

I liked him wrapped around me like this.

"Is that a threat or a promise?" I purred, and he growled, gripping my waist and pulling until his hard length notched against my ass and the base of my tail.

"Drive," he barked, and I engaged the throttle with a press of my thumb.

The breeze did nothing to cool the hot ache radiating from my protective pouch. My tail pulsed, charged with restless energy, where we pressed together.

A shower of neon lights dotted the air as the hoverbike stirred up a swarm of winged starbugs. Constellations formed and broke around us as they buzzed by.

I wanted to ride in this haze of lust forever, but we reached the sono in a span of minutes.

Geo sat with his arms around me long after the hoverbike went silent. A few starbugs lingered around us, flashing. Despite the cold air, his body provided all the warmth I needed. It was as if the goddess Sola had reached deep into my mind and recreated my perfect moment.

His reluctance to leave was palpable as he shifted his feet onto the ground. "I'll just unload these supplies, and you can be on your way." Geo's voice puffed against the back of my neck, spreading heat before he walked stiltedly to the trailer. He lifted the sheets of lamar off before stacking them in neat piles in the storage bay.

With Geo's warmth gone, I shivered. "Let me help." I followed his slow steps, his tool bag slung over my shoulder. He turned the corner into the dark storage area, out of sight.

I squeaked when Geo thrust me into the rough wall, hard muscles pinning me there. His nose pressed into my collarbone as he inhaled me in deep drafts. "Fuck, you smell good."

"Finally," I gasped, tugging the tool bag from my shoulder until it landed with a thunk at our feet.

"I can't control myself around you, Makir." The point of his tongue traced my collarbone, and he nipped me with his square teeth. "Tell me to stop if you don't want this." Vulnerability threaded through his deep voice.

My heart thudded against my rib cage. Why did he care so much about control? "I want this so much I'm afraid I'll scare you away."

He grasped my chin between his forefinger and thumb and dipped it to face him before his mouth slowly met mine. "Not a fucking chance."

Geo's plump lips yielded as I pressed and sucked and pressed again. Then, like a live wire snapping, he took control. His rough tongue massaged past my lips and slid inside.

A purr rattled deep in my chest. My tail brushed along the exposed skin on Geo's arms, over the curve of his bicep and mingled with the hair on the back of his neck. Not enough. It wanted to be under his overalls and coiled around the girth of the iron bar in his pants. Does it have moisture beaded at the tip already? I purred deeper as I succumbed to the press of his mouth against mine.

"Stop purring. I can't think," Geo groaned.

Does he really want me to stop?

"I can't help it. I don't have control over it." I tried to clear my mind and quiet myself. "You're pumping out pheromones like crazy."

"Sorry, little lion, purr all you want. I like it," he whispered into my neck, then suckled. I melted against him as his palms traveled over each bump of my rib cage and pulled me closer.

His lips weren't on mine, and mine weren't on his. We just stood and hugged. But the world stopped while we embraced. I wanted to be held like this, safe in Geo's massive arms forever.

"Wish I had my own place. Want you to be in my bedroom on Earth right now." His deep voice rumbled against my chest.

I couldn't help the purr in my voice. "My place is your place."

He pulled me in tighter, his voice a choked gulp. "Fuck, don't say that to me." He pushed away, his fingers still tangled with mine, and led me back to my hoverbike. I was in such a daze that he had to help me on. His brows furrowed, but his eyes were bottomless pools flashing between hunger when they met mine and uncertainty when he stared at his shuffling feet.

What's happening?

"I'll see you new week, Makir. Dinner and swimming. We're on still, right?" His soft grip on my hand contrasted with his brisk voice. Plus, my mind was still stuck on sex in the storage bay. He leaned in for one last deep inhale before he nipped my ear. "Goodnight, little lion. Sleep well."

He ran his palm down my back, hard and heavy, and smacked my ass, sending me off into the night dizzy with want.

The end week market vibrated with energy. I waved at the enforcer curtained behind colorful swaths of fabric, admiring his Interplanetary Gems sign. Maybe I could do something similar for my mittens. My eyes watered as I dodged the acrid black steam that rose from a table covered in strange orbs where a line of Lizards stood. Dark-skinned Boolas, white-feathered Nacers and tawny-furred Tigs shopped and socialized along the narrow dirt street. Thrown-together booths built from scraps lined either side.

I shifted my heavy backpack onto my other shoulder. Cold seeped through my linobee vest from the frozen mantu I hoped to trade today. Only a few short weeks ago, I'd been living off rations and meals from Raz. Now I had credits to burn and goods to trade because of D'irk, D'Rasma and D'Argon.

I set the paper-wrapped package on D'ovey's counter while he bagged my graneth puffs. My wristport flashed green with credits from my trade. "D'ovey, that's too much."

The deep brown skin around his eyes crinkled. "Not at all. This mantu will make me many credits. I will bake my mother's meaty and flaky fire cakes. First one's free for you."

I laughed. "I see your strategy."

I wondered if Geo liked spicy food. As I thought his name, someone called it, and I spun to find him. I bid a hurried goodbye to D'ovey as I rushed to follow my tether. Geo's overalls did nothing to hide his bulging muscles where he stood in line at D'irk's grill. The savory aroma of mantu wafted to me, and I crept into the front of the long queue beside Geo, nudging him with my hip. A group of enforcers stood nearby, mingling as they snacked.

Geo's wide eyes matched his smile, and he hooked his pinky finger around mine, like a chaste kiss, before letting go.

My cheeks hurt, and I knew I must have looked like a lovesick fool, but I couldn't stop grinning.

"D'irk." I tipped my chin in greeting and held up three fingers, transferring the credits over and shoving two skewers at Geo before he could blink. Then I turned back to D'irk. "Would you like to join Geo and me for dinner new week?" Geo stiffened beside me, his skewer of mantu forgotten. "I really need to get some recipes from you. Someone..." My eyes rolled. "Left me more mantu than I know what to do with."

"Never turned down a dinner invite in my life, not about to start now. Com me the details." D'irk chuckled and nodded to the next person in line.

Geo offered me his second skewer, his jaw tight. "I would've paid."

I petted his round belly. "I've got to keep you fed." He sucked in his stomach, and the knob in his throat bobbed before he craned his neck, looking around the market as if searching for anything besides me to focus on.

"D'Argon, D'Rasma," Geo called out as we joined the nearby enforcers' discussion. "Do you have a second? I have a favor to ask of you...well, your sister."

"Geo, you never fail to entertain." D'Argon's pointed teeth flashed.

"What obscure part of Tern will you steer us to next?" D'Rasma's laughter carried above the din of the crowd.

"You won't be rescuing me again," I replied cheekily. Geo's gaze caught mine and dashed away, but not before I read the adoration in it.

"That's a relief." D'Argon's lips flattened into a straight line. "We've got enough to think about with everything going on in the Starry Mountains." The two brothers' foreheads wrinkled with concern.

"The Starry Mountains?" I raised my eyebrow in question.

The brothers made eye contact, speaking to each other in a silent language only siblings understood, then focused on Geo and me.

D'Rasma lowered his voice. "There's been a lot of disturbance, vibrations in the ground causing mini rock falls."

I gasped and reached for Geo's hand. "There's more than one of those monsters?"

"Shhh... It hasn't been confirmed. Sisip has asked us to keep it quiet for now. The mayor doesn't want anyone to panic."

All four of us frowned at the mention of the mayor.

"Anyway, what do you need our sister for?" D'Rasma asked.

Geo leaned toward me. "Makir mentioned she researched the impacts of the Fires That Cleanse?" The warmth from his hand in mine shot straight through to my protective pouch.

D'Argon and D'Rasma nodded.

"Would she give the all clear on some plants and a few domestic animals I would like to import from Earth? My friend's visiting in a few weeks, and I hoped she could bring seeds and seedlings and maybe some birds humans commonly eat."

D'Rasma chewed his mantu while he spoke. "She loves researching how life-forms interact. Com the list, and I will forward it on." Then, he and D'Argon headed back over to the group of enforcers.

I'd briefly mentioned her research while the worm monster had us trapped. "You remembered that?" When I turned to face Geo his warm breath ghosted over my shoulder. It had been a passing thought. And he remembered. Past alphas who'd serviced me during a heat had not even recalled my naming celebration.

"I remember everything you tell me, Makir." Geo's voice was low, and his neck flushed. I wanted to press my nose into the heat there and nuzzle.

He straightened, looked around and stepped away from me. The noise of the busy market grew loud again. "I need to get some"—he scuffed his toe in the dirt and cleared his throat—"scheduling done for tomorrow." He squeezed my wrist in a gentle pulse before he headed back toward his office.

A pang of sadness burned me between the eyes. Is he embarrassed by me?

My tether tightened with every step he took away, pulling me toward him. I forced myself in the opposite direction toward the cantina, and traded the rest of my frozen mantu for a few containers of the orzfoam Geo enjoyed. I spent the whole time trying to decipher Geo's mixed messages. How could I broach the topic at our swimming lesson tomorrow?

Never in a million annums did I think I'd look forward to getting into water.

19

I CIRCLED THE AREA in front of the sono and deepened my breathing. Stance wide, I bent my knees and spread my arms, allowing the push and pull motion to lull me away from distractions—mainly Makir pressed against me in the storage shed last night. Weeds had started to make their presence known in Yurstille, and every pivot tangled me in a new one.

Grasps bird's tail...stork spreads wings...carry tiger up the mountain...

I'd been a mess all day, Makir a constant presence in my mind. Since my fall off the cliff's edge, it was as if the cord tying us together strengthened each moment I spent with him. I couldn't stay the hell away. His draw was much too strong.

...carry tiger up the mountain...carry tiger up the mountain...

Damn it. I shook out my arms, my fingers squeezing into fists. When would this restlessness stop? Nothing worked. No amount of tai chi settled me and my behavior had grown frustratingly erratic.

"Boss man?" JayJay's booming voice startled me out of my 'unrelaxation.' "Quit dancing out here." The deep vibration of his laughter moved up my arm when he passed me a bottle of wine.

"What's this?" I tilted the bottle and nodded at the familiar red fruit on the label.

"It's the dinner gift you meant to get for Makir."

I bit the corner of my lip. He was right. I should've thought to bring something over.

"It's swimming lessons." Or it had been supposed to be, anyway. Then I'd gotten tricked into dinner. "Thanks, JayJay." I gestured at the bottle. "I can't string two thoughts together." The bandage wrapped around my finger where I'd hammered it carelessly today was a testament to that. "Might have to visit Dr. Ten again. Pretty sure something's wrong with me," I mumbled.

"Bish, there's nothing wrong with you. You've been hit with the goddess's blessing." He pushed me toward Makir's, bottle in hand, his deep chuckle carrying behind me. "Enjoy your...swimming lessons."

Goddess's blessing... What's he talking about?

The frosty air turned my breath into clouds while I walked to Makir's. His linobee mittens would be in high demand soon. I waved to D'ovey as he turned the sign on the bakery to Closed for the day. The woodskies squawking song turned much longer than its summertime call. Ripe graneth seed heads dangled from long stalks where they dropped and filled cracks in the dry pink earth.

Warm light and laughter spilled from Makir's entryway. The door stood propped open. Even though he was expecting me, Makir's lack of personal safety burned like gasoline in my veins.

"Makir, why did we put a lock on your door if you won't use it?" I shouted through the house.

Fuck, why did I always yell when I came here? I loved this place.

D'irk and Makir worked side by side making dinner. Soft music played in the background, and Makir wore some type of silky-looking fabric, presumably for swimming, that swayed with his every movement. A loose white shirt hung open, framing his mouthwatering torso. D'irk's arm went behind Makir as he reached for the salt on the counter.

A hot wave of anger turned my vision red. My muscles bulged and tightened under my suddenly too-small shirt. Now isn't this the perfect picture of domestic bliss. Makir turned his gaze toward me, then dropped it to his feet in submission.

I rubbed the back of my neck and unbuttoned the top two buttons on my shirt. Shit, he hasn't broken eye contact with me in a long time. My muscles expanded across my back, prickling each nerve ending as they stretched. D'irk continued to prepare food, hip-to-hip with a frozen Makir, unaware of me about to lose my shit.

D'irk dusted the mantu with some type of seasoning. "Then you spread the paste on, roll it into a tight bundle and tie it off."

Get it together. D'irk's not a threat. I'm pretty sure he's straight.

I prowled toward the counter, where D'irk provided instructions in the bright kitchen. Makir's shoulders rolled inwards. Fuck. I'd done that.

I plastered myself to Makir's side, one arm wrapping around him and pulling him in tight. I needed to touch him. To claim him. "How can I help?" I growled, slamming the bottle of hiscus wine on the concrete slab countertop so hard I was surprised it didn't crack. Makir whimpered and softened like a limp noodle in my arms.

Damn it. Get control. I inhaled, but Makir's ginger and juniper perfume only increased my possessiveness.

D'irk finally faced me His eyebrows rose, and a moment later, his teeth flashed in a playful grin. He finished stuffing the piece of mantu in front of him with the savory herb mix that spiced the air and nudged Makir's shoulder. "Makir and I are getting to know each other a little better, aren't we?"

Makir's gaze was pinned to the ground, his tail coiled around his waist.

Part of me understood D'irk was just playing around, but part of me—the alpha, maybe—burned like fire under my skin, so feral I was one step away from showing my teeth. I grabbed Makir's wrist and pulled him out of D'irk's range. D'irk didn't miss that.

"Blant, Geo." D'irk washed his hands impatiently and dried them on a towel hanging from a hook on the cabinet. "Take it easy. We're only making dinner."

Makir's neck turned toward me in complete submission, and his gaze was still pinned to the floor. My fists clenched and released, clenched and released as I tried to regain control. Short, panting breaths heaved beneath my rib cage.

D'irk shook his head and took pity on me. "I'll pop these in the oven. They'll be ready in one sun." A timer notification pinged on Makir's wristport.

"Makir?" D'irk called out. When Makir didn't respond but sank deeper into my side, D'irk glared at me. "We'll do this another time." He waved an irritated hand in front of the oven and moved to grab his jacket off the back of the chair.

"Geo, cool down, get in the pool or something. Tomorrow, com me." The "com me" sounded like a death sentence. "There's a right way and a wrong way to do this." D'irk spoke slowly, like he would to an animal before he turned and left.

What an idiot. My shoulders dropped, and I blew out a breath. But at least I could put a label on it this time, and I was already calming with D'irk out of the picture. The last time the alpha in me had risen to the surface like this, it wouldn't settle until... It would take more than a swim and dinner. The alpha needed contact. Intimate contact. It needed to claim.

My strength surprised me as I placed my palms on Makir's waist and lifted him onto the long concrete countertop with ease. He yelped, and his eyes flickered to mine and darted away. I growled, wanting his trust back. Makir's tail wound around his torso in a hug.

I dipped my head to the velvety fur where his collarbone met his neck and drowned myself in the ginger and juniper heaven there. The heady aroma tightened my groin. As I licked and sucked at Makir's neck, his hands clutched my biceps, and his high-pitched whine loosened the taut tether. Then, I dragged my nose along the edge of his smooth jawline and worked my mouth toward his full lower lip.

"I'm sorry, little lion."

Makir's tail unwound, and its fluffy tip brushed the back of my neck. "It's okay. I should've known standing next to an unmated male would trigger you."

I moaned as he continued the soft graze of his tail over my neck. "It's not okay. D'irk's not a threat." My fingers clenched on the cool ledge. "Yeah, I really need my scent on you right now. Can I?"

His lavender eyes fixed on mine with unnerving alertness. The contrast from his delirious gaze when he was in the throes of his heat left me feeling even more unsteady.

Driven to touch him, I plunged my tongue between his lips into the warmth of his mouth. He tasted like the herb mixture he'd been preparing, exotic and fresh.

"My alpha craves your consent."

Makir's silky swim trunks were so thin that every dip of his muscled thigh rippled as I swept my hand up his long leg. On a long groan, he replied, "An incomplete bond leaves an alpha's claim unsecured. It's a constant fight, or so I've been told."

The velvety fur over his knee brushed against the side of my belly where my shirt rode up. A cascade of shivers surged through me. I slid my hand up his leg until the material bunched around his groin.

"I love claiming you, but when you're not compromised by your heat, I want you to decide. I want you to say 'no' if you need to. You have free will with me." A growl rumbled low in my belly as my thumb pressed against the base of his balls sheathed inside their protective pocket.

"I can't believe you're for real," Makir muttered, his long fingers clutched at my biceps, and his eyes grew glassy. "Yes, Geo. I want you."

The heaviness of the moment grew too much for me, coupled with the relief his 'yes' brought. I blurted, "Are there lots of gay Lornians?"

My free hand traced each bump of Makir's rib cage before my mouth dipped forward to taste his nipple. They were a lighter blue, free of the velvety fur covering most of his body.

"Gay?" His whisper-soft tail fluttered up my spine. "We don't go so far as to separate people that way, but yes, there are many same-gendered matches." With nimble fingers, Makir unfastened the buttons he'd sewn on the other night.

Heat consumed me. The tether, even stronger with Makir's consent, vibrated between us as my belly clenched in anticipation of his touch.

"Lift." My voice was gruff as I coaxed his hips off the counter.

The lavender of his eyes swirled with desire. I focused on his swim trunks, which I removed in one smooth motion before tossing them to the floor. His swollen purple head peeked out of its protective pocket when I lowered him again. Saliva pooled in my mouth, and the surface of my skin grew so hot it might power a nuclear reactor.

"Have to taste you," I groaned. My fingertips teased the inside edge of his protective pocket, a horizontal slit that extended across where his belly button might have been if he'd had one. In a flash, I tucked it under his large, hairless balls.

Makir purred so loudly it overpowered the music, and he leaned in to kiss me. "You're going to taste *me*?"

"No, I have to taste you." I dragged my nose down his torso, over the sensitive skin under his exposed protective pouch, drowning in the stronger scent pooling there. On instinct, I dove to the wide base of his cock, lapping up traces of ginger and juniper with long sweeps of my tongue. I rubbed my bristled cheeks and chin along the underside of Makir's firm balls.

"W-w-what are you doing?" Makir writhed on the countertop. The fluffy tip of his tail spread open, and he suctioned little darting kisses behind my ears.

I grew harder than the concrete he sat on as his purr vibrated up my spine. His scent filled my nose and his juniper taste melted in my mouth. I licked up the smooth blue skin of his shaft and twirled my tongue over the fat purple head.

Makir's purr turned to whimpers, and he lifted my chin with a gentle hand. "Geo. Stop. Alphas don't pleasure omegas this way."

"Not happening. I want this. I need to apologize." My jaw widened and unhinged over the fat head of his cock. I brushed off the momentary panic before accepting it as another adaptation to his omega call. His musky flavor spread over my tongue, and I lapped like a starved man. Every nerve buzzed and snapped like a live wire. The suction of his tail latched onto my nipple, and he drew on it, sucking in a way that drove me insane. He left me no choice but to release his throbbing dick, throw my head back and roar, "Hell yeah!"

Makir pulled my head back down to his groin. "Geo...please."

Before swallowing another mouthful of cock, I mumbled, "I knew you'd love it."

With the calloused pad of my thumb circling the small protrusion he called his tine, I watched his blue lion's mane tumble wildly around his shoulders. I pumped his long shaft with the other hand and rubbed my lips over his ripe and leaking head.

Makir's purr turned into a whine. "W-what are you doing to me?"

I kicked my leg behind me and snagged one of the wide stools under Makir's table closer with my foot. Now I sat at the perfect height to grab his ass and pull him to the counter's edge.

"If you like that, little lion, you'll love this." My voice was a deep baritone I didn't recognize.

Makir placed his feet on either side of the stool for balance, hips writhing, but I forced them back to the counter and wrapped my lips around his cock, pistoning him deep into my throat. His eyes were squeezed shut, and every taut muscle pulsed, needing release. When Makir picked up the rhythm on his own, I reached up to his nipples and tugged on them.

As he fucked my face, pleasuring himself, satisfaction filled me. The beautiful length of his spine arched, pushing him deeper into my throat. The new position pressed his nipples into my palms as he whined, purred and garbled nonsense. Finally, he stilled. His release pulsed down my throat in hot spurts. Our eyes locked, his gaze so wild and hungry that I almost spilled.

I placed his hand around my throat, squeezed it right over his pulsing dick, and took deep breaths through my nose.

"Blant, Geo. You're so sexy." His thumb pressed gently over my Adam's apple, right where his tine was lodged, into his softening length.

It'd never felt like this before. This need to absolutely dominate and be owned at the same time. I massaged my thumbs deeply into Makir's thick thighs above his knees. His muscles clenched, but he still held his cock in my throat.

When Makir's senses returned, his eyes opened, and the lavender swirls shifted from contentment to concern. He pulled out of my throat slowly and jumped down from the counter, soft cock swinging, and gently wrapped his long fingers around my throat.

"Geo…" He focused on the ceiling and prayed. "Oh! What have I done? Are you all right? Can you speak? Will you be able to eat, drink, breathe?"

Where the suction of his tail kissed along my throat, blissful zings of energy erupted. The laughter about to burst out of me at Makir's reaction morphed into elation as the electric waves turned me into a moaning mess. His tail's suction seemed to amplify emotion, and my release barreled through me, soaking the front of my swim shorts.

Makir glanced at the wet spot on my shorts, and my gaze dropped to where his tail and hand were still wrapped around my neck, and we burst into laughter.

"I guess you're okay then." Makir reluctantly unwound his tail from my neck and propped his elbow against the counter, his long, lean body on display.

I wasn't sure why he created distance between us, but space was the last thing I wanted, so I stood from the stool and pressed the length of my body into his. I tipped his face down to meet my mouth before gently sucking his lips. My hands rubbed up and down his soft, velvety arms and stilled when our fingers threaded together. Our kiss deepened.

Makir pulled back, his voice soft. "I thought I choked you and..."

"And stopped me from eating, drinking, speaking and...breathing?" I teased before I smoothed my palm up and down his spine. I couldn't stop touching him and pressed my lips to his again.

He pinched my waist, and I didn't even care when my muffin top pushed against his lean hips. "Don't tease me. What if I'd hurt you?"

"I loved it." I fixed my eyes on his, willing him to see the truth there, while I circled my thumbs on the inside of his wrists.

Makir grinned. His voice became so eager he sounded like a child. "Does that mean we can do it again?"

"Abso-fucking-lutely."

"Now?" he purred.

"Quit it." I tugged his tail. "No more purring."

When I released him to gather his swim trunks from the floor, he whimpered. I worked his feet through the legs, ran my thumb possessively down his half-hard cock and gently tucked it back in his pouch. Finally, after a quick peck on his nose, I pulled his shorts up the rest of the way and tied the drawstring in a neat bow.

I leaned away for a second, trying to gauge his expression. The tether hung slack and heavy, the alpha in me content, but I didn't like the uncertainty in his eyes, as if he wasn't sure what to do with this kind of attention. He worried his lip.

"Hey, I don't care if it's not something alphas do. Did you like it?"

His tail wrapped around my calf, and he nodded, eyes on the floor.

"Look at me." I tipped his chin up. "Then I'm going to keep doing it for as long as you like it, 'kay?"

His eyes swirled, and the way his lips curled in a tentative smile looked a lot like hope.

"We've got a swimming lesson to take care of." I smacked him on the ass. "And I can't wait to have that mantu. It smells fucking amazing." With a smile, I looped one arm under his legs and lifted, cradling him in my arms as I walked to the lounge chair in the courtyard and laid him on it. "But first"—I nestled in behind him and rested my arm in the crook of his waist—"we cuddle."

20

Silky fabric floated over my legs in a direct contrast to the heavy plod of my steps, each foot dragging as if chained to an anchor. The pool lurked in front of me, its placid surface a deception. Soon it would break and ripple and attempt to swallow me. My hair was braided back so the wet tendrils didn't turn into tentacles attacking me as I sank into the unknown depths of hell, but perspiration still soaked my hairline.

Geo's voice startled me from my funeral march. "Makir, you barely ate any dinner. Are you feeling okay?"

At this point, a heart-to-heart with my parents would have been preferable to this torture.

"Yep. Just great." My high-pitched voice and over-eager smile convinced no one, including me.

"Fuck, Makir, you're trembling." Geo's hand cupped my elbow at first, and when my body wouldn't stop shaking, he pulled me into him and wrapped a warm arm around my exposed back. "Hey, I won't let anything happen to you."

His voice—no more than a rasp—worked its magic, loosening my clenched muscles. *I'm safe.* With each exhale, more awareness returned. Geo wasn't wearing a shirt. Our chests touched skin to skin, his curly black fur to my smooth torso. The scent of summer fields filled my nose, and I dropped my cheek onto his shoulder.

But my mind would not settle. With one threat out of the way, the next loomed, and thoughts shuttled through my brain like a meteor shower.

How could I have used my tail's healing power on him? Again! But I'd been so worried about his throat after he... Why would he do that to me?

"Close your eyes." Geo turned me away from the pool. "We're going to go nice and slow, 'kay?" He rubbed his palm from my shoulder to my smallest finger, his other arm snug on the small of my back as he slowly slid us backward, inching toward the pool. "Tell me what Sisip said about the mittens you made her again?"

My heart ticked faster as water lapped at my ankles.

When I said nothing, he asked, "How many more orders do you have?"

Why was being in the water harder today? It had been so much easier when I'd shown Raz the pool, trying to drum up business for Geo.

"Let me try something else." His low voice practically hummed as his lips coasted over my chest, missing my nipples. My breathing remained shallow, but for an entirely different reason now. I clutched his waist hard when he skimmed his palm over my trunks and cupped one cheek.

"Have I ever told you how much I like your silky fur?" He peppered kisses over one shoulder as the water knocked at my knees. "And your delicious scent." Geo's nose dipped to my armpit and nuzzled. My swim trunks grew wet. "Or your lion's mane." He fingered the tail of my braid.

My heart kicked into overdrive, and a long whimper escaped me.

Geo's soft voice guided me toward the deeper end of the pool. "You're doing great, little lion."

I never want him to stop talking to me like this.

"Stop, would you?" I said, gazing straight into his soft green eyes now that the buoyancy of the water had leveled our heights. Geo treaded water as I stood on my tiptoes, his hands secure on my waist as the water lapped between our chests in a soft caress. "I don't know how to deal with you when you're like this."

Geo waded into shallower water, then stood to support me with his hands on my waist. "Like what?"

He walked me backward until my feet lifted off the ground, and my heart jumped into my throat. "Nice," I gasped as my breaths turned into pants, and tension built in my muscles.

Geo cringed and squeezed my waist before he broke eye contact. "So, we're not going to swim today."

My breathing evened out a bit at that revelation, but I wanted his eyes back.

"I want you to lie back in the water, ears under, and float. Take some deep breaths, close your eyes if you want and allow yourself to get comfortable with having your head in the water. Notice the different sensations that come while your ears are submerged."

Panic! Fear!

I snorted in disbelief. 'Comfort' and 'water' were not compatible words in my vocabulary.

"I'll be with you the whole time, okay? There's no need to be scared." His deep voice was calm, and now that he'd claimed me for the night, he'd transformed into a new person. Softer, kinder...

My voice wavered. "You're telling me to put my head underwater, and you don't want me to be afraid?"

Geo lifted my legs, one arm supporting my knees and the other under my neck, and tucked me in tight so the water rocked my rib cage against his soft belly. "I've got you. I'm here."

I whimpered.

"Shhhh…" His alpha voice coaxed me along. "I'm not going to let go until you relax."

I all but stopped breathing, locked rigid. I would have been dead weight at the bottom of the pool if it weren't for Geo holding me.

Then a deep, melodic vibration climbed from the back of his throat, and I let myself close my eyes. He was humming. I inhaled and took another breath, then another… His music, the water's sway and his cradling arms almost lulled me to sleep. I wondered if this sensation of warmth and safety I was currently wrapped in was akin to what a youngling felt in its parent's womb.

"You're doing so well." Geo kissed my forehead. "Now open your arms and legs just a little bit more." His alpha voice projected a sense of safety that calmed me. Geo withdrew his arms.

"Geo, I'm doing it." I grinned. "I'm floating."

"Yeah, you are, little lion." Water droplets beaded on Geo's eyelashes like tiny gems, magnifying the sparkle in his eyes. "You're doing amazing."

Ignoring the little lion bit—*because, ugh, I'm not a cat*—I grinned bigger. When his gaze focused on me again his eyes shone like bright stars.

I cranked a bolt tight on the undercarriage of the hovercraft above me. The pit Geo had built for my hovery was a stroke of genius. My back no longer ached at the end of a long workday. With my high-pressure wand, I blew out the fine pink dust that had settled in the down thrusters of the machine, blocking air movement and preventing its launch. Every hovercraft presented nearly the same problem, and the monotony of this tune-up turned my thoughts to Geo.

The last few weeks had been amazing. Each time Geo had come over, he'd been so feverish with desire that his need to possess me was palpable. He would suck on my cock like a lifeline and transform into another male with his release—one who was calm and patient. That version of Geo taught me to swim.

I hummed the tune Geo used to soothe me as I maneuvered my torque jack to replace the dust-free undercarriage. Swimming the length of my pool came with ease most days now, and more importantly, my heart didn't trip in fear when I entered the water. Never in a million annums would I have guessed that swimming would become one of my favorite pastimes.

It's not swimming that's your favorite pastime.

The torque jack skidded off the last bolt, nearly stripping it, and I refocused on the task at hand only to drift off again seconds later. After our lessons, we'd sit down for dinner and talk and talk and talk, greedy for each other's company.

I climbed out of the pit using the short ladder and swept up the pink dust I'd blown everywhere before rolling the repaired hovercraft into the last empty spot in my parking lot. My fists clenched, and I muttered, recalling Geo's remote gaze when he'd told me about his past partner, Cameron. Blanting idiot wouldn't even agree to watch their dogs for a year.

While notching my tools back into their spots on the pegboard, memories of last night sent my tail twirling. When the moon had hung high in the sky, and we'd talked long past when we should have, he'd pressed me to the door and kissed me senseless before heading into the cold night.

A long yawn stretched my mouth. Under all the perfection, one thing still had my brain working overtime. The sex. While omegas didn't technically need penetrative sex when not in heat, I craved the intimacy of having him buried deep inside me. Maybe it was a human thing, but Geo seemed to have no interest.

I wasn't sure how to broach the subject. 'Geo, I love it when you suck my cock, but am I ever going to feel you inside of me again?' It sounded so...ungrateful? The limitations on how he let me pleasure him wreaked havoc on my omega sensibilities. I appreciated an alpha's need to care for his omega, but I wanted that close connection with a desperation I'd never known. An omega tended to their alpha in all matters, and Geo kept stopping me.

I slid the door shut to the hatch on the pit, scrolled through my jobs for tomorrow and locked up. After showering, I cut open a graneth puff and filled it with cold mantu, eating over the sink. The closer the arrival date for the visitor shuttle his friend would be on came, the less I saw of Geo. And making dinner for one had no appeal.

My wristport chimed, an incoming video com from Jast coming through.

Her light blue mane, normally coiled in neat curls, was tangled as if she'd run her hands through it repeatedly. "Makir, thank the goddess you answered. Your overbearing alpha brother is driving me to the end of my patience," she teased, but one hand swept through the hair by her ear and pulled, revealing her underlying frustration. "You must deal with him. Just this morning, he insisted we must get a reclining nest to ease my back pain. I don't have any back pain. Silly parenting manuals."

I laughed. "Even if I had any sway over Bonic, how do you propose I do that?"

She threw her hands up in the air before they landed on her belly. "I don't know." Her shoulders slumped. "W-what if we came for a visit?"

"Are you serious, Jast?" My heart ticked with cautious optimism.

Her lips flattened, decision made, and she nodded. "Yes, I couldn't be more serious. I'll get him there, even if I have to threaten to visit alone."

"This is perfect timing!" My tail flicked the air. "You can meet Geo, see the dwelling he built me, and I can't wait to kiss your belly and meet my little nephew or niece."

Some of the tension lifted from around her eyes. "We've missed you too, Makee. See you soon."

I waved goodbye, and my heart lifted and filled with sunshine. My tail twirled, and I rushed to the spare room. Round windows dotted the space below the ceiling and lit the area with silvery moonlight. "This space will be perfect." I piled my softest linobee pelts into the nest and replaced all the towels in the bathroom.

"Damn it. I won't be there." Geo's harried voice carried over my wristport. "There's a problem with the geothermal spring at the mayor's, and his pool house has an inch of water on the floor." Geo's long sigh mixed with the shouts of his crew in the background as they instructed each other on how to stop the leak. "Count on me for dinner tomorrow, though." His low rumble soothed how let down I was.

My disappointment that Geo wouldn't be at the landing platform to greet my brother and Jast saddened me more than it should have, but an emergency was an emergency. So, I rid my voice of any dissatisfaction. "Get here when you can. No rush."

The majority of the spaceport was manned by Tigs, and the one who checked me through security had pointed ears on top of her tawny head, with long white wisps flowing from each one. She scanned my ident card embedded in my wristport. "Ah, so you're Makir." She smiled as she waved me through. "My sister, Sisip, has shared stories of your adventures."

"Is that what she calls them?" I laughed. "More like midnight rescues." I waved as I passed through the detector into a hangar. Hilt drills and hammer drivers whined as I walked past the construction to the private shuttle arrivals dock and through additional security. The newly finished walls were marbled with a liquid metal encased below a clear surface. Copper and aqua alloys mixed and then repelled each other, as if alive.

Alone in the arrivals area, I wished for Geo. I smiled, picturing him buried up to his ankles in pink mud. *What will Bonic think of him?* The distinct *whoosh* of the air-lock engaging refocused me. I glanced at my wristport. Right on time. I would expect nothing less.

Bonic's quick stride ate up the distance between us, and the next moment I was wrapped in his embrace. "Makee! So good to see you, brother." The warmth and familiarity of his arms around me placed me immediately back on Lorne. When Jast's smaller frame snuck around me too, I opened my eyes, surprised to be standing in the private arrivals room.

I hadn't realized how much I longed for family until this moment. "I missed you guys so much." My tail wrapped around Bonic's, and my lips found the crest of Jast's belly. "Welcome to Tern, youngling. When you get out of there, I'm going to be the best uncle ever."

With both of their hands in mine, I pulled them toward the exit and security. Janny, Bonic's personal guard, shadowed us, and a hover lift floated behind with their bags. "Good to see you too, Janny," I called over my shoulder, and he tipped his head in reply.

For some strange reason, Raz also happened to be at the spaceport. He scanned the open space of the regular arrivals area, his gaze dipping between his wristport and the blank arrivals board. When he glanced toward me, it appeared he might approach for a moment, but his steps froze when he saw my brother. Odd, but for the best. The last thing I wanted to do was introduce my brother to my neighbor.

"I have so much to show you." My gaze drifted to Jast's belly. "It's about half a sun, would you like to walk or hire a hovercraft?"

She faux-glared at her mate. "Don't you start babying me too, Makee. That's the whole reason we're here." She smiled. "I'm fine to walk. Show us your new home."

21

I TRIED TO TAME the growl in my voice, smoothing my hands over my pants. "My friend is arriving from Earth, due in about"—I dropped my gaze to my wristport—"five minutes." My teeth were grinding together, but I was keeping my cool. "And she has brought a lot of stuff with her—"

The Tig guard was questioning my need for a giant hover trailer in the cargo bay for the third time.

JayJay turned toward me and leveled me with a look that said 'Shut the fuck up.'

If he only knew what I wanted to say to the dumbass guard.

In truth, I was worried. Worried about meeting Makir's brother and his wife, worried Ginger wouldn't like it here, worried the plants and seeds and chicks would somehow trigger Tern's next plague, just plain worried. JayJay had agreed to load everything while I met Ginger at arrivals, but I couldn't even get past this ass to drop off the trailer, something that should've been simple.

"I'll need a copy of the permission granted by Mayor Yurst to allow the cargo off premises." The hardass interrupted me.

JayJay pressed his palm to my shoulder with more force than necessary. "Let me handle this, boss man. Go get your friend."

I focused on my wristport once more. Two minutes. Fuck. I glanced at the tight-lipped guard and a stoic JayJay. *I'm just making things worse.* "Thanks, JayJay, you're a lifesaver." I squeezed his arm and jogged through the polished concrete balustrades marked with blaze-orange tape. The narrow chutes were color coded, and I ran toward the neon green arrivals gate.

I swiped the back of my hand across my brow and plopped down next to a vibrating Sully. His excitement was contagious, and my toe tapped alongside his as I gripped the edge of my seat.

"I haven't seen TeyTey or my younglings in nine turns of the moon." He finally stood up, his eagerness unseating him.

That was a long time without seeing your wife and kids.

How would I feel if Makir were gone for nine months? I shuddered, not able to consider it. "She's going to love it here, and the kids are going to live in that awesome swimming pool you built."

Sully rocked back and forth. "What do you think the delay is?" He wrung the treat bag he'd picked up from D'ovey's tighter and tighter until the contents squished. "The arrivals vid-screen indicates that they've docked."

I rolled my eyes. "If I had to hazard a guess, I would say there is a holdup unloading the cargo."

Finally, the light above the arrival gate doors turned green, and the handful of people waiting jockeyed for the best position. One *swoosh* later, the air came alive with boisterous welcomes.

Sully was nearly taken down by a much smaller female Rock Dweller and two boys already the size of their mother.

A Lizzard passed through next, eyes scanning and tail thudding against the floor when no one arrived to greet him. He typed out a com on his wristport.

Three Boolas with floating baggage joined an enforcer who might have been part of my rescue in the wastelands, and a stream of new colonizers flowed through and headed to the same orientation room I had months ago. My worries lifted, and a lightness grew in my chest. At last, Ginger appeared, harried looking, with two Jack Russells pulling on their leashes.

"Ging, over here." I rushed toward her, wrapped her in a one-armed hug and stole the leashes. Charz and Pika's tiny paws bounced off my shins, scrambling for my lap when I crouched. Months away from me amplified their usual whimpers. I settled cross-legged on the floor so we could get our fill of each other. This was heaven on Tern. As they slathered my beard in doggie kisses, I looked up at my best friend. "I missed you."

She plunked down beside me in a heap. Her deep brown leather pants matched the cuffs she wore as bracelets, and wispy pink fabric draped loosely around her in various folds belted by some type of large chain. "I am *not* meant for space travel." She dropped her head onto my shoulder and idly petted Pika's rump as she continued to attack my beard with love. "Thank God I'm on solid ground again." Black bangs framed Ginger's face, and her stick-straight white hair slipped over one shoulder when she sighed.

The dogs eventually grew interested in their surroundings—too interested—and we hustled outside. Ginger's boot heels clicked over the polished floors.

"Wow, what is this?" Ginger snapped a picture of the liquid metal moving under the floor's smooth surface. "That aquamarine copper blend will work perfectly for my next costume."

"Something unpronounceable." I grinned at the familiarity of her comment. She may have been on another planet, but some things never changed.

"It's so...pink." Ginger scanned the landscape around her as we ducked under the arrival bay door. "Kinda reminds me of badlands a bit." She shivered and pulled out a long white coat with a floppy neckline from her large carry-on.

"I haven't learned to fly a hovercraft yet, so I thought we could walk."

"Why am I not surprised? Your aversion to change is shocking at times." She hugged my arm, silver-white hair swishing as she shook her head and then turned to face me. "But holy muscles, Geo, you weren't kidding. You're like the poster child for steroids." My lips turned down as she prodded my biceps. "In a good way, of course. You look incredible."

Her praise had me strutting down the center of Yurstille toward the sono like I owned it. With my dogs in one hand and Ginger in the other, I oozed pride. My small family was with me again. The only thing missing from the picture was Makir.

"Hey, I've taken some rather large steps for a guy who doesn't like change." D'ovey waved from his shop entrance, and a few enforcers called out hellos as we passed, their eyes focused on Ginger, Charz and Pika. Men outnumbered women here ten to one.

Oblivious to their interest, Ginger patted my arm. "That you have."

"So." I sucked the inside of my cheek. "Are you sure you'll be okay without me for a couple of hours?" The sono was quiet when we entered, and I showed Ginger her bunk opposite mine. "Sully will be here with TeyTey and their boys soon, and the rest of the crew will show up for dinner in about half an hour."

"Geo, I get it." She rolled her eyes. "Of course, you must go meet Makir's brother and his wife. He's only here for a couple of days." Ginger's black bangs highlighted shadows under her eyes as she yawned. "Plus, I'm beat. I'll just have a quick nap with the pups." They jumped onto the bed when she patted it, instantly nuzzled under the blankets, and curled into balls. "TeyTey and I have been traveling together for two weeks, Geo. We're friends. Honestly, I'm fine. I know all about Rock Dwellers. I'm good." She pushed me away from where I hovered over her. "Now, shoo."

22

B ONIC SAT AT MY long kitchen table with a container of whiskey in front of him. "When will I meet this alpha who has swept my brother off his feet?"

Bonic had been my protector my entire life, and while I was happy his pheromones no longer affected me in the same way, it signified my independence and saddened me. Though he would always protect me as a brother, his role as family alpha existed firmly in the past.

My tail whipped behind me in excitement, giving away the forced calm of my voice. "He'll be here any minute. His best friend just arrived, and he's getting her settled." I washed away the pheromones Bonic fanned my way as he tried to calm my jangled nerves. His alpha instincts to soothe me as he had done my whole life had been triggered. My eagerness to have Geo at my side was tempered with nerves over him meeting my brother. "Quit it. He'll be frustrated if he smells you on me."

Jast held her round belly, laughing at my expense. "Finally, there's someone who understands Bonic's alpha in hyperdrive." Her light blue fingers smoothed over the rich fabric covering her firm belly. "It's been working overtime ever since this seed was planted."

My tail brushed over Jast's knee. "Better you than me. I've been dealing with him ever since his alpha designation revealed itself."

"Fine." Bonic huffed in a very un-alpha-like manner and slumped into his chair. "I know when I'm not welcome."

A knock sounded at the front door. My heart tripped, and I spun to face my brother before forcing myself into a calm walk to answer it. "I expect your best behavior." I pointed at him.

His shoulders slumped farther as he let out a "Hrmph."

"Hey, hey, Mak." Raz's tongue slithered over the nickname he'd given me. His heavy hand landed on my shoulder, and my fur stood on end before I stumbled backward.

Blant. I should've looked through the door hole. Raz had made himself scarce after Geo's threat.

"The delicious s-s-smell coming from your dwelling is wafting through my door." The sharp outline of his spiky teeth flashed in his open-mouthed grin. "I thought I would come and ask you for the recipe s-s-since you kindly shared your mantu with me."

My fists clenched at my sides. I'd suspected when I'd given Raz some mantu that he might take it for more than face value—me paying back a debt, as any Lornian would. He'd fed me often when I'd lived off nothing but ration bars, and I owed him.

Raz's talons clicked across the polished concrete floor as he strode toward my brother, uninvited, with an awed expression strangely out of place on his long jaw.

"I wouldn't have interrupted if I knew you had visitors-s-s." His tongue rattled on the 's' sound.

What is he up to? He'd seen me with my brother and his mate when they arrived.

"Makir's sharing a recipe from his friend D'irk with us." Jast's helpful voice carried from the kitchen, where she filled a container with water.

Raz's unnatural focus on my brother wavered as his gaze locked on Jast's pregnant belly. He dipped his head as he neared my brother and bowed forward in a formal greeting. "I, Raz S'Lant of the Third Clan of Hotner, am indebted to you, Bonic Tuniga, High Commander of the Elite Protectors of Lorne, for the aid given while Hotner was under siege from the Jugga."

Strange. How did Raz know my brother? I stood behind my chair, shuffling my feet from side to side.

Bonic rose and placed a solemn hand on Raz's shoulder, and Raz's head lifted to meet his gaze. "There is no debt to bear, Raz S'Lant of the Third Clan of Hotner. Your slate is clean. Hotner has paid the price in those lost."

Bonic's ability to slip into his role as high commander awed me, and Raz's unexpected sincerity had me second-guessing how quickly I'd judged him.

"Well, you must join us for dinner, Raz, and tell us of your time on Tern." My brother's commanding voice brooked no arguments.

Raz's lips turned up in a smug smirk at the invitation as if he had expected it. My stomach dipped. Even if I were curious about how Lorne had aided Hotner, I did not want Raz at my dinner table. "Ah, Bonic...I'm—"

Distracted by the loosening tether, I turned toward the open door, my anxiety easing, and my steps turned light and floaty. I hadn't seen Geo in days.

"Makir!"

My smile flattened, and as I neared Geo, I was slammed with a wall of summer fields pheromones. Geo's tense arms were clamped to his sides, trying to rein it in, but the alpha in him broiled too near the surface, and he blew.

"Why the fuck is the door wide open?"

Yep, there it is. His singular focus narrowed on me, and I shivered under the intensity of his pale green eyes.

From the table, Raz asked, "Are you going to let a barbaric Earthling s-s-speak to your brother like that?"

At Raz's slithery voice, Geo's thick knuckles turned white where he gripped a bottle of hiscus wine. The tether between us snapped with electricity. I took a tentative step closer to calm him and bared my throat. Bonic growled in the background, but I ignored him. I suspected Geo lacked awareness of his surroundings, which was confirmed when his possessive gaze nailed me. I needed to get his beast under control.

As I approached, his skin flushed deeper, and perspiration beaded across his forehead. I brushed my knuckles over the back of his hand to loosen his clenched fist and slowly peeled back his fingers until he released his stranglehold grip. I placed the wine on the side table beside the door and threaded my fingers with his in exchange. Geo's heavy arm snapped around my waist, pulling me to him with a grunt, and the air squeezed out of my lungs.

"Mine," he rumbled. He ran the coarse hair along his chin over my shoulder where Raz had touched me, then nuzzled into my neck. I sank deeper under the spell of his pheromones as he suckled behind my ears, rubbing his face everywhere he could touch skin.

"Mine, mine." His raspy voice reverberated through me, sending a bolt of heat to my groin. My womb clenched. The empty void wanted to be filled. His fingers moved to unbutton my shirt, and his hard length pressed into my thigh.

I had to be the sensible one and move this show somewhere private. Geo was going to be mortified over the first impression he'd made on my brother and his mate once he returned to himself.

"What a dis-s-sgusting lack of control," Raz commented from the dining table. "Certainly, this behavior is not condoned among the High Hold on Lorne?"

Jast's laughter rang out in the background. "Nope, a possessive alpha over an unmated omega—practically unheard of."

"C'mon, I wasn't that bad..." Bonic's teasing voice trailed off.

With a quick tug on Geo's rough palm, I pulled us toward my nest.

Immediately, the tension bled from him as the scent of our togetherness surrounded us. I loved that my sleeping furs smelled of the two of us. I'd been making a habit of not showering before bedtime, and as a result, Geo's summer fields scent lingered on my furs even though he'd spent next to no time in my room.

Geo's tongue swept up my neck, from the top of my chest, where he had my button undone already, to the tip of my ear. His attention remained there. My ears seemed to captivate him. He was particularly enamored with the points, and my tail wrapped around his calf in anticipation.

I loved every part of Geo, including the alpha asshole, but we had company to entertain, and his timing was garbage. Though, I was sure they were far from bored.

Geo fumbled over the rest of the buttons on my shirt. "Why do you smell so fucking good?" He dragged his face over the smooth skin on my belly, yanked down my pants and nuzzled deep into the short fur between my leg and groin.

I let out a groan when he reached into my protective pouch and pulled out my straining cock. The tip was wet and shiny and ready for more. I moaned as his mouth closed over my head, and his tongue polished my round knob. It glistened, reflecting the pinks and oranges of the setting sun floating through the lamar ceiling.

I laced my fingers through Geo's short hair and tugged him back up, whispering in his ear, "Not a chance. It's not just about me today." When the soft fabric of his shirt dragged over my sensitive nipples, I moaned. Geo's hot mouth latched on to one, tugging it with his blunt teeth before slathering it with long licks.

Unused to removing anything but his overalls, I scrabbled with the zipper of his pants. At last, I reached into the stretchy fabric of his undergarments and pulled out his fat cock, drooling at the sight. He may not have been long, but I could barely wrap my hand around his girth.

I notched his plump cockhead below my dripping one and wrapped both hands around us. Juicy with our combined essence, our dicks glided against each other. His head ground down on my sensitive tine. He growled, and I whimpered, my mouth pooling with saliva. I arched back, my lower body pressing into Geo's solidness. He wrapped one hefty arm around my lower back, his bicep rippling.

He whispered as he hunched over my bent body, "God, so good." Geo pulled back, and I whined as our dicks separated. He pressed a calloused palm over my heart before he lowered my pants, then kicked his off and carelessly flung them across my room.

Geo picked me up and placed me on my back against the soft white linobee furs. "Yes," he whispered, his warm lips brushing along the shell of my ear. "That's it. Purr for me, little lion."

Until now, I hadn't noticed the deep, reverberating purrs coming from my chest.

He palmed his thick cock, groaning as he milked himself and collected his thick dew, only to line us up again and wrap his slippery hand around us. His weight settled on me as I spread my legs to accommodate his size and twisted my calves around his. My tail wrapped around the bottom of his ass and snuck between his legs, and the suction hidden amid the furry tip of my tail kissed along his full balls.

His hips jerked forward. "Damn, you don't play fair."

My hands gripped his hard biceps as he rocked against me with a heavy, slow slide. His plump head bumped my tine over and over until I wriggled, delirious with need.

Geo's voice was threaded with dominance, and I overheated when he placed two firm hands on my hips to lock me in place and said, "Stay still."

A pleading whine escaped my mouth, and he slowed to a painful grind.

"I'll give you what you need—now wait for it," he growled. My tail wrapped around his balls and tugged. "Fuuuck..." The word dragged out long and low as his grip tightened, and our lips smashed together. His tongue curled around mine in a sinuous coil, overwhelming my heightened nerves.

"Geo, please, I need to release..." I begged.

"Not yet." He pulsed slower, pressing his fat head against my tine. Saliva pooled in my mouth as I watched him handle his cock, expertly trailing the plump head sideways over my tine again and again. My toes clenched as he drove me to new heights, and the fluffy part of my tail brushed over the tight pucker of his entrance. I brushed a featherlight touch here and a suctioning kiss there as he kneaded our cocks together.

The heat ratcheted higher and higher, the smell of summer fields and musk an intoxicating drug. But it was the intensity in Geo's pale green eyes, a direct line to my soul, that toppled me over the edge. "Goddess, the things you do to me," I breathed.

Geo's eyes flared at my release. He tasted my ejaculate before coating his dick and finishing himself off, groaning as he watched his release coat the blue skin of my stomach like the white icing on my favorite cake.

"So hot, little lion." Geo's voice, now soft, had me never wanting to leave my furs again. If only I could have stayed wrapped in his warmth for eternity. All too soon, my blissful glow morphed into a reality check as muffled conversation drifted to us from the dining area.

Geo's head snapped up, and his neck and face flared red. "Fuck," he muttered as he stood, went to the bathroom and returned with a damp cloth to clean me up.

"I'm sorry, Makir. I fucked up again." His eyes flicked from mine to where he cleaned up my belly, and his lips pinched together. "I'm just going to head home the back way." He gestured to where the sliding doors opened onto the courtyard. Then he pulled on his pants, his undergarments forgotten in his distress.

Would wonders never cease. An alpha apologizing to an omega? Twice now.

"Hey, slow down." I stood up and moved closer. "We've got this." I smoothed my palm over the coarse hair on his face and leaned in for a kiss.

I unbuttoned his shirt, then rebuttoned it so the holes lined up correctly and scanned him from head to toe.

"My, aren't you handsome this evening?" I brushed the palm of my hand over his shoulders, smoothing the crisp fabric.

He bit the inside of his cheek at my apparent approval. "Ginger brought me some new clothes."

I dragged my hands down the arms of his navy button-up shirt and clasped his hands. "Feeling better?"

His chest heaved when he inhaled. "Let me put my underwear on."

I took that for a yes and let go of his hands. With his clothes on the right way, I wove my fingers through his once more. "Ready?"

23

THE NAVY BUTTON-UP SHIRT Ginger had brought me itched against my sweaty skin, and my belt buckle dug into my belly. It had been so long since I'd worn a dress shirt and pants that I'd forgotten how stifling they were. The confidence I'd built from Ginger's constant oohing and ahhing and her occasional prod of my bicep had disappeared entirely. If I were Makir's brother, I'd deck me.

When I'd found his door wide open earlier and the scent of two males on him, I lost my shit. I knew I'd gone overboard, dousing Makir in my smell. He now reeked of me, but I loved it.

I should've listened to JayJay when he told me to bring my 'puppy doojies' to help me relax. Charz and Pika were having so much fun with Sully's younglings that I hadn't dared take them with me, fearing they would give me evil looks for the rest of my life.

Instead of a short walk to the open kitchen where the dining table was, it was a torturous slog. As if my legs were mired in mud and plodding through a never-ending tunnel. Makir's grip on my sweaty palm was the only thing grounding me.

Much larger than his brother, Bonic approached us from the long dining table. With his lips pressed into a straight line and his stride purposeful, getting a read on him was difficult.

"He's not as scary as he looks. Try not to worry," Makir whispered in my ear as his tail wound around my calf.

Bonic bowed and then rose to his full height. "You must be the male who has changed my brother's eyes?" His lavender eyes scanned me from head to toe.

Makir's grip loosened in mine, and his gaze focused on the floor. My forehead wrinkled in question.

Why is he talking about the color of Makir's eyes like that?

His brother towered over me. Despite his regal bearing, I was still more embarrassed than afraid of him. As I wiped a sweaty palm down the dark fabric of my pants, I wished I'd asked Makir a lot more about his family. The lack of a heads-up that I might have to bow seemed like an enormous oversight on Makir's part at this stage of the game.

My head dipped forward, and I tucked one arm behind my back and the other around my stomach while I leaned my body toward Bonic in what I hoped resembled a bow. I forced myself to not roll my arm in a flourish.

"I'm pleased to make your acquaintance." Then I repeated the gesture and greeting toward Jast. When I rose, I placed my hand on Makir's back, kneading out the tension I found there in hopes of drawing his eyes off the floor.

Jast lowered her chin toward me. "I, Jast Tuniga, lifemate of Bonic Tuniga, happily meet you, Archbuilder Geo."

Okay, that wasn't so bad.

Raz's voice rattled. "Archbuilder, anyone who knows-s-s anything about Lornians knows that a true mate has been found when their eyes turn from silver to lavender."

My blood boiled at Raz's pompous voice. *Why is this jackass here? And how the hell did he know so much about Lornian culture?*

Now that Raz mentioned it, I hadn't seen the silver in Makir's eyes since the night he'd rescued me after falling off a cliff. But I ignored what *true mate* might mean and leveled my gaze at Raz instead. "What are you doing here?"

"I am a gues-s-st of the High Commander of the Elite Protectors of Lorne." His tail smacked the polished floor where he sat with authority, as if he believed his presence was welcome in Makir's home. The home *I'd* built.

Makir whined beside me, distressed. I straightened my shoulders and turned away from Raz, cupping my hand around Makir's neck and forcing myself to concentrate on what was important. After showing zero restraint earlier, I needed to be on my best behavior in front of Bonic and Jast.

Bonic's jaw tightened, and his gaze snapped between Makir, Raz and me. He opened his mouth, but before he could say anything, Jast ran her hand down his whipping tail and lifted her brows in a 'you're not in charge here' look.

"Makir speaks highly of you, Bonic." I pulled out an empty chair for Makir and gestured for him to sit before taking the one beside him. *I am perfectly capable of ignoring Raz and being polite.* "Why don't we all sit?"

On a deep inhale, I gathered my nerves. "Please accept my sincere apology for my inappropriate behavior with Makir. It was inexcusable." Makir's rigid posture relaxed beside me as I addressed my poor conduct.

Bonic ignored Raz's snort. "Four alphas and an unmated omega...it's to be expected." He brushed off my apology with a wave of his hand, and the tight collar of my shirt loosened a bit.

"Four?"

"My guard, Janny, is currently doing laps in Makir's pool."

His brother came with a guard? I squeezed Makir's knee, steadying myself. Though woefully unprepared for this meeting, I could work with the few things I'd learned. "I've heard many stories about your childhood adventures trapping bush-tailed monties."

Makir turned toward his brother and Jast. The eagerness in his voice blunted Raz's presence. "I hope there's time to take you out trapping linobee. The same snaring technique we used as younglings seems to work. And, Jast, you'll love the hot springs."

I nodded at Jast, hoping it would appeal to her. "Is hot water okay for pregnant Lornians?" It might be enjoyable for her if she didn't stay in too long.

A smile tipped her lips. "That sounds wonderful, Makir, and you must join us, Geo."

Makir breathed a sigh of relief, and I thought I might have just scraped the surface of saving face after my barbaric entry.

"Makir, why don't we make arrangements for this trip tomorrow at first sun?" Bonic said.

"That's perfect." Makir scraped his chair back and rose, and I followed behind him into the kitchen, a little lost. "Dinner will be just a moment longer."

"Smells good in here, little lion." My words were soft as I ran my hand up his tail. The mixture of mantu and fresh herbs lingered in the air, and my mouth watered. I wished we were alone so I could lean into Makir and tell him about my day wrestling hot water under the idiot mayor's direction.

"It's D'irk's recipe." Makir brushed his fingers down my throat, and a soft purr drew me closer as images of the last time we'd had D'irk's recipe freeze-framed in my brain.

Jast sighed. "You two are the cutest. The grand omega's sure to see a connection."

I stole a piece of mantu from the platter Makir was preparing. "Who's the grand omega?"

The disdain in Raz's voice prickled every nerve under my skin. "Only the most important omega on Lorne."

Makir shook his head at me when I opened my mouth to reply, and he placed a large platter of herbed mantu in my hands. "She's the true ruler of Tern. My parents are the regents and for the most part she lets them rule, but the grand omega has all the power. She and Bonic split responsibility. He handles everything security related."

What the ever-loving fuck? Makir was royalty? "Why didn't you say anything?" I stared at him, dumbfounded. I'd thought we'd gotten closer. My stomach bottomed out as if my feet had been swept out from beneath me.

"This looks divine." Jast took the platter from me and placed it in the middle of the concrete tabletop. Frowning at Raz, she cupped my elbow for a moment. "She communes with the goddess Sola and her wisdom is sought by all Lornians, not just omegas. One of the many gifts she has been blessed with is her ability to see true mates."

Her genuine smile helped ease my tension as Makir dodged my questioning looks. I took a second to appreciate the differences in the first female Lornian I'd met. Jast's fur was the color of the sky on Earth, and she was slender like Makir, about my height. Her baby bump stood prominent against her thin frame. Straight blue hair framed her face rather than Makir's messy mane. It happened to be in a neat braid today, but a few strands had worked loose while I'd claimed him. They softened his high cheekbones. His brother favored a top knot, with the remainder shaved to a short buzz, and he wore a dark navy uniform with boots so polished they must have been spit shined.

"When is your baby"—I corrected myself—"youngling due?"

Makir placed the sliced hiscus he'd marinated alongside a fragrant oil to dredge the crusty loaves of graneth bread through.

Raz cleared his throat and punctuated it with a dramatic tail slap. "Are we going to ignore the fact that the archbuilder stormed in here, was unspeakably rude to Makir and then proceeded to"—he waved his tiny arms in front of him—"claim

Makir in the bedroom. Where we could all hear, I might add. Then, as if that weren't enough, has the audacity to slight the high commander and his mate with an uncivilized introduction."

Bonic began to rise, but Jast placed a hand on his arm.

The table appeared to grow larger before me as if I was shrinking under the weight of Raz's words. It was as if I'd consumed a drink-me potion and spiraled down a rabbit hole. Sweat dampened my shirt, and Raz's voice pounded like nails piercing my skull.

Shame overwhelmed me. I'd botched foreign customs. I didn't know shit all about Makir's family and I'd behaved like a wild animal unable to control my lust.

Makir's whimper forced me to unclench my jaw and take a deep breath. I willed the table to return to its normal size. Everyone stared, lips pursed.

Raz placed his taloned hand on Makir's shoulder. "Nothing to say, Archbuilder? You're unworthy of a Lornian omega."

Makir nearly jumped into my lap to get away from Raz. Anger pumped through my blood and rushed through my veins. To hell with the shame rolling through me. I may have been ignorant, but I wasn't a dick. I dug deeper into the simmering rage, honing it to a sharp point and directing it at Raz.

When Makir's focus remained on his feet and his tail stayed wrapped around him in distress, it stoked the fire in my blood higher. Fuck, I hated when he reacted that way to anything, but it was ten times worse coming from this useless Lizzard. Makir was the spark of life meant to bring joy to a room, and here he was, diminished in his own home by this crocodile-lipped dick.

Well, fuck that.

Bonic's jaw tightened, and Jast forced a smile onto her face as she passed the food around the table.

Raz's voice rattled higher and higher as his indignation built like a politician controlling a room. "Plus, are you willing to disregard the fact that he appears to have no idea that he has initiated a formal mating bond with one of the heirs to the High Hold of Lorne?"

Makir whined, and he sank deeper into his chair.

Enough is enough.

My chair skidded over the floor and fell with an abrupt thud when I stood. I loomed over Raz, who still sat at the table with his long jaw tipped up and his arrogant eyes flashing. My fists clenched and unclenched, adrenaline pumping through me until the anger could no longer be contained.

"Raz!" My deep voice boomed, filling all the space in the room. "I have no idea how you weaseled your way into Makir's home, but I've told you on two other occasions not to even *think* about sharing Makir's space. Under any circumstances." On fire and fueled by rage, my cheeks heated and my biceps bulged. "Do you need a reminder?" I grabbed his collar and lifted.

Raz's feet shuffled underneath him as he tried to gain traction. "There would be consequences-s-s... Y-you said there would be consequences."

"Fucking right, I did."

I dragged a squealing and kicking Raz by the shirt collar and smashed him against the wall. My thick forearm pressed against his neck, and the heel of my boot mashed his tail into the concrete. The tip lashed like a limp noodle under my boot's weight.

"Elite Protector Tuniga," Raz coughed, "I beg you—" His plea went unanswered.

"Now, I don't want to offend my guests..." I may have been in Makir's home, but something deep inside had me treating Bonic and Jast as if they were *my* guests. When I turned my head to look over my shoulder, Jast and Makir were leaning into each other, tails linked, and Bonic sat at the table with his chin cradled in one hand, lips curled in a lazy smile.

My attention snapped back to Raz as his tail wriggled loose and snapped me in the hip.

"I demand to be treated with respect," the Lizzard wailed.

"Like the respect you've shown me?" With a quick shift backward for momentum, I launched my knee straight into his gut and flattened his tail once more under my boot. "As you've been ever so polite in pointing out the Tunigas' impressive lineage to ignorant little me, I'm willing to take this matter outside to settle. Is that respectful enough for you?"

Raz shook his head back and forth, his eyes watering. Held up by his throat and unable to speak, I took that as a no.

I turned my head for a moment, chasing Makir's whimper. Makir and Jast were huddled under his brother's arm, eyes pinned on me.

"Geo's got it, Makir, don't worry," Bonic said.

I winked at Makir before returning my attention to a begging Raz.

"I knew we could see eye to eye." I patted his green cheek, maintaining the chokehold I had him in, although my knuckles itched for more.

Bonic snickered in the background.

Ready to be rid of Makir's nosy neighbor, I hauled him, sputtering, to the door. With my elbow firmly locked on his windpipe, I opened the door and threw him into the cold night. His scaled tail knocked him in the face, and he landed on his ass in a puff of pink dirt.

"Now, lose this address. And by the way, you now hold the illustrious position of being the last name on my list for dwelling upgrades," I spat out after him.

I stood there a second longer, impervious to the icy cold that misted around me as my lungs heaved from the residual anger.

Raz scuttled away, one hand clutching his neck and the other rubbing his backside.

"Fucking bully," I said to his retreating back. "I hope you take the visitor shuttle back to your home planet and get sucked into a black hole."

The tether snapped and sizzled as Makir approached, and the heat from his body warmed me as he leaned into my side. Adrenaline still simmered in my veins, but when I looped my arm around his narrow waist and we faced each other, the gratitude that shone back at me weakened my knees.

Makir hitched a leg over my hip, and when I grasped it, he wrapped his other leg around me, clenching my thick waist. His thick purr melted the tension from my body. "That was amazing."

Thank fuck for that.

The last time I'd turned to rage had not gone well, but a lapful of pleased Makir was more than enough reward. The only thing better would be a taste. I dipped my tongue past his soft lips and sank into his embrace. This time, I sampled Makir's lips only long enough to remain in control. No matter how much Makir's purr called to me, I would not let my base urges take over.

"Let's go eat, little lion." I ran my hand down the blue velvet of his tail and lowered him. His pupils were blown, the lavender barely visible. I took his hand and tugged him back to the dining table.

Jast and Bonic stood as we neared. Bonic's slow, resounding clap filled the air, followed by Jast's. Makir beamed at me, and I stood taller.

"This one will do, Makir. This one will do just fine." Bonic smiled at his brother first, then me.

Even though I was confused by their easy acceptance of my outburst, my hands loosened at my sides, reassured by Bonic's words. Apparently, my alpha asshole tendencies were not something to be ashamed of in the High Hold of Lorne.

"It appears my charming brother may have left you in the dark about a few things." Bonic's deep laugh filled the dining area as Makir spooned herbed mantu onto my plate.

Yeah, no shit. Heir to the High Hold of Lorne... Initiated mating...

I filled a tumbler with my favorite whiskey—Ginger had brought me a bottle as a gift—and offered a glass to Bonic before taking a long draft. The heat warmed my throat, and I exhaled, sinking deeper into my chair.

Makir had some explaining to do. "Heir of the High Hold of Lorne?" The easiest question stirred in my mind.

"I planned on telling you..." Makir's shoulders curled inward. "But the right time never came. Plus, Bonic is the first heir. Now that Jast is having a youngling, there is very little chance the High Hold would ever come to me. Not over my parent's dead bodies anyway." His last words were so quiet I strained to hear them.

"Nonsense, Makir." Jast's sweet voice eased the tension in the air. I guessed that was her omega. "There will always be a special place for you in the High Hold of Lorne, and I already know you will be the favored uncle of this small one." She patted her belly.

"I'm the only uncle, sweet talker."

"Jast is right, Makir." Bonic's commanding voice softened. "I understood your need and supported your move to Tern. You have done very well for yourself." Bonic gestured to Makir's home and hovery. "But I wish every rotation for your return to Lorne. You have proven you can be independent. Our parents will welcome your return."

"You fool yourself, Bonic." Makir's tail wound around his calf, and his gaze fell to his plate. "The regents have never approved of anything I've done."

My heart clenched, saddened by his dejection, but panicked at the thought of Makir returning to his home planet. I'd never even considered it before. In a desperate move to change the topic, I pushed back my chair. The loud screech echoed through the room before I polished off my drink. Then, pouring another, I forced a smile. "Have you been able to take advantage of the pool? Why don't we bring our drinks out back, relax and get to know each other a little more?"

Jast's eyes crinkled at the corners. "That sounds wonderful, Geo. Why don't we all get changed and meet in the courtyard?"

I attempted to focus on the ingenious way the Rock Dwellers had created a dome from lamar panels. They'd transformed the courtyard into a year-round solarium. But the list of reasons why this relationship could never work kept growing. I tacked on 'he's royalty' right after 'I lose control around him all the time.' The number of things working against us weighed me down like an anchor tied to my ankle.

Makir was distant as we sipped our drinks in the shallow end of the warm pool. Time crept by as water lapped over our toes. The moon reflected in the water's surface, bright white and stark against the pool's red glow. Bonic and Jast took an inordinately long time to get their swimwear on.

"Makir..." My eyes fixed on a long scar on his muscled thigh. "Do you think you'll return to Lorne?" I had many questions for him, but I couldn't hold this one in any longer. It left me aching with an eerie aloneness, as if he were already gone.

I inhaled the solarium's humid heat, awaiting his response, my breaths growing shallower and shallower. The smell of the rich soil from all the plants filling the courtyard thickened the air. The silence grew suffocating.

"There's nothing for me on Lorne."

That didn't answer the question. "And here?" I turned toward Makir, my heart stuck in a holding pattern, on pause until he replied.

But my pleading eyes went unnoticed. Makir stared into the distance before he replied with a hollow, "I've made nothing but bad decisions my whole life when it comes to partners, Geo. I need to trust myself first."

My heart kickstarted with a heavy thud. His words were not the answer I'd hoped for, but at least they weren't Cameron's.

"Geo, I always knew you were delusional, but if you think I'll wait a year for your fat ass and small dick, think again."

I could work with Makir learning to trust himself.

I reached for his hand under the water. "If you can learn to swim, you can learn to trust yourself. I believe in you." I bit the inside of my cheek. "But more than anything...I want you to trust me."

His lips lifted in a smile.

24

I DIDN'T RECOGNIZE THE version of Geo standing outside his office this morning, but his unabashed happiness had me smiling to match his, and my heart soared.

"Hey, you, stud muffin, come here and give me some love." A female human with sleek silver-white hair and a black bangs laughed when Geo scooped her up effortlessly. Her tall boots lifted off the ground, and pink dust floated from his puppy doggies, who pawed at his legs. I couldn't help but notice the dark smudges under her eyes, but dismissed them. She'd spent the last two weeks on a space shuttle, and maybe it was an everyday look for humans. I only knew one other.

"Quit teasing me, Ging." Geo's cheeks glowed as he let Ginger down. Finally letting her go, he swept up his dogs next, and they bathed his face and beard with their little tongues. His eyes sparkled when he turned toward me, and the smile on his face grew even wider, sending my heart into a full gallop.

Ginger's hips swung as she sashayed toward me. *Is this how all Earth females look?* A cloud of something flowery enveloped me as she wrapped me in her arms. She was as tactile as an omega, and I immediately liked her. "I don't know what you've done to my friend, Makir, but I thank you from the bottom of my heart."

She would have had to be blind to not see the hearts in my eyes. If Geo had changed because of me, I'd changed even more so.

I shrugged. "There was nothing to do. He's always been great." I might've been pushing the truth a little, but making a good impression with the best friend was important.

"What's a stud muffin?" My lips pursed over the translator's images—a creature labeled 'horse' and what appeared to be some type of handheld bread. Neither reminded me of Geo.

Ginger laughed at the confusion that must have been clear on my face, throwing her head back just as JayJay exited the sono. He stilled with one foot outside and the other planted inside. Geo and I peered at JayJay, who appeared frozen by Ginger's laughter.

Ginger bent down to pat Charz and Pika, newly released from Geo's arms. "A stud muffin is a silly expression back on Earth that describes an attractive male with lots of muscles and the good looks to match." She glanced at JayJay, still in the entryway, then back to me. "Though technically, a stud is the finest male livestock used to breed females and produce strong offspring, and a muffin is a breakfast cake."

"English is a strange language." JayJay's deep voice rumbled. The dogs bounded toward him, and he crouched to greet them.

I tested Ginger's words. "Hey, stud muffin, come here and give me some love."

Geo prowled toward me, his hungry eyes eating me up. His alpha pheromones transformed the lighthearted moment. The muscles in his thighs bunched, drawing the fabric taut, and his strut had my tether zinging as he drew nearer.

The predatory look in his eyes turned my mouth dry, and I gulped. Fragrant warm summer fields mixed with Geo's fresh-from-the-shower scent engulfed me. I purred as Geo's cheeks flushed and his calloused hands wrapped around my wrist.

The dogs' piercing cries alerted me to the new arrivals, and I dragged my gaze away from Geo's and over my shoulder. Bonic and Jast were currently mesmerized by Charz and Pika's exuberant greeting.

Bonic brushed pink paw prints from his shins. "Enough of that, brother of mine." He glanced at where I still had my hands cinched in Geo's shirt. "Or else we will never make it on this adventure you and Geo have planned." Bonic's announcement caused Geo's cheeks to flush further.

Jast and Ginger stood to the side, smiling like fools.

Geo brushed the inside of my wrist, and his calloused thumb sent sparks through my body. I raised my eyebrow at him and forced myself to step away.

"Happy morning, brother." I rushed to my brother and Jast's side and wrapped my tail around their already joined ones.

"This is Ginger, Geo's friend visiting from Earth"— I gestured to them—"and JayJay, Geo's foreman."

Geo ushered Bonic and Jast toward the warehouse after greetings were exchanged. "Sully has loaned you his hoverbike for the day," he said. Sully and his family waved from the doorway. They'd come to the sono to visit their friends for the rotation.

Sully's younglings ran out to play with Pika and Charz, and laughter rang through the air.

"Are you sure you don't mind watching them for the day?" Geo asked Sully for what must have been the fifth time.

"You will be lucky if you get your puppy doggies back, Geo. Now go have your picnic." Sully gazed at Charz and Pika as they jumped in and out of the laps of his younglings, a fond expression on his face.

"Ginger, you're with JayJay," Geo said, and soon the hoverbikes were loaded with supplies.

I waved at Janny where he leaned against one of Makir's loaner bikes in the distance, nearby but never intruding.

"Why does he have a mask dangling around his neck?" Geo asked Bonic.

"Janny's an unmated alpha and an unmated omega in heat could trigger his rut. Wearing a mask is the best way to avoid messy conflicts. If he were a beta he wouldn't require one—they're less affected by alpha and omega pheromones."

I scuffed the ground with my toe. Guilt plagued me. All those nights Geo and I had chatted after swimming lessons, and I hadn't bothered to explain even the most basic nature of my people. I just hadn't wanted him to view me as some helpless omega. Now he had to suffer through a youngling crash course from my brother.

"So if I wear a mask around Makir, I'll be able to control myself?"

"I'm afraid it's too late for that." Bonic tried to hide his smile but lost it when he looked at a giggling Jast. "You wouldn't want that anyways."

Hadn't I shown Geo how much I loved it when he lost control? I knew just the way to ease him past his fixation, but my plans would have to wait. Ginger stopped at the hoverbike beside me, where JayJay strapped on supplies.

"You want me in front or in back, stud muffin?" Ginger tossed her hair over her shoulder. JayJay, usually the first to crack a joke, sat on his bike, frozen. Ginger ignored his lack of response and swung her leg over in front of him. "You're so big. I'm going to ride in front so I can see, 'kay?" When she turned back and patted JayJay's leg, his hands clenched as if he didn't know what to do with them.

Geo climbed on behind me. "What's that about?"

"I'm getting the impression there's a lot we don't know about JayJay." I engaged the ignition, waiting until everyone hovered near me, and then we flew toward the rocky outcrop. The sun warmed my face, and graneth grass mixed with other wispy yellow and green vegetation dotted the pink soil that whizzed by

.

Any jitters over a monster lurking under the ground were erased as Geo's arms wrapped around me. D'irk was convinced daylight would keep the sun-sensitive bastard at bay, and that was enough for me.

I parked my hoverbike next to JayJay's. He already leaned into the glassy ebony rocks, chanting in his low voice as he pressed a hand to the hot surface.

"Distant cousin?" Ginger teased JayJay. Strands of her hair ran over the back of his hand, disturbing his meditation. He stumbled as she turned to grab a backpack.

Geo approached JayJay. "Everything okay?"

"Ya ya, boss man." JayJay ducked his large bald head.

My eyes darted to where Ginger rifled through her bag out of earshot, and I passed Geo his water container before I asked JayJay, "Are you sure?"

"Bish, I've never met an Earth female before, is all." His rasping voice was a soft rumble.

"Well, she is something else." Geo smiled and tapped his friend on the elbow in a gesture of comfort.

Jast and Ginger admired the leg coverings I'd made for everyone as I passed out thick mantu hide gloves. Ginger oohed and ahhed over their quality and snapped a picture with her device before she laced them. As the group hiked through the jagged ebony shards of the rocky outcrop, Bonic hovered protectively over Jast.

Janny shadowed them, slipping on his mask now that he was nearer to me.

Jast slapped Bonic's hands away from her. "I'm no fragile flower, Bonic. I can walk on my own." She huffed. "Alphas, honestly."

"Say it again, girlfriend." Ginger tapped her knuckles to Jast's, Jast looped her elbow through Ginger's and they walked off, leaving Bonic trailing after them.

The full sun beamed through the glass-like rock, sending silver sabers of light into the sky. Stumbling across the hot spring with the enforcers on our full moon hunt had been a stroke of pure luck. The entrance was better guarded than the High Hold of Lorne.

"Makir…" Bonic's deep alpha voice reverberated through my spine. "How much farther?" Jast was back at his side, and the tip of his tail rested on her belly.

I dipped my head involuntarily, and Geo inserted himself, blocking me from my brother.

"We're past the worst." Geo answered for me, his voice deeper than usual, unknowingly clashing with Bonic's. "We'll go down from here." He tried to ease the tension coursing through me from my brother's overprotectiveness, but my emotions see-sawed like a toy balanced on a string.

"Blant, Ginger, get away from there." JayJay pulled Ginger away from the cliff that plummeted to the plateau below.

"Relax." She placed her hands on her hips and pointedly fixed her eyes on JayJay, then Bonic and finally Geo. "What is it with you men today?! I'm on another planet for the first time, and you think I'm not going to take advantage of this amazing vista?" Ginger continued muttering while JayJay shadowed her steps along the precipice like an elite protector on Lorne.

We wound down the trail to the plateau—Geo's palm on the small of my back, JayJay on Ginger's heels and Jast fighting against being carried. Janny was unnoticeable.

I needed to get some food into this crowd.

"This is the perfect spot for our picnic." I sighed happily. A warm breeze invited us to rest on the short grass cropped by the herds of mantu grazing in the distance. I spread out a red blanket and placed the graneth buns and roast mantu on it along with a jar of something called 'dill pickles' that Geo insisted on and the horrid smelling 'cheese' that Ginger had brought. Geo added a large skin bag of hiscus juice, and Jast set down a mysterious box.

Bonic's long legs stretched out in front of him, and the food before us quickly disappeared. "We may have to take some mantu back to Lorne with us. And imagine a family nest lined with linobee fur. What do you think, Jast?"

"Jast, what's in the box?" I interrupted. Curious, my tail whipped out, and Geo gathered it around his wrist, sending shivers deep into my belly.

She leaned forward from her cross-legged position and picked up the white package, giving it a little shake. "Ah, this?"

Geo laughed as she teased, and I nodded vigorously. She cleared her throat with a flourish. "I thought you might be missing a little something from Lorne." She lifted the lid and passed the parcel to me.

I sucked in a breath as my mouth watered. "Zilnas? Bless the Goddess Sola, Jast. You're officially my favorite sister-in-law ever!"

"I'm your only sister-in-law, Makir. Now pass them around." The tip of her tail vibrated happily.

"Absolutely not. These are mine. They can have the...cheese." I unwrapped my tail from Geo's wrist and hugged the box to me before popping three in my mouth, humming at the delicious sizzle.

Geo pulled me to his side a moment later, his voice gruff in my ear. "Stop it with the purring, or we'll need a private moment in the cave."

Zilna and a private moment in the cave sounded perfect to me, but we hadn't even arrived at the hot spring yet, so I stopped.

"Makir?" Ginger's fingers wiggled toward the box in question.

With a mock huff, I passed the treat around. "If you must." I leaned into Geo for a kiss and then popped one into his mouth when he least expected it.

His lips turned down in an adorable frown as he crunched through it. "These are...interesting."

"What is it?" Ginger poked the half-eaten snack in her palm.

"It's fermented zilna rolled in a rota coating," Bonic replied, one corner of his mouth turned up. "The better question is, what is zilna?"

I'd been present many times when Bonic had gifted this treat to foreign dignitaries. His typical decorum was replaced by the carefully concealed amusement he found in their varied, often disgusted expressions when he explained what the small brown balls were.

"Okay, hot shot, I'll bite." Ginger still chewed on hers, and by the way her nose twitched back and forth, she was undecided whether she liked it or not. "What's a zilna?"

Jast elbowed her husband as he sucked in a dramatic breath. Bonic grinned, the pleasure he took in drawing out the punchline evident. "Zilna, my lovely Earthlings and Rock Dweller, are the larvae of a hard-shelled black insect, a real blanting pest. The larvae are fermented in salt and their own juices and then covered in rota, which I've been told is similar to chocolate on Earth and cava on Yagras." Bonic pointed his chin in Ginger's and then JayJay's direction.

"Welp." Ginger swallowed. "I like to say I'll try anything once, and that was my once." She laughed.

JayJay could not keep his eyes off her. His treat melted on his fingers.

"What do you think, King Kong?" Ginger asked JayJay.

Rota dripped from JayJay's fingers into his lap. Woodskies swooped in the sky overhead, and the lowing of mantu filled the plateau. I leaned into Geo's side, my cheeks tight from the grin I held back as I waited for JayJay's response. Ginger smoothed her hand over her leg coverings. Jast cleared her throat.

"What?" Startled by JayJay's overloud voice, the woodskie that pecked in the grass near us took flight. He'd finally realized Ginger had asked him a question.

"The zilna..." She pointed to his pants, now smeared in rota. "Do you like it?"

He placed it in his mouth and licked his thumb. "I—it's fine."

"It's blanting better than dill pickles." Bonic's reply had everyone smiling, and the picnic was packed away.

"I liked the pickle," Jast said, smiling at Geo.

When Geo replied, his gushy smile filled me with joy. "It's universal—pregnant women and construction workers galaxy-wide love pickles."

"So, hot springs or trapping linobees?" I asked the group at large.

"I can't be with you in that hot spring, Makir. You smell too damn good." Geo's whisper thickened with lust as he nibbled the tip of my ear. "I'm going to try and redeem myself with the High Commander of the Elite Protectors of the High Hold of Lorne. Now that's a mouthful."

My shoulders rolled in as Geo's lips straightened into a tight line. *Blant, he's still upset I didn't tell him about my royal lineage.* I dropped my gaze in response to his displeasure.

At my reaction, he smoothed his calloused hand down my tail and smacked my ass. Then, he gave me a cheeky wink that ignited like wildfire in my groin before he strutted toward my brother.

"Ah...that would be hot spring all the way for this little lady." Ginger folded the blanket and placed it in her backpack.

"For this little lady too," Jast chimed in.

"Hot springs." JayJay's baritone voice carried a distinct reverence as he focused on the cave's entrance.

Bonic nodded at Janny and motioned for him to follow Jast.

"All right, alphas, enjoy your trapping, and we'll see you back here in"—I checked my wristport—"about two suns." I brushed my lips over Geo's before he left with my brother.

Though the light was dim, my keen eyesight tracked JayJay as he trailed his blocky fingers down the curved cavern wall leading us to the hot springs, his jaw slack. Janny remained at the entrance, his hulking shadow looming. The air grew hot and thick, weighed down with moisture and sulfur. JayJay's somber attitude quieted the girls, and my mind turned to Bonic's words.

"You have done very well for yourself. But I wish every rotation for your return to Lorne." My hovery was performing well. I had a beautiful dwelling. It appeared I could trade my linobee designs for enough mantu to never go hungry again. But, most importantly... My breath caught in my throat.

"I've found my mate." My quiet voice cracked like thunder in the dark, steamy tunnel. I had no desire to return to Lorne.

"Of course you have, Makir. I'm certain the grand omega would sanction your union." Jast reached for my elbow and wrapped her velvety hand around it. Her tail twisted around mine in a soothing gesture omegas practiced with close family. One I hadn't known I'd missed. My heart swelled.

I revered the grand omega, but with or without her blessing, I was certain Geo was my true mate.

The grand omega had been kinder to me as a youngling than my mother. The only thing omega about my mother was her ability to birth younglings, and even then, she was affronted by the submission that required. I'd rarely been touched growing up, and it went light-years in explaining how starved for affection I was and how badly that had worked out for me.

We walked deeper into the cave. "It feels so real now that I've said it aloud."

"Well, it's real to anyone who cares to see." Her tail squeezed.

"But he's not Lornian..." Whenever I thought I'd finally accepted it, the disbelief that my mate could be from off-planet surfaced again. Geo had sent me Dr. Ten's report findings. The evidence of compatibility was undeniable, but doubts lingered.

"Wow!" Ginger caught up to us, slipped off her leg coverings and shoes and dipped her pale toe into the spring. Her gaze was locked on JayJay's shoulders as he moved silently through the water. My lips twitched. Was she exclaiming over the hot spring or JayJay?

"Bless the goddess Sola." Jast's tail squeezed mine again as she scanned the chamber.

With no risk of drowning this time, my gaze caught on the long silvery ribbons draping the thick air and reflecting off the water. Sunlight beamed through the pinprick holes in the cave's ceiling.

JayJay sank into the deep pool before us. He hadn't made a peep the entire way down, but now a low vibrato resonated from his chest, and he swam through the water and into another chamber without a backward glance.

"Is he okay?" Ginger asked, folding and piling her clothes neatly on a rock beside her. "Do you think we should follow him?"

"He mentioned that the energy here reminds him of a sacred place his ancestors on Yagras went to for guidance. I think we should give him some space," I said.

"Yeah, you're probably right. His humming is so beautiful and soulful." Ginger walked into the warm water as if drawn toward JayJay. "It reminds me of the Tibetan Monks' horn back home."

I shrugged, but now wasn't the time to address language confusion.

"I'm not surprised by his connection—this is a special place. The goddess feels closer. Thank you for bringing us here." Jast took in the moisture that condensed on the stalagmites overhead, and the heavy beads that plipped into the pool with a slow drip, drip, drip, as mesmerizing as the center of a flame.

Ginger's attention turned to Jast as she reached for her hand. "Oh my God, look at your swimsuit. Come back out of the water for a moment." She plucked at the shimmery fabric of Jast's suit. "What is this? I must take a picture."

I chuckled as Ginger marveled over Jast's swimwear.

All was quiet except for the soft lap of water and JayJay's distant chanting as the three of us floated on our backs.

Ginger broke the silence. "So...what does being a mate mean to you, Makir?" She swam toward the wall, and I guided her and Jast to a stone shelf where we rested, submerged to our waists in healing waters.

As if she sensed my difficulty gathering words, Jast took the lead. "For Lornians, true mates are rare. When the bond is complete, it allows the free exchange of thoughts and emotions through a mental tether." The slow current swirled water around us. "One of the first external signs is the shift in eye color."

I swam toward the pool's center and trod water—something I would never have been able to do without Geo's help.

"I did everything in my power to remove myself from alphas. Who the blant would've guessed I might be compatible with a different species?" My voice rose in frustration, and I kicked the water beneath me as if I were fending off the giant ringa from home.

Ginger's forehead furrowed. "You don't want to be Geo's mate?"

"He doesn't know what it means to be mated to an omega. His erratic behavior is driving him crazy." My tail slashed through the water before my voice grew soft. "In no time, he'll tire of servicing me every full moon."

"So, tell him," she implored.

"He won't want to complete the bond with me." I sighed. Then, deflated, I said, "I'm broken."

"Now, there won't be any talk like that." Jast pulled me back beside her onto the bench. "There is more to an omega than the ability to bear young." She turned to Ginger. "Geo's behavior will settle as soon as they are fully bonded. All partially bonded Lornians are a nightmare."

"You can have children?" Ginger gasped, ignoring the comment about Geo's behavior normalizing.

"No." I hung my head, defeated.

Jast wrapped her tail around my shoulder and pulled my hand onto her hard stomach. "Makir was attacked by an alpha in his last heat on Lorne. The encounter left him...barren."

Her unborn youngling stirred under my palm and drew me out of my head. "I felt it." I stared at her distended stomach in wonder and held my hand over the wiggling mass. "Jast, you'll be an amazing mother. My brother is so incredibly fortunate to have found his true mate."

"I'm the lucky one," Jast said easily. "The youngling loves this water." Jast had both hands on her belly as she leaned against the cave wall, the perfect picture of contentment.

JayJay's deep rumble pulled me back to the real world. "It's been almost two suns." He tapped his wristport with a gray knuckle. "Let's return."

Jast, the only one smart enough to have brought a towel, loaned it to Ginger while I shook off. JayJay worked his wet limbs into his clothes before we followed him up the sloping tunnel.

Ginger fell into step beside me, her stance rigid. "Makir, I'm sorry if I was insensitive. I was so blown away that a man could bear children that I didn't listen to what Jast was saying." She nudged my shoulder. "I'm sorry that was taken from you." Her hand cupped mine. "He won't care, you know."

I met her soft eyes squinting in the dark, searching for the truth.

"He won't care that you can't have kids," she repeated quietly with a little smile. "Gay men on Earth can't have children with each other. If they want to be parents, they adopt, and most don't bother because it's so complicated." Ginger dropped back to walk with Jast.

He won't care, I thought to myself over and over again. Her words took root in my mind, and I reached for the tether between Geo and me.

25

H EAT RADIATED FROM THE sunbaked rocks, and I wiped my brow with a corner of my shirt while checking the last few snares with Bonic. Our time together passed in comfortable silence, but when I checked my wristport I realized our private time together was coming to an end. I wanted Bonic to understand how much I cared for his brother and that I wasn't an overbearing buffoon all the time.

"These will make a wonderful lining for our family nest. Jast will be pleased. Only the softest fabrics are used to cradle new lives, and these are among the softest I've ever felt." Bonic admired the brilliant white fur of the brace of linobee he'd trapped in the craggy rocks.

"Here"—I passed over my two linobee—"you might as well add these."

"Thank you. Our youngling will be very comfortable." He ran his large blue hand over the fur.

"Makir has enough linobee pelts to start a fashion line. They won't be missed." I chuckled.

Bonic nodded as he wound the snare wire up and handed it back to me.

"So, you and Makir are kind of a big deal?" Finesse was not one of my finer character traits.

Bonic's deep laugh echoed off all the jagged ebony surrounding us.

"Will you make Makir leave?" I blurted before he could respond. The question had been constantly on my mind since dinner yesterday.

Bonic secured the linobee to his brace. "You're a strange alpha. I've never met one so uncomfortable in his own skin. Why do you doubt my brother's love for you?"

Huh? That wasn't what I'd expected him to say. More like—'You're no match for my brother. He's worth ten of you.' My lack of ability to be a good alpha was what I doubted. And maybe my ability to hold Makir's interest as a lover.

Then the rest of his words wiped out every thought, blanketing my mind like an avalanche, turning everything arctic white. He thinks Makir loves me?

"Geo, are you coming?" How had he got so far ahead of me?

I stuffed our snaring supplies into the backpack so hard my fist almost drove through the bottom of the bag, then hustled to catch up. "That's because I'm not truly an alpha. I'm just a fat gay guy from Earth who's had one terrible relationship and happens to be good at building houses."

Shit, did I say that out loud? Heat rushed to my ears, and I ducked my head.

I searched for a reaction from Bonic's tail as he spoke. "You've got the tether, am I correct?" Except for when he wrapped it around Jast, Bonic's tail gave away no emotion, unlike Makir's.

After unscrewing the lid from my water bottle, I took a long drink. "I can sense him. It's like he's attached to me in some way. I found him when he was in trouble out here." I looped snare wire idly in and out of my fingers. "But it's more than that. I didn't just find him. I was driven to find him." Like my whole life's focus suddenly existed to ensure his safety.

"You're an alpha, whether you choose to believe it or not. You protected my brother from Raz. My brother's eyes have turned, and he now submits to you over me. The start of a true bond is in place. His song calls to you. When full, the tether will become stronger." His intense lavender eyes met mine, so different from his brother's soft looks. "Lornians search their whole life to find their true mates, and many settle for a lesser bond, which can be very fulfilling, but nothing compares to a true mate bond."

I followed Bonic through a narrow section of the trail.

"This is rare and should be cherished, not feared," he said. Bonic found shade under a flat rock and folded his long legs over the cool moss that grew there in springy curls. I ate up every word he said. "It's painful for true mates to be away from each other for extended periods." He unhooked a linobee from his belt and carefully scraped and prepared the pelt for travel. "You'll find that Makir will not want to be away from you, and you won't want to be away from him."

Yeah, no kidding.

"He won't return to Lorne without you." Bonic's lips flattened.

My heart floated like a helium balloon as I packed a layer of moss over the hide to help it cure. "Well, all that means is we'll have to visit Lorne when the youngling comes."

Bonic's shoulders relaxed, and the corner of his mouth tilted slightly. I'd said the right thing. With a quick movement, I rolled the treated linobee and placed it in my backpack.

The wind gusted, and the air grew heavy and ominous. Slivers of rock pitched and heaved as the ground shook, sending us to our knees. The tether snapped like a live wire. Makir's in danger. My heart leaped into my throat.

Bonic and I jumped to our feet in a flash. Vibrations rolled under us as we tripped and staggered, bolting toward our buzzing tethers. The quakes matched those from the last time the worm had surfaced. Chest heaving, I ignored the burning stitch in my side. The hot spring entrance was still much too far away. Makir...

"Fuck, they're underground," I shouted as chunks of rock snapped off around us and burst through the ground at odd angles below us.

They were in the worst possible place they could be. The tunnel could collapse at any moment. The tether tugged urgently, increasing the pounding of my heart. My lungs stung, searching for more air, and my legs strained as I ran faster than ever before. Idiot, why had I thought we would be safe? My alpha instincts to protect reeled. Once again, I'd failed Makir.

Bonic whipped around the sharp corner as if his life depended on it. I followed, practically on his heels. Linobee pelts smacked against his legs as he jumped the shards strewn across the path.

Pink dust filled my lungs, the displaced earth in the air choking me.

As abruptly as they'd started, the quakes stopped, and the monster grew quiet.

Why? Had it caught its prey?

Panicked, I reached for the tether hard, pouring all my desire and will for Makir to be alive and well into our bond. The message caught and held, and a sense of warmth spread throughout me.

A lifetime later, we arrived at the cave entrance, panting. My heart plummeted. An enormous boulder blocked their exit.

"Blant!"

"Fuck. They're trapped." Bent over with my hands on my knees, I sucked in air. Bonic's tail lashed beside him, and I straightened and laid a hand on his elbow. "We're getting them out of there."

His gaze never moved from the boulder, but his chin dipped, and his jaw clenched so tightly a crowbar might not have been able to pry words free.

"We're coming! Hang on!" I yelled, hoping Makir could hear and praying for his safety.

"We're all right." JayJay's booming voice, scarily muted, carried from inside the cave. The rock rolled slightly, then fell back again.

JayJay must have been trying to push it up and out. From the grassy plateau, the bastard worm shrieked an ear-piercing warning that chilled my bones.

"Follow me. I have an idea." I tore down the path to the plateau, scanning for the beast, but it must have retreated below ground. It was like déjà vu, only this time Bonic was in step beside me. "There." I pointed to the mantu rib cage I'd hoped would remain and exhaled a sigh of relief. "We should be able to use those as levers."

Bonic clasped my shoulder. "Good thinking."

The unwieldy bones jostled between us over the broken ground as we rushed back toward the entrance. Soon a long, curved bone was wedged under each side of the boulder blocking the entrance. "On the count of three." I tipped my chin toward Bonic.

Bonic's neat top knot had unraveled, and his long mane whipped at my cheeks. "JayJay...on three, heave," he shouted.

JayJay's muffled reply was barely audible.

In unison, we roared, "One... Two... Three..."

The gap grew, and JayJay's grunts of effort were music to my ears. My muscles bulged and my heels dug into the ground, but no purchase could be found. Before my feet skidded beneath me and the rock slipped back into place, Makir's panicked cry rang out. "Geo, I can't breathe."

He'll pass out if I don't get him out of there.

"Again," Bonic bellowed.

"One... Two... Three... Heave!" I shouted.

The long rib creaked and bent as I pried. Please don't snap, I begged.

The boulder gave way, and the relief flooding me left me lightheaded.

Thank you. Thank you. Thank you.

I was engulfed by a bundle of gingersnap and juniper as I marveled over how thankful I was that Makir had been trapped with an eight-foot Rock Dweller.

"Bless the goddess Sola, you're all right!" Tears ran down Makir's face. His lavender eyes overflowed with love. "You're hurt." He manically rolled my hands palm up and down, examining cuts I'd been unaware of, then drew a finger over a large gash in my pants. "What happened?"

I gulped. My heart hurt so much, but in the best of ways. No one had ever looked at me like that before.

"Shhh... I'm fine now. I've got you, little lion." My hands smoothed over his pointy ears, his hips, down the tip of his tail and over the zipper covering his protective pouch. "You're fine. We're fine." I pulled his face down to my chin and breathed deeply into his mane. The sounds around us slowly drifted in.

Ginger joined us, clinging to my elbow, her arm trembling, and I pressed her to my side until her knees grew solid in our huddle.

From our circle I watched as Jast reassured Bonic. "Yes, I'm positive I'm all right." Jast cupped Bonic's jaw. "The youngling's fine—feel for yourself." She gathered his hand in hers, and with their fingers intertwined, she placed his palm on her belly. "Janny hovered over me the entire time, just as you would've." She smiled at her guard, and Bonic slapped him on the back.

Ginger moved to stand behind a stiff JayJay and planted her hands on her hips. "Let's get the hell out of here. I don't want to be around when that screaming thing returns. It gives me the major creeps."

With Makir safe and his tail wound around my calf, my mind wandered. What I felt for Makir was uncontained. It escaped and spread like glitter, no matter how hard I tried to rein it in. My emotions were a force of their own whenever Makir came near. That was part of the problem. I hated the constant roller coaster. I didn't know how to alpha.

Would it mean behaving like some dude bro for the rest of our lives? Maybe Dr. Ten had a prescription for that. An anti-alpha medication. There must be something like that, right? But if it meant experiencing this kind of love...this adoration...this want to never be separated, then I'd do whatever it took.

Screw my plans for a construction company of my own on Earth. I was never leaving Makir's side.

Bonic's arms were wrapped around Jast, his hand splayed over their unborn youngling. She wasn't complaining about his fawning for once as he carried her over the sharp rocks back to the hoverbikes. Ginger was shaken but held up remarkably well, holding my hand as we navigated the churned ground. Makir's tail was wrapped around my wrist, and JayJay's jovial personality was nowhere to be found as he marched through the rocky outcrop like a Rock Dweller on a mission. Janny took up the rear scanning for danger.

A shriek rent the air. Like a thunderbolt, the crack sent a flight of woodskies into the air as we reached the miraculously unharmed hoverbikes. The monster worm's message was loud and clear.

I'm still here.

JayJay grew unnaturally still, almost haunted. "Hellsna." His lawnmower-like voice rang out. He had everyone's attention. "That thing—you named it a worm monster—it's a 'hellsna.' We fight them on my home planet Yagras. I'd recognize that scream anywhere."

Makir's tail unwound from my waist and leashed my wrist, cuffing our hands together.

"You used to fight those things?" I gasped.

"JayJay, if you would come with me to visit Mayor Yurst before my departure regarding this matter, I would be in your debt." Bonic's authoritative voice coaxed a reluctant agreement from the giant Rock Dweller.

"I'm glad you know what we're dealing with and all, King Kong"—Ginger let go of my hand and strode to JayJay—"but can we get the hell out of here?" She tugged on his rigid arm and pulled him to his hoverbike.

At the private departure lounge the next morning, I wiped a stray tear from Makir's cheek and pulled him closer to my side. One hand drifted up and down his rib cage, the other waved goodbye to Bonic and Jast as they passed through the final security checkpoint with Janny on their heels.

Bonic turned back for a minute, lashing his tail. "Mayor Yurst is about as competent as a batsa, but the message was driven home. He will take action. You have nothing to fear with JayJay in your arsenal."

Makir rushed toward the gate for one last goodbye. "I'll miss you." Their tails spiraled together.

"Me too, brother."

"Best of luck with the delivery," I called out as Jast brushed away her tears.

I embraced Makir as Jast and Bonic departed through the gate. Through the tether, I sensed a hollowing in Makir's heart. His sadness ate at me until it became unbearable. I would do whatever I could to erase it.

My palm smoothed over Makir's long spine. "What's a batsa?"

His tears turned to a choked laugh. "It's like the putty a youngling plays with. It forms into balls and long rolls and whatever shape you wish."

"Ah, Play-Doh." I stood in front of him and brushed my thumb over the skin under one blurred lavender eye. "That sounds about right." I chuckled, then smiled up at him with a depth of emotion I couldn't quite place, but it left my heart a little less empty. I hoped he felt it too. "We can go and visit them any time you want. I can't handle you so sad."

He swallowed hard and nodded.

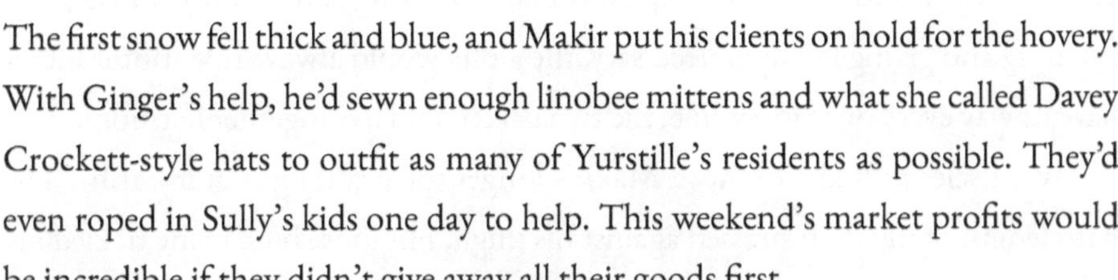

The first snow fell thick and blue, and Makir put his clients on hold for the hovery. With Ginger's help, he'd sewn enough linobee mittens and what she called Davey Crockett-style hats to outfit as many of Yurstille's residents as possible. They'd even roped in Sully's kids one day to help. This weekend's market profits would be incredible if they didn't give away all their goods first.

I found them sitting together—Makir's messy blue hair mingled with Ginger's silvery-white—consulting on a new pattern on the long concrete dining table I'd built. Dusk's sunrays glowed over the entire scene. Charz and Pika lay in the nest Makir had made for them after they'd taken over his. They were crashed out under the table in it. The kitchen air was rich with the scent of roast chicken, and saliva pooled in my mouth at the savory aroma. My heart filled with a sense of domestic bliss that was entirely new to me.

What if this could be mine forever?

"Smells good in here." My entire front crowded Makir's bent form at the table, and I nuzzled into the place on his neck where the fresh juniper scent concentrated, hardening instantly. His fragrance grew more appetizing each day. "I'm hungry," I growled, licking into that delicious spot.

Makir whimpered.

I was likely pumping out alpha pheromones, but when Makir smiled like that, some other part of me took over.

"Woah, Nelly." Ginger fanned herself with her hand.

"We'll be back in a minute." The deepness of my voice surprised me.

Makir squealed as I scooped one arm under his long legs, the other supporting his neck, carrying him bridal style to his room. Our room. Then, shoving my embarrassment down deep at having Ginger see me like that, I nudged the trailing dogs out of our space and closed the door with my foot. I recognized the signs now, and when the alpha took over, he was in charge.

Stop being embarrassed about it and accept it.

That was what D'irk had said, anyway. In our talk, he'd made it clear that treating Makir the way I had over dinner that night wasn't okay, but he understood I'd never learned to control my alpha. If I kept resisting and fighting it instead of listening and giving in when necessary, the alpha would always rule. But if I let it have its way every once in a while, the two parts could live together harmoniously.

My muscles pulsed with heat. Makir's longer torso was light in my arms. The hard length of my shaft pressed against his thigh. His loose blue mane tickled my hot cheeks, shooting sparks deep into my groin. His scent grew so enticing that I couldn't keep my mouth from his.

He purred softly as his mouth opened to mine, and our tongues intertwined. He tasted sweet and spicy, like hiscus juice and the zilna he hid in a secret stash somewhere in this room. Though I had no interest in his horrid snacks, I found it cute that he concealed them. His lavender irises swirled, drawing me in.

"Fuck, why do you smell so good, Makir? It makes me crazy." We slipped into his nest. Thank fuck he wore his hovic jumpsuit. My clumsy fingers only had to fumble over one zipper. Naked and aroused, I laid him on the white furs where our mixed scent lingered. My erection leaked as my nostrils flared in an attempt to inhale more of his scent.

"The full moon must be getting closer," Makir purred. His tail snapped back and forth in front of his pouch, drawing my eyes to where his long blue fingers reached in and teased the opening. My mouth watered as the tip of his cock popped in and out of the protective pocket.

"Thought you were hungry?" Makir teased. Moisture beaded on the blue tip. He smeared it around with his thumb. I could already taste his gingery juniper musk. "Are you going to come and get it?" Makir stretched out an arm, highlighting the solid ropy muscle, and held his thumb toward me. "Or are you going to stare at me all rotation?" His scent, a flicker of his sweet smile and his purr all called to me like a thousand sirens.

"Little lion," I rumbled, "I can't think when you do stuff like that."

Makir licked his thumb. "You know what I love?" he purred. "When you don't think. When you lose your tight grip on control."

After stripping out of my overalls lightning fast, I straddled Makir, my soft belly hugging his pouch. My lips dipped toward his outstretched hand, eager to suck his thumb into my mouth. I savored every morsel before releasing it with an audible pop. Then, I licked my lips and stared into his mesmerizing eyes. "Tastes fucking amazing."

I sat back and swatted Makir's hand away from where his fingers were running up and down his dick, then reached into his warm pouch, pulling him all the way out so I could hold what was mine.

"Give me that." I trailed my work-roughened fingertip down his length and tugged his tine gently. His slender spine arched, and another bead of liquid freed itself.

I grunted when Makir grabbed my ass and spread my cheeks. He was much stronger than his lean body suggested.

The shift put us close enough for him to wrap his long blue fingers around our stiff lengths. Mine short and fat, his long and blue, we fit together perfectly. My mushroom head plumped, and the lip rubbed over the bump on Makir's cock. So slippery with our juices, his tine hit the rim of my head with each pass. I wouldn't last long.

I bent forward and painted a long line up his throat with my tongue. His velvety fur changed to smooth skin, and I chased his mouth. At last, our lips found each other and clung, and Makir increased the pace, fisting our cocks, sending me to the edge and hovering. His song filled me.

Makir's tail reached behind me, and the soft, fluffy tip tickled the sparse hairs on my balls. The suction buried inside the fluffy tip zinged over my balls with every kissing clasp and release.

"I need more. I want you inside of me." My voice sounded harsh to my own ears.

"You want me inside of *you*?" Makir repeated, dumbfounded, as he walked his tail's suction back, baby step by baby step, until my cock leaked all over his pouch and the slide and drag between our cocks had me panting.

"Yes, now! I don't want to cum like this. Want you inside." I put as much alpha influence into my voice as I could.

"But I've never done that, Geo. I should've told you—" He shuddered as I palmed his cock. "I thought you knew."

I mouthed the tendon up the side of his neck until I met his ear and exhaled hotly. "But do you want to?" With deft fingers, I plucked his tine. "Wanna see what this feels like in me."

Makir gulped, and I chased his slender throat with my tongue. "I want to." His voice was so low I might not have heard it if he hadn't lifted my chin to meet his steady gaze. I bit and licked at him, eager to deepen our connection.

"Like this." I pulled the base of his tail closer and rubbed the puckered hole under his tail with two fingers, gathering some of the waxy slick. Then I leaned back into the furs and spread my legs wide before grabbing my knees.

Makir stared, and his tail stilled.

When I inserted two lubed fingers into my hole, Makir's eyes widened. The suction of his tail met my wrinkled pucker as if on instinct, and the combination had me writhing. A frisson of heat vibrated through me, sending me to a higher frequency, and—

"Not yet," I begged. "Closer." I hooked my heel around the curve of Makir's ass until his hips were cradled between my spread legs. The wet heat from his dripping cock slid over my hole.

Makir squeezed his eyes closed, and I began to doubt myself. Was I pressuring him? Had I used my alpha influence to sway him?

I pulled his rigid body up onto my chest and lowered my legs. "Hey, I'm sorry." One hand smoothed down the long curve of his spine. "We don't have to if you don't want."

His stiff cock gently rocked into my belly, making my toes curl.

"Really, I meant it when I said you can say no. This isn't just about me." His tail softened as I ran it through my fingers.

Makir lifted his head from where he nuzzled my armpit and met my eyes. "I want it so bad, Geo, but when I tried with Reinik, well, he..." Tears blurred his beautiful lavender irises.

"Shhh..." I knuckled away his tears. "I suspected you'd been hurt before, but it'll never be like that again, I promise." Anger brewed deep in my gut, but I threaded my fingers through Makir's mane and dug deep to find calm. Now was not the time to release the rage boiling under my skin. This was about Makir trusting himself. Trusting that whatever he wanted was valuable. "Follow your instincts, Makir." I squirmed my hand between our stomachs and squeezed his flagging cock.

His lips met mine, and he kissed me so softly I thought I might melt. "You're the best thing that's ever happened to me."

I squeezed my eyes shut, wanting to hold the syrupy sweetness running through me inside forever. If you only knew.

Makir's long cock prodded at my hole, and he eased through the tight ring so slowly that every muscle clenched, waiting for release. "Just like that, little lion." I grunted.

He placed his palms on my bent knees and leaned into me, driving deeper. "This is incredible." His arms trembled as he held still above me, eyes filled with wonder.

I jerked when his tine met my prostate. "Right there," I gasped. My knees clasped his waist as his balls touched my skin, and I worked myself against his fleshy protrusion. "Oh God, don't move."

"I thought this was about what I wanted." His eyes sparkled as he sped up his thrusts, rocking into me in a perfect rhythm.

"Not going to last." My legs were already starting to seize, a sure sign that this would be over sooner than I wanted.

I shifted onto my elbows, took one of Makir's pale blue nipples between my teeth, and bit down. He jerked against me, shouting, "Geo!"

"Makir," I cried in unison as his warmth flooded me and ribbons of my cum splashed his torso—a perfect blue sky streaked with jet streams.

The tether hummed, loose and sated.

"Can we do that again? Did you like it?" Makir lowered his gaze and turned away.

"The evidence is on your chest. I more than liked that," I growled, turning his face back to mine and kissing him fiercely. "That tail of yours is nothing short of magic, and your tine, I have no fucking words for."

His smile blinded me before he mashed his lips to mine in a graceless kiss.

He's let his guard down at last. *I've got you, little lion, all of you, every single part.*

I held him until the world around me came into focus. The dogs scratched at the door manically. Music blared from the kitchen, and the mouthwatering aroma of roasting chicken sent my stomach rumbling.

I untangled myself from Makir and walked to the bathroom, returning after cleaning up with a warmed washcloth. Naked, I crouched behind Makir, setting him in the V of my legs, and dabbed him clean. I needed a minute to come up with the words that were just out of my grasp.

"Makir, I'm coming to terms with it. I really"—I cleared my throat—"like you, and I want you to do what you want when we're, ah..." I gulped. "Together like this."

Like him? You mean love him! Find your words, asshole. Coming to terms with it? Jesus... It doesn't get much more romantic than that. Just tell him you don't want to lose control. You don't know how to be an alpha—yet.

"Okay..." He met my eyes. "I like you too?"

"Are you ready?" I switched gears, failing once again at expressing myself.

"I'm ready for everything with you, Geo." The depth of truth in his voice turned my mouth dry, and my thumb rubbed vigorously up and down his tail.

"Um...I meant to head to the kitchen and get reamed by Ginger." My cheeks grew hot, and I swallowed hard.

His eyes flickered uncertainly, but he still linked his fingers with mine and pulled us to our feet. "Let's get dressed."

26

WIND BLEW THROUGH THE sliding doors into my bedroom, stirring the leaves of the plants that had been brought inside. Even though it was now cold, I liked to leave it open a crack, enjoying the freshness it left in the air. But I didn't like the gust that slammed the door behind us or the way I jumped as we walked down the hall. Like the door was sending me a message straight from Geo's heart as he shut down again. After his heartfelt but strange declaration of liking me, I was more confused than ever. I'd made it abundantly clear that I was ready for everything with him.

And what had I got in reply? Nothing!

Blant, it sucked to be an omega almost in heat, driven by the full moon.

Why couldn't my mind lead the way instead of my hormones?

I was Geo's shadow as he walked toward the kitchen, still in awe that he had wanted to submit to me in that way. My parents would disagree, but generally speaking, my decisions were sound. When my omega needs took over, I was at their mercy and life tended to turn upside down. Without a complete bond, the insatiable lust and need to breed left me at the whim of an alpha who could fill me with their cock. It didn't matter if they were a low-life criminal or my father's best friend. Although, they ranked the same in my experience.

Geo ignored his puppy doggies bouncing around his feet. He needed space. But I couldn't separate from him. I needed to touch him and, more importantly, have him touch me.

When we entered the kitchen, Ginger turned down the music and slow-clapped before rolling her hand in front of her as she bowed. Any embarrassment caused by my actions as an omega had dissolved long ago. Ginger's teasing would only rub one of us the wrong way, and the target sucked his stomach in and squared his shoulders.

"Warn a girl next time there's going to be a performance, and I'll sell some tickets." She leaned her hip against the counter where she'd been preparing vegetables.

"Yeah, yeah." Geo's cheeks flushed. His chest would be hot and lovely under my fingertips. He cleared his throat. "Let me help." He opened the oven, and out came the roast chicken. He placed it on a serving dish while I stayed on his heels, flustered. An omega required reassurance from their alpha.

"If only Cameron had been a fly on the wall for that show." She laughed.

Geo tensed, and I wound my tail around his waist.

"What a player." Ginger rolled her eyes. "Did I tell you he asked to move back into your house with me after you left? As if!" She snickered with disbelief. "Money problems."

She winked at me over Geo's shoulder, forcing me to suck in a surprised breath. "I'm so happy for you. Makir is wonderful. You truly are a stud muffin." She slapped Geo's ass, and he shoved her shoulder gently. The tension popped like a bubble.

Geo placed a fork and knife next to the chicken and carved it. "Fuck...why was I so hung up on that guy? He wouldn't even watch Charz and Pika." Geo's gaze lifted, knife suspended, caressing me with his eyes. "Now, I know what having everything means."

I swallowed the knot in my throat and clung to Geo's waist with my tail.

Judging by Geo's contented expression, the remains of the first of many roast chickens lay before us.

"I'm stuffed." It tasted remarkably similar to the prized Nu on Lorne, an underwater creature made popular by the regents and even more rare because of it. I patted my full tummy and squeezed Geo's thigh with my hand as he reloaded his plate. "We should sit in the hot pool this evening."

"Yes, let's..." Ginger paused. "Shit, my bag is back at the sono. I'm not going anywhere in the dark with giant-ass worms on the loose." She frowned, shivering at the blue snow drifts piled against Raz's dwelling, visible in the silvery moonglow through the lamar.

Geo picked up his plate and gathered Ginger's and mine, taking them to the kitchen. "That was too close of a call." Geo's gaze met mine. "I hope Mayor Yurst has a plan."

"Yurstille is far enough away from the rocky outcrop that we don't have to worry." The quaver in my voice had Ginger's eyebrows rising.

"Anyway," Geo said to Ginger. "I thought you might want to stay here for the rest of your time on Tern. It's awfully crowded in the archbuilder's sono." Geo's gaze snapped to mine, brow raised as if to say 'is that okay?' before he lowered the dishes into the sink.

"Of course. I should've offered as soon as my brother left." I spun to face Ginger. "Think of all the mittens and hats we'll be able to make before the market if you stay."

Geo's shoulders relaxed as he turned on the water to wash up.

"I'll stay too." Geo's alpha voice hit low in my stomach. "To keep Ginger company." Still facing the sink, his back stiffened. "Shit," he muttered. A spike of pain rippled along the tether, and he

held his finger up before pinching it.

My chair skidded backward as I darted to where Geo stood. Bright red blood dripped through the soap bubbles into the sink, turning them pink.

"I've got you," Ginger yelled as she jogged to the bathroom. Cupboard doors slammed from down the hall.

"I'm fine." Geo pressed the edges of his cut together with his thumb as I leaned into him. His heat calmed me. "Just a dummy, that's all." His pale green eyes met mine, full of apologies that had nothing to do with his injuries. I reached for his finger, taking hold of it with the lightest touch and blowing on it.

My tail unwound from where it hugged Geo's waist and rose between us. "Let me take care of this." His gaze consumed mine, finger long forgotten.

"Where the hell are your Band-Aids, Makir?" Ginger called from the bathroom.

Band-Aids?

The fluffy tip of my tail parted, exposing the suction pad hidden within. It latched on to Geo's throbbing wound, sending pulses of healing energy. The tether lit up with sparks of joy, contentment and...love? The sensations shuddered through me, and another thick strand wrapped around our temporary bond, strengthening the connection.

"Fuck, that's amazing." Geo's pupils dilated. "What are you doing to me?"

His thick arm warmed my waist, pulling me closer. I pressed my lips to his. His mouth tasted of spice, roast chicken and the whiskey he loved. I whimpered at the closeness, the vibration of the healing energy weaving between us, knitting us tight together.

"Well." Ginger huffed, flicking her long straight hair over her shoulder. "Here." She held out a small sticky length of fabric that definitely hadn't come from my bathroom. "I thought it would be a bloodbath out here, but you're lip-locked instead." She emptied the water in the sink and refilled it. "Must have been a near-death experience."

Under Ginger's curious gaze, my tail dropped away from his finger.

Her brow wrinkled. "Honestly." She shook her head and pushed Geo away from the sink. "Let me finish up here before you cut your finger off altogether."

Blant, I shouldn't have done that. My hands trembled as they kneaded my tail. It was understandable to heal someone when unconscious, but healing a non-life-threatening cut was off-limits. Not to mention that Geo had been perfectly aware, and Ginger had been just down the hall. Bonic would have my head. Every Lornian youngling knew by heart that this precious gift required secrecy.

Geo waved his finger in front of him in awe. "That's incredible." His voice dipped low so Ginger wouldn't catch it. "How did you do that?"

"It must not have been as bad as you thought." I brushed his question off with a false smile.

"You can trust me, you know. I'm good with secrets." Geo's voice rang with sincerity, and I tipped my head to the side. His lips were pressed into a thin line, but he threaded his warm, calloused fingers through mine, and his rough palm sent shivers along my tail. The perfect mix of hard and heart.

Not ready to disclose anything, I tried to distract him. "Why don't we com JayJay and ask if he can bring over Ginger's things? You can't see when it's dark." I squeezed his hand. "And you need your stuff too, since you need to keep Ginger company."

I teased him, but my heart swelled. Despite his want, he couldn't outright say he wanted to stay with me. The next few weeks spent with Geo would be a dream come true. Maybe I'd convince him to stay when Ginger returned to Earth.

"Let me show you your room." I pulled the drying towel from her hand and reluctantly unwound my tail from Geo before we walked to my guest room.

The space was bright and cozy. A nest of linobee furs filled one corner next to an oversized chair, and a shelf stood beside it with a couple of books Jast and Bonic had brought me. "You won't be able to read these." I ran a finger over their spines. "But there are some spectacular pictures of Lorne if you're interested in my planet."

The books, combined with the picture Jast had commed earlier, weighed down my heart. The blanket she'd made from the pelts of the linobee Bonic and Geo had trapped was spread over her pregnant belly in the image. 'With gratitude and love,' the sweet message addressed to Geo and me had read. A wave of longing swept through me.

Charz and Pika nudged my ankles, wanting to be picked up, and Ginger nudged my shoulder. I needed to mention the shadows under her eyes to Geo.

Ginger flopped into the nest. "I've wanted to know what it's like to sleep in a cloud of furs. Thanks for letting me stay."

A knock at the front door interrupted my melancholy. JayJay's deep laugh filled the dwelling as he teased Geo for his poor night vision.

The laughter abruptly stopped when Ginger and I entered the front hall, and she walked toward him to retrieve her bag. "Thanks, JayJay. You want to come for a swim?"

JayJay stood and stared, his silence thickening the air, and then he belted out a resounding, "No."

Ginger shrugged, the open expression she usually wore replaced with an out-of-character blank one. I'd worn a mask for most of my life, so hers was easy to identify. She nonchalantly turned away from him to take her stuff to her room.

"So, you won't be staying at the sono anymore?" JayJay asked her retreating back in his overloud voice.

She turned to look over her shoulder. "Probably not. Makir and I are trying to make as many—"

JayJay cut her off with an abrupt, "That's good." He shuffled his feet awkwardly, then stared only at Ginger before his sharp "Bye" echoed throughout the dwelling. An avalanche of snow slid from the roof as the door slammed behind him.

Ginger's knuckles turned white where she gripped her bag. "Is something wrong with my translator?" She tapped behind her ear. "Everything I say around that guy, he takes the wrong way," she mumbled. "I'm going to go change into my swimsuit. I could use a glass of that hiscus wine, Makir, if you have any more?" She whistled for the dogs to follow her.

"JayJay won't like it when I suggest he see Dr. Ten about Rock Dweller and human compatibility." Geo burst out laughing as he pushed me toward the bedroom. "Go get changed. I can't be in a room alone with you right now. You smell too damn good."

He was on to something, though. JayJay's personality turned upside down whenever Ginger neared.

Moonglow on the blue drifts collecting on the panes of lamar overhead turned everything into a purple oasis beneath. The rippling water shadow-danced against the pink walls of my dwelling.

"You should stay, Ging." Geo was easy to read right now. His broad shoulders were propped along the tub's edge—one hand petting Charz, fast asleep beside him, and the other arm a comfortable weight on my shoulder. His tummy was relaxed.

Ginger sighed as she sank into the smaller, hotter pool and sipped her glass of hiscus wine.

"Oh my gosh," she gushed. "I think I love Tern."

"Mayor Yurst is recruiting women. Do I need to ply you with brochures?" Geo's deep laugh warmed my insides.

"Watch what you ask for, you may just get it." Ginger finished off her container of wine and sank deeper into the warm water. "I plied Geo with brochures for years, hoping he would accept a position. And he finally did, even if it is for just a year."

Just a year? My heart started to race.

The evening passed in easy conversation between Ginger and Geo. Meanwhile, I was on the edge of my seat, wondering what would happen when Geo's contract ended. Certainly, Yurst would offer him another. Everyone loved the dwellings he and his team were building.

But would he stay?

For the next three rotations, I woke blissfully content. Geo's warm body pressed against my back, and my nest smelled of summer fields. My dwelling was filled with a comfort that had been absent my entire life in the High Hold of Tuniga. Geo prepared coffee from Earth each morning and delivered a warm mug to me where I lingered in my furs. His attention was addictive, but when the caffeine hit, so did the revelation that Geo might leave Tern. Every time it was like a fresh jolt shocking my nervous system.

The morning of the market, the sun shone bright and clear. The mist from our breath crystalized in the cold air, and white clouds formed while we piled my hoverbike trailer high with furs.

"One minute." Ginger reached to grab a hat and mittens from the top. "I'm keeping these." She tucked her hair behind her ears and pulled the hat over her head. Its white fur contrasted sharply with her black bangs.

My wristport dinged. Incoming vid com: High Regent Tuniga.

Geo grabbed a hat and tightened the flaps around my ears, leaning forward to kiss my nose.

My cheeks bunched so tight they hurt.

"Blant, it's my father." My voice trembled, and Geo reached for my mittened hand. Why would my father be contacting me? He had not even bid me farewell when I left Lorne, emphasizing how little my departure would mean to him or my mother.

With a swipe of my finger, I picked up the com. My tail frantically beat the snow around me. Was Bonic okay? And Jast? Oh, bless the goddess Sola—was it the youngling? "Father?"

My father's angular jaw had just started to purple with age, but he could not be mistaken for anything but royalty. With his face projected in the air, he held his chin high and his eyes pierced me with expectation. His thin lips were pressed into a straight line, sealing in his unvoiced words. Nothing new. He was always stoic.

Ginger sucked in a breath, awed as she and Geo glimpsed the projection of my father. For some reason, he wore his official crown, and the formal high collar embroidered with a giant ringa—a beast from Lornian folklore—screamed business. I stepped to the side, concealing them from my father's view.

Blant, I hated these lessons. Every conversation with my father was a guessing game. What does he want me to say? I inhaled till my ribs ached—get yourself together—while my tail kicked up snow drifts behind me.

"High Regent Tuniga." I bowed my head. "To what do I owe the honor of this call?"

Is that adequate?

"You are formally summoned to return to Lorne for your nephew's naming." His eyebrows pinched, a small tell that he was doing something distasteful. "My personal shuttle will arrive in Yurstille tomorrow. Prepare for your departure." He reached to end the call.

I blew out a breath, surprised to discover his alpha voice no longer compelled me to do his bidding.

"Wait, Father…" I gulped. "The youngling's time is not for three weeks. How is Jast's health?"

"You will refrain from addressing me as father." His jaw clenched as he spat out the words. Disdain bled through his usually emotionless voice. "The youngling has come early. Also, I expect you to be attired in an official capacity. You can leave that ridiculous head cover behind." The com ended with the same abruptness it had begun.

It's nice to see you too, Father. I'm doing great. Thanks for asking.

My tail swooshed off the ground, showering snow and hugged my waist. "I need to com my brother and make sure everything's all right." My hands shook so much that I couldn't correctly hit the commands on my wristport.

Geo tugged me into his side, settling my jangling nerves, and he typed in the request for a vid com to Bonic. Moments later, my brother's happy smile appeared in front of us, and I collapsed into Geo's side, exhaling a huge lungful of air.

"Congratulations, brother!"

"Congratulations!" Geo and Ginger shouted.

"How are Jast and the youngling?"

"They are well and resting happily in our nest." Bonic beamed. "How did you know? It's only been a short time." His eyes narrowed. "Ah, Father commed you. Mother's going on about the naming ceremony and how the advisers are outraged that the High Lord Tuniga will not be present. Apparently, he has buckled under the pressure." He snorted distastefully.

"He has commanded my return," I said quietly.

"Although Father's being Father and forcing you, I'm happy you will be present. I know you'll love my son with all your heart no matter where you live." A newborn cried in the background. "I must be off now." Chest forward, he ended the com, a new father with a purpose.

"Congratulations, Uncle." Ginger hugged me. "Or should I say High Lord Tuniga?" She placed her hands on her hips and shook her head. "Off-planet for the first time, and I meet royalty too. I wondered about Janny. You certainly have moved up in the world, Geo." She wandered away to get more furs from the dwelling, muttering, "That Jast is going to get an earful from me. I spent two days with her, yet not a single mention of royalty. Hmmm...I wonder what the market might have for a royal baby?"

"She's a bit of a galactic storm, isn't she?" I reached for Geo's hand and chuckled at Ginger's tendency to drift from topic to topic in a heartbeat. "Hard to keep up with her." Then my smile dropped. No matter how much I wanted to meet my nephew, I had no desire to return to Lorne.

Geo turned to face me and pulled my forehead down to his. "Hey, are you okay?" His mitts slid over my bulky jacket in a soothing gesture. "That was a lot."

"Yeah." I'd not fully digested the conversations yet. "I'm an uncle, Geo." Then I straightened my shoulders.

"Yeah, little lion, you are." Geo kissed the tip of my cold nose again.

"My father's alpha voice has no power over me any longer."

He clasped both of my mitted hands. "That's a good thing, right?"

I nodded, my words stuck in my throat.

Geo's alpha voice wrapped around me like a warm blanket, and my nose filled with summer fields on a crisp snowy morning. "Here is what we'll do. You and Ginger will sell your mittens and hats. We'll get gifts for the baby and your family"—he swung my arms a little—"and make a plan for the dogs and Ginger. It'll be fine."

It'll be fine...

Blant, it wouldn't be fine. My parents would never accept an off-worlder as a potential mate. Geo can't come. My heat was nearly on me. It would be absolute agony without him. He has to come. I could handle my parents' wrath, but I couldn't handle the abuse they'd rain down on Geo. He has to stay here.

With the cold season upon Tern, the bustling market had migrated indoors. The windows of a giant greendwelling, operated by a couple of enforcers as a side project, dripped with condensation, and the potted plants we walked through spiced the air with their exotic scents. Ginger carried my beat-up duffel bag loaded with hats and mittens. While we unloaded our goods, my mind remained unsettled, plagued by indecision.

Everyone shed their warm outer clothes as they met the steamy inside air. I wished I could shed the doubts about my trip to Lorne so easily. Thankfully, Ginger took on most of the transactions. My sole purpose diminished to plastering on smiles in response to customers eager to purchase our dwindling supply of hats and mittens.

Ginger answered another question about her hair as she sat beside me. Most of Yurstille's residents had never encountered a female from Earth before, and they were curious. JayJay loomed nearby like a silent guard, awkwardly out of speaking distance, but noisy in his presence. And Geo had disappeared amid the masses, but the tether would lead me to him if needed.

My com port dinged with a message.

Bonic: Talk to Geo and prepare him.

That didn't help one bit. My deliberation paused when Geo returned. His presence eased my jumbled nerves. He tucked a few packages under the table, and one of the chicks Ginger had brought from Earth at Geo's request pecked at the strings tied around the parcels.

The chicks had caused quite the stir, running freely, but once they were determined to be no threat, the enforcers' entrepreneurial side had taken over, and they charged for handfuls of graneth seed that could be strewn across the floor to feed them. TeyTey and Sully's boys were their best customers.

Geo stood behind me. "Wait until those chickens are old enough to lay eggs, then we'll see some profits, and I can buy the High Lord Tuniga whatever he desires." His warm palms spread across my shoulders, and he dug his thumbs into my tense muscles. The wonderful contact turned my insides to mush.

Geo had never mentioned my position before, or that I might be the one left wanting in our relationship. Doesn't he know I don't care about money? I just wanted him to stay.

I looked over my shoulder. "You have been everything I desire from the moment you followed me into the wastelands. I don't require more than that."

He blushed, staring at his boots as if they were made of sul, Lorne's most precious metal.

Ayla Rowtee's presence returned my attention to the table of items before me. She stood fascinated, white feathers fluttering, staring at our goods. "That's lovely." She pointed at Ginger's creation.

Ginger demonstrated the holder she'd worked on between customers throughout the rotation. "If I may." She approached Tarik, Ayla's husband, with a long swath of fur. "You want to loop the opening around your shoulder and place the baby in the little pocket. Fur side would be best for this weather, but in the summer, the fur side out will be cooler." Ginger gestured for Ayla to place her youngling in the fur wrap hanging around Tarik's neck. The happy youngling nestled in and promptly fell asleep, and the proud father was sold.

"We'll take it," said Tarik.

"Wonderful," Ginger exclaimed. "I'll make you your very own sling. This one's a gift for Makir's new nephew." She smiled at me.

My heart hiccuped. "Not even my parents would criticize such a fine gift. Thank you, Ginger."

She straightened her already straight bangs with her palm. "You're welcome."

Tarik's beak clacked, and the youngling stirred in the holder, picking up on her father's agitation.

I spread a few furs in front of the new father. "Tarik, you must select the best linobee for your sling," I soothed, sensing Tarik's frustration.

Ayla tipped her head my way in gratitude as I smoothed Tarik's ruffled feathers. It wasn't just Lornian fathers who coveted what they felt their younglings needed. The only saving grace was that I happened to be close enough with the Rowtees to have been at their youngling's naming ceremony. I could get away with anything after helping Geo install lamar openings for their nursery.

The market's busy hum quieted as the day came to an end and we stacked packages of dried mantu skewers and bottles of hiscus wine onto the back of my trailer. At the same time, Ginger compiled all the custom orders she'd collected after we sold out. While securing the packages with straps, I silently debated whether Geo should stay or if he should come. He was not prepared to meet my parents.

I'm not, either.

By the time evening came around, I'd succumbed to emotional exhaustion.

"Come here, little lion," Geo rumbled from my nest, though, with each passing rotation, our nest seemed more appropriate. He lay on top of the furs in the second-skin shorts he wore as underclothes. I loved that he didn't suck in his belly anymore.

I stripped off the jumpsuit I wore every rotation even though I hadn't been in my hovery much this week and climbed in beside him, forcing away visions of the stuffy formal clothing I'd soon be in. The ones I'd left behind forever. I purred as I ran my fingers through the coarse fur on his chest and the trail on his relaxed belly.

"You're tired, Makir," Geo growled low.

The effects of my purr prickled his skin with goose bumps, and I soon drowned in his pheromones. He slipped his arm under my side and grasped my ass, effort-lessly positioning me on top of him like a blanket. I luxuriated in his heat as his calloused palm smoothed up and down my spine and tail, lulling me to sleep.

27

M Y MOUTH WATERED AS Makir's house filled with the dark, bitter aroma of my favorite coffee. I mentally thanked Ginger for the case every time I took a sip. She'd saved me from the sludgy javae.

Over steaming mugs, she reassured me that everything was under control. "Of course you have to be with Makir for his visit home." She reached over the table to rest her hand on mine. "You'll only be gone a few days. It's fine. Quit worrying."

Makir needed to be my main focus, one that would continue forever if I had any say in the matter. I predicted that the arrival of High Regent Tuniga's shuttle would not allow for a leisurely sleep-in this morning, but I hoped luck would be on our side and we'd be the only passengers on board to ease Makir's worries.

A loud knock rattled the front door, drawing my eye. Ginger opened it, revealing two alpha males, marked by their wide stances, confident bearings and my desire to slam the door in their pretty faces.

A Lornian, no taller than me, clicked the heels of his tall laced-up boots together. "We've come to escort High Lord Tuniga home."

This is his home.

Our bags were already waiting in the entryway. First thing this morning, I'd organized everything when I slipped away from under Makir's long warm body.

Ginger squatted to settle the dogs. "Would you like to come in for a cup of coffee while you wait?"

The taller of the two nodded a friendly greeting toward Ginger as I sat at the dining room table, saying, "Is that what I smell? Seems like the perfect thing to keep me awake. We've had a very early start." He winked while crouching to pet Charz and Pika as Ginger had done the moment before. "What are these creatures?"

Leave it to my dogs to break the ice.

The older Lornian escort stiffened behind the first. "The High Regent has declared time is of the essence." The disdain on his face amplified his frown as he shook his leg free from Pika jumping on him.

Ignoring the men, I carried a graneth puff spread with peanut butter, a glass of hiscus juice and a mug of coffee to our room. I paused, basking in the peacefulness. Makir lay curled on his side, buried in linobee pelts. His lashes appeared longer in his sleep, and both hands were tucked under his chin. In a perfect world, I would linger here forever, but Makir would want to get ready, so I woke him with a kiss on his forehead.

"Your father's men are here, little lion."

He purred softly as his eyes drifted open. "Geo?" My name dripped like molten lava from his tongue, and the sound beckoned me to crawl right back into his nest of furs.

The next moment, he shot out of the bed and threw on his jumpsuit, naked underneath. "They're here!" Not bothering to guide him into anything different, I ran my hands down his arms to soothe him. There would be time to change into appropriate clothes on the shuttle.

"Sit. Drink and eat." My low voice forced his submission. "They can wait." And when the graneth puff was gone, I beamed, pleased with myself for finally figuring out when to turn on the alpha and trust my instincts.

He dusted the crumbs from his jumpsuit and twisted his hair into a knot on his head. "I'm ready now."

I couldn't stop myself from leaning into his luscious lips, stained a deep plum from the hiscus juice, for a long kiss before we left our quiet sanctuary.

"Makir!" The taller Lornian reached for Makir and hugged him, and I prowled toward them. "I haven't seen you since Hovercraft Flight Academy. How have you—" His nostrils flared. "You smell enticing." The tall man's alpha voice rumbled and his nose dipped to Makir's collarbone.

"Wen. It's good to see you, friend." Makir ducked out of his embrace and closer to me, eyeing me carefully. "Bonic was thoughtful to have sent you." He dipped his chin toward Wen. "Geo and I have a bond. I'm no longer an available omega."

The other Lornian's gaze jumped to Makir's lavender eyes, while he fingered the giant ringa embroidered on the high collar of his uniform, and a frown twisted his lips. "The regents will be displeased." Then he stood tall, formality replacing indignation. "High Lord Tuniga." He offered a shallow bow as an afterthought.

Makir's juniper fragrance flavored the air, attempting to calm the alpha energy that permeated the room. Instead of feeling soothed, my skin grew prickly and itchy.

"Ginger, Geo, this is Wen, Bonic's second in command, and Tunt, one of my father's personal guards." He motioned toward the Lornians with a long sweep of his arm. "Wen, Tunt, meet Geo and his best friend, Ginger."

"Enough of these pleasantries," Tunt barked, unaffected by Makir's attempts to project serenity. "We will be on our way at once."

Wen picked up the bags by the door and moved outside. "Tunt, you're out of line. You'll treat the High Lord Tuniga with the respect he's due."

"This is not off to a good start." Makir's tail smacked the floor as he yanked on his boots. His glassy eyes found mine when he stood, and his fingers trembled.

Ginger fanned her hand in front of her flushed cheeks. "Mamacita, there's more testosterone in this room than a whole chain of Gold's Gyms." She hugged Makir and passed him the wrapped sling for the baby. "Good luck. You'll be back before you know it." Her smile was full of encouragement. "Take care of him, stud muffin." Another hug for me, and she pushed us out the door while wrangling the dogs in, shivering from the cold draft.

I faced Makir and buttoned his wide-open coat against the biting wind. Fresh tracks lingered behind us as we walked to the docking port in the newly fallen snow.

"Wait, the wine..." Makir turned back.

"Packed." I pressed my lips together and held in my grin.

"Oh, and the jerky..." He turned around again.

"Got it." I soothed my hand up his tail, and he shivered.

"What about..." He pulled away again.

When Makir wouldn't settle, I hugged him and trailed a finger down his pointed ear, warm beneath his furred hat. "Everything's taken care of."

The increased traffic flattened the snow, and the path grew icy as it led to the spaceport. Loud with construction, the spaceport hummed with energy. Makir's forehead beaded with sweat, and his fingers fumbled over the buttons of his coat. I guided him, my palm resting above his tail, toward the first security clearance, and he flung his jacket to the ground. Sheltered from the wind but by no means warm, I bent down and folded it over one arm.

A Tig worked the detector. The long hairs on the tawny ears topping her head flew around under the enormous overhead fan. She efficiently scanned Tunt and Wen's ident cards.

"Makir, back so soon." She smiled as Makir raised his wristport to her, the ident card embedded.

He dropped the gift in his arm that Ginger had passed him at the last minute. "Sisip's sister, right?" His voice wavered as he wiped the back of his hand over his sweaty brow.

She nodded. "Please proceed."

When the gate opened, I lifted my wristport, proceeded through and snapped Makir back to my side. "Everything'll be fine." I plucked the package from his hand before it unraveled from his fidgeting.

The back of his neck was slick when I placed my palm there. "Are you okay?"

"Not now, not now..." Makir clutched his stomach and shuddered. "Oh, bless the goddess Sola. I can't think." His tail fluttered behind him like a kite string full of ribbons.

"Finally." Tunt stamped his boots. "We can leave this frozen wasteland."

We wove through the private departure bay, and I barely had time to appreciate the liquid metal encased in the walls. The copper and aqua swirls repelled each other. That would make a fantastic floor.

Makir was leaning into me so hard I practically carried him. A small, dark shuttle emblazoned with a giant beast on the side came into view. Relief flooded me when there appeared to be no other crew besides Tunt and Wen. Makir was a wreck, and the fewer people around, the better. I needed to get his nerves settled.

The shuttle door closed, and Makir shuddered as he leaned more of his weight into me. He unzipped his jumpsuit, and I placed my hand to stop his as it reached his belly button, and he rubbed against me like a cat in heat.

Fuck! Why now?

In the confined space, his fragrant odor overpowered me. My knees grew weak, and our time together in the cave for his first heat returned to me. If my fingers were to dip into the crease between the firm globes of his ass, I guaranteed they would return slippery with his wax.

My muscles bunched and thickened. My shirt almost burst at the seams. The itch from earlier was nothing compared to the colossal need pounding its way free from under my skin. I pawed at Makir's exposed chest, where his jumpsuit gaped open.

Wen groaned, his nostrils flaring, and his tail stood stiffly upright. "Damn, you smell good, Makir."

My fingers latched on to Makir's zipper and dragged it up as he whimpered in my arms. "He's mine," I snarled, placing myself between the much taller Lornian and Makir, who I tucked behind me. Makir's arms clasped me from behind, and his lips nuzzled below my ear.

Wen may have been taller, but with my new alpha pheromones, I'd grown thicker and more muscled than most men on Earth. Even with a gut, I was no pushover. I could hold my own against the elite protector and any other who tried to claim my omega.

This incomplete bond is bullshit. Makir was my mate. He was mine for keeps.

Wen's nostrils flared as he took in more of Makir's heady scent as the small cabin filled with his mind-numbing flavor.

My cock stood at full attention, ready for duty.

"What's the holdup?" Tunt turned from the open cockpit door and assessed the situation. "Blant the goddess Sola." He stormed toward Wen. "Unmated alphas and blanting useless omegas in heat. They'll be the death of me. Where's your blanting mask?" Then, with a strength that shocked me, he dragged Wen into the cockpit, belted him into the seat, turned on the overhead ventilation and sealed the door before returning to us.

"Now listen up, Earthling." Tunt's lips curled in a snarl. "We need two of us to fly this shuttle, and an omega in a mating frenzy will not make me late, especially a broken one." He eyed Makir from head to toe.

"He's not fucking broken!" My hands turned to fists at my side as Makir undid his jumpsuit zipper once more.

"I can't stand the feel of it on my skin." He moaned, grinding his pelvis into my side.

I wanted to wring Tunt's neck as he snapped the fastening on his cuff together, likely offended that it would dare come undone.

Tunt's nose wrinkled. "As no unmated alpha of suitable rank is available to service this omega, and the High Regent will certainly not approve of you..."

Makir's purr sent sparks of desire up my spine while Tunt prattled on.

"I command you to refrain from touching the High Lord." Tunt brushed invisible lint from his uniform coat. "A suitable alpha will be made available to tend to his needs upon his return to Lorne."

The fuck he will. "That's Makir's choice now, isn't it?" My control fizzled, nerves snapping, wanting to both pummel this jackass and get Makir naked.

Tunt's stance grew rigid. "It's clear alphas from Earth know nothing of what an omega needs." He spun on his heel, strode to the crew access hatch and engaged it. Wen, now masked, lifted his hands in an apology from his co-pilot seat, clearly having heard the whole exchange.

The doors swished shut along with my ability to reason, and I spun to face Makir like he was the air I needed to breathe. Before I could question what had happened, Makir had unbuckled one of my overall straps and started on the next. He splayed his velvety blue fingers through my hair, nipping my ear, oblivious to Tunt's commands. My mind grew foggier and foggier by the second.

But one thing remained clear. If another alpha serviced Makir...it would result in their immediate death.

"Fuck, you smell good." Saliva pooled in my mouth as I unzipped the final stretch of his jumpsuit, and my knees dropped to the plush carpet.

"Up here. Now." Makir hauled me by the armpits and scrabbled to take off my clothes. After he unclasped the second buckle, my overalls dropped around my ankles. Purring, he led us to the long couch against the cabin's wall.

The cabin lurched. The far recesses of my brain registered that we must be taking off, and we should probably be strapped down. I wrapped one arm around Makir, and the other grasped a handhold dangling from the ceiling. Makir straddled my waist, his calves hooked behind where my heels jammed into the floor. We were as secure as my preoccupied brain could get while he pulled his erection free from his protective pouch and rubbed his hard length against my shorter, fatter one.

His tongue lashed against mine in desperation. Makir's mane was dark with sweat around his face, and his hot skin burned my fingertips.

He broke our kiss, his voice a deep purr. "Geo, I'm on fire. I need you."

Our cocks bumped together, sticky white webs clinging between them as they knocked and kissed each other.

One moment he sighed, "So good." And in the next, he whimpered, "Not enough, I'm burning up." His tail lashed against the carpet and rose, snapping like a lion tamer's whip in the air. "Need you inside."

Inside? Why didn't I want to go inside again?

I vaguely recalled that someone had hurt him, and I couldn't let the same thing happen again.

Makir licked my neck and inhaled deep drafts along my collarbone. My thighs clenched. He shifted to nip and lick the tops of my swollen pectoral muscles. I strained under his needy fingers as they pinched and pulled my nipples, and they stiffened to rocky peaks.

I massaged his velvety ass and grabbed one firm globe, then the other, opening him. The round muscles were like putty in my hands, and slippery wax leaked out. I squeezed the thick base of his tail. His cock tine ground into my soft tummy, painting a trail of pearly fluid over the coarse hairs as he let out the most delicious moan.

"Now, Geo." He flattened his tongue along my neck. "Inside me now. Everything hurts." His needy whimper called to me, and the tether flared with urgency. I barely registered his weight as I lifted him with one hand, circled my thick dick around his entrance, and stopped, reason returning.

"No, Makir. I can't. I won't hurt you like he did." I pumped my hand up and down his hot length, determined to relieve him. More waxy slick ran down the inside of his thigh. His tail coiled around my base as if he would drive my dick into him of his own accord.

"I'm in charge here." I pinched his tail until he released my thick erection.

"I need you, Geo, please. I'm begging you." He squirmed with desire as I held him above me, just out of reach. "It hurts so bad. Put it in me, please." He leaned forward, cooing in my ear, and sucked my lower lip into his mouth as if nursing from it. "I promise you won't hurt me."

"There are other ways, Makir." I fisted our erections together, dipping my hand lower to collect his waxy slick and returning with it to create a seamless glide.

"No..." he whined. "The only thing that eases the ache is your seed." He trembled in my lap, liquid eyes pleading before he squeezed them shut. "Please, Geo, I ache for you."

My conviction wavered. His distress was so great. "You promise to tell me if I'm hurting—"

"I promise." He rubbed his torso over mine, heat radiating like a furnace. His eyes flashed open, locking on mine, and he mouthed, *It hurts.*

"Unh..." I gripped the base of my cock and circled his slick entrance. One push breached the tight ring of his opening, and Makir's whine rang through the cabin loud and clear—a siren's song. Keeping him suspended above me with a palm on each cheek, I slowly eased the rest of the way in.

Makir's clasped my face, and his eyes rolled back as he tried to focus. "It doesn't hurt, Geo. It feels amazing. Only I need...more." He forced himself down until my balls slapped his fuzzy cheeks.

He started bouncing, setting a mind-boggling rhythm in and out of his greedy ring, squeezing my fat cock like a vice on each entry. The delirious need to devour him took over, and I swallowed all his needy cries with eager lips. Any reservations had evaporated into thin air.

"Geo, your lock," he pleaded. "Give me your lock. I need your seed. I'm so hot." His lavender eyes pierced straight to the essence of me. In all my life, I'd never known a connection like the one I had with Makir. The tether between us zinged, like the elation that takes over when you laugh so hard you start to cry.

My hand released the soft fur of his ass before I ran it up his spine to the nape of his neck and gently squeezed, letting him take control. At once, he swallowed my erection like a starved man. I rubbed and bumped over a rough patch deep inside him, my girth encased in his tight, slick channel.

His back arched—fuck, he's beautiful—and I memorized the perfect line of his body. I trailed my calloused fingers down his sternum and wrapped them around his long blue penis, joining his tail, already hard at work, slowly milking it. The rough patch he drove my erection against deep inside softened and opened.

I thought I'd imagined this part.

And then I slipped into heaven. My already engorged cockhead expanded inexplicably, swelling until it locked me inside. Inside of my mate.

"My mate," I growled.

Makir's undulations stopped, and he grasped my shoulders in a grip so firm it would bruise. He buried his face in my neck, and his reedy whine triggered my release. I sank deeper into the couch, pulling Makir even tighter to me as I released into him over and over, washing his womb with my cum. "Jesus Christ, that's good."

We dozed in our post-lust haze, the tether loose and sated between us, the urgency gone. The bond leaped like a child skipping down the sidewalk. Much too soon, my lock released, and a gush of our combined fluids forced my softened cock out.

"Oh, goddess Sola, that's a mess." Makir's head dipped, mortified. "But I feel so much better now." He kissed me on the cheek, shy and vulnerable.

His smile lit me up inside as if I'd won every prize at a carnival.

"Blant. Are we on my father's shuttle?" He scanned the shuttle's cabin and hopped off my lap, and I followed to where he opened a concealed bathroom door and ran a towel under the water. He wiped me down, not making eye contact, rinsed out the towel and then wiped himself clean. "You were supposed to stay on Tern." He admonished me halfheartedly, then pulled a comb out from a cabinet and quickly unsnarled his mane. His fingers trembled as he attempted a braid.

"Here, let me." I smoothed my fingers through his long mane. "I'm not about to let you face your parents alone." The alpha need to protect and control had dulled to a simmer for now, until the next wave of his mating frenzy would take over, but the need to care for him dominated my mind.

I sifted my fingers through his tangle-free locks, massaging his scalp and pulling a deep moan from him. Then I spun him around and bound his soft hair into a tight French braid.

I was thankful for the horrific show Ginger had been contracted to work on. There had been so many elaborate braids required to complement her costumes that I'd learned how to French braid so she didn't have to panic about it any longer.

I kissed his shoulder, admiring our reflection in the bathroom mirror. "You're beautiful."

Makir's shy eyes dipped away from me.

"Hey now, look at me, Makir," I rumbled softly.

The ship banked, preparing for descent.

My eyes sought Makir's. "Shit, how long do we have?"

"Not long enough. It will never be long enough. We must have gone through a worm hole to get through the Reiner System so quickly. We should have had more time." His frantic hands opened another concealed door, searching for something before he sighed in relief. "Thank you, Bonic." He kissed his knuckle—a gesture of thanks, I presumed—as he pulled out two formal-looking uniforms and pairs of high boots, passing one to me.

He pressed the stiff maroon fabric to my chest. "Quick, get dressed, and we might make it through this nightmare."

I was lacing my boots when the shuttle's landing gear descended.

"Here, let me see." Makir pulled me to standing, tucked a long swath of fabric around my back and knotted it before he wound a sash around my neck and over my shoulder. He patted my chest and stepped back to admire his handiwork. "Now, aren't you a handsome sight?"

Makir in his hovic jumpsuit full of grease was adorable, and Makir in a swimsuit was mind-melting, but the Makir that stood before me at this moment was every bit the High Lord Tuniga.

My heart swelled with pride that a man this kind and capable could be mine. He stood taller, more regal. His braided hair threw his cheekbones into sharp relief. The same beast insignia as on the shuttle marked his left shoulder above a long sleeve of badges. Surely they stood for all the outstanding accomplishments he had achieved on Lorne. I vowed to learn the meaning behind every single one of them.

We stood side by side, fingers laced, as the cockpit opened and the shuttle's exit door unlatched.

Tunt marched by us and engaged the mechanism to lower the ramp. "It reeks of sex in here." He tapped out a com on his wristport before the door had swooshed all the way open. "You did not heed my warning, human. The regents will hear of this."

"Do what you need to. I have nothing to hide." My eyes fixed on Tunt as Makir adjusted the sash crisscrossing my chest and beamed at me.

Wen, more reasonable since he had donned the facemask unmated alphas wore around omegas in heat, bowed to Makir and shook my hand before departing. "Congratulations, Lord Tuniga. I wish you and your mate the best."

Pheromones poured from me as I tried to ease Makir.

"Stop it." He swatted at me, purring, "You're going to trigger my next wave. We need to find a safe place for the next couple of days. My parents will be furious. Geo, please brace yourself."

"Hey..." I turned him to face me, pulling his lips down to mine and brushing over them. "No matter what happens, remember we can do anything as long as we do it together." Makir's lavender eyes sparkled, and the shared certainty of our near-complete union fused our tether into unbreakable steel.

28

United, Geo and I disembarked, my leaden feet rattling on the ramp's metal grate. Wind howled against the domed windows of the arrival's hangar, and lyre tree leaves the color of Geo's bruises slapped the roof angrily. The residents of the capital city, Navra, should've been tucked in their dwellings out of the storm. Instead, nearly all of Lorne stood gathered, awaiting their wayward lord.

Jast and Bonic were unsurprisingly absent, but my parents stood front and center, flanked on either side by their personal guards, minus Tunt, who stormed ahead of us on the ramp. A host of advisers fanned out behind the guards.

The thin thread of sanity I hung on to stretched taut and threatened to break as I struggled through each minute of fanfare. I glanced at Geo. "Here we go."

Hundreds of Lornians—alphas, betas and omegas, each with their tail linked to their neighbor's above their heads—bowed toward me. A gentle purr rose from the omegas, welcoming my return and warming my heart. They calmed the alphas in the cavernous space, and my shoulders relaxed bit by bit.

I swept my hand in front of me, and the hangar grew quiet. Even the howling wind cooperated. "Thank you, citizens of Lorne. You bring me great honor with your fine welcome." From the top of the shuttle ramp, my voice carried over the masses below. In my head, it quavered like a loose tooth.

Geo's shoulders rolled back, and he squeezed my hand. His obvious approval helped fortify me. His maroon uniform fit snugly over his broad shoulders, and even if I hadn't been in between waves of my heat, I wouldn't have been able to keep my hands off him. A long sash crisscrossed his barrel-shaped chest as an indication he was tied to the royal line. I shouldn't have been surprised by how well Lornian clothes suited him.

My father's face contorted in anger, one fist clenched at his side. His glare moved from my changed eyes to where my hand clasped Geo's. "You claim him as your mate. He's not Lornian!" The staff he always carried scraped across the metal floor of the port with the force he exerted. His roar was all alpha, and those who gathered quailed in submission.

My mother gripped my father's elbow. He would pay for his outburst with a bruise. I'd experienced her steely clutches more times than I cared to remember.

"Regent Tuniga, let us greet our long-lost son more privately." She leaned closer to one of her guards, who signaled for the elite protectors to disperse the crowd as she marched us toward the loading docks.

I obediently trudged between the guards with Geo at my side.

"Your father seems like an interesting guy." The absurdity of Geo's comment immediately dragged me from the pit I'd been stewing in.

It took me a second to compose myself before I dipped my mouth toward his ear. "Stop, you're going to make me laugh."

His cheek pulled to one side in a smile just for me. "And..." Then his face sobered. "Makir, I don't give a flying fuck what your parents think of me." His warm hand brushed down the gold-threaded seam on the spine of my jacket. "I'm here for you."

I bit my lip to hide my overflowing emotions. Never had I been so glad to have someone stand beside me and give me their support as in this moment. Geo doesn't care what my parents think.

Geo and I, along with my parents, a member of their guard and an elite protector, were ushered into a small, sparsely furnished room. A pile of fabric heaped in one corner urged me to make a nest.

My mother's nostrils flared. "You're in heat." She snorted as soon as the door closed. With a practiced motion, two unmated males in their entourage donned their masks.

No matter how much I wished it didn't, her disgust still crushed me when she showed no compassion for needs I had no control over. But I shouldn't have expected more. My mother was the least empathetic omega I'd ever known.

"Regents." I bowed toward my parents, one arm locked on my leg to stop the tremble. "May I present my true mate, Head Archbuilder of Tern, Geovani Natali."

Geo's hand tightened around mine—the only sign of his surprise over my knowing his full name. Had he thought I wouldn't quiz Ginger a little during our time together? My lips twitched.

Geo bowed. "Regents." His deep voice grounded me, but the greeting went unacknowledged by my parents.

My father's staff screeched across the floor before the sharp point was directed at Geo. "Under no circumstance will an omega from the Tuniga line ever be serviced by an off-worlder."

I cringed at my father's outburst. His lack of decorum bordered on cruelty, and was so unlike his typical stoic behavior. His disdain, always clear to me, usually had to be peeled back from under many layers for outsiders to glean the same knowledge.

Geo stood steadfast beside me as perspiration beaded my brow. I ignored my father's words, more worried about my mother than my blustering father, as she whispered to her guard, who slipped out the door a moment later.

What's she up to?

I addressed my parents with as much poise as I could gather, but my fluttering tail gave me away. "We're bonded. The tether's engaged."

I was moments away from losing all reason. A sharp pang nearly buckled my knees, and I clutched my cramping stomach. Geo turned to face me and loosened the buttons on the high collar at my neck. The heat bubbling beneath my skin turned unbearable.

My father's eyes narrowed to slits. "Tether? You lie. What a fool you take me for, High Lord Tuniga. Not even you would tether with an off-worlder." Disgust furrowed his brows as he spat out words of disbelief. "You have known from birth that no one of the royal line will ever be mated without a full bond—without evidence of true matehood."

Geo smoothed his cupped palm along my tail, coiling it around his wrist to stop its relentless lashing against the floor. "I would like to request privacy. Makir needs my attention. We would be happy to resume this conversation—"

The door to the small room burst open, and my mother's guard returned alongside another alpha.

"Ah, finally." My mother smoothed her palms over the front panel of her long skirt, chin held high.

I recoiled. Reinik.

All but climbing Geo, I turned to him to keep me safe. How could my parents be so...heartless?

Geo's firm grasp cuffed my wrists together. "Shhh…I've got you." He gathered me into his arms effortlessly.

Terror turned to desire as I lost focus and succumbed to my heat, shamelessly rubbing myself against Geo, trying to rid him of his handsome uniform. Why did it have so many damn buttons and ties? My womb clenched, and I blinked back the tears pooling in the corners of my eyes.

A small part of me was distantly aware of a conversation I could no longer participate in.

"Ah, my dear friend Reinik," my father addressed the new alpha in the room. The long scar Reinik had seemed to smirk at me from temple to chin where it distorted one side of his face. His cold, rapacious eyes had not left mine since his entrance.

Cradled in Geo's arms like a youngling hiding, I ignored the weight of Reinik's gaze. My legs dangled over Geo's muscled arm, my hands were bound, and I turned my nose to press against the spot behind his ear that smelled of summer fields. I was lost to need.

My father spoke to his closest friend, not caring that he had ruined my life. "Your timing is impeccable. High Lord Tuniga has worked himself into quite a state, and your shared past will allow you to fulfill his needs."

Geo's grip tightened uncomfortably. "Hold on, little lion. I need to take care of this." His deep voice rumbled, a balm to my jagged nerves, stirring the desire more.

My mother's tail stood high in the air beside her. "A fine choice to get him through his special time, my dear."

My father linked his arm with my mother's, claiming the decision to call upon Reinik as his own—a common practice.

Geo's warm summer field scent grew stronger. "Clear this room…now!" Geo growled. "Makir and I require privacy."

The tension in the room swelled to a thick, uncomfortable silence save for the hiss of forced air through the overhead vents.

Reinik advanced toward the corner of the room where Geo cradled me in his arms. "You have one thing correct, intruder." The scar across Reinik's face froze half his mouth, and his lips twisted in a familiar mangled sneer. "The room will be cleared immediately. Only I'll be the one doing the servicing." His eerie laugh sent cold shivers rolling through my body.

I wrestled my hands out of Geo's grip and placed them protectively over my stomach, shielding my womb from the remorseless male who had broken it. Chest heaving, my locked elbows trembled and my legs kicked out as Reinik moved to gather me in his arms.

"Now, now, sweet lord... I'm here for you. Quiet yourself." Reinik's tail wrapped tightly around my elbow. "I know you missed me. It will only be a second until I soothe your fears away."

Geo's growl had the hairs on my arms rising in a prickling warning. "That's close enough, asshole."

Geo's alpha voice rattled my bones and commanded the room. Even my father took a small step back. But Reinik continued to advance, caught in the thrall of my heat. In one swift move, Geo threw Reinik's tail to the ground, crouched low and nestled me softly among the old fabric, stale with disuse.

Geo twisted, releasing like an sprung coil. The heel of his hand shot into the soft underside of Reinik's chin. His head snapped back, sending a line of bloody saliva into the air, and my first heat partner roared and launched himself at Geo in a full-blown alpha rage.

An elite protector rushed from my parent's side.

"Leave them," my father commanded.

The fabric, though dusty, was soft and inviting. My need was so intense that I itched everywhere, and my clothes against my fevered skin were agony. They had to go. I wove my shirt into the dusty fabric of my nest, and my pants followed suit. They had Geo's scent on them, and my nest was one hundred percent improved.

The masked protector turned toward me, his shoulders hunched away from my parents' view. With an assessing gaze and tense shoulders, he typed a message into his com port.

After burrowing into the nest, my flaming skin finally freed from my itchy uniform, my gaze found Geo.

He moved like a dancer. His fluid bulk countered every move Reinik threw his way, stealing my breath. Arms overhead one minute, knees deeply bent the next, on his toes and twisting in the span of a breath, then pivoting as if second nature. He controlled the room and his opponent.

My heart drummed a longing beat. I was mesmerized, like a starbug to a flame.

Reinik lunged, ripping off Geo's Lornian sash, and maneuvered to wrap the long fabric around Geo's neck. His scar stretched as his face contorted into a smile sure to scare the most hardened criminal. "You think a mere human has a chance against me?" Reinik's maniacal laugh chilled me to the bone.

Geo had rid himself of his fine coat, but Reinik had torn the white high-collared shirt beneath. The shreds stuck to Geo's sweaty torso, plastered in damp patches over his swollen biceps. His muscles throbbed and bulged, and I couldn't keep my eyes off the round balls of his shoulders when he quickly reversed their positions and launched fists like hammers into Reinik's gut.

I wanted to collect the scent gathering in the fuzz between his blocky pectoral muscles with my tongue. The maroon sash floated to the ground like a white flag saturated in blood—peace never negotiated.

Hidden deep under the base desire of my heat was a sense of redemption so strong that the long-tattered pieces of my heart were being sewn back together. Geo was healing the fragments of me Reinik had so callously broken.

Geo caught my eye and roared. As if fueled by my red-hot need, he drove his knuckles into the skin above Reinik's eye. His long scar split wide, and blood dripped down his face, blinding him in one eye. My hero slammed the much taller Lornian to the wall and pinned him with one meaty hand around his neck. "Have you had enough?" Geo snarled.

Reinik's blue fur, purple with matted blood, showed a large bruise on the exposed skin of his stomach, his shirt long shredded. He panted, and his eyes drifted toward my father. "Regent Tuniga, I beg you to end this farce. Certainly, my prowess has been demonstrated."

Geo shook him, and Reinik's head slammed against the wall. "You will sub—"

Bonic burst through the door with the grand omega at his side.

My heart fluttered even as my hands kneaded my thighs. Bonic and the grand omega took in the scene: me naked in a pathetic nest, whimpering with need, Reinik pinned against the wall by Geo, and my parents—avid spectators—protected by their guard.

"Father, how could you let that"—Bonic balled his fist into his palm and squeezed—"creature near your son after what he did?"

My mother straightened the large amulet hanging from her neck. "How nice of you to join us, Bonic." She smiled politely. "I have no idea of what you speak. We only have one son in this room."

My father shuffled his feet, and his lips turned down as he dropped my mother's arm.

My newly fortified heart shielded me from my mother's harsh words, and my father's reaction buoyed me. Her crowning achievement had been birthing the high commander of the elite protectors. Her entire identity was wrapped up in my brother. She'd never gotten over the fact that she had also birthed an omega, the pinnacle of weakness, even though she was one herself. Over the years, her poison had infected my father, her omega sway only used to manipulate.

Bonic's stance grew rigid, regaining the staid composure rarely broken since he had taken on his role as High Protector. "Place Reinik in custody." Two elite protectors advanced at Bonic's command.

I fisted my sweaty hands around the nest's fabric. Would justice be served at last?

Geo growled, near animal, as the elite protectors attempted to pry Reinik from his death grip. He smashed an elbow into Janny's eye and swung his heaving body around before he slammed his heel into Wen's knee as they cornered him and endeavored to free my worst mistake.

"Geo, I will not allow him to go free. He'll be in my custody. Release him." Bonic's command went unheard, and he motioned for two more of his men. "Don't injure my brother's mate."

My mother hissed at my brother calling Geo my mate.

Mind muddled, stomach roiling in pain, waxy slick oozing down my leg, I could do nothing but burn up until Geo filled my needs. Wait...there was one thing. My gentle purr filled the room. Geo's ravenous gaze locked on me. The raging alpha settled, and Janny coaxed him to release his prey from his stranglehold.

Clutching his neck and choking, they marched Reinik toward the exit.

My mate bolted toward me.

The whole room shuffled or averted their gazes when the grand omega spoke.

"Evlyn..." Her disappointment, although directed at my mother, radiated through the room.

The grand omega rarely intervened, allowing my parents to rule Lorne on all matters outside of security, but that didn't change the fact that she had the final word.

"Makir is of your womb and is an omega in need." She ran knobby knuckles through a long purple mane threaded with silver that skimmed the floor as she walked toward me. "When it comes to your designation, you've turned your head and closed your eyes for long enough. Without omegas, there's no future in Lorne. I had high hopes your reign would be a strong voice advocating for omega rights, but the truth is I've gone far too long without righting your shortcomings."

Chagrined, my mother dipped her head, joining my father's already bowed one. The way his fist tapped the bulbous jeweled top of his staff clearly indicated his discomfort. My mother was the better actress though, her acquiescence likely temporary.

The grand omega lifted a graceful chin toward Bonic, but her words were for my parents. Combined, they were the true rulers of Lorne. "This will be rectified when I meet with your advisers new week." Although an omega, her omnipotent presence filled the room.

A wide grin spread across my brother's face. "Protector Sim, please escort Reinik to Station Eight. I understand they require people of his skill set to guard the imprisoned Snaks held there."

I gasped and whispered to Geo, who nuzzled at a spot under my ear. "Station Eight is one of the most feared penal colonies in the galaxy."

Geo wrapped his warm hand around the base of my tail and squeezed. "Too little too late if you ask me."

"My Regents," Reinik begged. "I've only taken what you freely gave." He pleaded as he was dragged away, heels scuffing across the floor where he flailed.

My body shuddered in protest. I had to say something, but it went against every omega instinct. "It wasn't theirs to give!" I lurched to my feet, shouting. Geo threw his jacket over my shoulders and stood behind me, his strong hands on my waist a grounding force. Buoyed by his strength, I looked directly into Reinik's twitching eyes. "To survive Station Eight, you'll have to show true courage."

"Then he'll be dead on landing," Geo growled, pulling me back into our nest.

My father's knuckles turned white where they gripped his staff. Had the grand omega's presence finally convinced him of the atrocity of his friend's crime?

Bonic's men led Reinik from the room. Courage was not a character trait I would have ascribed to the bastard who had left me barren, and I wouldn't shed a tear if he fell prey to a Snak within the week.

"Come, my dear." The grand omega lowered herself to my side with regal grace. While I lay swaddled in discarded fabrics, she ran her hand over my sweaty curls, sending cooling peace over me and my cramping womb.

"Out, now!" Geo growled, nearly animal, as his need grew to match mine. He gathered me in his lap, running his palms over my arms, down my tail, and up my torso. Claiming me. I sighed.

Her hand was tiny against Geo's shoulder, where she patted the beast, voice laced with reassurance. "Only but a minute more now, alpha." She stood tall. The air shimmered as her hands arched to her sides and swept over her head, weaving energy as her medallioned belt jangled in a symphony of bells. "A true mate bond has been found. The rarest and most beautiful of matches. The connection sings to me. Makir, please rise and face your true mate."

Geo scrambled for his sash, haphazardly winding it around my middle.

"The goddess Sola has spoken to me." The grand omega's long purple fingers waved in the air in front of her as if she were plucking invisible threads, and her eyes closed. A quiet calm filled the air. When her eyes flared open, lavender and silver swirled like mist. "The ceremony will begin now." Her skirts chimed as she walked in front of us. "Do you, Geo, take Makir as your soul-linked mate while you walk this life?"

My heart thundered like a herd of mantu under attack as I waited for Geo's answer. He'd traveled with me unprepared and knew so little of my history. Even with no blanting idea what it meant to be bound by the grand omega as soul-linked, he stood unwavering, his green eyes wide open and locked on mine.

After Reinik had so callously used me to the point where I could no longer bear younglings, I had finally found myself in the place every omega dreamed of. Face to face with their true mate at a bonding ceremony performed by none other than the grand omega herself. It no longer mattered that in my dreams, we were dressed in luxurious finery, the room was filled with the fragrance of the Jas fertility flower, and my loving parents shed tears of joy. That dream faded. The only thing that mattered was Geo at my side.

This ceremony was a much better fit. Stripped down to the raw, naked love that shone like a bright star from Geo's eyes. A beacon of love so pure I basked in its glow.

"I accept Makir with all my heart." Geo twined his fingers through mine.

Tears fell unhindered down my face. Each landed on my trembling hands, made steady by Geo's solid grip and unwavering gaze.

"A fine answer." The grand omega squeezed her thin fingers around our joined hands. Her faded purple and pink fur denoted her age, adding to her mystical presence.

"Now, Makir, sweetheart." She smiled, her gaze brimming with acceptance. "I must ask of you the same. Do you take Geo to be your soul-linked mate while you walk this life?"

My mother grumbled in the background and my father paced beside her while Bonic gazed at the two of us with his heart in his eyes.

"With all that I am." My voice, true and clear, filled the space.

"Then, with the goddess Sola's blessing..." She waved a brindled hand in the air. "Place your tail's suction over Geo's heart and cover it with your palm. Good. Now, Geo, place your thumb over Makir's heart." Her wide-sleeved tunic shifted, exposing her thin arms. "Geo, with your free hand, take Makir's." Her serene voice carried to our ears only.

Her tail bound our wrists, and her powerful voice lifted me higher, commanding the tether to tug me to my tiptoes. A deep thrum came from Geo. His position matched mine.

"The goddess Sola gifts you with the energy that flows through your bond, providing enduring strength. Her golden light allows your hearts and minds to speak freely to each other. You have been blessed."

Heat burned through the tether, bolted down my tail and fused to Geo like a brand. My tail's suction was directly over Geo's heart, and the blazing gold it emitted flared and turned my blood molten.

Geo shuddered, the only sign of his pain as a fire-etched imprint of my tail's healing source stamped his heart.

His thumbprint scorched like lava, marking the same place on me, and my gaze clouded with stinging tears but never broke from his.

The grand omega's eyes rolled until only the whites were visible as her tail guided the bond.

My blood swelled, filling every cell with the hot syrup running in my veins. Every nerve was blackened, charred to ash and blown away, until all that remained was my connection to Geo.

Geo's love hurtled through the bond at light speed, incinerating any lingering doubts.

"Come now," the grand omega whispered in the background as she ushered everyone out of the room. "They'll need time together."

29

Alone at last, Makir pulled the final shreds of my shirt free, and I shimmied my legs until my boots and pants lay in a heap. Naked in my arms, Makir straddled my lap, and our mouths met. Fully tapped into his emotions—love you so much, need you, you're everything to me—our lovemaking overwhelmed me, and I groaned, relishing his unspoken declarations.

The door opened occasionally, and food and water slid through at frequent intervals over the next two days.

When the third morning dawned, I woke, and a languid warmth like a gentle hug replaced the urgency of Makir's heat. It was over, but his love for me remained. The sensation was so encompassing through the soul-link that I wanted to reach out, touch it and caress it with my fingers.

My soft thickness was still buried inside his smooth channel from his last heat wave, the fabric of the nest was soaked in our combined seed and his waxy slick, and it smelled like heaven. Idly tracing the mating mark over my heart as Makir slumbered, I marveled at its perfect mirror image with the pad on his tail. With care, I kissed the tip of his tail, my tongue running over the fine lines matching the ones now tattooed on my chest.

Makir's lavender eyes flickered open. "There you are," he said. The rough rasp of his morning voice stirred my cock, but it was too worn out to perform again. "I'm feeling so much better."

I ran my palm down his tail and squeezed the base while he purred. Bruised and scratched from his insatiable demands for sex, I should've been sore, yet nothing but peace filled my languid muscles.

"Can we go home soon?" I asked.

Makir traced his forefinger over his mating mark, then mine. "I've always wanted one of these." His lashes dipped when he glanced at me, and I brushed my thumb over his jawline. "But we haven't even met my nephew yet."

"Yeah, well, no offense, but let's get the little guy named so we can be on our way. I'm not a huge fan of Lorne so far."

"You haven't even been out of the arrival port." Makir slipped off my softened cock and out of my arms and stood, luxuriously stretching his stunning body before he pulled me to my feet. "I'm going to change your mind." His lips twisted up on one side, and his eyes sparkled. "My home planet is beautiful."

He pushed me toward the washroom in the room we'd been trapped in until his heat passed. I walked around a desk and chair that had gone unnoticed until now.

"Go have a shower and get dressed, and I'll give you a tour. My nephew must be named by now. We can meet him and be on our way by evening's light." His eyes glowed even brighter at the mention of the baby.

I called out to Makir as I scrubbed soap over my body. "What's this room used for normally?"

He passed me a towel as I climbed over the tall ledge of the shower stall. "Interrogations, mainly." He shrugged and cast his gaze to the ground. Embarrassment swelled along the tether, hot and reluctant. "We'll avoid my parents, but I really want to show you my special place."

His desire to show me the best of his planet spiraled through the tether, replacing his embarrassment.

My fingertips twisted with his for a moment before I gathered my clothes. I would give him whatever he wanted. "Show me the Lorne you love, but if I never see the regents again, I'll consider myself a lucky man."

Makir's eyes danced as he tapped a message into his wristport. "I'll arrange transportation for us."

"Make sure that jackass Tunt is not our pilot for the return trip," I growled.

Makir bent to kiss my nose. "Anything for you."

Janny tipped his chin in deference to Makir as we departed the interrogation room, guarding him from a respectful distance. I had no doubt that was a request from Bonic rather than the regents. After the quiet room we'd spent Makir's heat in, the spaceport on Lorne buzzed with an intensity I hadn't experienced since trying to find parking at a mall during Christmas.

The spaceport was enormous. A tiny shuttle, possibly big enough for two, buzzed beside us and landed as we walked. A hangar droid pushed it underneath a massive, sleek shuttle before the passengers, a species I didn't know, disembarked. All kinds of spaceships landed and launched, making conversation impossible.

Lornians and Tigs rushed to and fro with their luggage. Bright and loud, small bots filled the cavernous hangar, aiding with maintenance, offering glasses of something red—hiscus? Maps hovered over their heads when approached by visitors seeking directions.

Makir wrapped his slender fingers around my jaw, gently scratched my beard as he pushed my mouth closed. "We haven't even left the port yet, and you're acting like a tourist." His amusement zinged through the link.

Curved doors swooshed open under an enormous banner announcing: Lorne, Home of the Lyre Tree. Transparent buildings clad in long, glass-like sheets blended into towering cliffs that flanked a long U-shaped valley on both sides, turning them nearly invisible. A cool breeze laden with fresh citrus invited my lungs to inhale. When I cast my gaze up, an ivory sun belted with bronze, copper and gold rings cast its shimmering light high overhead.

"Damn, Makir, this is..." I squeezed his hand.

Makir led us to a much slicker hovercraft than the one he owned on Tern, but he piloted it with the same ease. Contentment hummed through the tether, and I pulled his hips back along the shared seat, nestling them against mine, wanting as much contact as possible.

The giant valley opened below us as we lifted off the ground. Bright rainbow meadows, not unlike the tulip fields in Holland, and vast expanses of towering turquoise trees blurred by.

"Now I can see why you were so happy to find lamar," I shouted so the words weren't blown away.

Makir nodded vigorously, his mane whipping in my face. "Lornian dwellings are bathed in light, but none compare to the beautiful windows you created for me."

Our full bond pulsed with sincerity, and I ran a finger over the back of Makir's pointed ear before clenching my thighs around his, sloppily braiding his mane and tucking it under his collar.

"My dwelling." Makir slowed his hovercraft as we coasted through a long archway formed by the reaching arms of the lyre tree that led to an entrance flanked by half a dozen elite protectors.

'Dwelling' was a dramatically inadequate word for the palatial tower rising above us, the sunlight casting the lamar cladding entirely in bronze.

"Holy shit." I'm mated to royalty. Nerves reared their ugly heads as we passed Bonic's men, heads tilted in deference, and my palm grew sweaty against Makir's.

He purred as we entered a courtyard, loosening my shoulders, and soft grass cushioned my steps.

Jast squealed, rushing toward Makir and crushing him in her arms. "Congratulations! I'm sorry I missed the ceremony. I heard it will go down in history books." She beamed at me and hugged me too. "Welcome to the High Hold of Tuniga, Geo."

Shit, shit, shit! I hadn't thought this through. Royalty. No way, I couldn't be. I was a construction worker, for fuck's sake.

A soft gurgle drew Makir's attention to Bonic and Jast's baby, but my gaze froze on the new grandparents sitting beside where Bonic had their newborn cradled in his lap. His father gazed adoringly from his rather distant perch while his mother stared straight ahead, spine stiff, examining one of the courtyard's columns. They sat on elaborately decorated cushions on a large rug emblazoned with a huge beast—the same beast that adorned the royal uniform's high collar.

"Let me see. Let me see," Makir said, dashing toward his brother, his tail linked with Jast's. "I can't believe I'm meeting my nephew," he purred. "Can I?" He turned pleading eyes on his brother.

"Brother, you don't need to ask." Bonic scooped up his baby and placed him in Makir's waiting arms.

A wave of emotion crashed through the bond, and Makir's eyes grew glassy. Caught up in the moment, my own eyes teared. Makir linked his tail with his brother's, and Jast twined hers around them as they gazed at the linobee-wrapped bundle. He cooed to the little boy and lifted his gaze to mine. "Come meet him."

The sun appeared to mark time by the color of its rings, and as I approached the happy family, the mirrored walls of the courtyard turned from bronze to copper.

"Stop!" Makir's mother rose from her cushioned throne, her voice dripping with disdain. "You will not get any closer to the new heir, human."

Fuck, I hate these assholes. The need to protect this child from his grandparents threatened to overcome me. I didn't even know his name, but the urge to prevent this perfect new life from being subjected to the negligence and lovelessness that had left Makir so vulnerable thrummed through my veins.

"Do you love this grandchild with your heart? Or only as a tool to continue the Tuniga line?" I asked. The regents stepped back, gazes hardening at my implication.

Makir's mother frowned and with words full of vitriol, spat out, "How dare you question—"

I interrupted her tirade with a voice so steadfast it could not be misinterpreted. "Because I'll do everything in my power to prevent you from hurting this child like you did your own."

I hadn't sensed Makir at my side until his tail wrapped around my waist and he leaned his weight against me.

"I will too." The force of Makir's conviction caused his parents' frowns to waver.

"Bonic, do something." His mother moved toward where Bonic cradled the baby in his arms once more.

He passed the sleeping boy to Jast. Bonic's gaze hardened, encompassing his parents in its lethal glow. "You're right." His father's shoulders eased as Bonic continued, "It's well past time I did something. I will not tolerate my youngling or any omega being treated as lesser by you any longer." Makir's mother's knees trembled as Bonic's eyes narrowed to slits aimed at her. "I've turned a blind eye and made excuses for you over the years, but they are wide open now. You will heed my words if you wish to be part of his life. Love my youngling as if he's the most precious thing on Lorne, or you'll have no place in this family."

Bonic called his guard over. "Janny, escort them from the courtyard so they can think about their choices."

"Bonic, please," his father said, "I already love him. There is no need for this, I beg of you." While his father's remorse was evident, his mother walked rigidly beside the guard until they vanished from view.

"Makir, Geo…" Bonic motioned us forward, smiling as if he hadn't just admonished the regents of the kingdom and sent them packing. "You'll have the honor of being the first to know our youngling's name."

Jast purred as she held the baby out to me. With trembling arms, I cradled him like he was the most valuable thing in the world. Makir's purr blended with Jast's.

"His name is Telya." At hearing his name spoken by his mother, the baby boy opened his eyes and fixed them on me before his own purr ignited like a little motor.

"He likes you." Makir laughed.

The copper turned to gold, and Makir insisted we say our goodbyes. I reluctantly passed off Telya to his mother, kissed Jast on the cheek and shook Bonic's hand. Makir's sadness resonated along the bond as he hugged his family one last time.

"We'll see them again soon." I pressed Makir to my side.

Makir's somber mood turned gleeful as we flew through the valley. The hovercraft dropped suddenly, and the contents of my stomach dropped with it. Makir tucked us into a private turquoise alcove and turned off the ignition.

He inhaled deeply and held his breath, as if trying to swallow enough sweet air to last him until the next time. "This is my special place."

My fingers traced the branches of the tall trees surrounding us. Their limbs embraced the space with their enormous translucent bat wing shape. They turned the view overlooking the floating island we were on ocean colored. Their veins transformed the island into a vast cat's eye-marbled dome. With the hovercraft engine stopped, the quiet was deafening.

"Little lion, this sanctuary is like you—a rare gem. Are you okay? Are you happy?"

"Feel it, Geo." He dropped one hand to my thigh behind him, where I sat on his bike.

Makir opened his connection to me fully. Elation, wonder and profound satisfaction coursed through me. If I were a mountain climber, I would've just summited K2. My heart thudded, and I jerked back.

Is he feeling the same as me? Supercharged? Like bright light...and fizz...full of the mettle to defeat any challenge?

Now that my most pressing questions had been answered and our bond confirmed as unshakable, it was time to resolve what had plagued my mind for too long.

"And Reinik..."

Makir immediately tensed under my hands.

"That's the bastard who sent you fleeing to Tern?" I growled. My biceps throbbed, and my knuckles itched with the need to pummel something.

"When you took on Reinik like that, in front of my parents..." He paused, overwhelmed. "It was everything. My parents knew of his abuse but blamed me for encouraging him while I was blinded by my heat. Bonic tried to banish him, but my father pulled out all the stops to protect his best friend." He choked, tears turning his eyes liquid lavender. "I never imagined I'd find my true mate in fleeing."

I gathered Makir into my arms, lifted him from the seat and walked toward the smooth tree trunk. After sliding my back down to its base, I tugged Makir into my lap.

My fingers untangled what remained of the braid in Makir's mane. "So Reinik didn't want to be your mate?"

"My eyes never turned for him." He cupped my cheeks. "I'm so blanting lucky."

Never had I been so thankful. "I'm the lucky one."

His glassy eyes met mine before he continued. "I don't feel empty anymore. Reinik took away everything. I thought I loved him. My parents were pleased with me for once. He was my dad's best friend. And then he ripped it all away." Tears streamed down his face. "I can't have younglings anymore. He took that from me."

The bond yanked so hard that I jolted. Happiness surged through our connection like a cresting tsunami.

"But I have so much more now. I have you. I don't feel purposeless anymore." Makir's tail massaged the mating mark over my drumming heart. "I love you, Geo... Feel it." His lips skated over mine. "Can you feel my love for you?"

The bond quaked and surged into a glorious ache. Impossible to imagine, the foreign emotion flooded through me, and I had no choice but to believe the love traveling through the bond was real. I'd learned that the key to becoming a strong alpha was knowing when to submit.

I swallowed hard and nodded. "I love you, little lion." My eyes stung as I gathered Makir's tears with my thumb. "I promise, I never wanted kids anyway. We'll be the best damn uncles ever."

30

EPILOGUE

"How could you get married without me?" Ginger exclaimed, throwing her hands up in the air in disbelief. Charz and Pika were settled at my feet, and a cup of coffee sat in front of me in the home I now shared with Makir.

Makir had stars in his eyes as he spoke of his new nephew. "Believe me, Ginger, the whole trip was a disaster except for meeting Telya." Smile lines creased the corners of his eyes. "Wasn't he the sweetest thing you've ever seen, Geo?"

He rushed on before I could say, 'yeah, he looks exactly like you.' Would his designation be omega too?

"Oh, and Ginger, Jast adores the sling you made for him. She's the envy of all the new moms, and if you're interested, you're welcome to sell your wares on Lorne."

Ginger smiled and tapped a long, lacquered nail against the polished table.

I cleared my throat and rubbed the mating mark over my heart. "So, the only good thing that happened while you were on Lorne was meeting your nephew?"

Makir pressed a long finger to his lip. "Well, Reinik's ass-kicking and banishment comes to mind." A deep chuckle made his tail swish. "And have I failed to mention that the grand omega blessed us in a soul-linking ceremony like no other?" His voice transformed from teasing to awed, and the lavender in his eyes turned liquid with love.

I leaned over to kiss Makir on the cheek. "There was that little thing."

"You guys are nauseating." Ginger groaned as she pieced together a few pieces of mantu hide in front of her, pins stuck between her lips.

Ginger was right. We couldn't stop touching. The tether fizzed with the heady newness of our love, and the constant feedback loop of undisguised reciprocation made me needy.

"Ginger, just how many orders have you accepted?" My eyes swept over the huge pile of cut-out hides stacked on the table. "You can't possibly sew all that before the next shuttle leaves, unless..."

She plucked a pin from her mouth and wove it between the layers of hide. "Now, don't you go getting any big ideas." She bit back a smile. "As much as I love designing costumes for horror movies, I can't stand watching them, and there is a huge freaking horror show creature on this planet, Geo." Her eyes widened comically, but underneath the humor, a glimmer of fear lurked in their depths.

Makir fiddled with one of Ginger's patterns. "JayJay said we don't have to worry for a while. Winter will send it deep underground where it's warmer."

Ginger rolled her eyes as I leaned into Makir for a real kiss. She cleared her throat as I reached for his zipper. "I'm going to pack my bags and stay at Jay—I mean, the archbuilder's sono for the next couple of days so the two of you can have a bit of a honeymoon." She exhaled, sending her bangs flying off her forehead. "Though I'm not sure what'll be worse—handling you two lovebirds or dealing with JayJay. I've seen teaspoons with more emotional depth."

Makir pressed the translator behind his ear and jumped up, clapping. "Yes, a honeymoon. That's what we need." He waved goodbye to Ginger.

"Give JayJay a chance. He's a good guy." I hugged my best friend and left her in the kitchen, organizing her projects.

"You, my true mate"—Makir tapped the button on my shirt—"will learn how to fly a hoverbike. Let's go to the hot springs." Then, with a finger over my lips, he silenced any objections.

I scooped Makir into my arms and walked to our bedroom. "But first, sleep. You've exhausted me."

Makir bounced as I dropped him into our nest. "Blant. Warn me next time, would you?" he yelped before discovering the gift I'd given him. "Goddess. What is this Sola-blessed thing?" He scrabbled the furs back from the nest to reveal the custom-made mattress I'd requested Ginger bring to Tern. He reclined on it, pushing at it with his heels, hips, shoulders and head.

My mouth watered as he rolled and pressed his body into the soft cushion.

"I think I've landed on a cloud."

I pounced, landing with my knees on either side of him and licking a long stripe up his stretched-out neck. "You like it?" I growled.

He wiggled deeper into the new mattress. "Geo, we're never leaving the nest again."

Makir's tail brushed over my heart, and my thumb over his mark. The suction from his tail weakened my knees, and I drew in a breath.

"Show me what you've got, stud muffin."

Thank you for reading my story. You fill my heart with thanks!

Did you enjoy 20% Stud 80% Muffin?

If so, please consider leaving a quick review on Amazon or wherever you read. I'd love to know what you think of Geo and Makir!

Bonus Content

Would you like to see Geo and Makir's soul-linked mates ceremony from Geo's perspective? Then, sign up for my <u>Newsletter</u> today to unlock the access code and read this exciting chapter for free.

www.chrisredd.ca

Sneak Peek

I'm excited to announce *80% Beef 20% Cake*, Book 2 in the *Alien Fated Mates* series, is coming spring 2025. Read on, to catch the first chapter early!

80% Beef 20% Cake

One year ago on the planet Yagras...

JayJay

The courtroom swam before my eyes. A sea of gray-skinned Rock Dwellers stared down at me from their steep seats. Three vertical inclines, filled with pinch-lipped faces, surrounded the podium I stood on far below. Their haughty gazes reduced my worthiness to a speck. I swallowed hard.

"I did not commit this crime." I ignored the citizens in the crowd and turned toward the councillors, willing them to see the truth.

Light glinted off the polished head of the man standing on the raised dais before me. Devile. A sharply pressed sash cut across the deep indigo of his representative uniform in a slash of bloodroot fungus red. Behind him, seven supreme councillors fanned out—one for each Yagras district. Draped red cloth hooded their heads, cloaking their decisions with anonymity.

"The time for pleading your case has concluded. The verdict has been passed." The more the public nodded, the louder Devile's voice grew, bolstered by the hive-mind energy of his large audience. "For the calculated planning that led to a female's death, the supreme councillors of Yagras have come to the decision—"

The crowd roared along with my racing mind. Surely this can't be happening.

Devile raised a three-fingered hand to hush the districts' eager citizens.

My heart thundered inside my ribcage. The curved bones, once protection, had transformed into prison bars. Sweat stung my eyes as I scanned the crowd for the distinctive white worm emblazoned over the hearts of my soldiers' uniforms. Every time I caught a glimpse of white, my shallow breathing eased.

Poised beside their hollering neighbors, frowns etched the hard mouths of my elite guard. Strewn among citizens demanding answers and retribution, they were the voice of reason. With their unconditional solidarity anchoring me, my breaths grew deeper. I stood taller, shoulders squared. My team would not see me falter under pressure.

How could I have fallen from hero to villain in such a short time?

The crowd grew riotous. Under my tight grip, the podium vibrated. Representative Devile waved his raised fist to no effect.

I hope he's trampled under the masses. I aimed all the hatred running through my veins at Devile.

As the citizens' rage built to a deafening roar, the supreme councillors rose and turned as one. At once, the crowd went silent. The councillors nodded to Representative Devile to continue.

Devile swept his hand down the length of his red sash. "For the intent to kill a sentient being, a female..."

Females are revered. Who would stoop so low? My legs grew weak, and I leaned against the podium. Blant that lying bastard!

Livid, the crowd surged forward, their wrath-filled words hurled at me like poison darts. "Kill him. Kill him. Kill him." Even as a respected male commanding many guards, the misplaced hatred pierced through my brain, sharper than any headache.

Each supreme councillor unfolded their draped hood. Bloodroot-red fabric dripped down their backs as they exposed their stony faces to the mob. Without a word uttered, the citizens of Yagras calmed.

With a theatrical turn of his wrist, Devile circled the raised dais like a stage. "The Rock Dweller before us...Lead Protector of the Yagras Elite Guard, JayJay Atlason, shall be exiled to Tern."

Exiled to Tern? But who would take my command?

The crowd sighed in collective relief, and an arrogant sneer curled the representative's upper lip.

At the supreme councillors' nods, guards approached me from each side. My second in command gathered one arm. "I do not wish to cuff you, Lead Protector." Though his gruff words said 'Lead Protector,' his glassy eyes and gentle grip said 'friend.' A new recruit hooked his arm through my other elbow.

The supreme councillors' ruling was final. No matter how much I wanted to scream, 'I'd never kill a female,' a Lead Protector would never degrade himself with such a show of emotion.

I cleared my throat. "I will not fight."

Empty-handed, chin high, I walked the long hall, exiting the courtroom. Behind me, boots pounded metal stands as hundreds of Rock Dwellers stomped out their support for the verdict. A hovercar awaited. Instead of finding relief at not being terminated as the citizens so vehemently demanded, numbness spread through my bones.

Stunned, I flew through the arched gate lined with sharp teeth. Loss prickled my skin as I passed through the barrier constructed in the image of a hellsna's giant mouth—the beast I was charged with protecting Yagras' citizens from. My people, what would become of them?

My friend's warm hand landed on my lower back as I exited the hovercar. He ushered me through the departure bay, up the grated ramp and into the shuttle. Bent on one knee, an arm crossed to his opposite shoulder, he bowed his head. "Until I see you again, Lead Protector."

With every silent step he took away from me, I wondered, Is this the last time I set eyes on a Rock Dweller?

The small shuttle jolted skyward. Alone with only a pilot behind cockpit doors, I dropped my face into trembling hands and scrubbed my head.

An AI system pinged, and a sunny female voice announced, "We'll be arriving at Tern, a remote outpost in the Reiner System, in approximately thirty-two suns. If you wish to know more about Tern, please scroll through the options menu on your armrest. Topics include its recent recolonization after a plague, a map of the only settlement, Yurstille, and a gallery of goods for purchase at the local bakery. Please do not hesitate to ask me if you have any questions. My name is—"

"Enough. I wish for quiet." Beneath me, the black rocks of the Nara district grew smaller. Everything I knew and loved faded away before my eyes until all that remained was a hollow ache. A jungle cat perched on the high peak above the tree line lifted its head as if saying goodbye.

I whispered, "I'll be back."

It had been a year since I was driven from Yagras' lush forests to Tern's barren rolling hills.

"Blanting pink dust." From under the worksite's roof, I stared through the space a wall would soon occupy. Endless blue snow-covered hills stretched far into the distance.

One dwelling at a time, the building crew I was foreman of had transformed Tern for new colonizers. Where a vast pink desert once sat, the settlement of Yurstille now thrived.

Sully, the mech-grader operator on my building crew, drove past, kicking up dust while leveling the ground for our latest client's accommodation.

A curl of smoke spiraled from Yurstille's bakery. Even two streets over, the yeasty tang filled my nose, and the honey-sweet aroma of graneth bread melted over my tongue as if I were eating it.

Sully's deep voice bounced off the studs going up, pulling me back to the moment. "We're going to knock this one out in no time." A much-larger-than-called-for grin plastered his face. "I'm disappointed they don't want to put in a pool, though."

Sully's family had arrived on Tern from Yagras among the new batch of colonizers, and since then, he'd been obnoxiously happy—rightly so. Finding a mate was every male Rock Dweller's dream. Except mine. Way too much work.

Despite the rarity of Rock Dweller females, the compulsion that had driven my friends to Tern to find compatible mates was foreign to me. I'd been satisfied with my career. A female would never have been enough motivation for me to leave Yagras voluntarily.

For a moment, a sliver of guilt shot ice through my veins. A year ago, someone had killed a rare female on my home planet. That meant one less male would find their mate. But who had set me up, and why had they risked our dwindling population?

Beside me, Sully positioned the hydro-tamper over the loose soil, shouting over the loud whirring, "Bish, JayJay, cheer up. Geo will be back any rotation now."

Though I missed my human friend and boss, that wasn't the reason for my sullenness. This rotation marked the first anniversary of my fall from worthiness. A year ago, Representative Devile had done everything to break me, but nothing could dampen my love of home, not even banishment to this desolate land of pink dust and endless blue snow. I longed for Yagras.

"I have just the thing to brighten your rotation." A swath of compacted soil followed in the wake of Sully's machine. As he worked it over a tricky rocky spot, the wide grin spreading over his face had me bracing for the opposite. "TeyTey invited Ginger for dinner. You should join us."

My spine snapped to attention at Ginger's name. My three fingers loosened as her image came to mind—pale-faced and silver-haired—and the shovel slipped from my grip. Ginger lurked in the shadows of my mind, tiny and clever, like the jungle cat on Yagras that always stole by me.

Nuh-uh. No way. Voluntarily sharing space with Ginger was out of the question, even if my boss had expressly asked me to watch over his best friend who was visiting from Earth. I might consider it if I didn't freeze in her presence like some towering bald idiot.

Sully's grin faded, and he paused his work to focus on me. The hydro-tamper bumped against a reclaimed beam where it idled. "Before you say no—" Sully swiped a grimy hand across his sweaty brow. "—you know TeyTey will ask you herself. I'm just preparing you."

Disgusted by my incompetence around a female, I rolled my shoulders back. I was a fierce fighter, with dozens of hellsna dead at my hands to prove it.

With a new resolve, I committed to fulfilling my promise. Geo would be back any time now, and Ginger would be his responsibility. I could suck it up until then. Besides, I would never turn down Sully's mate. "Fine."

"You need more practice talking to females if you ever hope to gain the attention of a mate." His laughter rumbled through the building's skeleton frame and dampened when it hit the berm of blue snow surrounding the construction zone.

Blant. Rock Dweller females were revered on Yagras. Their rarity made it nearly impossible for a male to do anything that might displease them. Despite that, TeyTey was far from the spoiled princess I'd expected.

Females confused me to begin with, but one in particular confused me so much that my brain didn't seem to connect to my mouth in her presence. Ginger was so different. She was much smaller and more fragile than a Rock Dweller female. No Rock Dweller female would visit an unfamiliar planet on their own. Well, maybe TeyTey.

Plus, Ginger had hair, and when the silvery curtain swirled around her face, it awoke something I couldn't grasp inside of me. I wanted to touch it.

I passed the hydro-tamper back to Sully. "What time should I come?"

Sully's jaw clamped tight as he held back his grin. "Sundown, and bring some of that hiscus wine. Ginger's raving non-stop about it, and my female loves it."

Great. Now a looming dinner with Ginger would occupy my mind for the rest of the blanting rotation. The dwelling could wait. "Let's wrap up here." I needed to wash away the grime, polish my head and find something besides overalls to wear.

Avoiding TeyTey, I snuck into their solarium and relaxed near the lazy river Sully had installed behind his dwelling. One finger smoothed over the leaf of a frilly plant lining the humid oasis, and my thumb pressed into the tiny bumps on its underside.

"Blasterball," YimYim shouted, tucking his knees into his chest and jumping.

I jerked as he doused me in warm water. Thrown back into the moment, I wiped the droplets off my head, preparing to battle Sully's eldest son. Eight annums old and as tall as Ginger, he could easily throw her into the pool if she were here.

"Gotcha good, Uncle JayJay. Watcha doin' out here all by yourself?" YimYim ducked under the water, jetting through the gentle current before I could retaliate.

"It's like that, is it?" I wiped any levity from my voice and fake-stomped toward a hose coiled along the pink earthen wall. With as much stealth as I could muster, I turned on the faucet, lever in hand, and leaped toward him. "Now who's the boss?" I drenched him with cold water.

"No fair!" YimYim screeched as he scrambled to get away, his smile so big he choked down mouthfuls of water.

The see-through door separating the courtyard from the kitchen snicked over small wheels as it unfolded. TeyTey loomed in the opening, arms crossed. Her dress billowed, and the purple linnea leaves on the patterned fabric fluttered the same way they would if caught on a breeze at home.

I blocked out a sudden longing for Yagras brought on by the matching wrap tied in an intricate twist over her smooth head.

"JayJay, get in here this instant and say hi," TeyTey said.

I stood, limp hose in hand. Guilty as charged.

TeyTey turned on one foot and marched back into the kitchen. "Unmated Rock Dwellers—unbelievable. I'll have to teach them all manners so they can find females."

I ducked my chin and shrugged at YimYim before following.

YimYim spun toward the pool. "Manners are overrated."

My mouth watered. Rich roasting mantu and tangy graneth bread flavored the air. "TeyTey…" I opened the cooler and placed a bottle of hiscus wine inside to chill. "Thank you for inviting me. I was only getting a breath of humid air."

TeyTey juggled an armful of spiky black tubers. Her brow ridges jumped at my excuse, but she let it pass. "JayJay, if that's hiscus wine, you'll be my friend forever."

I suspected she wouldn't mind if her wine was a little warm, judging by the eagerness in her voice, so I returned to the cooler and poured her a container. Sure enough, she took a long sip and sighed.

TeyTey put on gloves before removing the spikes from the tubers. "Ah, here they are."

An icy blast blew through the front entry, but it did little to chill me as Sully motioned Ginger into the warm dwelling.

My mind grew foggy as she approached, so I ducked behind a tall plant to avoid looking stupid. Most of Ginger's straight white hair hid under a warm hat. In my imagination, my fingers threaded through the strands, and they were as soft as clouds.

Ginger hugged a wet YimYim, patting him on the head even though he was her height. "TeyTey, it smells soooo good in here." They embraced next, and YimYim rushed back to the pool.

When will she take her hat off and reveal her pretty hair? I smothered a cough. What the blant was going on with me? I did not need a female who caused me to abandon reason whenever she neared. A leaf tickled my nose.

Sully kicked off his snowy boots. Water pooled on the geothermal floors while he walked to TeyTey's side and wrestled against her solid hold on the oven door. "Bish, sweet TeyTey, just a morsel…"

Sully and TeyTey's teasing drifted into the background as Ginger monopolized my attention. She removed her coat and hat and hung them on the ball hook hanging from a ceiling chain. Her black forehead hair cut straight across her eyebrows and framed the amber, green and gold of her eyes in sharp contrast to the otherwise silver-white length.

Pink tubes encased her legs, highlighting the small mounds of her calves, and as my gaze swept up to the fabric sheathing her body, my mouth went dry. Brown leather crisscrossed in a vee at her neck and flared at her knees and wrists like a tunic. Little animal shapes were punched out along the hems, and a sparkly pendant hung from a gold chain around her neck, nestled at the top of her—

I forced my chin up.

Wide-eyed, Ginger scanned the home while she snapped pictures on a handheld device. I swore her eyes narrowed as they met the plant I was staked out behind.

"This is breathtaking, TeyTey." She walked through the folded door to the courtyard, and her slender fingers glided over the same plant mine had lingered on a moment ago. "Oh, drat." She bit her puffy lower lip. "I forgot my gift outside. It'll have turned into a popsicle." She rushed to the front entrance then returned, rubbing her arms vigorously after pushing a giant plant similar to the one by the lazy river into TeyTey's arms.

TeyTey ducked her head between a gap in the leaves. "Thank you. This will look beautiful by the lazy river." Then Sully scooped the plant from her arms.

"Ginger?" TeyTey said, playfully shoving Sully away from the oven when he snuck up behind her. She reached in and pulled out the roast mantu, shielding it from Sully's wandering fingers. "YimYim has lost his lovely mittens. Do you have any more?"

Ginger clicked a picture of TeyTey and Sully. "Dang. No, I don't." She pursed her lips. "And shoot... I've used up all the linobee pelts." Her pink tongue darted to the corner of her mouth. "Oh, I know, after our hoverbike lesson, I can fly to the rocky outcrop and do some trapping."

"Bish, TeyTey. I'm hungrier than the elite guard after a battle with the hellsna." Sully's mention of the hellsna jolted me from the camouflaged position I'd been using to follow Ginger's every move. "Let me have a little taste."

All the breath left me as images of the elite guard I'd trained over the annums dying in the giant worm's vice-like grip flashed in my mind's eye. I'd spent my entire adult life responsible for protecting Rock Dwellers from hellsna on Yagras. How had they gotten to Tern?

"I don't know what the elite guard is, but nothing seemed hungrier than that giant freaking worm. Talk about terrifying." Ginger shuddered, her hands rolling down the front of her tight dress. As if she'd known my location all along and was speaking to me directly, her hazel eyes locked on mine. "But a certain somebody did a helluva job rescuing us."

Sully stiffened and lowered his head in embarrassment. The few Rock Dwellers inhabiting Tern were the only ones who knew of my banishment. "Blant, JayJay, I meant no harm."

"You owe us five credits for swearing, fata." Sully's younglings hollered from the open doors to the solarium.

Sully rubbed his head. "I know it was hard for you to leave that part of your life behind." He squinted at me through the leaves, giving away my position behind the too-small plant.

A scar on my head throbbed, and my stomach roiled. I had no soldiers to command here, and rescuing Ginger after she'd been trapped in a cave had me yearning for my old uniform and bloodroot darts.

"It's all in the past," I said as I tipped my chin at Sully.

But the fact that Ginger thought I might have the answers…that she sought me out for reassurance… It stirred the same part of me that wanted to find out whether her hair felt as silky as it looked.

I plopped down on the stool beside Ginger. "You're planning a trip to the rocky outcrop?"

Startled, Ginger jerked the plate TeyTey had just passed her, and it dropped from her hands, shattering on the polished floor. Blant, I'd forgotten how loud she found me.

"Shit." She crouched down to pick up the large shards. "Well, hello to you too, JayJay. Interesting plant?"

Blant this female and my lack of tact. I had gone full-on lurker, studying his prey.

Seconds later, I'd found the pan and broom and nudged her out of danger. "Who's accompanying you?" I quickly filled the pan with the broken pieces and dumped them in the container.

"Oh, my day was great. Thanks for asking." She pursed her lips as she grabbed the broom from my hands and completed another pass over the floor. She smelled like the rich vegetation of Yagras. "I worked on the designs for some mantu coats I'm sewing, fed the chickens at the greendwelling and transplanted some of the veggies I brought from Earth. They're growing fabulously, by the way." Ginger's smile was intact but held about as much enthusiasm as one of Mayor Yurst's stale bulletins.

Instead of the embarrassment I should've felt at her scolding, my stance grew wider and my vision tunneled, as though Ginger were the target at the end of my sighting scope. "The rocky outcrop is dangerous. It's cold, and there's snow on the ground. Who will accompany you?"

TeyTey and Sully stood side by side in the kitchen, Sully sneaking mantu from the platter on the counter and openly eavesdropping. TeyTey's brows pinched together, unimpressed, while a bent-over Sully barely held it together. The younglings' splashing in the pool carried through the open folded door.

Ginger's eyes narrowed as she looked up. "Not that it's any of your business, but TeyTey's giving me hoverbike lessons, so I'll be going by my little lonesome. Me, myself and I." Her enticing chest shoved out when she planted her hands on her hips. "Problem?"

I patted my hip, only to find it empty, my old blaster nowhere to be found, and swore when I found myself mentally unarmed. Blant, this female unsettles me. "I'll accompany you."

Her hair swung around her like the frilled neck of a Yagras jungle cat. "Jeez, do you have to talk so loud?! I can handle the cold, JayJay. We have snow on Earth, ya know. I don't need anyone to accompany me."

I wasn't loud, yet I found myself lowering my voice. "I promised Geo I would protect you, and I'm a male who keeps his word."

YimYim ran into the kitchen, trailing water behind him. "Mata, I'm starved."

"All right, have it your way, King Kong," Ginger huffed while she passed the broom and the emptied dustpan to YimYim. Her face softened as she met the youngling's smiling one, even though he made a bigger mess with the water pooling around his feet.

Yim Yim's voice echoed from inside a cupboard. "Ginger, what's a King Kong?"

Although YimYim had asked the question, her laser focus pinned me. "King Kong's a giant make-believe gorilla that tries to protect women, I mean females, from things they can handle just fine on their own."

TeyTey snorted and nudged me with her elbow as she placed a dish of sizzling mantu on the table. "Sounds like every Rock Dweller male I've ever met."

Sully protested in the background while YimYim squinted, likely processing the image the translator sent to his brain.

Ginger's chair scraped across the floor, and she tucked it under the table, as far away from me as possible. She showed all the signs of a ruffled fledgling after its mata had nosed it from the nest—elbows locked, arms crossed over her chest and spine rigid.

I would protect her whether she liked it or not. The hellsna on Tern didn't behave the same way they did on Yagras, and who knew where they would surface next?

She planted her balled hands in her lap. Ginger's black bangs shot toward the ceiling as she blew out a breath, and silver-white strands jerked over her narrow shoulders as if affronted. Then, more composed, she turned and grinned. "Fine. But I'll do the flying, and that's not negotiable."

Coming Spring 2025

Alien Fated Mates
20% Stud
80% Muffin
CHRIS REDD

Chris Redd has been dreaming up stories since she can remember. Her attraction to the romance genre began in the dusty corridors of her tiny local library, browsing the curled corners of *Sweet Valley Highs* and *Sweet Dreams*. Now she writes her own twist on romance.

She loves crafting vivid sci-fi worlds where flawed humans fall in love with equally flawed aliens. Chris is the author of the steamy *AlienFated Mates* series.

When she's not writing, you can find Chris Redd exploring the forests and the coastline with her Toy Aussiedoodle or trying to capture the perfect video of her daughter's rabbit doing a binkie.

Connect With Me

Subscribe to my newsletter

www.chrisredd.ca

Facebook

Instagram

TikTok

www.ingramcontent.com/pod-product-compliance
Lightning Source LLC
Chambersburg PA
CBHW021233060726
47590CB00005B/1746